MW00368350

Praise for Previous Work

Madison House

Winner of the 2005 Langum Prize for American Historical Fiction

"Peter Donahue seems to have a map of old Seattle in his head. No novel extant is nearly as thorough in its presentation of the early city, and all future attempts in its historical vein will be made in light of this book."
— David Guterson, author of *Snow Falling on Cedars* and *The Other*

"Every page reflects Peter Donahue's meticulous and imaginative recreation of a lively and engaging moment in American history. I loved reading this novel..."
— Sena Jeter Naslund, author of *Four Spirits* and *Ahab's Wife*

"Peter Donahue crafts a resplendent novel examining life in Seattle in the early 20th century, complete with a Dickensian cast of unforgettable characters."
— *Seattle Post-Intelligencer*

"An ambitious novel. . . Donahue's story is a paean to a significant part of the city's history."
— *The Seattle Times*

"Peter Donahue has penned a memorable chronicle of life in the Pacific Northwest one hundred years ago."
— *The Historical Novels Review*

"Peter Donahue is producing the same kind of historically accurate, thoroughly researched study of his city as William Kennedy did with his Albany novels..."
— Don Noble, host of *Bookmark*

The Cornelius Arms

"Donahue's stories introduce a group of tenants who, in their varied, decidedly non-affluent circumstances, define a pre-dot-com city on the verge of overwhelming change …*The Cornelius Arms* stories deliver a cumulative effect that is quite powerful."
— *The Seattle Weekly*

"This is fiction to remind you why you read: to see into the heart of human life."
— Thomas E. Kennedy, author of *Passion in the Desert* and *The Copenhagen Quartet*

"*The Cornelius Arms* is a place where the down-and-out rub shoulders with the hip, the bitter, the persistent, the abandoned, the exiled, and the mad. A wonderful, illuminating portrait of both Seattle and of an unsanitized and peculiarly rich life."
— Brian Evenson, author of *Altmann's Tongue*, *Contagion and Other Stories*, and *The Open Curtain*

"Donahue introduces a kaleidoscope of characters and tone to give a rare, intimate view of tenants' lives … Donahue is an extraordinarily talented writer."
— *The Birmingham News*

"In *The Cornelius Arms*, Peter Donahue has gone to the hidden heart of Seattle … This is a lovely collection that will draw readers into his Seattle-centered world and keep them there."
— Peter Bacho, author of *Dark Blue Suit and Other Stories* and *Cebu*

"I am put in mind of story collections as established in our tradition as Sherwood Anderson's *Winesburg, Ohio* and Mark Costello's *Murphy Stories*."
— Gordon Weaver author of *Long Odds* and *Four Decades: New and Selected Stories*

Clara and Merritt

CLARA AND MERRITT

PETER DONAHUE

La Grande, OR • 2010

Copyright © 2010
ISBN: 978-1-877655-66-1
Library of Congress Control Number: 2010922060

First Edition:
June 2010

Cover art: Yvonne Twining Humber (1907-2004)
"Business District," 1947, oil on board
Courtesy of Martin-Zambito Fine Art, Seattle, WA
Cover design: Kristin Summers,
redbat design, www.redbatdesign.com
Author photo: Jay W. Shoot

Published by
Wordcraft of Oregon, LLC
PO Box 3235
La Grande, OR 97850

www.wordcraftoforegon.com
editor@wordcraftoforegon.com

Member of the Council of Literary Magazines and Presses (CLMP)
and Independent Book Publishers Association (IBPA)

Printed in U.S.A.

For my brothers, Steve and Neil,
and for Susan, Tana, and Elizabeth

Life only avails . . .

—Ralph Waldo Emerson, "Self-Reliance"

We're waltzing in the wonder of why we're here.

—Arthur Schwartz and Howard Dietz,
"Dancing in the Dark"

TABLE of CONTENTS

BOOK ONE

Though There Be Rain and Darkness

Seattle Waterfront, 1934

The way the shipping and stevedore companies were running the hiring hall with their speed-ups and shape-ups and dishing out as much work to the casuals as the regulars, Carl Hamilton would never make enough to support his family—his wife, two growing boys, and young Clara. The Depression had hit the country like a rusty rail stake to the chest. He'd been working on the waterfront since 1923, two years after the failed strike of '21 that led to the union being busted up. He typically worked as a hold man on general cargo, though now and then he was put on a shoveling gang, working ore, bone meal, or copra in a ship's hold with his pick and shovel. No way around it, it was hard, spine-splintering work.

Carl sometimes thought it a sad blessing on the family when little May, their fourth child, died in infancy. When the doctors gave no explanation, called it crib death, and told Carl and Glenora it happened to about one in every thousand newborns, Glenora turned her back on modern medicine and took up Christian Science as the only surefire way to safeguard her family from further illness or harm. That was three years ago, before the latest round of union organizing following passage of the National Industrial Recovery Act in '33. The family had just moved into Glenora's parents' three-story house in West Seattle after the bank foreclosed on their own small home in White Center. And unless the union could win its demands this time around, get the shipping companies to give up control of the hiring hall, stop the speed-ups and shape-ups, and guarantee wage increases, overtime pay, and work equalization through a shorter work week, Carl knew his family would never live in a house of its own again. In their bedroom in her parents' house, Carl hung a framed photograph of FDR next to Glenora's framed drawing of Mary Baker Eddy—each portrait a testament to the faith both of them, respectively, held in the future.

And sure enough, less than a year after Roosevelt's Recovery Act, the union rolls on the West Coast jumped from 800 to 7,500 longshoremen, stevedores, dockers, and warehousemen. And yet, just when the union was beginning to flex its muscle and show some strength again, the president of the International Longshoremen Association, Joseph Ryan—"From the East Coast, wouldn't ya know it," Carl remarked one day to his fellow longshoremen—started undermining them. Overnight Joe Ryan and Dave Beck, the Teamster boss who ran West Coast trucking from his roost in Seattle, buddied up to do everything in their power to avert the waterfront strike, especially in Seattle.

"That bastard Beck thinks his union's the only one in town," Carl declared one day down at the Liberty Tavern on Western Avenue. The tavern served as the unofficial union hall, where men could voice their grievances against the maritime companies, poll one another on strategy, and bandy about opinions on the strengths and weaknesses of current leadership. "And I say *his* because he thinks it's his union and his alone, and to hell with the rank-and-file. I'll hand it to the plug-headed sonuvabitch, he knows how to organize."

Someone stood Carl a schooner of beer and he drank it down. It was his third, and he could feel himself warming to the cause. "The problem is Ryan's too damn cozy with the maritime employers. He wants shared control of the hiring hall. Yet men like Frank Jenkins and Shaun Maloney, good men who go to work on the docks and in the cargo holds every day, know that's just giving them the rope to hang us with."

Jenkins and Maloney were local ILA organizers who opposed Joe Ryan's more conservative approach to dealing with the maritime companies. Yet a handful of die-hard Ryan supporters remained within the ranks, and one of these stoolies nearly killed Carl one day when he was working below in the No. 2 hatch aboard a freighter out of Los Angeles, loading cartons of canned salmon onto the sling board, cross-stacking the cartons eight high. The Ryan man was the hatch-tender, the guy up top who signaled the winch driver when to hoist the sling board up from the hold. He gave the winch driver the hoist-away sign, and when the sling board heaved up, Carl lost his balance, grabbed at a line attached to the winch cable, but missed and fell eight feet, a dozen cartons of canned salmon toppling down on top of him.

"Whoa," the hatch-tender shouted from above.

Carl lifted himself off the wet and rusty hold floor, pushing aside the fallen cartons, and spotted the sling board swaying above his head. He ducked to the side and looked up through the hatch, where the hatch-tender, the Ryan man, was silhouetted against the grey sky, peering down into the poorly lit hold.

"What the hell, Smitson," Carl barked at him. "You damn near killed me."

"You okay down there, Carl," the hatch-tender called back. "I can barely see you."

Carl removed his floppy wool cap and wiped his brow with the sleeve of his canvas jacket. He knew Smitson was a Ryan man. He'd overheard him the other day call Harry Bridges, the vocal strike chairman down at the San Francisco local who refused to take Ryan's fink deals, a "dirty Commie bastard," and declare, "They should ship him back to Aussieland."

While Carl hated to see dissension among union members—*After all, weren't they in this together?*—he'd be damned if he was going to let some company stinker send him home with a broken back.

"I'll tell you when," he shouted up through the hatch, his voice booming in the half-emptied hold. "Now tell Hagen to lower it back down—Slowly!"

When Carl knocked off work that evening, he went straight across the road to the Liberty, and as soon as he walked in he spotted Smitson at the bar, smoking a cigarette. He went straight up to him and backhanded him across the shoulder. Smitson spun around on his bar stool.

"Hey, Carl," he said and poked his cigarette out in an ashtray. "Let me buy you a beer."

Carl grabbed Smitson by the collar of his jacket, yanked him off the bar stool, and slammed his back against the bar.

Smitson swatted Carl's hands away. "What's the big idea?"

Carl poked two fingers into the middle of Smitson's chest. "You know good and well. It's about you trying to give me a ride on that sling board. Thinkin' maybe if I got killed, that's one less vote against your boy Ryan."

"You're cracked, Hamilton. I don't know what you're talkin' about. Accidents happen. You ain't immune. No more'an the rest of us." Smitson tried to sit back down. "Now bug off."

Carl shoved him up against the bar again. But this time Smitson pushed back, and when he did Carl landed a roundhouse right across the side of his face. Smitson went stumbling into the bar, knocking over a pitcher of beer.

Two other longshoremen jumped off their bar stools and pulled Carl away as Smitson picked up a glass full of beer and hurled it at Carl's head. The glass missed and shattered on the floor, but not before soaking Carl and the other two longshoremen.

"You'd better watch yourself out there, Hamilton," shouted Smitson. "Like I said, accidents happen."

Carl wrenched himself free from the two men holding him back. He stormed out of the tavern and made his way to his trolley stop down the block, while across the road the starkly lit pier remained as busy as ever with men loading and dispatching freight among the forest of cranes, booms, and rigging.

ONE
Clara, Fall 1943

Clara lit two candles on her drawing table, and despite her better instincts glanced at the shadowy reflection in the bedroom window. She was pretty enough, most of the time. She kept her wavy hair pulled back from her face with half a dozen bobby pins and though not the most fetching, or modern, way to do her hair, it served its purpose. It was practical and showed off her long, slender neck and what her mother called her "big Irish features, from your father's side." She was proud of those features—her prominent forehead, distinguished nose, long jaw line, and wide, sloping cheeks. They gave her a striking countenance, *arresting* even, which was how the movie magazine she'd leafed through that morning described Ingrid Bergman. The Swedish actress, like Clara, also enjoyed above-average height—5'9", according to *Movie Mirror*—though the last time Clara checked, she still measured two inches taller than Miss Bergman. Just shy of freakish, she liked to think.

She threw open her wire-bound sketchbook, exasperated at herself—*Why did she look at those ridiculous movie magazines?*—and began to draw from memory. First she drew the wizened old man in the dirty work apron who tended the West Seattle newsstand that had all the movie magazines on display. Then she made an unflattering sketch of the stout and visored transit driver who every morning refused to greet her when she boarded his bus. She drew fast, filling page after page. The beat cop tarrying at the corner of First and Pine where she got off the bus downtown. The Civil Defense warden in his khaki uniform and white pith helmet. Prim and proper Mrs. Berner at the Reading Room. The young mother in tears outside the Post Office, her frightened toddler in her arms. The soldier seated inside the Seattle Service Men's Club, gazing out the window as Clara walked by. Mr. Katevatis at the Athenian lunch counter in the Farmer's Market, who served her the liverwurst sandwich she ordered for lunch that day (instead of her usual pimento cheese). She drew whatever faces lingered in her mind once her day was done, logging each into her sketchbook and always, *always* using both sides of each heavy-weight sheet to conserve paper.

When she looked up from her sketchbook, she gave a start to find her reflection glowering back at her. Did she really look so glum or was it just the dimness of the candlelight, the waviness in the old window glass, the darkness outside? Last week after dinner, her mother had asked her if something wasn't the matter. "You look so woebegone," she remarked as Clara washed the dinner plates at the kitchen sink. Clara didn't know how to respond. She considered herself a rather high-spirited individual, someone inclined toward good cheer, who liked to latch onto the affirmative. Yet lately she'd been thinking of her brothers, Freddy and Ken, off fighting in the war, and how it had been more than two years since she'd seen them—and that's what had gotten her so down.

"Just thinking, I suppose," she told her mother, setting a plate in the dish rack, and wondered if it had really been so long ago that her family had sat around the radio on the Monday afternoon following the attack on Pearl Harbor and listened to President Roosevelt address the nation, asking Congress for a declaration of war on the Empire of Japan after its "unprovoked and dastardly attack" on America.

"We'll see this through," her father said at the conclusion of the President's address, and her mother recited the Lord's Prayer and asked the family to share in a silent prayer. "In the oneness of divine Mind," she intoned, "where true brotherhood prevails."

Four days later, after Germany declared war on the United States, Freddy announced he'd quit his longshore job and was enlisting in the Army. This prompted Ken to declare he was going to drop out of high school—five months shy of graduation—and enlist as well, despite their mother's protests. And the next day both boys drove straight down to the Army enlistment office and signed up. Two days later their father drove them to Fort Lewis in Tacoma for their induction, and a week after that Clara and her parents stood on the train station platform in Seattle and waved goodbye to Freddy and Ken, attired in their starched khaki uniforms, as they boarded an Army transport train that would take them all the way across the country to Fort Dix in New Jersey.

For the longest time, Clara would tear up just thinking of her brothers and what they must be going through overseas. It was as if her daily life, brimming with so many trite activities, was a disservice to them, a betrayal of both family and country. To thwart this dilemma, she'd decided back in high school to put away her artwork and devote all her spare time to the war relief effort. For the next two years she tended the neighborhood Victory Garden, helped with the church clothing drive, and knit Red Cross socks at the rate of one pair per week. Then, after she graduated last June, sacrificing her art on behalf of the war effort suddenly seemed like a silly schoolgirl notion and she once more took up her pencil and sketchbook, vowing never to forsake her creative gifts like that again. And to make up for lost time she drew like a fanatic—still tending the Victory Garden, still working on the clothing drive, still knitting socks for the soldiers—but now taking care of what she needed to do for herself as well, which meant her art.

In January she even took the bold step of enrolling in a drawing class at the Cornish School of Allied Arts on Capitol Hill. Her teacher was Mark Tobey, the famous modern painter, Seattle's most renowned artist. He'd studied in Paris before the war and knew many great artists, including Picasso. Yet despite his international acclaim, he'd chosen to return to Seattle to teach at Cornish, probably because of the war. He was an animated sort, though with a sullen, nervous aspect to him, always pacing about, pulling at his ashen goatee. Maybe he felt compromised, stuck in this Northwest outpost teaching local yokels like herself. All the same, though, he proved to be a dedicated teacher, urging his students to share his passion for art, to understand the interplay between line and shadow, to create with their hearts as well as their minds. In his enthusiasm to see his students excel, he could turn fierce, especially if he deemed a student was settling for mere competency—"Anyone can draw competently," he would bark—though his tirades always concluded with a practical suggestion and several words of encouragement.

"Not so rigid, Miss Hamilton. Allow more grace into the line," he urged Clara during last Thursday's class, peering over her shoulder and giving a flourish with his hand. "Loosen your elbow. That's better." With the exception of an older man who was bald and pudgy and a young man with metal braces on his legs, the class was made up entirely of women, which seemed to make Tobey even more demanding.

Upon Mark Tobey's insistence, the Cornish School had recently recruited its first nude models, which incited a minor scandal among the school's trustees. Rumor had it that Tobey threatened to resign if he could not hire at least two models—one male, one female—for the instructional benefit of his students. "Old biddies," he called the trustees during studio class the week after the controversy. "Every last one."

Clara was abashed the first time the class pushed its drawing tables into a circle and the model, a woman in her late twenties, stepped onto the center platform, dropped her robe, and stood naked awaiting Tobey's instructions on how to pose. Tobey told the students to concentrate on attaining a sense of contour and weight in their drawing of the model. And just like that, as soon as Clara began drawing, her embarrassment passed and the woman's shoulders, breasts, hips, and limbs became like so many apples and pears assembled in a fleshy bowl—that is, until she came to the model's face. Tobey had also told the students to focus exclusively on the form of the body, but Clara was intrigued by the compliant, oddly alluring expression on the model's face and spent the second half of the period sketching her facial features, trying to capture that expression. When Tobey passed behind her table and saw what she was up to, he became livid.

"This is *not* a portrait class, Miss Hamilton," he reprimanded her. "It's not

17th-century Holland, nor are you Frans Hals! Do I make myself clear?" and with that walked off.

Tobey also insisted his students draw every day, without exception. "Draw, draw, draw," he commanded them, "anything and everything," emphasizing that this was the only way they would rise above mediocrity and have any hope of achieving mastery. Nothing was off limits, he told them. People, objects, landscapes. "Even faces, Miss Hamilton."

Clara took Tobey's decree seriously, which was why she set to work each night at her drawing table upstairs in her bedroom and didn't stop until well into the predawn hours.

After she had drawn all the faces she could recall from her day, she turned her attention back to the model from class, especially her hands and feet. The model had long, graceful hands and what another student, pointing to the model's long second toe, called "Greek feet." She tried several detailed sketches on the same page—true studies, she thought, in the manner of da Vinci. But upon turning the page, she returned to the model's irresistible face. The downturned eyes, slightly arched brow, tapered jaw, and small, nautilus-like ears. She didn't know why she was so taken by the model's face. Perhaps it was the challenge of the impossibility it presented. The same impossibility that all faces presented. Perhaps she felt compelled by her Christian Science upbringing to ignore the body and seek infinite Spirit in the one region where Spirit found most expression, where essence and reflection were unified and body and soul merged. The face.

For now, though, as she finished drawing and prepared to blow out the two candles and crawl into bed, the only indisputable fact was that she had filled another sketchbook and, first thing the next morning, would need to replenish her stock.

Seattle Art Supply was located four blocks from the downtown Christian Science Reading Room where Clara worked Tuesday through Friday, 8:00 a.m. to noon. Since rarely did anyone come into the Reading Room so early in the morning and the art supply store opened at 9:00, she could sprint over, buy her sketchbooks, and be back before anyone knew she was gone. She placed the morning *Post-Intelligencer* and yesterday's *Christian Science Monitor* on the newspaper rack up front and waited out the first hour of her shift knitting her one-hundred-and-twenty-ninth pair of combat-green wool G.I. socks. She liked to think that at least one pair of the socks she knit would make it onto her brothers' feet. And when nine o'clock rolled around, she donned her raincoat and, leaving the Reading Room unlocked, hurried up the street.

Seattle Art Supply was on 6th Avenue and Virginia Street. Mr. Abbott, the store's owner, was just settling into reading the morning paper when Clara rushed in, carrying a good bit of rain with her. Coming to the art supply store was one of the great pleasures in her life. Despite the war shortages, the store remained stocked with everything a working artist could need or desire, and Clara could barely contain herself whenever she entered.

"Another wet day," Mr. Abbott called out from behind the front counter as Clara brushed the rain off her coat and caught her breath.

"How are you, Mr. Abbott?" Clara looked out over the tables and shelves piled high with art supplies. "I need more paper."

Mr. Abbott leaned across the counter. "You bought three pads last week," he said. "Mind, I'm just saying."

"I'm drawing as much as I can," Clara replied. She appreciated Mr. Abbott taking notice, but she was in a hurry. She picked up a wooden mannequin from one of the tables and asked how much it cost.

"Which size?"

"Eight-inch." Clara adjusted the limbs of the mannequin to the contrapposto position the nude model had assumed in her drawing class last week.

"Two dollars," Mr. Abbott answered. "But with the aspiring artist discount, which is good only on the days you come in—one-fifty."

Clara knew she shouldn't buy it. Even with Mr. Abbott's generous discount, it was an extravagance. On the other hand, she knew she would make good use of it, and so she set the mannequin on the counter and walked to the back where the sketchbooks were kept and picked out five different sizes of the Winsor wire-bound sketchbooks that she preferred.

As Mr. Abbott tallied the cost of the five sketchbooks and one mannequin, Clara knew she'd dallied too long and would be in big trouble if anyone from the church stopped into the Reading Room and didn't find a librarian there. She tucked the sketchbooks beneath her raincoat and the mannequin in a front pocket and thanked Mr. Abbott.

She arrived back at the Reading Room breathless, and just as she was reaching for the door, it pushed outward and a young sailor in a dark peacoat, white pants, and white sailor's cap blocked her entry. He seemed as startled as she was. He stepped aside and held the door for her, and yet as she turned to greet him, the door swung closed behind her and he was gone. She dropped her sketchbooks onto one of the armchairs and stepped back out onto the sidewalk.

"Excuse me," she shouted.

The sailor turned around, his hands stuffed into the pockets of his peacoat. He was tall and rangy, not unlike the hundreds of other sailors on the streets of Seattle since the start of the war. He wore round, rimless eyeglasses that magnified his dark pupils and gave him a scholarly look, like someone you might bump into among the stacks of the public library.

"I'm sorry I wasn't here when you came in," she called across the stretch of sidewalk separating them. "May I help you with something?"

The young man looked at her through the thin rain and replied, "I just stepped in to dry off."

Clara nodded as if to say *Ah, I see,* and pondered the odd figure before her. It was unusual to see a sailor walking about by himself. They usually formed small packs, clusters of four or five, when they caroused about town. It was even more unusual that a sailor—or soldier—came into the Reading Room, especially this early in the day. If one did, once he learned the Reading Room was neither a bookstore nor servicemen's canteen, he quickly left.

"Well, come again," Clara said. "Even if it's not raining." She liked the look of the sailor, his peculiar mien, and smiled at him. "I'm here most every morning. Honestly."

"That's all right," the sailor answered as if fearful she might start proselytizing to him. "Thank you anyhow." He then raised his hand to his sailor's cap.

"Bye then," she said and gave a faint wave.

Sailors, she thought as she returned to the warmth of the Reading Room and remembered her brothers' warning to stay clear of them.

She removed her raincoat and at the desk in the back corner took out her pencil case and made several rapid gesture drawings of Mr. Abbott in one of her new sketchbooks. Sixty seconds each, with light, quick flourishes. Yet she couldn't focus, and the drawings became more caricature than character study. She kept thinking how if the funny sailor with the round glasses had entered the Reading Room while Mrs. Berner was on duty, her supervisor would have engaged him in friendly conversation and made certain he left with a copy of *Science and Health* and half a dozen brochures Had she failed in her duty by not inviting him back inside and introducing him to the splendors of spiritual science? She recalled the surprise on his face when he opened the door and saw her blocking his exit, and abandoning her efforts to draw Mr. Abbott she flipped to a clean page and began sketching the leggy, bespectacled sailorboy.

TWO
Merritt, Fall 1943-Winter 1944

Merritt's first impression of Seattle when he arrived in early November—after eight weeks of basic training at Camp Decatur in sunny California and three months of special training at the Naval Administrative Base in the bone-dry Utah desert—was of unrelenting drear. It rained every day, all day, his first week in town. He'd never seen the like. He didn't witness his first sun break until well into the third week when a feeble yellow light filtered through the haze-gray sky for a few hours. Otherwise, a perpetual marine cloud hung over the city like a bad head cold, making everything damp and obscuring the top of any building over four stories high. He eventually tried to come to terms with this morose weather—*What choice did he have?*—and carry on as best he could.

The downtown was lively enough during the day, especially in and around Victory Square where Navy PR officers held daily events to boost morale and sell war bonds, or at Westlake Plaza where the department stores kept busy with shoppers and window displays, or throughout the Public Market where farmers and vendors hawked their produce and other goods. Come night, however, it was another story. With businesses locked up, streetlamps turned off, windows covered, and automobile headlights blindered with tin—all part of the mandatory black-out—the city turned downright grim. It was scary to walk the streets after dark, which at this time of year and this extreme latitude descended upon the city at four in the afternoon. Merritt regularly heard of newbie seamen, drunk off their rocker, being rolled in downtown alleys. They would show up at the Recruitment Station the next morning, begging for a couple of dollars and a liberty chit to get them back to base before being declared AWOL.

Because of limited housing at the Sand Point Naval Air Station, Merritt was placed on subs-and-quarters, which gave him $2.30 per day for room and board, on top of his $45 monthly base pay as Seaman Second Class. He and five others assigned to the downtown Recruitment Station took rooms at the Loring Hotel, a fleabag SRO with a sink in the room and a toilet and shower stall down the hall. When Merritt wrote home, he told his parents he lived close to work and two blocks from a cafeteria, which was all they needed to know. He stopped at Manning's Cafeteria every morning for coffee and a bear claw. For lunch he got a hotdog at Bartell Drugs on Westlake, a little pie-wedge building with a lunch counter upstairs that overlooked the street. Sometimes he went to one of the Chinese joints on First Avenue and ordered a big plate of pork fried rice and a bottle of Oly for a buck-ten, the best lunch deal in town.

A lot of the guys from the Recruitment Station hung out at The Turf Club right next door. It had a restaurant and bar up front and card tables, billiards, pull-tabs, dice, two guys taking numbers, and various other gambling opportunities in the back. Someone in recruitment would shout, "The smoking light is lit," and two or three guys would get up from their desks and head down to The Turf Club for a smoke and a round of drinks. During boot camp Merritt had smoked at night to help him relax before climbing into his bunk. Now he averaged a pack a day. Something about the rain made him want to stand at a window or beneath an awning with a cigarette dangling from his mouth. Each morning at 7:30, he entered The Turf Club and bought a pack of Chesterfields from the cigarette girl at the front counter. Dressed in his regulation blues, he would stand on the sidewalk beneath the restaurant's green awning, loosen the knot on his white seaman's scarf, give his soft cap a push forward, and smoke his first of the day. Then he would flick the butt into the gutter, straighten his crackerjack and Dixie Cup, and head up to the office and the eagle-eyed scrutiny of his C.O.

Six months had passed since he left Vermont. It was as if he'd been dropped in this cloud-clogged city and told to pass the days as best he could until the war was over. He had his duties to perform, typing and filing forms the live-long day, but otherwise his time was his own. The tedium of it all eventually made him regret ever having done so well on the Navy classification tests. He'd scored highest on the general test, which measured ability to think and reason in terms of words, and the clerical test, which gauged one's ability to observe fast and accurately. In other words, as he told his older sister in a letter back home, he could look, think, and speak all at the same time without getting confused. In fact, it was his test scores, along with his ability to type 60 words per minute, that got him sent to the Administrative Base in Utah for clerical training and that, for better or worse, was the sole reason he hadn't been shipped out along with 99.9 percent of the other enlisted men.

As the holidays rolled around, he felt more forlorn than ever. He spent Christmas Eve by himself, leaving the Recruitment Station at eight and eating a hamburger at The Turf Club, then walking up Capitol Hill and sitting in a lounge on Broadway Avenue for two hours nursing a couple of rye highballs, and finally shuffling back downtown and then to the waterfront where he sat on a creosote-soaked beam and smoked until the distant church bells rang in Christmas morning.

By mid-January he couldn't remember ever feeling so blue, even as he told

22

himself it could be far worse. At least no one was shooting at him. He was walking to the office, thinking about what it would be like to ship out, when he got caught in a morning downpour and ducked into the nearby Christian Science Reading Room. The sign in the window said "Open to Public - Servicemen Welcome," so he figured he might find a cup of coffee inside. He paused inside the doorway and looked about. There were four armchairs with a couple of floor lamps near the front window, two round tables farther back, then a rack of newspapers, a shelf of books, another table with brochures and booklets arranged upon it, and way in the back corner an unoccupied desk. That was it. No attendant, no coffee. He immediately felt as though he were trespassing, but just as he turned to leave a young woman appeared before him in the doorway, almost bumping into him. She looked flustered, so Merritt stepped aside and held the door for her—she was tall, nearly as tall as he—and then left.

It was the brief exchange they had on the wet sidewalk a moment later that left him so befuddled. When she pulled several strands of hair away from her face, all he could do was gaze at her. She had that rare loveliness, and accompanying sex appeal, of someone who doesn't know how beautiful she is—someone who never recognized the effect she could have on men. When she asked him if there was anything she could help him with, he only stared at her. He muttered something finally, though he didn't know what, and she said something in return and smiled ever so sweetly at him. And then, like a frightened little animal, he scurried off.

As he fled, he felt bad for her. Maybe she'd hoped to find a convert in him. He didn't have a clue what Christian Science was about, or what kind of religious fanatic she might be. The name of the religion had always struck him as oddball, especially as it appeared on their churches—*Church of Christ, Scientist*—as if Jesus had traded in his dusty tunic for a lab coat. Yet the simple way she had smiled at him, her eagerness in chasing after him in the rain, made him want to know more.

So two days later—her damp face, ash blonde hair, and clear-eyed look still vivid in his mind—he returned to the Reading Room. He entered more tentatively this time, removing his wet cap and peacoat and hanging them on the coat rack beside the door. Again there was no attendant, yet rather than leave, he picked up the *Christian Science Monitor* and sat in one of the armchairs to wait. He was perusing an account of the campaign for the Marianas when the door flew open and the same young woman rushed in carrying a large black portfolio case under her arm.

"Hello again," she said, recognizing Merritt, and walked to the back where she put her portfolio case down and removed her coat. A moment later she came up front again. Only then did Merritt remember how tall she was. She wore a kind of make-do-and-mend dress—as his mother called them—trimmed with lace about the collar and cuffs. She stood at the front window and peered down Union Street. "Rain, rain, go away," she trilled and turned to Merritt. "Are you getting out from the rain again?"

Merritt watched her. *Gosh damn,* he thought, *she's really something.* "Yes," he blurted, "and to read the paper." He held the newspaper up for her to see. "Is that all right?"

"Yes, it's all right. You're more than welcome," she said and took a deep breath. "I'm afraid this is the second time you've caught me neglecting my post." She looked about the Reading Room. "Oh well," she said and added, "Let me know if I can help you with anything," and retreated to the back.

Merritt resumed reading the newspaper, but every few seconds glanced back at her seated at the desk. She was writing, and he figured she was composing a letter to her beau off fighting the war. He imagined the letter sodden with expressions of devotion and longing and littered with *X*'s and *O*'s, and eventually he returned the newspaper to the rack and retrieved his cap and coat. As he readied to leave, the young woman looked up, smiled ever so sweetly at him, and said, "Our hours are eight to four, Monday through Saturday."

"Thank you," he called back, and as he opened the door noticed she'd already returned to her letter.

All the same he went back to the Reading Room several more times. The next time it was in the afternoon and an older woman was there, a Mrs. Berner, who gave him a copy of *Science and Health*. From then on he returned only in the morning and each time found the young woman at the back of the room, seated at the desk, either writing or drawing. She would greet him as he hung up his cap and coat, but she never got up from her desk. Finally, on his fifth visit, he mustered up the nerve to walk to the back of the room.

"Excuse me," he stammered. "May I apply for a library card?"

"A card?" she said. She closed her sketchbook, but not before he saw that she'd been drawing a man's portrait, and once more figured it was her boyfriend, perhaps a member of her church, maybe even her fiancée.

"Since I come in so often, I figured—"

"We're not a lending library," she explained, "though you're welcome to borrow any book you like, and we also have books for sale. Mostly people come in to study the daily lessons or to read the newspaper."

He was a fool all right, he thought, and said, "I see. My misunderstanding."

"There's some literature over here I can give you," she offered and led him to the table arrayed with various church publications. She handed him a brochure and stood back. Wasn't she going to sell him on the virtues of Christian Science or invite him to attend Sunday services, or ask him whether he believed in God? As far as she knew he was a raving heathen.

24

"I'm stationed a couple blocks over at the Recruitment Station," he said and eyed the cover of the brochure, which read *The Christian Science Reading Room. For the Study of Spiritual Healing and Understanding.* "My name's Merritt."

"It's nice to meet you, Merritt." She put her hand out and Merritt took it. Her palm was cool and dry, her fingers soft and firm. "I'm Clara."

"You like to draw, do you?"

She glanced at her sketchbook but didn't say anything.

"May I see?" he asked, feeling emboldened.

"Well . . ." she demurred, obviously uncomfortable. "They're just some sketches. Nothing worth looking at really."

He instantly regretted being so forward and wanted to beg her forgiveness. But even more, he wanted to tell her how beautiful she was, stunningly beautiful, and just how loopy he'd been about her since their first encounter on the sidewalk two weeks ago. He wanted to let her know how sad and lonesome he'd been since coming to Seattle and plead with her to let him take her out just *once*—her boyfriend be damned—because he knew an evening with her would transform his sorrowful existence and make his world a joyful, sun-lit place once more. He curled the brochure in his hand and twisted it hard.

"In any case," he said, "may I buy you lunch?"

THREE
Clara, Winter 1944

Maybe she should have spoken to him about church precepts, the triune Principles, and Mary Baker Eddy's *Science and Health and A Key to the Scriptures*. Maybe she should have asked what church he attended, whether he read the Bible and prayed everyday, whether he even believed in God, and so on and so forth. Instead she let the lanky sailor take her to lunch at The Continental, the new restaurant on Bell Street that, according to an ad in *The P.I.*, featured "flaming service," which turned out to be nothing more than chafing trays. Not only that, she also agreed to go to a movie with him Saturday afternoon. So maybe she wasn't the best person to serve as a Reading Room librarian after all.

Merritt had that awkward way that boys often displayed around her, an attitude she attributed to her height. Yet Merritt was rather tall himself, standing two or three inches above her. He was also courteous, holding her chair for her at the restaurant, as well as extremely nervous, which she could tell from the way his hands trembled. Over lunch he asked her about growing up in Seattle—"West Seattle," she corrected him—and she asked him about Vermont and whether he missed it—"The foliage," he replied. They talked about Christian Science, though this made Clara uncomfortable, as if she might be seen as proselytizing to him. So she changed the subject by asking him what he planned to do after the war. When he said he didn't know, that he hadn't thought that far ahead, she appreciated his honesty. She'd only been on three dates her entire life, and each time the boy had tried to impress her with what a big success he was going to make of himself in life, which always left Clara with the sense of being told she ought to hook her star to his while she still had the chance. Such presumptuousness never failed to make her laugh, and think how most boys had more swagger than common sense.

Merritt was different. He was shy, which she found appealing. He also seemed to be the same person Saturday afternoon when they went to a movie as he was three days earlier over lunch—intelligent and kind and a thoughtful listener. After the movie, a matinee of *The Fighting Seabees*, when they were having a bite to eat at the corner diner, he let her prattle on about her drawing, Mark Tobey, and her desire to take up oil painting, without once glancing at his watch or looking about for the waitress to bring the check.

When he finally said something, it was to compliment her on her commitment to her artwork, and then, out of the blue, to ask if she liked to dance. The question didn't register with her at first, but when it did she said, "I don't know. I've never been."

"That makes two of us," he replied and sat up eagerly in the booth they shared. "But I know where we can get a free lesson."

"Are you asking me out again?" she asked. "To go dancing?"

He blushed bright red, but then cleared his throat and said, "Do you mind?"

He had to be the cutest boy she'd ever met, she thought, and shook her head. "When?"

He thought a moment. "If I remember correctly, the coupon isn't dated. It's for one free lesson at the Hollywood Dance Studio near Liberty Square. We could get a bite to eat before hand."

"That would be nice," she said and folded her napkin in her lap. "I have class on Tuesday and Thursday nights. Otherwise I'm free."

"How about next Friday then? I can pick you up."

"Or I can meet you," she said. As far as she knew he didn't own a car, and she didn't want him to have to borrow one and drive all the way over to West Seattle when she could just as easily take the bus. She also didn't want her parents to know about him just yet. So they agreed to meet for dinner at The Continental at five and then walk over to the Hollywood Dance Studio for the 7:00 p.m. dance lesson.

"Friday at five then," he confirmed as they slid out of the booth.

"I'll wear my best dancing shoes," she replied.

Two consecutive dates with the same boy had been her standing record. Plus, she hadn't gone out with anyone since her junior year of high school, nearly two years ago. Of the three boys she'd gone on dates with, one had joined the Army and the other two had moved on to more glamorous girls. The one who joined the Army was the only one she'd ever made out with. So even though she hadn't been nervous during her movie date with Merritt, she was now about to enter a new stage with him. This was going to be an evening date. Dinner and dancing. They hadn't even held hands yet and here they were planning to go dancing.

After tarrying about the Reading Room that Friday afternoon, she walked the five blocks to the restaurant and found Merritt waiting for her outside. He was not in uniform. Rather, his brown sports coat and glen-green plaid pants— "plaid-'n'-plain," it was called—made him look like a college boy trying too hard to be some kind of sport. She nonetheless admired his tan knit tie and well-polished shoes. The outfit, she figured, might have been the same one he'd worn to his own prom not too long ago. He also wore a fancy felt fedora with a small scarlet feather stuck in the silk band.

He greeted her with a handshake and held the restaurant door open for her. When she removed her coat and handed it to the coat-check girl, he complimented her on how nice she looked. She thanked him, and as the maitre d' led them to a table she straightened out the navy-blue poplin dress she'd ironed with rose water—her only decent dress—after recovering it from the recesses of her bedroom closet that morning. She'd also used her mother's metal curlers on her longish hair to give it the off-the-shoulder swoops that made everyone these days look like one of the Andrews Sisters.

Throughout dinner, they said very little to one another. Clara ate modestly, picking at her food, and Merritt hardly ate at all. When the waiter removed their plates and reprimanded them for not eating more, they both gave a nervous laugh and told him they had to stay light on their feet. The beginners lesson at the Hollywood Dance Studio commenced at 7:00 p.m., Merritt reminded her, and so they agreed to forego dessert.

It was a short cab ride to the Hollywood Dance Studio. A street-level entrance led up a flight of stairs to the second-floor studio space, where a glossy hardwood floor stretched the length of the building. Long, narrow windows overlooked Seventh Avenue and floor-to-ceiling mirrors lined the back wall. Half a dozen couples were gathered in the studio, waiting for the lesson to begin. In due time, the instructor introduced himself as Mr. V. Markum Lerner and his female assistant as Miss Jeannie Northrup. He went on to explain that he'd been a senior instructor at the Arthur Murray Studio in San Francisco for six years prior to opening the Hollywood Dance Studio here in Seattle.

"We shall begin this evening's lesson with a basic fox trot," he said and informed the group that the fox trot was the foundation of all dance steps, hence its nickname the "get-acquainted" dance. Several couples tittered at this, including Clara and Merritt, and then V. Markum clapped his hands and signaled the couples to space themselves out across the floor. Next he and Miss Northrup demonstrated the proper stance. "Good posture is a must," he insisted. "The gentleman positions his right hand gently on the lady's mid-back, and the lady rests her left hand softly but securely on the gentleman's shoulder. The partners hold their free hands palm to palm, shoulder-height."

Clara and Merritt exchanged bashful smiles. She felt a bit awkward being nearly as tall as he, yet as she cupped his shoulder and he placed his hand on her back, she saw that they matched up better than she'd expected. They joined palms and awaited V. Markum's next command.

"We'll begin with a basic walking step and side-step," he instructed, "keeping time to a 4/4 beat." Miss Northrup moved over to the phonograph and set the needle down on a standard Dorsey Brothers number. She and V. Markum then demonstrated the basic fox trot steps, after which they stood aside and signaled the couples to proceed. As everyone stepped carefully across the floor, V. Markum exhorted them to keep tempo with the music and control their timing. "Move smoothly and continuously. And for goodness sake, try not to look at your feet. Make eye contact with your partner."

Clara and Merritt soon found their rhythm and, after initially stumbling over one another's feet, moved across the floor with some ease. After two more practice dances, Miss Northrup stopped the music and V. Markum announced he was now going to introduce them to the basic slot step, part of the "sophisticated swing" that Arthur Murray himself had developed. "In this step, the lady moves toward the man."

"About time," a fellow in a blue suit cracked and tugged his pudgy blonde partner toward him.

Everyone was feeling loose now and had a good laugh at this, including V. Markum and Miss Northrup. Then, to Clara's surprise, Merritt reached down and held her hand as the two instructors demonstrated the new step. She felt her face warming and her palm beginning to perspire. When their turn came, and feeling rather emboldened herself, she slid straight toward Merritt, the skirt of her poplin dress lifting away from her calves, her hair floating off her shoulders, her eyes meeting his as their bodies touched and they swirled into the next step. When the dance ended, they stepped back from one another and in silly imitation of high school dance etiquette, she curtsied and he bowed.

Two more practice dances followed before the hour-long lesson concluded, at which point V. Markum explained that if they returned for the intermediate lesson he would teach them several new steps, including taps and shuffles, coaster steps, and the underarm pass. "That's when the fun really starts," he said. He ended with a pitch for signing up for six lessons for the price of five, with a special discount for servicemen, and then thanked everyone on behalf of himself and his lovely assistant. The dancers applauded their instructors and then set about retrieving their coats and hats.

Back out on the street, Merritt lit a cigarette, the first time he'd smoked in her company, while Clara buttoned her overcoat. "That was great fun," he said.

Yes, it was great fun, she thought. "We're a regular Fred Astaire and Ginger Rogers," she said, and as they walked down the street she put her arm through his. "It's been a pleasure being your dance partner," she said.

"The pleasure's all mine," he said and tossed his cigarette into the street. "Where to now?"

Though it was only half past eight, Clara knew she really ought to be getting home. She'd told her mother she was meeting some friends downtown to have a knitting circle, and when her mother asked why they had to meet all the way downtown, Clara had to improvise and tell her mother that one of the girls lived in a studio apartment, and then promised to be home by ten.

"The Bohemian Café has excellent desserts," said Merritt. "Can I entice you with a piece of apple pie? Maybe a cup of coffee?"

She leaned forward and kissed him on the cheek. "That's so sweet," she answered, "but I promised my mother I'd come straight home." She seriously considered breaking her promise, but decided she couldn't. "You can wait with me at the transit stop, though," she said and gave his arm a playful shake. "Doesn't that sound like fun?"

He laughed and told her it would be an honor.

Twenty minutes later when her bus arrived, she let him kiss her on the lips as the bus door opened and they said their goodnights, and all the way back to West Seattle she wondered what it would be like to actually fall for someone like him.

Two days later, on Sunday, Clara fell ill and had to ask Mrs. Berner to fill in for her at the Reading Room. In the past two weeks, she'd grown accustomed to Merritt stopping in during his morning break to chat for a few minutes before he had to return to the Recruitment Station. Now she wished to phone the station or leave a note with Mrs. Berner, letting him know she'd had a delightful evening on Friday and would be back in a day or two. But she was too drained by her illness to do even this and let it pass, hoping she would be able to return to the Reading Room before the end of the week.

Her sickness lingered, however, and by the weekend, despite her mother's healing ministrations, it had worsened to a racking cough, congested lungs, rasping breathing, headache and backache, and night fevers. Try as she might, she couldn't pray away the symptoms. She grew frustrated with her mother's insistence on calling in a Christian Science practitioner, as her mother had done once when Clara was a young girl and fell seriously ill. How many times at Wednesday evening testimony held in the large church meeting room had Clara heard true-life accounts of the divine power of scientific healing? Illness was a mere error in thinking, simple spiritual misguidance, which enough prayer and proper study of the Scriptures and *Science and Health* could rectify. God wants us to be healthy. That's what her mother believed, and as best as Clara could tell in her feverish condition, it's what she herself believed.

Of course she wanted to be healthy—*Who didn't?*—and so by the end of the second week when she still hadn't gotten better, she agreed to let her mother call in the church practitioner. Her father protested, wanting to take her to a doctor instead, but her mother said that such an action would be a grievous concession to mortal error and would only worsen their daughter's condition. So the next morning the practitioner, her mother's good friend Mrs. Holmquist, sat at Clara's bedside and the two prayed in silence for more than an hour. Then

30

Mrs. Holmquist read that week's assigned passages from the Scriptures while Clara read the accompanying lessons from *Science and Health*. In the two hours the practitioner was with her, Clara rarely coughed. She breathed more easily and seemed almost to forget that she was sick. And after Mrs. Holmquist left, she slept for seven straight hours.

She woke up in the early evening, though, with a devastating headache. If there had been aspirin in the house, which there never was, she would have gulped a fistful. She just wanted the pain—mortal error or not—to be gone. When her mother came into her bedroom with a glass of water, Clara was nearly in tears. Her mother held her hand and told her she looked better and that God's pureness would have her back on her feet in no time. Clara smiled wanly at her mother's words, and then her mother said, "A young man telephoned earlier this afternoon asking for you."

Clara released her mother's hand and tried to sit up. "Who was it?" she asked. "Did he say?"

She was no longer certain how long she'd been bedridden. It could have been months. Her dancing date with Merritt, while still vivid in her memory, seemed like an event from another era in her life, or maybe something she'd dreamed during one of her night sweats.

"Mervin or Milton," he mother replied. "I can't quite recall."

"Merritt?" Clara said.

"Yes, that's it. *Merritt*. How could I forget such an unusual name."

"What's wrong with his name?" Clara demanded, looking sharply at her mother.

"Nothing, dear. It's a fine name. Just not one you hear very often." Her mother patted the top of Clara's hands, which lay on top of her bedcover. "Is he someone you know?"

"Yes," she said and settled back down. She wanted to ask her mother what day it was. "Did he say why he was calling?"

"Well," her mother allowed, deliberating over her answer, "he said he wished to know how you were doing?"

"And . . . ?" Clara said. "What did you tell him?"

"I explained that there was only health in God's Truth, and that you were closer to that Truth every day."

"Oh dear," Clara muttered. She had only ever spoken in vague, general terms about Christian Science with Merritt. Though he said he wanted to learn more, she knew he was only being polite. And quite frankly she was reluctant to go into the technicalities of her religion, since admittedly it was an unusual faith—a beautiful faith, but one that often left people scratching their heads at its more challenging precepts and practices.

"He also asked that you contact him as soon as possible. He said, 'Please tell her it's urgent.' Now, dear, you know I respect your privacy, but is there something going on here your father and I should know about? What could be so urgent as all that?"

Clara listened to her mother and gathered her wits about her. "No, mother, he's just a boy I met. He came into the Reading Room a couple of weeks ago and we had lunch."

"Does he belong to the church?"

"No. But he's very nice. He reads *The Monitor*." Clara felt badly that she was whitewashing the details of her acquaintance with Merritt, but she had neither the strength nor will to go into a long explanation. "Did he say anything else?" she asked.

Her mother shook her head no.

"Did he leave a telephone number?"

"It's downstairs on the secretary."

With this Clara threw back the covers, swung her feet past where her mother sat on the bed, and stood up. Yet the sudden motion sent blood rushing to her head and she became faint, grasping the headboard and nearly fainting before her mother could reach out and guide her back into bed.

FOUR
Merritt, Winter-Spring 1944

"So how was she?"

"I bet those legs could wrap around a fella two or three times. How tall's that girl anyway?"

"Did you wank her?"

After his movie date with Clara, Merritt made the rookie mistake of telling his fellow squids in the Recruitment Station about her. When he'd mentioned he was taking her dancing the following Friday, they howled like hyenas, whistled, and made obscene gestures until he was thoroughly red in the face. Even the new recruits lounging around the office got into the action, including a large group of young Teamsters from Everett, Seattle, and Tacoma who'd come *en masse* to enlist.

"All right, all right," he told them all. "It may be that way with your two-bit swoozies, but this gal's got class."

"That's right," Lieutenant Seaman Boyington shot back. "She an *artiste*, right, Driscoll? She gets *nude* rather than nekked."

That's when Merritt decided to take his cigarette break. He hadn't seen or spoken to Clara since kissing her goodnight as she boarded the bus to West Seattle. Throughout the weekend, he couldn't get his mind off her. He'd never kissed a girl before. Twenty years old and never kissed a girl—it was hard to believe. All of which made Clara that much more memorable.

But what he was feeling, he knew, was more than just an infatuation. This could be the girl for him. He hardly dared admit it to himself, but that's what he was thinking. And damn if she wasn't fine looking. After he'd mentioned her to the guys in the Recruitment Station, two of them strolled over to the Christian Science Reading Room and peered in through the front window to get a gander at her. When they returned to the office, they confirmed it.

"The chickie has a figure on her all right."

"I about popped off in my dress blues when I saw her."

Merritt was pleased and embarrassed. Clara did have a striking figure. Some girls that tall—and she had to be nearly six-foot—were either gangly or horsey or downright freakish. But she struck the perfect balance between these physical possibilities and came out perfectly proportioned. She also had such a lovely face and heart-melting smile that . . . well, he was stumped to figure how he'd gotten so lucky. What's more, she seemed to like him too.

After the drawn-out weekend, he was eager to stop into the Reading Room and thank her for the wonderful evening, as well as suggest they go out again during the week. When he entered the Reading Room on Monday morning, though, he found Mrs. Berner seated in Clara's place at the back desk.

Mrs. Berner recognized him from their first meeting. "Why hello again," she said. "Come in, come in."

"Good morning, Mrs. Berner." Merritt knew from Clara that Mrs. Berner hailed from Massachusetts and claimed to be related to Mary Baker Eddy, the founder of the Christian Science church. "Is Miss Hamilton in this morning?" he asked.

"No, not this morning," Mrs. Berner replied. "Maybe I can help you. Today's *Monitor* hasn't arrived yet, but maybe you would like to look at *The Sentinel*."

Merritt had loitered about the Reading Room enough over the past two weeks to know that, whereas *The Christian Science Monitor* was a respectable newspaper, *The Sentinel* presented the straight church perspective. Besides, he had no interest in either paper today.

"I was actually just following up on a discussion about painting that Miss Hamilton and I had the other day," he said and looked about the Reading Room for any trace of Clara's portfolio or sketchbooks. "Will she be in later?"

"No," Mrs. Berner replied, sounding a more dour note, "she's taken the day off."

Merritt turned his eyes to her. "Is she sick?"

"She's resting at home," was all Mrs. Berner would say.

He didn't know all the in's and out's of Christian Science, not by a long stretch, but he knew what most people did, that they frowned on doctors and preferred to heal themselves through prayer and study—or something along those lines. He didn't know how far Clara bought into such nonsense, but if she worked in the Reading Room he figured it was pretty far.

He thanked Mrs. Berner for her time and asked her to pass along his regards to Clara.

"I'll do that," she replied. "And do come again."

Merritt could tell Mrs. Berner had him pegged as someone more interested in young, attractive Miss Hamilton than crazy, old Mary Baker Eddy. There was nothing he could do except hope Clara showed up tomorrow, and so he returned to the Recruitment Station and worked steadily the rest of the day, anticipating her return. Yet the following morning, when he strolled back into the Reading Room, Clara was again absent.

This went on for another three days and by the end of the week he began to fear Clara might not be sick at all, but might be giving him the dodge, figuring he'd eventually get the message and go away. After all, who stayed sick in bed an entire week? Or maybe it was something else altogether. Maybe, he thought, it was her parents. Mrs. Berner might have tipped them off about him, and once they'd learned he wasn't in the church, they'd forbid Clara from seeing him, going so far as to hold her prisoner in her own house. Religion made people do all kinds of crazy things, so it was possible.

He did his best to tamp down such thoughts by working late each night and afterward taking a stool at the bar in The Turf Club and drinking beer until closing. All the same, he couldn't keep himself from reviewing every detail of his two dates with Clara to figure out how he might have offended her. Why the hell, for example, had he taken her to see a war movie, especially one about the Navy? The war was the last thing someone on a date wanted to think about. But Clara said she'd never been to the Orpheum Theatre and heard it was marvelous inside. "I like Susan Hayward," she also said. "One of my favorite movies is *Among the Living*." And that settled it. Yet then why had he been so foolish as to take her back to The Continental before their dance lesson? They'd just been there for lunch. Also, how many times had he stepped on her feet while dancing? It was a miracle she could even walk afterward. Maybe he shouldn't have put his hand so low on her back (even though it felt good there). And then there was the kiss. After the peck she'd given him on the cheek outside the dance studio, he felt encouraged and tried to kiss her on the lips before she boarded the bus, but she was already halfway up the steps, the driver waiting to close the door, when he reached up, took hold of her arm, and planted his lips on hers. Jeez louise, how awkward could a fella be! She must have known right then the kind of rube she was dealing with.

By Saturday morning when he arrived at the Recruitment Station hung over, he wasn't certain of anything anymore. Maybe Clara *was* sick. Really sick. What kind of cracked religion didn't take a sick person to see the doctor? She could die and he would never know. It was this notion that led him to get out Polk's City Directory and look up her address and telephone number. He would check on her for himself. If she didn't want to see him, she could tell him so. The thick directory listed three Hamiltons in West Seattle: Ian Hamilton, Gust and Maggie Hamilton, and Carl and Glenora Hamilton. He figured the second or third listing was Clara's since both her parents were alive. But phoning her, now that he thought about it, might seem too forward, and he didn't want her to think he was keeping tabs on her. And what if one of her parents answered the telephone? The whole situation had him in a knot, and so maybe, he decided, he just needed to accept the fact that she didn't want anything to do with him.

By Wednesday he stopped mentioning her to the guys in the office, and by Friday they stopped ribbing him about the leggy new dame he was dating. By the end of the day on Saturday, two full weeks since he'd seen her—and not a word between them—Merritt was fully resigned to the fact that he and Clara were through. What was, was.

He went down to The Turf Club with Boyington at about 7:30 and threw back three rye highballs before the clock struck nine. When the lieutenant stood up from the bar and told him he was calling it a night, Merritt implored him to stay.

"I'm buying," he said.

"Not at your pay grade," Boyington replied.

Merritt saluted his superior without standing up from his barstool, and Boyington told him to go easy on the rye. "We call that Kentucky kickass back in Ohio."

Merritt knew he was just feeling sorry for himself. Sure, it had only been a couple of dates, but why'd she have to do him like that? Why not just tell him she wasn't interested in him rather than disappear like that, without a word? What kinda way was that to treat a fella? Here he was twenty years old, he'd never even been with a woman, and already he knew what it was like to be dumped.

He was finishing his fourth highball and was set to take off when a seaman in dress whites sat down next to him and offered to buy him another. The seaman introduced himself as Leigh Rivard. "Ensign Leigh Rivard," he said, "but you can call me Leigh."

Merritt introduced himself as well, thinking the ensign looked familiar and that maybe he'd seen him over at the Sand Point Naval Air Station when he delivered the enlistment roles each week.

"You're in the Recruitment Station next door, right?" Rivard asked.

"Sure am," said Merritt, his tongue slow and heavy in his mouth.

Rivard was at least a decade older than him, with gray hair laced through his sideburns. Merritt figured he'd come into town from Sand Point to spend Saturday night carousing. Most nights of the week, Seattle's taverns and burlesque joints teemed with sailors on leave from the half dozen naval stations and shipyards in and around the city. The streets became a swirling sea of crisp navy white, with a pair of baton-twirling, helmet-wearing SPs posted every few blocks. By closing time, the scene always turned ugly—fights erupting, bottles smashed on the pavement, vomit spewed across the sidewalks, piss flowing in the alleys. Since Merritt was stationed downtown, he had the benefit of never having to put in for leave to partake of the debauchery. As long as he had his butt back at the Recruitment Station bright and early the next morning, he was free to indulge to his heart's content. So when Ensign Rivard offered to buy him a round, he told himself why not and signaled the barkeep to bring him another rye.

The two continued to drink and just before midnight, having lost count of how many he'd had, Merritt stood up from the bar, steadied himself, and weaved his way past the gamblers in the back room to the head. When he came back, Rivard stood at the bar as if waiting for him. He handed Merritt his peacoat and said he had a bottle of bourbon and some beer back at his room.

"Let's go," he added. "Have you ever had a boilermaker?"

Merritt knew that as a Seaman Second Class you didn't turn down a superior officer when he offered you a drink, even a petty officer like an ensign. He'd learned long ago that the Navy often came down to a drinking chain of command, in which sipping scotch with Naval Commander "Bull" Halsey was the pinnacle of one's career. So he took his peacoat from Rivard and told him to lead the way.

They staggered out of The Turf Club and walked to the corner of Seneca and Eighth where Rivard had a room at the Exeter Hotel. Merritt couldn't figure why the ensign had a room downtown if he was stationed at Sand Point, and when he asked, the ensign told him he kept it so he wouldn't have to haul himself all the way back to the naval base every time he wanted to go downtown. "A lot of officers do it," he added. "And if you're having company, a fella needs a place of his own, if you get my drift."

Merritt nodded. The remark made him think momentarily of Clara and what might have been. He entertained a glimmer of hope that she would show up at the Reading Room on Monday—yet then reminded himself of his vow not to go by and see her even if she did. Also, he figured he and Leigh might go out later and round up a couple of hussies just to let the world know he could get some whenever he wanted.

Rivard's room on the second floor looked like every other SRO room in the city. Iron bedstead and sunken double mattress, a dresser drawers and mirror, a table upon which sat a hotplate and coffee percolator plugged into the wall socket, two rickety chairs, one on either side of the table, and a small armchair in the corner piled high with discarded clothes. Rivard took the bottle of bourbon off the top of the dresser and set it on the table with a couple of shot glasses and two glass beer mugs. He opened the room's only window and retrieved two bottles of beer from the ledge where they kept cold. He popped the tops off the bottles, poured the beer into the mugs, then screwed off the top of the bottle of bourbon and poured the shot glasses full.

"Bombs away and down the hatch," he declared, and with Merritt following his lead, he dropped a shot glass of bourbon into one of the beer mugs and in four gulps downed the whole thing. Merritt slammed his mug down on the table and the two sat back and smacked their lips. "That's a boilermaker," said the ensign.

They kept up this pace for the next hour or so until Merritt stumbled out of the room and reeled down the hallway to find the toilet closet. He found it, but when he couldn't locate the pull string to the light, he peed into the dark until he heard the splash of toilet water. When he returned to the room, Rivard

37

handed him a straight shot glass of bourbon, which he took and threw back. He then dropped the empty glass at his feet and collapsed onto the bed.

He didn't want to get a whore any longer—or ever, he decided. "That's not me," he muttered as the room wobbled and spun.

"What's not you?" he heard Rivard say from the table where he sat.

"Whores," Merritt answered.

Rivard laughed, and Merritt watched as the ensign came over to the bed and picked up his feet, pulled Merritt's shoes off, and swung his legs onto the bed.

"Thanks," Merritt said as he stretched out and closed his eyes. "I'll get up in just a bit. Pour me another."

His eyes remained closed, though, and when he rolled over on the bed and opened them, the room was dark and a body lay next to him on the narrow mattress. So he rolled back the other way, trying to remember where he was, and closed his eyes again.

He was on his back when he stirred next. His pants were undone, all thirteen buttons, so maybe he'd tried to undress himself before falling asleep. Or maybe he'd been to the head again, he couldn't remember. He tried fumbling with the buttons to do them up, but couldn't manage and gave up.

When he came to again, it was still dark in the room, but something was going on. He had an erection and was softly stroking himself. But no, it wasn't him at all, but the person lying next to him. He kept perfectly still, pretending to remain asleep, and tried to figure what was happening. Maybe he was only dreaming. He'd had wet dreams before, including once in the barracks at boot camp, after which he'd had to hide his stained skivvies until he could find someplace to dispose of them. Now, though, he didn't know what to do. He was about to do something, anything, when he heard Rivard say, "At ease, sailor," and then raised his head just enough to see Rivard taking his member into his mouth. It was as if he became someone other than himself in that split second, someone apart from who he was, another person altogether . . . and yet still himself, still there, still present and accounted for, alone in a dark room with another sailor about to bring him off.

He shot his wad and the next instant rolled off the bed and stood up. Rivard neither said or did anything as Merritt hitched up his pants, found his shoes and peacoat, then lurched through the door, down the stairwell, and out onto the street where a dense pre-dawn fog obscured every building and parked car he reeled past.

The next day was Sunday, so he didn't have to report for duty until noon. Just the same, he showed up a half an hour late and his C.O. chewed him out.

After he finally settled down to work, Boyington strolled up to his desk and told him he looked like hell.

"You didn't take my advice, did you?"

Merritt didn't dare look at him, and kept his head bowed, his left hand pressed to his forehead.

"I guess not," Boyington said and walked off.

The rest of the day Merritt barely said a word to any of the other personnel in the Recruitment Station. He tried not to think about what had happened at the Exeter the night before—*Or was it this morning?*—telling himself he'd been too drunk to know what was going on, or that maybe it hadn't happened at all, he couldn't be sure. The whole incident was that bizarre. Nothing this creepy, this unsettling, had ever gone on with him before. All he knew with any certainty, he told himself again and again, was that he wasn't that way. He'd just been stupid was all. And drunk. More drunk than he'd ever been. And this is where it got him—hang-dogged and shame-faced. After an hour at this desk, his stomach soured and he had to scurry to the head to throw up, catching the eye of his C.O. as he shambled back to his desk. At three o'clock when Boyington asked if he wanted to go down to The Turf Club for a little hair of the dog, Merritt told him no, he was off the booze for good.

"Taking the pledge, eh," the lieutenant snorted and headed out.

Merritt worked until seven that evening, got a sandwich at Manning's, and returned to his room at the Loring. He worried about seeing Ensign Rivard and resolved never to enter The Turf Club again. He would also arrange to have another seaman spot him when it came time to bring the enlistment rolls out to the Sand Point Naval Air Station. If Rivard came looking for him, he would do whatever it took to ditch him, even at the risk of insubordination. He tried to read for a while but couldn't keep his mind off what had happened. It was so much worse than the embarrassment of his wet dream in the barracks. It was worse than his bunkmate at boot camp getting caught jacking off in the latrine, then being made to wear black socks when their company had its photo taken, the only seaman of the entire group without white socks, marking the poor jack-off for life. And for what? What Merritt had done—or rather, had done to him—was far worse. Yet at the same time, mortifying as it was, it was something he knew he'd just have to get past. It was a mistake, it had happened, and now he had to put it behind him. No matter how often he replayed the incident in his mind or banged his head against the doorframe or buried his face in his pillow, nothing would change. He had to move on.

The next two days at the Recruitment Station passed uneventfully—given, of course, that the country was at war! The guys he signed up day after day were the same ones who in just a few weeks would be shipped off to the Pacific to fight and die. Only recently had President Roosevelt ordered the Department of War to release the conflict's true causality rates, and the numbers proved more devastating than anyone, even career officers, had imagined. Even after its defeat at Midway, the Jap fleet remained formidable, with Jap soldiers holding every thumbtack atoll and sand spit in the South Pacific to the bloody death. As everyone said, a good Jap would rather lie on his own hand grenade than surrender. All the same, Merritt kept at his job, enlisting two to three new young bloods every hour, and while initially he'd been grateful he didn't have to ship out, he began to question the rightness of his cushy assignment. Maybe he was just too cowardly to stand up and fight for his country—and for that reason didn't belong in *The Man's Navy!*, as the recruitment poster on the wall of the station proclaimed.

And his incident with the ensign only compounded such doubts, so that by mid-week he'd all but resolved to put in for a transfer. When his C.O. ordered him out to the Sand Point Naval Air Station to deliver the enlistment rolls, Merritt argued that he had a backload of recruitment forms on his desk to process, but the C.O. just scowled at him and said there was a jeep at the curb waiting for him. When he went down, Merritt half-expected Ensign Rivard to be behind the wheel, ready to escort him back to the Exeter Hotel. Once at the base, he kept his head down and wasted no time delivering the enlistment rolls and jumping back into the jeep, even though another half hour passed before his driver returned from the commissary.

Nerve-wracking as his excursion to the Naval Air Station had been, it got him thinking if he was careful, he might never have to see Rivard again. This notion restored his confidence, and on Wednesday morning he allowed himself to stroll past the Christian Science Reading Room and glance through the front window. Yet, once more, Clara was not there. Nor was she there the next morning when he walked past.

So that's it, he told himself. She's quit her job. Her conscience probably got the best of her when she remembered her boyfriend off in the war, the same one he'd seen her writing to. And then of course there were her two brothers in the Army, both of whom, as she'd admitted, told her to stay clear of sailors. And when it came right down to it, who was he to tell her they were wrong?

When he returned to the Recruitment Station after this last pass by the Reading Room and found a hand-addressed letter on his desk, he let himself believe for an instant it might be from Clara. It only made sense that a nice girl like her would write him a Dear John letter. Or maybe she was writing to tell him what a fine time she'd had on their date, and why she'd not returned to the Reading Room. He would read her letter and then phone her to let her know there were no hard feelings. Later they would meet at The Continental and afterward kiss and make up.

Yet when he tore open the envelope, pulled out the letter, and gave it a quick glance, he couldn't find a signature, and dejected sat down to read the brief, unsigned note.

I saw you with the ensign last Saturday. It's not smart to keep company with a flit like that. Of course you probably like that kind of thing, don't you? You see, the ensign likes to brag. He says you were his best ever. What if your C.O. found out? Or that sweet little thing you've been seeing? Something like that could really hang over a guy's head. Once people know about it that is. So you should think about what it's worth to you no one finds out.

That's all it said. The scrawl across the unlined sheet of paper was rough and uneven. Yet the message was clear. Someone knew about him and the ensign and he was being set up for a ride. It was blackmail, plain and simple, and as he realized this he peered about the office to see if anyone was watching him read the letter. He instantly became obsessed over who it might be. It had to be another seaman, someone who knew Rivard, and had also seen him with Clara, or else had heard him talk about her. Could it be someone from the Recruitment Station? He kept looking about the room, the metal desks lined up five to a row, a seaman clerk seated at each, interviewing enlistees, sifting through piles of paperwork, hammering away at typewriters. Had Rivard really said that or was the blackmailer just making it up to see how far he could get? At the very least, it was obvious Rivard had a reputation for this kind of thing. Then Merritt went heart-sick. Could the letter writer have already told Clara? Wouldn't this explain why she'd gone AWOL on him? He winced at the possibility, but there it was—a *real* possibility—and so without a word to his C.O. or anyone else in the office, he got up from his desk, walked out of the Recruitment Station, and made his way down to The Turf Club.

He couldn't sleep for several nights after receiving the blackmail note, wondering when the next note, the one extorting money, would arrive. He spent more and more time in The Turf Club, and twice his C.O. reprimanded him for slacking off, even threatening to call The Turf Club off limits for the entire Recruitment Station, which brought some flak from his officemates, who told him to shape up or ship out. Even Seaman Lieutenant Boyington, his friend, told him to buck up. "You've got it good here," he told Merritt. "Don't screw it up."

It was after this last warning that Merritt dragged himself back to his room at the Loring Hotel and for the first time since his troubles had started thought long and hard about his parents and what they must be going through during his absence. Though they never showed it, he could tell his father and mother had felt terrible the day he left to join the Navy. "Come home safe" was all his mother said to him, her arms crossed as she stood behind the screen door of the side porch of their house. Merritt could see she was holding back tears. His father, meanwhile, carried his cardboard suitcase to the car and stood talking to Mr. Addington, the assistant principal at Lyndonville High, who'd volunteered to drive Merritt and two of his friends, Reed Carter and Archie Harrell, to the First Naval District Headquarters in Boston for their induction. After placing the suitcase in the trunk of the car, his father slid a small manila envelop into Merritt's shirt pocket. "That should tide you over until you get to where you're going," he said and shook Merritt's hand.

"Say goodbye to Bardie and Henry for me," Merritt replied, remembering his older sister and her husband, who had two young children to look after and couldn't be there that morning.

That was the last time he'd seen his folks—almost ten months ago. He knew he could never face them again if they ever caught wind of his troubles in Seattle. The very thought of it made him want to take a powder. He wouldn't be the first sailor to do so. Every week another story circulated through the station of some seaman who'd slit his wrists or jumped off a building or tied an anchor around his feet and walked off a pier. He could do the deed right here in his room. His glossy black dress belt, the water pipe extending the length of the ceiling, the desk chair over there by the wall, were all he needed for a quick and tidy exit. How else could the situation possibly resolve itself? He could go AWOL, but with his luck the SPs would pick him up the moment he stepped out of uniform. He'd be charged with desertion by morning and spend the rest of the war cleaning latrines. Besides, desertion was even more cowardly than suicide. His only other recourse, he figured, was the one he was already on—drinking himself straight to the psycho ward or the grave, whichever came first.

The next afternoon Merritt was working his first highball during his lunch break when he encountered the boatswain's mate from the USS *Washington* in The Turf Club. The *Washington* had been towed into the Naval Shipyard in Bremerton several weeks earlier after colliding with the USS *Indiana*, another capital ship, during refueling maneuvers in the Pacific. While a new bow was being fitted to her, the boatswain's mate was on a five-day leave, spending most of it hunched over the bar at The Turf Club.

"Last time I was on shore leave I ended up in the brig," he told Merritt, who offered to buy him a drink. "So I'm staying right here on this bar stool and taking it nice and slow this time."

Merritt ordered them both another round and after a while complained to the boatswain's mate about being stuck with shore duty. "I'm sick and tired of being a lubber," he said. He'd already stretched his lunch break out an extra half hour and knew he needed to get back to the office. "This goddamn war's going to be over before I've had a chance to even fight in it."

The prospect of shipping out had taken hold of him the night before as he lay in bed unable to sleep, thinking how foolish it was to do himself in when there were plenty of Japs out there happy to do it for him. So the right thing for him to do, he told himself, was to ship out, even if it meant being a no-'count deckhand aboard some unescorted cargo ship. Better to become shark bait than keep living like this.

"Count your lucky stars," the petty officer told him.

Merritt had heard this line before, and wasn't having any of it. He told the boatswain's mate he'd give anything to get aboard a ship like the *Washington*.

"In that case," he replied, "tell your goddamn C.O. to get you billeted to her. I'm sure ol' man Cooley wouldn't mind picking up a few extra line handlers." He explained how T.R. Cooley, the *Washington*'s captain, had been appointed rear admiral of a division of ships for which the *Washington*, once she re-launched, would serve as the flagship. "If you get Cooley to okay the transfer, you'll be sailing the high seas in no time."

As soon as he returned upstairs to the Recruitment Station, Merritt submitted a formal request to go seavey. The boatswain's mate had told him the USS *Washington* was scheduled to rejoin the fleet in less than a week. "I want aboard her when she sails," he told his C.O., "and Admiral Cooley is shorthanded."

"You gotta be kidding," his C.O. replied, holding Merritt's request in his hand. No doubt Charley Oscar couldn't manage the Recruitment Station without his brilliant clerical skills. Yet Merritt held his ground. "I'll see what I can do," his C.O. said and waved Merritt out of his office.

The next morning Merritt again walked past the Christian Science Reading Room, and again there was no Clara. Almost three weeks had passed since their dinner-and-dancing date. Yet, even if she'd been seated at the desk in the back, he doubted he would have gone in to speak to her. At last, though, he decided he would phone her, even if it meant confronting his worst humiliation. He would wait until his afternoon break and then go down to The Turf Club and call her from one of the phone booths in the back.

The hours dragged along and at four o'clock he announced to Boyington he was taking a cigarette break and made his way downstairs. The Turf Club was in a lull between lunch and quitting time, so the backroom was empty when he stepped into one of the wood-paneled telephone booths, dropped a nickel into the slot, and dialed her number—ADmiral Way 8503. His hands shook as the phone rang. He would tell Clara he was sorry and let her know he'd put in for reassignment and might have to ship out at any time. He would let her know what a wonderful time he'd had getting to know her, and maybe, depending on how she responded, tell her how genuinely fond he was of her. Unfortunately, when someone finally picked up, it was Clara's mother who answered, and when he asked if he might speak to Clara, he was told she couldn't come to phone.

"I won't take much of her time," he assured her mother. "I just wanted to make sure she's alright."

Her mother seemed to demur but then said something about God and truth and healing, which left Merritt utterly confounded, and with the impression Clara might very well be on her deathbed.

"So she's okay?" he asked more stridently.

"She's sleeping," was all her mother would say, and then, "May I tell her who's calling?"

Merritt told her his name, gave the telephone number for the Recruitment Station, and asked that she have Clara call him as soon as possible. He was reluctant to hang up, but when he finally did, he thought that perhaps Clara really had been sick, and that perhaps he'd gotten worked up for all the wrong reasons. If he could only speak to her, he thought, everything would be straightened out, and they could arrange to see one another again and the past two weeks—almost three now—could be forgotten.

And so for the remainder of the day he hardly gave a thought to his incident with Ensign Rivard, the blackmail note, or his encounter with the boatswain's mate in The Turf Club. Instead he remained at his desk, waiting on Clara's call. By 6:30, though, when it still hadn't come, the old doubts and fears returned, and that's when a seaman passed his desk and tossed an envelop in front of him.

"From Charley Oscar," he said.

Merritt picked the envelope up and tore it open:

Seaman Second Class Merritt L. Driscoll to report to duty aboard the USS Washington, *BB 56, at Puget Sound Naval Shipyard, Bremerton, Wash., Saturday, February 18, 700 h.*

Beneath the orders, typed neatly on letterhead adorned with the U.S. Navy seal, his C.O. had scrawled, "Happy sails, Driscoll. You ship out tomorrow."

FIVE
Clara, Spring 1944

By the start of March, the cold winter drizzle ceded to spring storms. Clara recovered from the illness that had laid her up for nearly three full weeks in February. The ordeal had given her a scare not only about her health, but her faith as well. It was a mistake not to have seen a physician, a mistake that had likely prolonged her suffering. Whenever she'd become sick in the past, she'd been a kid who did whatever her mother told her. This last episode, though, was different. At times she thought she was suffocating from the congestion in her lungs, and the headaches and backaches made it so she couldn't even sit up in bed to draw or read. At night when she tried to sleep, her fever made her delusional. Yet through it all she never expressed her doubts to her mother. When she was finally able to make it downstairs to the front foyer and dial the number Merritt had left, three more days had passed and it was too late. No one in the Recruitment Station knew where he was. She realized finally that it had been three weeks since she'd seen him last. She'd been so sick that she'd lost track of everything—her drawing, her classes at Cornish, the Reading Room, and Merritt. To her despair, when she phoned the Recruitment Station again the next day, she learned that he'd put in for a transfer and had just received his orders to ship out the day before. The person with whom she spoke couldn't tell her which base he'd been sent to, and when she finally learned a week later that he'd been assigned to the USS *Washington*, the ship had already set sail. All she could think was that something had caused Merritt to flee—and perhaps it was her.

She resumed working each morning at the downtown Reading Room and attending night classes at Cornish and tried to forget about him. A couple of times she considered writing him but realized to do so would oblige him to write back and maybe he didn't want to. So she put her letter writing effort where it would count most, and doubled the letters she sent to Freddy and Ken, though her thoughts kept returning to Merritt.

She was fretting over it all, walking down Third Avenue, when she ran into Adel Worley, an old classmate from West Seattle High, just outside the Bon Marché department store. She hadn't seen Adel since graduation almost a year ago. With the exception of Latin two years straight, they hadn't shared many classes and only really knew one another in passing. Adel had been in band and orchestra, while Clara, she'd kept to herself through most of high school. Being so much taller than all the other girls (and most of the boys), she preferred not be gawked at. Still, she'd always liked Adel.

"Clara," exclaimed Adel and kissed her on the cheek. "I almost didn't recognize you."

"How are you, Adel?" Clara hardly recognized her either. Had they both changed that much in just one year? Adel had always been a real firecracker at Westside, one of the true free spirits. She'd always defied the dowdy trends by wearing tight brushed-wool sweaters and hip-hugging skirts that fell mid-calf. Rain or shine, she never wore a hat, and even now the wind lashed her dark hair about her face. She was one of the few girls to go straight into college after graduation. Most girls Clara knew from high school were raising a family already or else working as office secretaries or counter clerks. A few girls volunteered at USO Halls and other canteens around town, or campaigned for the Milk Fund or Red Cross. One girl she knew had taken a job at the Boeing plant assembling bombers and fighter planes, while another worked as a welder in the Moran Shipyard. A handful of girls had even joined the Navy WAVES. But wrong or right, Adel had pursued her own course and, as Clara had heard, now played flute and studied music theory at the university.

"Oh, Clara, I'm having a party this Saturday, You know, to celebrate the end of the winter quarter. You'll come, right?"

The invitation caught Clara off guard. Yet Adel had always been a straight shooter like that.

"I suppose," Clara answered. She hadn't been to a party since she didn't know when. The last party she attended in fact was probably Adel's sixteenth birthday party four years ago.

"Here's the address," Adel said and jotted it down on a store receipt. "It's in the University District. It'll just be some of us students and maybe a few other folks."

Clara thanked her and said she would check with her mom and dad—which sounded so juvenile she wanted to slap herself for saying it. Adel didn't seem to notice, though, and gave Clara another kiss and dashed off. Excited by the invitation, Clara forgot that she'd been thinking about Merritt and hurried back to the Reading Room to make a sketch of Adel with her wind-swept hair.

Four days later, remembering what her brother Freddy had told her in his last letter—"Have yourself a hot time while you can, Sis."—Clara looked up the cross-town bus schedule. Adel's party started at seven, but she wanted to give herself an afternoon in the University District. So right after her morning shift at the Reading Room (and following an awkward chat with Mrs. Berner, who wanted to introduce Clara to her nephew, a second lieutenant in the Army at

Fort Lawton), Clara boarded the bus for the U District. She couldn't remember the last time she'd had an outing like this, one intended for her pleasure alone. Maybe never. First she went to the University Bookstore and pored over all the big, glossy art books. Then she walked through the famous Henry Art Gallery—a museum really—which exhibited only modern artists. Afterward she stopped at a Chinese restaurant on University Street, which everyone called "The Ave.", where she ate Dim Sung for the first time in her life.

The highlight of her afternoon, though, was the Henry Art Gallery. The square, brick building on the edge of campus looked like a mausoleum from the outside, but inside it offered work by regional artists in oils and watercolors and less common media like gouache, tempera, encaustic, and collage. Many of the works were figurative or landscape paintings, but just as many were abstract. One of her favorites was a five-part depiction of Mount Rainier in various shadings by a Japanese artist. That the gallery dared to hang the work of a Japanese artist at all was itself quite startling. Everyone knew what had happened to Seattle's Japanese soon after the war started, silently understanding the reason for the empty classroom seats, the boarded up storefronts, the houses that suddenly had *For Sale* signs in their yards. Entire families had been put on trains and transported to the internment camps in California, Idaho, and Montana. So for museum curators to hang the work of a Japanese artist was nothing less than audacious.

One painting that she found especially provocative was a flat, cartoon-like bird figure against a reddish backdrop. It seemed at once playful and dramatic. Next to this painting was a triptych of rectangular canvases with overlapping spheres that invisibly connected each of the three panels. The interplay between the spheres and the artist's use of color made her think of the round watercolor pans in her trays at home. Finally she came upon two works by the only artist whose name she recognized, her instructor Mark Tobey. She contemplated the two paintings for a long time and concluded, finally, that the brushstrokes were just too frenetic and the colors unnecessarily muted—and not to her taste at all.

As she walked up The Ave after eating at the Chinese restaurant, she became uneasy about facing all the smart university people who would be attending Adel's party. When she found the building, she lingered out front several minutes before working up the nerve to climb the stairs to the second floor and knock on the apartment door.

Adel greeted Clara enthusiastically and pulled her inside. "It's wonderful you came," she said and guided her into the kitchen where she placed a glass of red wine in Clara's hand.

Good Christian Scientists did not drink. *I nothing lack—for I am His,* Clara could hear her mother admonishing her. Yet keeping with the general adventurousness of the day, she took a sip. The taste made her wince and smack her lips, but when she took another she could feel the wine's warm persuasiveness course through her, and decided she liked it.

Adel led her into the living room where the guests milled about, clustered in corners, lounging on the sofa, hovering near the table of hors d'oeuvres. It was a clamorous group and somewhere in the room a phonograph pulsed a piano number. Clara heard someone comment that he'd seen Art Tatum play the same piece at Jimmy Ryan's in New York last summer.

Adel raised her voice to quiet everyone and introduced the new arrival. "Everyone," she shouted, "I want you to meet Clara Hamilton. We went to Westside together. Rah Rah, Indians!"

People laughed and sent up a general welcome to Clara. She recognized only three or four faces, all West Seattle alums, among the thirty or so crowded into the small apartment.

"Hiya, Clara," someone called out from across the room. "Where ya been keeping yourself?"

"You remember Don, don't you?" said Adel and steered Clara toward a young man standing near the front window.

Don Oschner. Of course she remembered him. She'd had the worst kind of crush on him her freshman year. He was three years older than her and had been Editor-in-Chief of *Chinook*, the school newspaper. He was even more handsome now than when she'd seen him last. His shoulders had filled out, and a dark shadow of whiskers covered the lower portion of his face. He wore brown gabardines and a tweed jacket, and his white dress shirt was open at the collar, revealing a trace of chest hair.

"I'm going to get some more wine," Adel announced and just like that disappeared.

Clara could feel herself blushing as Don took her elbow and gave her a peck on the cheek. "So you made it out of Indian Territory," he said, referring to West Seattle High.

She took another taste of wine. "Just barely," she said and tried to smile.

"Is ol' Reed Fulton still in charge?"

"As much as ever."

Reed Fulton was the West Seattle principal. He enjoyed a minor celebrity as a literary man after publishing several mystery novels that received notice in the *Seattle Times* and *P-I*. While he had a small following of fawning female students—mostly members of the pretentious Calliope Club—true literary types like Don Oschner regarded him as a hack.

"Do you know he once told Dick Hugo he didn't have the guts to be a writer? Can you imagine? You know where Dick is now?" Don looked earnestly at Clara and she shook her head, trying to remember who Dick Hugo was. "He's flying bombing missions over Italy for the Army Air Corps. Tell me he doesn't have guts!"

"And what about you, Don?" Clara brought herself to ask. "What are you doing these days?"

"Funny you should ask," he said, and told her how he'd enlisted right after graduation but received a dispatch leave soon after when his mother fell ill, which was also when he began taking journalism courses at the university. "Mother died last November," he said somberly.

"I'm so sorry," Clara replied, and recalled her mother mentioning some time back how Mrs. Oschner had been ill. Her mother said at the time that she was going to recommend a church practitioner to the Oschners, though Clara remembered thinking she shouldn't interfere.

"So with Mom gone," Don went on, cheering up again, "I'm back in the Army, attached to the Communications Corp."

"That's wonderful," Clara exclaimed. "I mean, you'll be a journalist and all. Though I really just wish this rotten war would end." Her thoughts immediately returned to her two brothers. Ken was somewhere in Africa, but who knew where Freddy was? He didn't write as frequently as Ken and was much harder to keep track of.

When Clara looked up and saw Don watching her, it was almost as if the old flame she'd carried in high school for him began to rekindle, he was that good-looking.

"And what about you?" he asked. "What surprises does life hold for you?"

It was nice of him to ask, she said, but her life held no surprises. "I am taking a night class at Cornish," she added. "And I hope to go on. Studying art, that is."

Don gave her a bemused smile and said, "That's wonderful, Clara. Cornish is a swell place."

Yet she didn't appreciate his tone. Cornish had always had a reputation as more finishing school than bona fide college, and though Clara knew otherwise—knew that it was a real arts school with a rigorous curriculum—Don apparently did not. She took another sip of wine. It was the first time she'd ever blurted out her true intentions like that to anyone, ever really admitted not only that she wanted to study art but, in effect, wanted to be an artist.

"I should introduce you to someone," Don said, and just like that took her arm and led her across the room to a gaunt-looking man leafing through the sheet music on Adel's music stand.

"Eliot's an artist too," he said loud enough to get the man's attention. "Eliot Brasher, this is Clara Hamilton. She takes art classes at Cornish."

Eliot looked from Don to Clara and back at Don without acknowledging the introduction, making Clara wonder whether he had heard it.

"Eliot's from Spokane," Don went on, as if this fact explained his odd behavior.

"Are you a painter?" Clara asked, trying to break the ice.

He pursed his lips and nodded. He glanced skittishly at her and then away.

"Roger that," said Don, and just like Adel moments before left Clara to fend for herself.

She took a swallow of wine and looked over the top of her glass at this Eliot Brasher. He was an inch or two shorter than she—which was not unusual when she met someone. His torso had an almost imperceptible crook in it, as if he wanted to twist to his left to avoid facing her. He wore drab green khakis, a wrinkled white shirt, and a rumpled linen jacket of faded brown. His reddish hair was long and wavy with bangs swooping over his brow. He had a boney face, with skin that appeared soft, complemented by rosy, childlike splotches on his cheeks. His eyes, peering out from beneath his bangs, were sharp and black. Once past his general dishevelment, Clara found him curiously interesting to look at, and even somewhat attractive.

"Mind if I sit down?" she asked, feeling a bit tipsy. She dropped into an armchair, leaned back, and closed her eyes.

"I'd like to see your work sometime," she heard Eliot say and opened her eyes to see him perched on the armrest of the chair in which she sat.

She tried to sit up. "My work?" she said.

"I'll show you my portfolio if you show me yours," he said, keeping a straight face.

Clara blinked several times, uncertain how to respond, and placed her wine glass on the coffee table. She opened her handbag and took out several napkins from the Chinese restaurant where she'd eaten earlier and on which she'd sketched each item of Dim Sung the waiter had carted to her table. Underneath each drawing she'd written the name of the item. "There," she said. "There's my portfolio."

Eliot took the napkins from her and began scrutinizing them, while Clara waited for him to say something condescending. Instead, as he considered each drawing, it occurred to her that no one—not even Mark Tobey—had ever given such careful attention to her work. He handed the napkins back finally and said, "Very well done."

Clara thanked him and tucked the napkins back into her handbag.

"You must be very avid with your sketchbook if that's what you do with napkins."

And just like that he had her pegged. Clara picked up her wine glass. "Actually," she began, deciding to fess up, "everything changed for me today. It's just so odd." She knew this sounded a bit loony, but went on anyway. She told him about having sworn off her artwork at the start of the war and digging out her sketchbooks only last year after graduating. "Then today at the art gallery," she went on, "I decided I would start painting again."

She wasn't just making this up either, she told herself. Tomorrow morning she would retrieve her watercolors and begin painting again. The prospect excited her, and when she looked up at Eliot, expecting him to be gazing straight past her, he was actually listening.

"Have you been to the Henry?" she asked, changing the subject.

He pursed his lips again and nodded, then said, "I have a piece there."

"*Really*," Clara let out. What a self-absorbed ninny she was. The person she was speaking to about *her* art had a painting in the museum she'd just visited. This was astonishing! "Which one?" she asked.

"It's called *Endocrine*."

She couldn't remember the titles of any the paintings she'd seen and was afraid to ask what it looked like. "As in the gland?" she said.

"Exactly." He appeared pleased that anyone would know what the word meant. "There are five endocrine glands in all. So there are five paintings, each a series of secretions made by punching pinholes into the paint tube and smearing the paint directly onto the canvas." His hands came alive as he spoke, almost as if he were composing the painting before her very eyes. "I try to achieve an interplay between the colors as the surface receives the paint. And I never gesso the canvas. The five paintings vary in size, but the one in the Henry is about so big." He reached his arms out to indicate the painting's size. "Four by three, to be exact."

Clara knew exactly which one it was. It had a thick swirl of unexpectedly complementary colors—blue, brown, and burgundy—that gave the surface a peculiarly three-dimensional quality. She didn't know what it had to do with glands, though. The only fact she remembered about glands from physiology class with Mr. Sigrist, her science teacher at Westside, was the Islands of Langerhans, in the pancreas, which always sounded to her like a mythical archipelago in the Mediterranean. "I know just the one," she said. "I really liked it."

Eliot looked at her and almost smiled, but not quite. "Thank you."

When she asked what it was like to have a painting in such a famous museum, he told her about meeting Melvin Kohler, the museum's superintendent, which led to the Henry Art Gallery purchasing the painting. He referred to several of the other paintings in exhibition. They admired many of the same ones, and were equally unimpressed by Mark Tobey's. He then named two German artists, both of whom had fled Nazi Germany and were now in Vancouver, British Columbia, as well as a Norwegian artist living in exile in Seattle, impressing Clara with his knowledge of the local art world.

When she asked whether he'd been drafted, he admitted that yes, he had, two years ago, but that the draft board had classified him as 4F and sent him

51

home to Spokane. He didn't explain why he'd been classified 4F, and Clara didn't ask. He then told her how his grandfather had been the inventor of a tractor part now being used in Army tanks, and when the old man died last year Eliot received an inheritance from the estate that enabled him to come to Seattle and devote himself to his painting. He was now preparing for his first one-man show at the Willard Gallery downtown.

"I would love to come see it," said Clara, finishing her wine.

He seemed to smile at her finally, and asked, "May I get you another?" holding his hand out for her glass.

SIX
Glenora, West Seattle, 1944

No sooner had the strife with Carl and his union activity settled down than the war began and both her boys rushed off to fight. No matter how she tried, no matter the degree to which she threw herself into study and prayer, consulted Science practitioners, volunteered her time with church functions, or defended herself from the error of human will and mortal mind, she could not dispel the foreboding in her heart. It came in flashes that left a residue of dread—one of her sons would not return. Before the crib death of her infant daughter May twelve years ago, she would never have believed herself prone to such disquiet. Yet May's death—so sudden, so incomprehensible—had voided her of hope. She saw what it was to step into the shadow of the valley of death and have one's whole being thrown into fear and darkness.

But then, just three weeks following little May's death, while making her rounds in the West Seattle Juncture, five-year-old Clara in tow, she passed the storefront Reading Room of the Church of Christ, Scientist and saw in the window, on a child's chalkboard in calligraphic script, the following message:

Golden Text: "Thou shalt be perfect with the Lord thy God."
— Deuteronomy 18:13.

"The Christian Scientist has enlisted to lessen evil, disease, and death; and he will overcome them by understanding their nothingness and the allness of God, or good."
—Science and Health with Key to the Scriptures *by Mary Baker Eddy.*

The two passages resounded in her. The one perfectly complemented the other, the first setting forth the certainty of Scriptural truth, the second elucidating and reinforcing it—indeed, offering a key to it, a means to its very truth and wisdom. What's more, the singular notion of death's absolute nothingness struck at the core of her enduring grief. How right it was that in God's all-ness, death was nothing and sorrow naught. All that was required was a true and proper understanding of this spiritual *fact* for life to be restored in all its fullness and joy.

When she returned home, she set Clara to peeling potatoes in the kitchen and sat down in the hallway to telephone Mrs. Holmquist, whom everyone in the neighborhood knew belonged to the Christian Science church. She invited Mrs. Holmquist to tea the next morning, and when the well-postured neighbor woman came over she carried with her a St. James Bible and two copies of *Science and Health*. First Mrs. Holmquist read Glenora the Scientific Statement of Being, as given by Mary Baker Eddy, to which all Christian Scientists subscribed: *There is no life, truth, intelligence, nor substance in matter. All is infinite Mind and its infinite manifestation, for God is All-in-all. Spirit is immortal Truth; matter is mortal error. Spirit is the real and eternal; matter is the unreal and temporal. Spirit is God, and man is His image and likeness. Therefore man is not material; he is spiritual.* Next they reviewed that day's designated lesson, which, according to Mrs. Holmquist, was based upon the Golden Text scripture Glenora had been drawn to in the Reading Room window. By the end of their review, Glenora believed she had begun truly to comprehend the error of her thinking. To lend death any credence whatsoever (even to mourn) was to deny God's pureness of spirit, which was wholly expressed by Life effulgent and everlasting.

The next Sunday, Glenora dressed the children in their usual Sunday best, but instead of having Carl drop them off at the Free Methodist Church in Burien, the church in which her parents had raised her, she had him drive them clear across the Spokane Street Bridge and into Seattle, and then up First Hill to the resplendently white, four-square and domed First Church of Christ, Scientist. She was instantly taken by the clarity and simplicity of both the church interior and the service itself. Two readers stood behind a plain altar, a man to read from the Bible, a woman from *Science and Health*. Back and forth, they recited the passages from that week's daily lessons. Three hymns were sung (one written by Mary Baker Eddy), the collection plate was passed, and the service concluded. It was that simple, that honest and pure.

Six months later, after attending regular Sunday services and Wednesday testimonies and becoming a student of the Bible through the daily lessons, Glenora applied for membership to the church on behalf of herself and her three children—Freddy, Kenneth, and Clara. To her consternation, her husband, Carl, would have nothing to do with the church or the teachings of Mrs. Eddy. Just as he'd always refused to attend the Free Methodist services in Burien, he now refused to step foot in the Christian Science church. A determinedly unchurched man, he told her he believed in God and trusted to the Lord's Prayer and that was all he needed. As for the children, he said he knew she loved them and would do right by them in all matters concerning God and religion.

The fact was, the labor union had become Carl's church. Yet when hard times hit in the early '30s and they lost their house and moved in with her parents, she found guidance and great comfort through the church's weekly lessons as every morning she sat down with the children before school to read the passages from the Holy Bible and *Science and Health* assigned by the Mother Church. Meanwhile, ignoring all such spiritual matters, Carl threw himself into his union's organizing efforts. He spoke of President Roosevelt as if he were the workingman's Lord and redeemer, and when Marty Cole was shot dead during the '34 strike, it was as if the whole struggle became consecrated in that poor man's blood. Three years later when Harry Bridges came along to lead the West Coast longshoremen out of the old ILA union, breaking with its East Coast leadership, and form the new ILWU for West Coast longshoremen, it was as if Carl and his buddies down on the docks had reached the Promised Land. And certainly life improved for the family. Carl again had steady work on the waterfront, better pay, safer conditions, and by the time Mr. Roosevelt was elected president for a third time, the family was again in its own home.

Though he refused to attend church with her and the children, Glenora knew Carl was a good man. He provided for his family, doting on Clara and rearing the two boys to be honest, hard-working men like their father. However, after May's death, she refused to bear him any more children, a fact he blamed on the church—though on what basis, she couldn't say. She knew it rankled him whenever one of the children fell ill and she prohibited a doctor from coming to the house, but instead brought in a church practitioner to pray at the sick child's bedside.

"A bunch of hoodoo," he mumbled beneath his breath the first time, on the occasion of Clara running a fever that kept her out of school for a week. Even Glenora feared for her daughter, that old familiar dread seeping back into her heart as her darling girl suffered. But the very morning following the practitioner's visit, after four days of fever, Clara sat up in bed and asked for pancakes and Glenora knew she had acted rightly. It was her first direct witnessing of the divine power of scientific healing, and so the following Wednesday evening, with Clara at her side, she stood before the rest of the congregation in the church meeting room and gave a heartfelt testimonial of the Lord Christ's sweet promise to allow us to heal ourselves and our families through God's absolute Love.

Three months later when Freddy broke his nose, however, it was a different matter.

"How could you?" she demanded of Carl when he brought Freddy home from the hospital.

The boys were both in high school at the time and Carl, who'd been a boxer in the early years of their marriage, had recently set up a gym in the basement of the union hall in Seattle. Every Saturday morning he brought the two boys to the gym for boxing lessons. Kenneth, the quieter and slighter of the two, didn't much enjoy going, but Freddy, older by two years, had always been a roughhouser and took right to it.

"The boy's a natural, Glenny," Carl had reported the week prior, after Freddy had sparred with a much bigger boy. "He's got his old man's hand speed. And heart, plenty of heart."

The next Saturday, though, the same boy broke Freddy's nose and Carl took him to Harborview Hospital to be treated. Fortunately it was a simple break and didn't need to be reset. The doctor packed both of Freddy's nostrils with gauze and sent him home with an ice pack. Glenora was relieved her son had not been seriously injured but was enraged at her husband.

"He was bleeding and the hospital was just down the road, practically on the way home," was Carl's defense when she sent the children to their rooms and asked her husband to step onto the back porch with her.

"He needs to know Christ is the true healer, supreme and incorporeal," Glenora implored, her voice cracking. "I know it makes no difference to you, but the children's spiritual welfare is at stake."

"His nose was broke."

She knew her husband would never cotton to theological reasoning and so finally resigned herself to this fact, she said, "I know you did what you thought best. I just ask that you respect my wishes in the future."

"It's just that sometimes . . . ." He let the sentence trail off, though Glenora knew perfectly well what he meant to say and replied, "He shouldn't be boxing in the first place."

"He likes it," Carl said.

"Well, apparently it doesn't suit him," she returned and walked back into the house.

She'd recognized early on in the family's conversion to Christian Science that it might be too late for her oldest, Freddy. From the outset he was restless during the family's morning study periods, and as soon as he entered high school he complained of having to attend Sunday services. He would rather go fishing with his father, he said, and when finally he graduated, joined the union, and went straight to work on the waterfront, Carl could not have been more proud. Yet she was the boy's mother and so she worried—and prayed—and made every effort to keep the faith present before him.

Unlike his older brother, Kenneth surprised even his mother by taking right to the teachings. His fervency even concerned Glenora at times—since fervency, as the Rev. Mrs. Mary Baker Eddy had taught, could conceal false desire and lead to hypocrisy. Thankfully, Kenneth directed his into a true study of the Bible and *Science and Health* and, in time, carried forward the true Principle by teaching others as well. Yet occasionally—for instance when he invoked God as the Great Physician after Freddy sprained his knee playing football—he and his older brother would squabble over church matters. Otherwise, despite their differences, they remained close.

Clara was another story altogether. Glenora could never quite figure her out. She was barely six years old when the family united with the church, and so she'd been virtually raised in the faith. She participated in each morning's study session, joined in silent prayer, dutifully attended Sunday services and Wednesday testimonial meetings, and upon entering high school taught Sunday school alongside Kenneth. And now she even volunteered part-time in the downtown Reading Room. Yet it seemed the teachings never took hold with Clara the way they had with her brother. She evidently understood them. But did she experience *true* Understanding? It was hard to tell.

At the same time, during her daughter's school years, Glenora became concerned that Clara was becoming too absorbed in her artwork, drawing on old paper grocery bags until not a spare bag could be found in the house and then, when she and Carl bought her a set of watercolors and a sketchbook for her twelfth birthday, she painted.

"She's a regular Michelangelo," Freddy kidded her when she presented him with a pencil and watercolor portrait of himself on his seventeenth birthday. From then on, Carl called her his little Michelange*la*. And truth be told, she was quite good—"A natural," her husband again said—though it bothered Glenora how Clara saved her allowance each week only to squander her entire savings on new paints and more paper at the end of each month.

When the war started, everything changed. Carl said shipping would be vital to the war effort and urged Freddy to stay on at the waterfront. But he wouldn't listen, not even to his father. And once Kenneth learned that Freddy was going to enlist, he had to, too, despite her protests. When they saw the boys off at the train station was when—for the first time since May's death—dread again descended upon her, like a case of the dark willies, and no matter how thoroughly she insisted in her own mind upon the suppositional untruth that lay behind the evil and destruction of war, she could not escape the flashes of anxiety and foreboding that beset her. It came as a comfort to her, therefore, when Clara, still in high school, chose to put aside her artwork and devote her time and energy to war relief. Glenora commended her daughter for the decision, reminding her that sacrifices would now be required of them all. Yet the artwork was also why, when her daughter took it up again after graduating, she worried Clara had lost her resolve and might also slide away from the church.

SEVEN
Clara, Summer 1944

Clara felt as though her mother had never really supported her artistic endeavors. It was as if art was somehow antithetical to the triune Principles of Life, Truth, and Love by which her mother strived to live her life and have her children live theirs. Art was just another materialist—and hence deceptive—facet of the illusory world in which we wallowed. Though Clara would concede art was not *pure thought* in accordance with the Christian Science definition of that concept, it fostered the spiritual in her as strongly as any church service or silent prayer. More so. To her, art was a reflection of God, as well as God reflecting Himself in us. Indeed it was a *demonstration* of sorts, in the Christian Science sense, an active proof by means of which one cleared the mind and dispelled errors of perception. And like Christian Science, it demanded "a radical reliance on the truth." Clara understood it through her own direct experience, and the next time her mother accused her of refusing to put away childish things, she would stand her ground and declare—however blasphemously—that God and art were one!

The day after Adel's party, Clara retrieved her watercolors and brushes from the basement and began painting while her mother was out grocery shopping. She tried her hand at a few landscapes and still-lifes along the lines of the ones she'd done before putting away her supplies, but these no longer interested her the way they once had. So she began to paint people. Not portraits per se, but *people*, though the distinction wasn't so clear to her. Sometimes she meant to achieve a likeness, sometimes not. It didn't matter. She painted entirely from memory and let her love of color—bold, saturated, contrasting color—express her understanding of her subject.

Then, a few weeks after she'd begun painting again, almost as confirmation of her re-immersion into her art, she received a telephone call from Eliot Brasher, who wished to invite her to the opening of his show at the Willard Gallery in downtown Seattle. It was the first she'd heard from him since Adel's party. She still thought about Merritt from time to time, with confusion and a degree of yearning, but knew she couldn't dwell forever on him. Wherever he was, she told herself, she wished him well, but there had never been a promise between them—just a goodnight kiss—and so she knew her heart had every right to take her where it would.

It was a warm spring day the afternoon of the opening. Clara dared to wear a sunny yellow blouse and dirndle skirt that at first she thought might look too festive. But then she decided no, she was tired of the dour wool skirts and white blouses she typically wore and wanted to add more color to her wardrobe. When her mother saw her preparing to leave the house and asked where she was going, Clara told her she was meeting Adel Worley to go see a movie.

The gallery was on Sixth Avenue, not far from the Reading Room. The event commenced with Marian Willard, the silver-haired gallery owner, introducing herself and saying a short prayer for an end to the war and the safe return of the boys overseas. She then introduced Eliot, calling him an artistic prodigy and characterizing his work as conceptually challenging and technically innovative. "What you see before you, ladies and gentlemen, will, I am confident, influence artists of the post-war era for decades to come. I'm only afraid that our young Eliot's imminent renown will have him forsaking our quaint city to seek his fame and fortune in New York or Europe once this abominable war is over." She then signaled the guest of honor to step forward.

Eliot was dressed in the same rumpled manner as on the night of Adel's party, only now he wore a brown knit tie to go with his brown linen jacket. His hair was longer and shaggier than before. Yet, despite his appearance, and despite his bashfulness, it was clear he was enjoying the attention. The side of his mouth lifted in a half-smile as he looked down at his scuffed Thom McCann's and ran a hand through his reddish-brown locks.

"Thank you all," he began and glanced about the room. "Thank you for sharing in the excitement of having my work appear in one of the finest galleries in America. And thank you, Marian, for your encouragement and hard work on behalf of an unknown artist from Spokane." He caught Clara's eye at the back of the room and added, "Thank you also to my fellow artists." And with that he nodded to the group of forty or so people in the room and kissed Marian Willard on the cheek. When the applause subsided, he ambled over to where Clara stood.

"How was that?" he asked her.

"Splendid," she said. "Your modesty becomes you."

He accompanied her to the table of refreshments and poured them both a glass of wine from the half-gallon bottle next to the platter of hors d'oeuvres.

"I was glad to see a familiar face in the crowd. Most of these people are friends of Marian's," he remarked and clinked his glass to hers. "She assures me they'll buy two or three paintings even though I'm competing with war bonds for people's investment dollars."

Clara held her glass in both hands, looked at Eliot, and told him she wished she could buy one. In two swallows, he downed his wine. "I wouldn't allow it," he said. "I'll paint you one instead. Then you'll have to come out to my studio to pick it up."

Clara didn't know what to say to this apparent invitation. She'd never visited a real artist's studio. She didn't know any existed in Seattle, apart from the student studios at Cornish. She pictured Eliot's studio as a spacious, loft-like room with skylights, canvases tossed pell-mell about the room, an unimaginable clutter of brushes and easels, the air redolent with paints and varnishes and linseed oil, and asked when she could come see it.

"It's just a converted garage behind the house where I rent a room," Eliot admitted. "In Fremont."

She'd heard of Fremont, one of the city's more derelict neighborhoods, but had never been there. She imagined boarded-up storefronts, abandoned warehouses, rundown rental houses, and overgrown vacant lots. Just so, she couldn't wait for Eliot to give her directions. He told her he hauled his paintings around in an old Chevrolet ambulance and would be happy to drive out to West Seattle to pick her up in a few weeks, once the show at the Willard closed. But she told him no, she was used to taking the bus and could get there on her own—once again not ready to introduce the boy in her life to her parents.

When Eliot looked about the room and said he should probably mingle with his would-be patrons, Clara agreed and took the opportunity to look at his paintings. She liked the five paintings that comprised the *Endocrine* series, including the one on loan from the Henry. Some had more vibrant color than others, and there was evidence he'd applied a palette knife to three of them. Each painting was contained within a basic black frame and titled simply *Endocrine* #1, *Endocrine* # 2, and so on, so there was no telling which paintings represented which glands. She liked Eliot's other paintings as well, all of which played on various geometric shapes and a sense of motion through a thick, swirling application of paint. One painting was so dense with lines of paint that it looked as though he'd laid tree moss on the canvas and painted over it.

After a while Eliot introduced Clara to several of his artist friends, all of whom were quite a bit older than he and already well established in the Seattle art scene. She exchanged niceties with each of them, but for the most part they seemed uninterested in talking with her. The only woman Eliot introduced her to, Callie Porter, was the sole exception. She was probably in her forties, full in the hips and round in the shoulders, with hair that frizzed out on both sides of her head like a pair of ostrich wings. The maroon shift, beaded necklace, wool stockings, and lace-up boots she wore gave her the folksy appearance of a Russian babushka. They talked about art—drawing and painting, sculpture and printmaking, even so-called found art—and what it meant to be an artist, especially for a woman. Clara learned from Callie that she was unmarried and childless. "And I have no plans to alter this *très bon état*," she insisted. "I'm free to work day and night. Or not at all. As I choose." Her medium of late, she told Clara, was woodcuts. She'd been studying the carvings of the coastal tribes and making prints based on them, fascinated as she was by the natives' use of the ovoid and crescent. She then asked Clara what her influences were.

Clara was stumped. She didn't know whether she had any influences. "I'm not sure," she answered truthfully, and feared she might have revealed herself as the novice she was.

"That's okay," Callie offered. "Besides, I don't mean so-and-so or such-and-such. That's the kind of idol worship crap those guys over there go in for." She raised an eyebrow toward two of the men Clara had been introduced to earlier. She placed her hands over her midriff by holding a thick forearm in each hand—a curious gesture, Clara thought. Her hands were dark from the sun, the skin lined and calloused, and her fingernails were ragged and stained around the cuticles from ink, like Clara's father's hands always were after he came home from the print shop. "I'm talking more about what really gets your fire burning, what sets you to work, so your blood's racing and you're going to make a mess of some paper or canvas or whatever you're working with and you don't care but just know without knowing that something good's going to come of it. That's what I'm after. I believe the Spanish call it *duende*." She seemed to amuse herself with her own chatter and gave a wide grin that showed her thick tongue and yellowish teeth.

Clara wasn't sure how to respond, or whether she should say anything at all. "I like to paint people," she let out, and at this Callie roared, her head thrown back and her midsection extending outward.

"Yes," she declared once she stopped laughing. "People are good. I'd love to see some of your people paintings sometime." She then looked about conspiratorially and whispered, "I'm also going to leave a small book for you here next week. You can pick it up from Marian. It's by Helmi Eckenson. All about education and the woman artist."

"Thank you," Clara said politely.

"Don't forget," Callie said. "Helmi Eckenson."

"I won't," Clara assured her and turned to greet Eliot as he rejoined them.

Callie kissed Eliot on the cheek, patted his shoulder, and excused herself to go speak to Marian. Eliot held a full glass of wine. From the way he swayed, Clara guessed he was half-honked, as her father might say. He congratulated her on impressing so many of his friends with her charm and art smarts. "I see Callie's befriended you," he said and looked across the room in her direction. "She's a great ol' gal," he added. "But be warned, she's known for pursuing certain tribadistic interests."

Clara didn't know what this meant, figuring it had something to do with the coastal tribes Callie was studying for her woodcuts. It was one more detail from an event that, quite frankly, was beginning to overwhelm her. What would her church-going mother, longshoreman father, and servicemen brothers think if they saw the kind of company she was mixing with?

What's more, here was Eliot Brasher, the brilliant young artist, wobbling into her as he said, "Here," and handed her a slip of paper, "that's where my studio is in Fremont. I drew you a map."

Her mother, of course, wanted her to spend more time on the church sewing committee and less time on her art. As part of the church's nationwide war relief effort, the committee collected, cleaned, and mended garments which it then sent to its War Relief Shipping Depot in Portland, where the clothes were sorted and packed before being shipped to the Christian Science War Relief Committee headquarters in Boston. From there the thousands of coats, dresses, pants, and shoes were distributed to war needy throughout the world. Since the start of the war, Clara had been volunteering ten to fifteen hours a week with the committee. She organized neighborhood clothes drives, hauling boxes of children's clothing from people's attics and bringing them home to wash and fold. All the clothes had to be made like new before they could be sent out. "Every garment is a prayer objectified," the committee ladies were fond of saying.

Each meeting of the sewing committee opened with readings from the Scriptures and Mrs. Eddy's writings, followed by updates from the War Relief Committee Quarterly Bulletin on what garments were needed most, from baby clothes to work shoes. Clara's mother specialized in making quilts, featherstitching bits of silk from women's scarves and men's ties onto sugar sacks, then lining the quilts with durable flannel. In addition to being active in the church relief work, Clara tended the neighborhood Victory Garden, put in her morning hours at the Reading Room, and of course knit socks for the Red Cross. She knew her contribution—for which the animus, her mother frequently reminded her, was always spiritual love—amounted to nothing compared to what the boys in uniform had to endure. And for this reason, she continued to be tasked, emotionally at least, whenever she sat down to draw or paint and thought of her brothers fighting the Nazis, and had to keep reminding herself that the imagination, as embodied in art, was an ally against the "gross materiality" the Nazis represented—and was not the enemy.

One week after his show at the Willard Gallery ended, Clara visited Eliot's studio in Fremont. It was an old garage converted into a well-lit painting studio. His paints, brushes, palette knives, mixing trays, paint rollers, and other tools and supplies were scattered across a large worktable. Opposite the worktable his paintings were stored in a series of slotted plywood bins. Blank canvases leaned against the back wall ten deep. In the middle of the cement floor five separate easels were set up, four of which supported canvases in various stages of completion. One of the paintings, an 8-foot-by-4-foot canvas, stretched across two easels. Slashes of orange filled the lower portion of the painting, with a series of bluish moons above. There was also a loft at the front of the garage-studio where Eliot took naps. When Clara climbed the ladder half way to peer into the loft, she found a bare mattress with a bunched-up Army blanket, several books, a half-empty gallon jug of wine, and a glass tumbler with dried wine residue at the bottom.

After showing her around the studio, Eliot took her to a nearby tavern where they ate grinders and shared a pitcher of beer. Afterward they walked down to Canal Street, past the Burke Millwork where two women in overalls and work gloves stacked plywood in the yard, then along the poplar-lined ship canal where they watched a Navy transport ship heading toward the Government Locks, and finally back to the interurban bus stop where she let Eliot kiss her just as her bus arrived—just like her kiss with Merritt so long ago now.

That night when she told her parents about Eliot, her mother expressed grave concern, especially over their age difference. "The man is twenty-five years old," she said, "and you're just nineteen."

"So," Clara retorted, hating the childish tone of her own voice.

"*And* he's an artist," her mother added. "How in the world does he support himself?"

"He sells his paintings," she replied, knowing this was only half the truth, since Eliot lived primarily off his inheritance.

When her father, a veteran of the first World War, asked Clara why Eliot wasn't in the service, she explained that he'd been classified F-4. "I think it has to do with his hearing," she said, a brazen fabrication. She didn't know why Eliot was F-4, yet didn't dare tell her father this.

When her mother asked what church he attended and Clara told her he was Catholic, she half-expected her mother to quote *Science and Health*— "Whatever materializes worship hinders man's spiritual growth."—but instead asked whether he attended Sunday services, and when Clara said no, her mother looked dismayed.

On her second visit to Eliot's studio, they drank wine and climbed into the loft and necked. She began to speculate that Eliot might well be her first, though she couldn't say when or how, and knew she had to be careful. In Seattle, at least, a girl with a reputation meant only one thing—and it wasn't good.

It was during her third visit to Eliot's studio that she met Guy Anderson, a lean, balding man with a deep, soft voice and the dark complexion of someone who worked outside. He wore paint-stained khaki pants and a white t-shirt that showed off the viney muscles in his arms. It caught Clara's notice again how most of Eliot's friends were such well established artists. Unlike with Callie Porter, whom Eliot ridiculed as folk-artsy, he had the highest regard for Guy Anderson. The man was intelligent and composed and knew a great deal about art and artists, and yet never came across as a know-it-all. As Eliot and Guy discussed their work and Clara listened, she realized the triptych of paintings with the elliptical spheres at the Henry Art Gallery belonged to Guy Anderson.

"I'm moving to La Conner," Guy announced when Eliot asked him why he'd been out of town so much lately. "I found an abandoned horse farm up there. Got it dirt cheap. Morris is coming up to help me renovate it, and I'm going to get away from all the distractions of city life."

Morris, Clara figured, was Morris Graves, one of the artists she'd met at Eliot's opening. He was the one who'd painted the strange, ethereal bird she'd been so taken by at the Henry.

"Where's La Conner?" asked Eliot. He flicked the ash from his cigarette into a battered Savarin coffee can.

"La Conner, my friend," Guy explained, "is nestled in the tranquil Skagit Valley a couple hours north of here. You and Clara will have to visit." Clara looked up to see Guy's bright eyes upon her. He had an easy, self-assured manner, which she liked about him.

"What do you say, Clara?" Eliot asked. "Are you up to it?"

"I would love that," she said and stepped around an easel to give Eliot a kiss. "I've never been farther north than Everett, the time my father took me to a union meeting." Both men looked at her, apparently surprised by this comment. "When can we go?"

"As soon as I get settled in," Guy answered.

"How 'bout that, girlie," Eliot chimed in, putting his arm around Clara's waist and tugging her to him. "We're gonna take a trip."

EIGHT
Merritt, Spring-Fall 1944

It had been one of the proudest, and saddest, moments of Merritt's life when Captain Cooley ordered the USS *Washington* underway and the *North Carolina*-class battleship set a course through the Clair Inlet, north through Puget Sound, and out into the rough Pacific. He longed for and feared what he was leaving behind. He pined for Clara, and he dreaded the rotten blackmail letter he'd received after his unfortunate incident with Ensign Rivard. The more he tried to sort it out, the more frustrated he became, until finally he knew he would rather decipher pig entrails than try to figure out how circumstances went so wrong in Seattle. As he leaned over the stern rail, recovering from his first bout of seasickness, he could at least tell himself that none of it mattered any longer. His ship had sailed.

After a brief port of call in San Francisco and another at Oahu, the battleship steamed toward the Marianas to join the Fifth Fleet. Merritt's initial weeks at sea were spent in General Drills, swabbing the iron decks, scraping rust from grates, railings, and armor plates before repainting them, and greasing handwheels, roller paths, hatch doors, portholes, and anything else that swung, swiveled, rotated, or turned. His division twice had gunnery practice during anti-aircraft practice. Off-duty, he took his chits to the barber shop or soda fountain below-decks, then retired to his bunk to read or sleep. Meanwhile, he collected the letters he wrote home to Lyndonville and waited for the next transport ship to hand them off.

Out at sea he reminisced more about home than at anytime since he'd left almost two years ago. His parents insisted he graduate from high school following the attack on Pearl Harbor. The rush to enlist left guys like Merritt who remained in school feeling sheepish and less than patriotic. As a group they became shy and retiring. They turned serious about their studies, and Merritt knew his dedication to learning would not have been so strong if not for the war. He also knew that once his graduation day arrived, he would have to enlist, so he wanted to get in as much book learning as he could. He also thought about his mother and father back in Lyndonville, quiet, respectable people. He missed his two best friends from high school as well, Archie and Reed. After enlisting, they'd gone through boot camp together. Then Reed's regiment had been sent to Alaska. And Archie was sent straight to the Pacific, where he was killed near Midway Island when the Japs sank his PT boat.

Lying hour after hour in his berth compartment, Merritt listened to his shipmates yammering about their girlfriends and wives. Some guys bragged of high school sweethearts waiting for them back home, while others had gotten hitched before shipping out. The talk soon had Merritt musing about Clara. Tall, good-looking Clara sitting at the back desk in the Christian Science Reading Room, having lunch with him at The Continental, letting him take her to the movies, learning to dance, giving him a peck on the cheek on the sidewalk, accepting his kiss as she boarded the bus back to West Seattle. Clara . . . whom he never heard from again.

When the bluejacket in the bunk above his leaned over and asked Merritt if he had a girl, he said no, but a split-second later added, "Well, not steady like. But there's a girl I saw a few times before shipping out."

"Is that right?" his bunkmate said, sounding skeptical. "Some Seattle chippy, eh? What'd she cost you?"

Merritt kicked the bottom of the bunk with both feet. "Watch it," he shot back. "She's not that sort."

The bunkmate groaned out an apology and asked, "So you gonna write her?"

"Probably," Merritt said, and wondered if he ought to. He could send the letter in care of the downtown Reading Room. "Dear Clara," he would address it, "You probably don't remember me, but . . . ." But what? Of course she would remember him. How stupid was he? The whole idea was idiotic. She'd have a good laugh and toss it in the trash. Still, he thought, if she did write back, they might sort out what had happened and keep writing, and in time he might address his letters "My Dear Clara" or "Dearest Clara." She might even send him a picture of herself, one he could keep in his footlocker or pass around the berth like other guys did photos of their girls.

The tedium of General Drills ended a few days later with a call to General Quarters preceding the bombardment of Saipan. Merritt was above-decks when the 16-inch guns began blasting the 12-mile-long stretch of sand and rock. Nothing in basic training had prepared him for the bone-cracking din of the big guns, the discharge of white flames from the muzzles singing his eyeballs, the percussion of each shell pounding his eardrums until the ringing in his head would not stop. Each recoil rocked the ship and sent tremors through the deck as if it were made of tin, and Merritt wondered if the ship might just come apart at the seams and sink.

The fierce bombardment kept up into the night, and the next morning he was standing forward ship, helping secure the anchor chain, when he looked up and saw the first wave of Jap planes above the horizon, coming straight toward the Task Force. Within seconds the ship's crew was racing to battle stations as sirens sounded, bells rang, and a frantic voice over the speakers called "All ahead flank."

Merritt donned his helmet and flak-jacket and took up his position beside one of the foredeck 20-mm guns, just as he'd been taught in training. He flipped open the stacked magazines of antiaircraft ordnances at his feet and prepared to hand them off to the gunner's mate to load. As the squadron of Jap bombers and torpedo planes began to dive, he thought he might crap his pants, but he held tight when the gunner standing behind the splinter shield, his face pressed against ring sight, shouted, "What are we, seamen?"

Merritt hesitated, as did the gunner's mate, until the gunner looked over his shoulder and shouted again, "What the fuck are we, seamen?!"

This time Merritt and the gunner's mate shouted back, "Men-of-War, goddamnit!" and his nerves steeled up just as the first planes passed overhead and the score of small guns that ringed the ship's deck let loose with a snare of rapid fire.

The gunner swiveled as more planes buzzed the conning tower and strafed the deck. A charge detonated fifty feet starboard and sent a spray of seawater onto the foredeck, but no shrapnel. Merritt kept his head low and fed successive magazines to the gunner's mate as the attack picked up. At one point he looked at his gunner and saw him grimacing as he ripped a line of holes into the belly of a plane's fuselage and sent it barrel-rolling into the sea.

"This is a fucking turkey shoot," the gunner shouted and slapped the gunner's mate on the back, then said, "Which one of you boys wanna go at it?"

The gunner's mate instantly jumped behind the splinter shield, cussed the dirty Nips, and began firing at the next wave of planes. Merritt didn't have that kind of bravado, though, and kept picturing a bomb dropping onto the foredeck or a torpedo slamming the prow and the entire ship—and all 2,000 hands aboard her—going down in a sea of flames.

Two hours later the air assault ended just as abruptly as it had started, and the *Washington* came through virtually unscathed. A fire burned on the deck of a destroyer off to port side, but all reports were that the Task Force had incurred minimal damage. Merritt's first taste of battle, however, didn't leave him feeling very brave—and not nearly as boisterous as his shipmates, most of whom were hooting and hollering at having sent the Japs running. His nerves were shot, and as he made his way below-decks, he figured when it came to matters of life and death, he would keep expectations low.

After Saipan, life aboard ship returned to relative normalcy. The *Washington* detached from the Fifth Fleet to take on several scouting missions, accompanied by two cruisers and a handful of PT boats. They would have a few small skirmishes, but mostly cat-and-mouse stuff. The monsoon rains that came at night and oppressive heat throughout the day became harder to bear than any fighting they saw, and the only consolation was that the Japs had to endure it as well.

Several weeks after the attack at Saipan, Merritt turned restless and almost wished for another big battle. In one of the more lassitudinous moments beneath a make-shift parabola tent pitched on the open deck, he mentioned how fighting from shipboard made the war seem so impersonal. "All we're dong is shooting at a bunch of machines," he said.

A Marine instantly jumped to his feet and challenged him on the remark. He'd helped take Guadalcanal, he said, pointing a finger at Merritt, adding, "And let me tell you, the Nips ain't human no how." He then related how on the north end of the island he and several other Marines captured a Jap holed up in a cave, where they also found the uniform of a U.S. Marine. When they asked their prisoner where the Marine was, all the Jap said was, "Me eat him." And with that Merritt kept his mouth shut.

The *Washington* spent the next several months refueling smaller vessels, mostly destroyer escorts and light cruisers, and supporting air strikes on the Palau Islands, a stepping stone to re-taking the Philippines. Merritt began working on *Cougar Scream*, the ship's newsletter, to wile away the time. He interviewed seamen and officers and wrote short profiles of them. He also looked through the set of encyclopedia in the ship's library and wrote accounts of the South Pacific territories they were fighting to take back. He also read a lot. Sinclair, Steinbeck, Wolfe. All the good stuff in the ship's library.

When the *Washington* sailed into the Leyte Gulf in the Philippines in mid-October, the battle that ensued made Saipan look like a training exercise. The fight turned especially brutal off Cape Engaño where hundreds of ships engaged, exchanging nonstop fire as planes swarmed overhead, ordnances whistled past, and the air turned dark with smoke that choked the lungs. At one point when he ran up to the control room, the stable zenith instruments were gyrating out of control from the ship's pitch and roll and he knew if he didn't keep a steady handhold he'd be tossed overboard into the oily waters.

"Divine wind, my ass," his gunner shouted and doubled his fire at the kamikaze planes bee-lining toward the ship. After three hours of firing, the gunner collapsed from exhaustion and the gunner's mate pulled him from the mount and ordered Merritt into position.

Merritt hesitated, but then leapt behind the 20-mm gun and let tear at a fighter plane passing port side. He followed its path, unloading an entire magazine, and spotted what he thought was the pilot's stunned face in the cockpit fifty yards off port as the plane skidded into the sea.

For two days the battle at Leyte continued on without letting up, and when the Jap fleet finally turned tail, the *Washington* began bombarding the Luzon coastline. Toward the end of the campaign when he could finally go below-decks and drop his jangling body into his bunk, one phrase alone filled his thoughts . . . *still not dead.*

NINE
Clara, Fall 1944

Clara wrote her brothers every week without fail. The family had recently learned that Freddy was stationed in England, while Ken was serving in Italy, after having fought in North Africa. Every morning at 7:00 when Clara and her mother studied the day's lesson and silently prayed, they did not pray *for* Frank and Ken. Prayer wasn't meant for supplication, or for requisitioning God's intervention. Its sole and divine purpose was to achieve fuller consciousness of one's likeness in God, and by dwelling upon God's supreme Love and Truth they helped ensure no mortal error—through injury or illness—befell either Freddy or Ken.

Of the two, Ken had always been the more diligent in his faith. He wanted to become a practitioner, and according to his letters home he led fellow Scientists in readings from the Scriptures and *Science and Health* while bivouacked along the Elba River near Rome. "'The best sermon ever preached is Truth practiced,'" he told them in his most recent letter, quoting Mary Baker Eddy. Meanwhile Freddy, who didn't write home nearly as frequently, talked about how bored he and the other G.I.'s were waiting for the big invasion of France that General Eisenhower was planning.

In Clara's letters to Ken, she bragged about her war relief work and updated him on recent demonstrations of healing among church members. In her letters to Freddy, she avoided church talk and instead gossiped about the neighborhood, told him all about her drawing and painting, and 'fessed up about Eliot and their plans to drive to La Conner. She even divulged her newly hatched plan to apply for a job at the Frederick & Nelson department store downtown and eventually move into her own apartment.

She imagined Freddy and Eliot becoming fast friends after the war, and pictured Freddy as Eliot's best man at their wedding. Her mother, meanwhile, routinely reminded her that Roy Olmstead, Seattle's famous rum runner-turned-Christian Scientist, had a son her age. Yet Clara knew she'd already fallen too far from the church to entertain such a match. Each week she found herself inventing new excuses to skip Sunday services and Wednesday testimonials, and once she moved into her own apartment, she knew, she would stop attending services altogether.

News of the D-Day invasion left everyone both rattled *and* excited. General Eisenhower's order of the day appeared on the front page of the newspapers— "Soldiers, Sailors, and Airmen of the Allied Expeditionary Force! You are about to embark on the great crusade . . . The tide has turned! . . . We will accept nothing less than full victory"—swelling everyone's hope for a swift end to the war. She and her parents knew Freddy was part of the invasion, but that's all they knew. As the weeks passed, they continued to send their letters to him and awaited the postman's arrival each day for some word from him, no matter how brief, letting them know he was all right.

Another three months passed before Clara worked up the courage to apply for the position at Frederick & Nelson. For the interview she put on a two-piece copen-blue suit and applied a coat of leg make-up from the back of her knees to her heels. She also wore a pair of D'Orsay pumps that she'd filched from a clothing drive on fashionable First Hill. To finish off the outfit, she donned a hand-crocheted beret and gave it a jaunty tug to the right. While she didn't belong to the smart set of girls from Bush School and Holy Names Academy, she could dress with the best of them.

Frederick & Nelson was undisputedly the finest department store in Seattle. Maybe in the country. The five-story terra-cotta building on Fifth Avenue and Pine Street was a Seattle landmark. To show off the store's patriotism, the Pine Street side of the building had been draped in a colossal American flag. The Fifth Avenue side displayed an equally large banner commanding passersby to "BUY WAR BONDS". There were other department stores in Seattle—I. Magnum, Rhodes, and the Bon Marché—but not one of these matched Frederick & Nelson in sophistication. Even during the lean war years, the store maintained an impressive stock. And not only did Frederick & Nelson have the latest in fine and affordable apparel for both men and women, it had a complete children's section, a candy counter, a lunch counter, the newly installed Tea Room, a bookshop, and an extensive sporting goods department. It even had an art gallery, called The Little Gallery.

The afternoon of her interview Clara nervously took the elevator to the fifth floor business offices. In the Personnel Office she greeted the secretary, removed her beret, and was asked to please wait. When she was finally admitted to the office of the Director of Personnel, a heavy-set man with perspiration stains on his white shirt greeted her from behind a large oak desk. The green ink blotter in front of him was covered in doodles. Holding Clara's application, the man introduced himself as Mr. Boykin.

"I see by this, Miss Hamilton, that you've applied for a position in Ladies Apparel." He wiped his brow with a white handkerchief. It was a warm September day and the office was very stuffy.

"Yes, sir," she replied, but then, going for broke, she decided to reveal her true ambition. "I really want to work in the illustration department, sir. I've drawn nearly all my life, especially figures, and I know I can contribute."

Mr. Boykin placed her application in a manila folder and handed the folder across the desk to her. "Mr. Lundquist is in charge of our staff of illustrators," he said, "and I should tell you right now, he's a very temperamental fellow." He leaned back in his leather desk chair. "That said, there may, in due course, arise an opportunity for you to present Mr. Lundquist samples of your work. Do you have a portfolio?"

The question stumped her. It reminded her of Eliot asking her to show him her portfolio last March at Adel's party. "Not with me, sir, no," she answered. "But I can bring one tomorrow." She would stay up all night preparing it if she had to.

"That won't be necessary," Mr. Boykin assured her. He withdrew a fountain pen from an ink well on his desk and doodled on the ink blotter, then stopped. "Use your position in Ladies Apparel to familiarize yourself with the stock. We'll wait for the right occasion to approach Mr. Lundquist." He put the fountain pen down and extended his hand without standing up. Clara stood up and shook it.

"Thank you, Mr. Boykin."

"Give your folder to Mrs. Evans outside. She'll arrange your schedule."

Clara left the interview delighted with how it had gone. She'd stated her ambition forthrightly, and Mr. Boykin had given her room to hope that her opportunity to show Mr. Lundquist her portfolio would, *in due course*, arise.

As she waited for Mrs. Evans to fill out a weekly planner for her, Clara dared to ask why Mr. Lundquist was considered so temperamental.

"Mr. Lundquist," Mrs. Evans replied without blinking, "is a prima dona. Nothing a good sock in the jaw wouldn't cure."

"Oh," said Clara, astounded at Mrs. Evans' bluntness. She regretted asking and placed her beret on her head, and as Mrs. Evans handed Clara her work schedule, the secretary smiled and in a more pleasant voice said, "That hat looks darling on you."

By mid-October, Guy Anderson was settled in La Conner and let Eliot and Clara know they could come visit. She and Eliot had become much closer by this time, though their attachment remained oddly undefined. Were they dating? She couldn't say for certain. They didn't go on dates per se. The one time Clara suggested a movie at the Neptune Theatre in the U District, Eliot said he didn't like movies, that they sapped the imagination. Most of the time, Clara dallied about his studio, watching him work and drinking wine with him. Occasionally they climbed into the loft and made out. Otherwise it would be difficult to tell that they were a couple, at least as she understood that term.

The Sunday morning they were to drive to La Conner, she rendezvoused with Eliot in Fremont. According to her plan, once she returned from La Conner, she would tell her parents she was moving into her own place. She had located a one-bedroom apartment on Queen Anne Hill, along the counterbalance side, and had saved enough from her weekly paycheck for the down deposit and first month's rent. She would sleep in the main room and use the bedroom for her studio. Although she'd worked on several oils in Eliot's studio in the past few months, she badly wanted a place where she could create her own mess.

Eliot used his remaining ration stamps to fill the gas tank of his Chevy ambulance and by ten that morning they were off, each with an overnight bag. There were also two paintings in the back of the ambulance, one by each of them, which they planned to give to Guy as housewarming gifts. Clara also brought a cigar box full of pencils and charcoals and her stock-in-trade sketchbook.

Once they passed through the unincorporated neighborhoods north of the city and entered the farming country near Edmonds, she slid across the bench seat of the ambulance and snuggled up under Eliot's arm. She'd rolled her window halfway down to let in the cool, damp air, but as they reached Everett she rolled it back up to keep out the stench of the pulp mills along the Snohomish River. Once past Marysville, the air cleared, as did the sky, revealing a fresh dusting of snow on the Cascade foothills.

In Mount Vernon, a small mill town on the Skagit River, they stopped at a cafe for lunch. As they sat side by side in the booth, Clara wanted to tell Eliot how happy she was. It was such an adventure, she wanted to say, but feared sounding silly. When she finished the last of her apple pie and ice cream, she flipped the paper placemat over, took a pencil from her handbag, and began to sketch the waitress, a woman about her mother's age with graying hair. When the waitress came over to refill Eliot's coffee cup, Clara handed her the drawing.

"Is that me?" she asked, holding the placemat in one hand, the coffee pot in the other. "You've given me a *very* flattering figure."

"I draw what I see," said Clara.

"Well, thank you," she replied. "I'll pin it up next to the cash register."

Back on the sidewalk, Clara put her arm through Eliot's. Even through their two coats, she could feel a shiver run through his body. "Are you cold?" she asked and looked into his face. "We should buy you a hat."

He shrugged and said, "Do you always do that?"

She didn't understand. "Do what?"

"Pull a pencil out and start drawing people?"

She gave out a girlish titter. "Not always," she said and tugged at his arm. "Just when I'm inspired."

He smirked and pulled his arm free. "You mean to show off?"

She stopped. "Excuse me?" she said. She waited for him to turn around. "Did I embarrass you?"

"No," he remonstrated, stopping several feet ahead of her. He seemed chastened by her response. "It's just . . . I'm not used to it is all." He came back toward her. "I'm sorry I said anything."

Clara looked down at the sidewalk, biting her lower lip. "Well then, I'm sorry for my lack of decorum. I'm just excited to be with you. In this place." She thought she was about to cry, but then blurted out, "Wherever this is," and laughed to herself.

Eliot came forward and patted her shoulder, and Clara stood straight and declared, "Onward," and promised never to make another drawing in a restaurant, cafe, diner, or any other public establishment. "It's a bad habit, I know."

Yet, as they walked back to the ambulance, it occurred to her that she didn't really know what she was doing. Here she was a girl of 20, accompanied by a man of 25, going to visit a man in his mid-40s. Her parents would be mortified. When had she become such a reckless daughter? The tiff with Eliot had left her shaken, though maybe such flare-ups were inevitable as two people grew closer—like matches struck and tossed to the wind, here and gone. She didn't know. No more than she knew what she was heading for in accompanying him to La Conner.

From Mount Vernon, they crossed the Skagit River and drove west away from the mountains and into the valley's rich, moist fields. Hillocks rose in the near distance and, beyond these, larger hills that Eliot said were the San Juan Islands. Lush green marsh grass sprouted along the edges of the vast tideflats. They crossed one slough after another and then passed an apple orchard, the gnarled limbs pruned into vertical spears. At a dirt turn-off, a fruit stand advertised crates of Gravenstein and Jonagold apples for two dollars apiece. They drove up and over a dike, one side un-reclaimed mudflats, the other a pasture where cows grazed on winter wheat. They commented now and then on the scenery but otherwise said little as the road wound its way through a cluster of knolls and into the small fishing village of La Conner.

The plan was to meet Guy at a tavern located on a pier. Following Guy's directions, they drove down Main Street—two cafes, three taverns, a grocery market, a hardware store, and the storefront town hall—until it turned into a gravel track that paralleled the murky Swinomish Channel, from which a row of piers extended into the water. A half dozen fishing boats, trawlers mostly, were tied to the piers. Cormorants perched atop several pilings, ignored by the fishermen aboard their boats repairing gill nets and hook lines or applying a fresh coat of paint to the deck and rails. Just before reaching the fish processing plant, there was a short pier that the Purse Seiner Tavern shared with a fueling station. They parked the ambulance, and as they walked onto the pier Clara took in the heady marine smell of fish guts and motor oil.

The tavern was on the near end of the pier. A dry-rotted life ring hung from the door. Clara followed Eliot inside where the dark interior and beery aroma left her momentarily disoriented. A plate-glass window filled the wall opposite the entrance, creating an impenetrable white glare. To the right of the entrance was a pool table with a scuffed red felt top. A couple of men in grease-stained work jumpers milled about the table. The wall behind the long wooden bar was decorated with war bond posters, a large tides table, and a pin-up girl calendar. The month of October displayed a curvaceous blonde in a white swimsuit seated on a diving board above a swimming pool. Past the bar, a smaller window gave a view across the channel to several waterfront shacks with smoke rising from roof-top pipes. The bartender leaned toward a customer on the other side of the bar and rolled dice from a black cup.

Clara was the first to spot Guy, seated at the bar jotting notes in a pocket-sized notebook. Sitting by himself and wearing a black raincoat, he seemed to fit right in. A battered slouch hat rested on the bar beside his stumpy bottle of beer. When he finally looked up and saw who'd come in, he flipped closed his notebook and slid off his bar stool to greet them.

"Come over here, you old hound," he called out. "You, too, Clara." He shook Eliot's hand and gave Clara a peck on the cheek, then signaled the bartender to bring them three bottles of beer and led them to a table beside the plate-glass window.

When their beers arrived, he raised his bottle and said, "*Salut.*" They clinked bottles and just like that Clara felt cheered by the whole scene. What could be cozier? She could hardly refrain from pulling out pencil and paper and sketching the men at the bar, the two pool players, and Eliot and Guy. When the bartender set a bowl of peanuts on the table and Guy said, "Thanks, Jer," it was plain to see he felt right at home here.

They spent the next hour or more in the Purse Seiner Tavern. The big news Eliot and Guy had to discuss was Mark Tobey having won the Venice Biennale Prize, only the first American since Whistler to do so. Guy said the prize cemented his reputation. "It'll be good for all of us up here," he added.

As the men talked, Clara watched fishing boats putter up and down the channel in the fading light. It was the time of day that her West Seattle neighbors, émigrés from Finland, called "the blue moment," when day and night perfectly fused. It was nearly dark outside when the three decided to leave. Guy, who'd hiked the three miles from his house, had Clara climb into the cab of the ambulance so that she sat between him and Eliot. They drove out the west end of town and where the road turned left across the bridge to the Swinomish tribal lands or right into the fields and tideflats, they turned right. When they reached Guy's place, it didn't look like a house at all—and it wasn't. It was a large abandoned horse stable that, Guy explained, had belonged to a fellow who'd bred thoroughbreds in the '20s but went broke when the Depression hit. A few years later the main house burned down, and then last spring Guy purchased what remained of the property—the sturdy horse stable, a semi-collapsed hay barn, and four acres of surrounding pasture—and with Morris Graves' help converted the stable into his home and studio.

The hominess of the old horse stable surprised Clara. A faint mustiness, along with the lingering odor of horseflesh and hay, pervaded the interior. Guy had knocked down the individual horse stalls at either end and turned one end of the stable into the living room/kitchen area and the other end his studio, leaving two stalls in the middle for bedrooms. Two sofas and three leather armchairs occupied the living room, while in the corner a cast-iron cook stove with a stove pipe attached to the wall provided heat and a place to cook. Next to the stove, a hose extended from a spigot into the basin of a tin-topped table. Next to the table stood a wooden ice box, and on the other side of that an old watering trough that served as Guy's bathtub. The eating table was made of three rough-hewn boards from the barn laid across two sawhorses, along with an assortment of straight-back chairs. The walls were covered with a score of paintings reaching up to the exposed roof beams fourteen feet overhead, where there was also a former hayloft.

Guy escorted them down to the other end of the stable to his studio, where the odor of varnish and oil of cloves gave the air a kick. After turning on the bright mechanic's lights, Guy turned nervous, as if afraid his guests might see his unfinished work, and quickly flicked the lights off and led them away. He took Clara's overnight bag and set it in one of the bedroom stalls. Each stall had an iron bedstead and mattress, as well as a Pendleton blanket across the front for privacy.

"The lady's suite," he said. "The gentleman's is next door."

Clara and Eliot had agreed to leave the sleeping arrangements to fate since they didn't know what the layout at Guy's would be, and it appeared fate had dealt them separate rooms—or rather stalls. When Clara asked Guy where he would sleep, he said he would climb into the hayloft for the night.

Eliot then went outside to fetch wood from the wood pile while Guy opened a bottle of wine. When everyone was gathered again, he placed a .78 disk of Louis Armstrong on the turntable of his phonograph player, and as the Dixieland notes filled the stable he handed each of his guests a glass of wine. "To art," he said, raising his glass. "May we give it our damndest."

With a fire now going in the stove, Clara set about making cheese omelets and hashed brown potatoes in the two heavy skillets that hung from nails above the stove. While they sat about the sawhorse table to eat, they knocked off the first bottle of wine and Eliot went out to the ambulance to retrieve the gallon jug he'd brought up from Seattle. They kept drinking and the conversation grew more lively and at times even contentious. Guy defended Mark Tobey, one of his dearest friends, while Eliot berated Guy for idolizing the older artist. Clara jumped in by saying she didn't understand Tobey's objection to color and repeated his comment in studio class that color was for children. "Then I'm a child," she said. Guy tried to explain that Tobey was only being contrary when he said such things. "He saw too many Derains in France," he said. Eliot hefted the gallon jug and splashed out another glass of wine for everyone. "His paintings are pure parquetry," he sneered, and Guy guffawed and called Eliot's remark slanderous.

Clara eventually had enough of the Mark Tobey talk and cleared the dishes while Eliot and Guy retired to the leather armchairs. When she joined them, Eliot sprang to his feet and announced that he and Clara had come bearing gifts. He grasped Clara's hand and hurried her out to the ambulance. Moments later, braced by the cool night air, they carried their paintings inside and presented them to their host. Guy held the canvases up, one in each hand, and exclaimed over them. Eliot's was a mass of globular splotches in red and black and Clara's a vibrant portrait of Guy sitting in Eliot's studio. For the next hour, the three discussed which wall and at what height each painting should be hung. When at last they agreed, and after Guy had climbed a step-ladder to hang the two paintings, they refilled their glasses for another toast.

When she woke the next morning, everything was quiet. The narrow row of windows along the upper portion of the front wall let a flimsy light into the stall. She thought she should feel hung-over from drinking so much of Eliot's cheap jug wine, but she didn't. A sleepy sort of contentment came over her instead as she lay in the soft, lumpy bed. The evening had been more fun than she could remember ever having. A simple, honest enjoyment of life. She picked her wristwatch off the floor and was winding it when she heard the hatch on the cast-iron stove open and close and a moment later a light knock on the wall of her stall.

"I thought you might be awake," Eliot said as he pushed aside the colorful blanket that served as her door. He stood in his striped boxers and white tanktop. "I just put more wood in the stove, so it should warm up in no time."

She stretched her arms over her head and yawned a good morning.

"Good morning yourself," he replied. "How'd you sleep?"

"Splendiferously," she answered and realized she was still a bit tipsy. She then scooted to one side of the bed and tossed the covers back. "Come here," she said.

Eliot obliged by sliding into the bed next to her, and she pulled the covers up over their shoulders and turned to lie face to face with him. She then tugged his body to hers and began kissing his face. She figured he knew she was still a virgin, and as she pulled her nightshirt over her head and he kicked off his boxers, she also figured this was about to change. Beneath the weighty bedcovers, she nestled her warm body against his and reached down to touch him. He flinched and sat up and started squeezing her breasts. He promptly positioned himself over her and pried himself between her legs, and an instant later he tensed up as if someone had pinched him on the rear and with a deep exhale rolled off her. Without delay he slid from the bed, retrieved his boxers from the floor, and beat a quick retreat from the stall.

Clara watched his gaunt, white buttocks disappear behind the Pendleton blanket, not knowing if she should say something or go after him or what. She finally pulled the covers back up around her chin and nestled down into the bed and, perplexed by the whole experience, fell back asleep.

An hour or so later when she finally roused herself from bed and lumbered into the main room, she found Eliot seated on one of the sofas, fully dressed, staring at the wall of paintings.

"Where's Guy?" she asked.

"He took the ambulance to town." He looked at her rather sheepishly and returned his gaze to the wall. "I'm not sure we hung mine in the right place," he said.

"Do I have time to take a bath?" she asked. She came up behind him to kiss his neck, yet as she did so he twitched away and scowled at her.

"Maybe," was all he said and stood up. He then announced he was going to take a walk down to the beach and just like that was gone.

She couldn't understand why he was so fidgety, and could only guess that perhaps it had been his first time too.

She put more wood in the stove and then stepped outside into the chill air and pranced barefoot to the outhouse on the other side of the hay barn. After scurrying back to the warm stable, she filled every cooking pot she could find with water and placed it on the stove. When the water was hot, she poured it into the metal trough. As she took off her nightshirt again and let herself sink into the steamy water, she felt a new appreciation for her long, slender body—its assemblage of angles and curves—as well as her blemish-free skin, which her mother had always told her was her English inheritance.

She was still in the tub a half hour later when Guy returned from his errands, carrying a large box in his arms. "I'll be in the studio," he called out when he saw that he might be intruding on her.

"I was just getting out," she replied, and by the time Guy returned to the main room, she was dressed. She had also made a pot of coffee and was toasting cinnamon bread in the stove's fire hatch.

"You know you're very talented," Guy told her, pointing to her portrait of him on the wall.

"My mother taught me to cook," she said and set a plate of cinnamon toast on the table.

"I mean *artist*," he replied. "I haven't seen much of your work, just the one oil and a passel of drawings, but I'd say you've got genuine talent." He took a sip of coffee from the cup she handed him. "And something else too. Something more intrinsic."

"A certain *je ne sais quoi*?" she said.

"I mean it," he came back, watching her.

She couldn't tell whether his words were genuine appraisal or bald-faced flattery. "Thank you," was all she could say. She appreciated his taking notice of her work. She remembered Mark Tobey one evening quoting Freud on the two-fold foundation of human existence—Eros and Ananke, love and necessity. Did she now possess both, the one in Eliot, the other in her art? It was quite a notion.

"Are you going to submit to the Henry competition?" he asked her.

She brushed cinnamon off her fingers and confessed she didn't know anything about it. What's more, she doubted she would qualify.

"Bushwah," Guy said. "The deadline's in mid-March, five months from now. Begin working on something right now. You should also submit to the Northwest Annual at the museum."

Guy's unsolicited attention was beginning to embarrass her. Yet there was also something thrilling about it. Shamelessly so. She agreed finally to phone the Henry Art Gallery on Tuesday morning to ask for the competition guidelines, and Guy made her promise.

"I promise," she said.

When Eliot came back, Guy owned up that while in town he'd arranged to borrow a friend's motorboat—"A thirty-three-foot Gar Wood," he said, "a gorgeous boat."—in exchange for selling the friend a painting. And when he told Eliot and Clara that he wanted to take them up the Swinomish Channel to Padilla Bay, Eliot leapt at the idea, offering to buy the beer while Clara volunteered to pack them a picnic lunch—and before she knew it everything was back to the way it was the night before.

When she returned home late that Sunday night after the long drive down from La Conner, the magic of the weekend getaway was dispelled by the letter she received from her brother Freddy. He'd sent two, one to her parents and one to her, and hers had been placed on her pillow by her mother. Without removing her jacket, she sat down on the corner of the bed and opened the envelope. Though she knew her brother had participated in the D-Day landing, the only word she or her parents had received from him since then was a short note letting them know he'd survived. Just the same she'd kept up her weekly letters to him, praying they were received. She unfolded the two-page letter, the longest Freddy had ever written, and leaned into the light of the lamp. Immediately she noticed that it must have escaped the censors' scissors since, unlike previous letters from Freddy, it was intact, no paragraphs or sentences clipped out.

Dear Sis, it was addressed, and began with his usual apology for being such a lousy letter writer. *I appreciate all the letters you and Mom have sent and sometimes I think they're the only way I know I still have a family.* Clara paused at this, feeling she could cry then and there, but forced herself to read on . . . *When are Mom and Dad going to buy a camera so you can send pictures of everyone? I bet I'd hardly recognize you any more.* She laughed at this, but wondered if it might be true.

So you're really dating this fellow Eliot, eh? I'm sure he's a good egg. Otherwise you shouldn't give him a second look Have you told Mom and Dad yet? Go easy on them when you do. Mom will cry her eyes out, but Dad's liable to knock the lights out of any fellow he thinks isn't right for his little girl. And that goes double for me!

Also, what's this about your getting a job and moving out? Are you in your right mind? Maybe you should think this one through some more. But what the hay, who am I to talk? You're no longer the snot-nosed brat I said so long to three years ago. So you go ahead and do what's right for you. F&N will be lucky to have you. Plus I know how Mom and Dad can cramp a person's style. They mean well, but once a person's out of school, he wants his freedom, if you know what I mean.

She did, and couldn't wait to sign the lease on her new apartment.

It's got to be tough for a kid like you to grow up during this god-awful war and so I want you to know the men over here are terribly grateful for everything folks back home are doing to help out. That goes double for you. I don't even mind you and Mom praying for me once in a while, though I'll confess I'm more unreligious now than ever with everything I've seen over here. Of course Mom dragged me to the Scientists and filled me with all their loopy talk a lot later in life than you, so maybe you understand it better than me. It just never stuck with me is all, though with all the hurt and ugliness around here I can see why someone might want to say none of it's real, that it's all a bunch of mental error and such phooey. You see enough things and you come to realize that's not how it is. Let me tell you, Sis, it's plenty real. There's no mental error in the guy with his head half blown off or the fellow holding his guts in his hands, asking you what he should do. I'd like to see Mary Baker Eddy talk to these fellows about true Understanding.

Clara regretted hearing her brother sound so bitter toward the church, though she could hardly fault him for it. The horrors he described were beyond comprehension, and she found herself sympathizing with Freddy's expressions of doubt.

I'm sorry to go off like this, the letter went on. *I know the church means a lot to Mom and certainly Ken and probably you too. (We all know how Dad feels about it!) It's just I'm afraid things are going to get a lot worse over here before they get better. I can't tell you how many times I wished I was back working the waterfront. Sometimes I think I'd give anything to ride a slingboard into the hold of some rusty old tub again. I still carry my ILWU card with me and have run into a few union men in my regiment. We got together and told our commander we'd run the German ports once we take Deutschland.*

Yet these kraut bastards are mean SOB's and still got a lot of fight left in them. Someone should have told Uncle Omar this before he told the troops we'd all be home for Christmas. No one really knows when it will end, but like my pal Tig from Arkansas says, it ends when it ends, and hopefully we'll be around to see it.

On that sourpuss note I guess I'll say goodbye. This is a long letter and maybe my last for a while. I miss you all an awful lot, Sis. Tell Mom and Dad I love them. I hear Ken's regiment is in these parts, so maybe I'll catch up with him before too long. Wouldn't that be a kick? Keep well and watch out for those horny toad sailors!

Your big brother,
Freddy

Only after Clara had reread the letter and folded it back into the envelope did she allow herself to cry, muffling her sobs as best she could to avoid waking her parents. Even more than the horrors he'd seen, it was Freddy's tone that broke her determination to stay strong. He sounded so tired and weary—nothing like the boastful brother she'd always known him to be—yet at the same time apologetic about sharing his experiences, and trying so hard to sound cheerful. His tone, more than anything, conveyed his true suffering.

TEN
Merritt, Fall 1944-Summer 1945

After the battle in the Leyte Gulf, the Fifth Fleet deployed north bringing a short respite for the USS *Washington* that allowed her crew to recover from its battle fatigue. A couple of re-supply ships came and went, and on Thanksgiving Day the mess crew cooked up a large dinner complete with two kinds of pie. A radarman made a crack about the sad-sack G.I.s opening their golden cans of meat-and-veggie hash out there in the Philippine jungles, which got everyone in the mess yuking it up and backslapping one another until the chaplain rose from his chair to give the invocation and asked for God's protection of those same G.I.s.

As the Christmas season approached, the mood aboard ship became increasingly somber as men missed their families more than ever. Merritt wrote his parents every week and gave the letters to the mail clerk as if they would actually be sent off that day. He dug out of his footlocker the copy of the Emily Dickinson poem his sister had given him before he left Lyndonville, and he used a piece of chalk to scribble one of the lines from the poem onto the wall of his bunk—"This gave me the precarious Gait / Some call Experience."

When the fleet sailed straight into a typhoon the week before Christmas, no shipboard diversion could keep an overwhelming fear from seizing Merritt as the ship was tossed about. The massive battleship had been through heavy storms before, and he had dreaded every one, each making him more anxious and fearful than the last. Even more than the worst sea battle, the storms made him recognize his vulnerability and utter helplessness. He would feel every pitch and roll of the ship and become palsied with his own trembling. Eventually, hoping no one would see him in such a terrified state, he would hunker down in some corner of the ship's hull or curl up tight in his bunk and just wait out the storm as best he could. This storm, though, was different. As it came on—yet even before it reached typhoon proportions—the boatswain, a seasoned sailor who kept a nervous eye on the anemometer, turned to Merritt near the pilot house and told him it was the ugliest storm he'd ever seen, and was only going to get worse. For Merritt, who'd never seen the ocean until he joined the Navy, this was not reassuring news, and almost instantly a panic came over him

The winds soon topped 110 knots, with swells over 40 feet, and when

Admiral Cooley ordered all hands to don lifejackets and tie their whistles about their necks, Merritt knew that this was it, the ship was going down and he would perish with the rest of his shipmates. Everyone on board who wasn't an engineer or part of the bilge crew was ordered to ride out the typhoon in their berth below-decks. Merritt kept to his bunk, his hands gripping the side-rail. At one point when the ship abruptly rolled and first spun one way and then the other, he cradled his head in his arms and involuntarily let out a low moaning sound.

The howl and thrash of the storm were harsher than any bombardment or air attack he'd been through, and as he tried to hold his body against its uncontrollable shivering, it took every bit of self-restraint not to bolt from his berth, run to the top deck, and hurl himself overboard just to have done with it. He kept his eyes closed and pictured a surge of salt water breaking through the hatch as the ship plunged to the ocean floor. He would never see his mother or father again, his sister Bardie or her husband Henry. Never again see Vermont's autumn leaves or its winter snows or its gloriously green spring. And worst of all, his life would end without his ever having another chance with Clara. It was this thought that in a flash of recognition let him see how steadfastly, how earnestly he'd kept her with him all this while. And it was in this instant that he wished, more than anything else, to let her know how much she meant to him—and that he knew he would come through the storm okay.

Six months later when the *Washington* sailed back into Puget Sound for refitting, the crew was informed the ship would be reassigned to the Atlantic Fleet. Merritt pounced on the opportunity and put in for a transfer back to shore duty, which a week later came through. Assigned to the Pre-Separation Center at Naval District Headquarters, he would return to downtown Seattle. Apparently an official had figured out the war would soon be over and that Merritt was just the guy to process the legions of seamen who would be soon mustering out. Which suited him just fine. Fifteen months at sea had left him longing for solid ground. He knew every inch of the Mighty W, stern to bow, conning town to engine rooms, and after enduring the horrendous Christmas typhoon that eventually capsized three destroyers and drowned more than 800 seamen, as well as surviving a final attack by kamikaze pilots at Iwo Jima and the merciless bombardment of Okinawa, he wanted off.

One of the first things he did upon receiving his orders was to check if Ensign Rivard was still stationed out at Sand Point. He was not. He then went by the Exeter Hotel and asked the front desk clerk if Rivard still kept a room there. Again the answer was no.

During his long months at sea, Merritt had all but forgotten about his incident with the ensign, letting it pass for what it was—a drunken mishap. He also forgot about the blackmail letter he'd received two days after the incident. So much had happened since then, so many men had been transferred to other posts or shipped out—or killed—that he convinced himself he would never hear about it again. So much had changed—and was about to change—that the notion of being exposed had simply dried up and blown away.

Even while everyone knew that taking the Japanese home island would be a bloody undertaking, a good many guys were already talking up what they would do after the war. A fellow seaman in the Pre-Sep Center who was from Seattle talked about how he had a sweetheart job waiting for him at Vitamilk Dairy.

"All because of the union," he said, and when Merritt asked how that was, he explained that Vitamilk was a closed shop. "Teamsters," he said as a point of pride. "I worked for the company for two years before enlisting and was a dues-paying member the whole time. According to our contract, the company has to rehire any union member who resigned on account of the war. That's how it is. You stick by the union and the union sticks by you."

Merritt recalled the throng of Teamsters from Everett, Seattle, and Tacoma he'd processed back at the Recruitment Station and wondered if maybe his friend here had been one of them. He knew nothing about them except that they were truck drivers.

"Maybe I could get you on," the seaman offered. "You know what they say about the milkman," he added with a lascivious look.

Merritt didn't respond to this. The only thing he could imagine that might possibly keep him in Seattle once he mustered out would be his running into Clara again and, beyond that, their getting back together. Although he'd thought about her the first few weeks following his transfer, he knew he was only kidding himself. A girl like that didn't remain unattached for long. The Christian Science Reading Room was located halfway between the Hotel Commodore on Second Avenue, where he'd taken a room, and the Exchange Building, where the Pre-Sep Center was headquartered. His first few days back in town he would nonchalantly walk past the Reading Room and glance through the front window. But not once did he see her inside. In all probability, he figured, she'd married someone from her church and already had a kid or two clinging to her skirts.

He made up his mind to just do his job and log his discharge points as fast as he could. He also tried to stay out of trouble. He steered clear of The Turf Club and instead spent his evenings in the Seattle Public Library, the stone-block Carnegie structure just down the street from the Exchange Building. He speculated that once the war was over and he'd left the service, he would enroll in college, perhaps UVM in Burlington, and maybe study history or English literature. If the war had taught him anything, it was that he'd better pursue his heart's desire while he still could—a notion that, for better or worse, always brought him back to Clara.

ELEVEN
Clara, Spring-Summer 1945

The real trouble for Clara and Eliot came in March. Clara knew, though, it had really started several months earlier on the long drive back to Seattle from La Conner when she recounted Guy's suggestion that she submit a painting to the Henry Art Gallery competition. Eliot told her flat out not to, which startled her. Given Guy's praise of her work, she'd expected Eliot to be pleased for her. Plus, what harm could there be in her submitting one of her paintings?

"Everyone wants public acclaim, but no one wants to work for it," he told her. "Besides, competitions are a waste of time."

Yet his words were disingenuous, since he'd been one of three Honorable Mentions in last year's competition. Clara, however, said nothing further and let the matter drop.

Over the next few weeks she and Eliot saw a lot less of one another, even though her best friend at work, Jenny Rodale, had put Clara in touch with a physician who supplied her with the latest contraceptive device, called the Anna Health Sponge, so she wouldn't have to worry so much about becoming pregnant. Then, several days before Christmas, she and Eliot shared a bottle of wine in Eliot's studio and she spent the night with him. They agreed not to exchange Christmas gifts, especially since he planned to take the train to Spokane for the holiday. And even though she never mentioned the art competition again, she secretly made up her mind to submit a piece of work by the March 10 deadline.

After the New Year, Clara finally moved into the one-bedroom apartment on Queen Ann Hill that she'd had her eye on. She squabbled with her mother about the move—*Yes, it was an extravagance. Yes, there was a war on.*—but she would not be talked out of it. She put in longer shifts at Frederick & Nelson to afford the rent and devoted her nights to painting, leaving little time for Eliot or anyone else.

It was nearly February when Eliot phoned her with the astonishing news that the Seattle Art Museum wanted to stage a one-man exhibition of his work. The show would make him the youngest artist ever to have a solo exhibition at the museum. In the weeks following the public announcement, the Seattle art scene was abuzz with the news, calling Eliot the heir apparent to Northwest masters such as Mark Tobey, Morris Graves, and Guy Anderson, each of whom had had his own one-man show at the museum in years past. By March, he and Clara had decided to take another trip to La Conner so Eliot could consult with Guy about the exhibition.

It was a pleasant drive through the Skagit Valley, which was greening into spring, yet when they arrived at the stable Guy was not home. They let themselves in, since Guy never locked the door, and immediately Eliot turned his attention to the wall on which his painting hung. He turned silent, scowling at it, while Clara sat on the sofa and took out her sketchbook.

"I need to take that back," he said, pointing to the painting.

"I'm sure Guy will loan it to you for the exhibition," Clara said and looked up at it. It had never been her favorite of Eliot's. In fact she'd always imagined it one of his throw-away pieces.

"Loan it to me?" Eliot crossed his arms and looked over his shoulder at her. The brown-and-gray bowling shirt he wore with the name "Alex" stitched across the breast pocket was baggy on him, and his drab olive khakis hung loose on his hips. In the past three months he'd lost ten pounds, which he attributed to the phenobarbital the doctor had prescribed to help him sleep. With seven months to go to the exhibition, it was already weighing heavily on him. "It's *my* painting," he said.

She set her pencil down. "You gave it to him," she replied. "Just as I gave him mine." She looked at her own painting on the adjacent wall, the portrait of Guy which seemed rather amateurish to her now.

"Maybe you gave him yours," Eliot said, "but I don't just give my work away like that. Unless a person holds a certificate of ownership signed by Marian, the painting is only entrusted to the holder as the repository. If you'd ever sold a painting, you would understand the protocols involved."

Eliot's initial excitement had subsided in the weeks following the news of the museum exhibition and been replaced by a mounting anxiety. Understandably the exhibition carried a lot of pressure for him, and he worked night and day preparing for it. But this was no excuse for his increasing shortness with those around him. In just the past few days, his unpleasantness had worsened, and had turned on Clara. Just last night he snapped at her when he failed to respond to her caresses in bed, and now, as he kept his back to her and stared at his painting, she could feel the tension between them rising.

"Why would you say such a thing?" she asked him. "It's just plain mean."

He peered over his shoulder at her again. "Why must you always be scratching away like that," he said, indicating the sketchbook in her lap. She'd begun to draw the room, focusing on the dozen or so paintings on the walls. "Ever since I've known you, it's been scratch, scratch, scratch." He made an exaggerated drawing gesture, accompanied by an ugly, twisted-up face.

She closed the sketchbook and stood up. "You're a real ass sometimes, Eliot," she said and walked past him. "Put *that* in your exhibition catalog."

She didn't get three steps before he grabbed her upper arm, jerked her about, and slapped her across the face. She yanked her arm free and raised her hand to her face. He seemed to snarl at her, and more shocked than frightened, she stood there, staring at him. Yet as she opened her mouth to speak, he raised his hand, threatening to strike her again, and she turned toward the door and ran outside

She ran all the way down the dirt drive and only when she reached the road did she slow down enough to catch her breath. The left side of her face burned where Eliot had struck her, and as she kept walking she became even more angry at him. She wanted to rush back to the house and hit him square in the face, and knew that this was what her brother Freddy would have done. He would have given Eliot the beating of his life.

When a car raced past honking its horn at her, she screamed and threw a rock after it. By the time her head cleared enough for her to see where she was going, she'd reached the outskirts of town. She cut across a dirt lot where two men were mending holes in a gill net stretched across the empty yard. She stepped over their net and headed toward the channel. When she looked down, she saw that she still held her sketchbook and realized that even when Eliot had struck her, she hadn't let go of it. When she came to the main street, she spotted someone who looked like Guy approaching from a distance. In bib overalls, rubber boots, and slouch hat, he looked like some combination of old farmer, fisherman, and hobo. He'd apparently come from the Purse Seiner Tavern, and with his hands stuffed in his pockets and his head down, he didn't see her as he neared. Clara quickly wiped her eyes and greeted him only after he was directly in front of her.

"Clara!" he said, astonished at finding her standing before him. "Where's Eliot?"

She leaned forward and gave him a hug without answering. "He's back at the house," she said and released him from the hug. "You look deep in thought."

"I've been sitting in the Al K. Hall too long," he said with a beery grin.

Clara smiled back.

"Eliot let you drive the ambulance to town?" he asked.

"I walked."

"That's a long ways," he said and leaned forward to inspect the side of her face. "Did he do that?"

Clara nodded and turned away, looking across the channel. Guy then put his arm around her and asked, "Are you okay?" and before she could stop herself she was crying again.

"Come on," he said and guided her back down the street to the Purse Seiner. "I'll buy you a beer. Two, in fact. One for you to drink, the other to put on your cheek."

She laughed at this and put an arm around his waist as they walked.

The tavern's dim interior was just the place to soothe her hurt. Guy sat her down in a back booth, went up to the bar, and brought back three bottles.

"That was a rotten thing he did," he said and took a pull from his own beer.

Clara didn't speak. She alternated drinking from one bottle and pressing the other against her tender cheek. Guy was kind enough not to say anything more about it, and so they stayed like that for a good long spell, sitting quietly in the warmth and stillness of the tavern.

After a while, though, Guy leaned forward and said, "He's a remarkably talented painter, Eliot is."

"I know," she said.

"—but it's the kind of talent that feeds on itself, and on others too." He peeled the wet label off his beer bottle. "You understand what I'm saying?"

"I don't understand much of anything right now," Clara answered and wiped the back of her hand across her runny nose. "Mostly I wish I could get back to *my* work. At first Eliot liked that I was painting. But after I told him about the Henry competition, suddenly everything was wrong with it. And he *really* hates that I draw all the time." She tossed her sketchbook onto the table.

Guy looked at it.

"Mostly it keeps me busy," she said and let out a derisive snort. "Idle hands, you know."

Guy pulled the sketchbook toward him and asked, "May I?" and she nodded.

She watched as he turned one page after another. The first drawing was of a beach shack. The next was a figure faintly resembling Eliot. The next few pages contained sketches of people she'd seen on Seattle streets. There were always those, she thought. Guy leafed through the dozen or so drawings and came to the last, the one she'd been doing when her fight with Eliot erupted.

"May I have this?" he asked.

The request surprised her. "Of course," she said, and taking the sketchbook from him tore the page from the spiral bounds and handed it to him.

"You have to sign it," he said and handed her the fountain pen he pulled from the pocket of his overalls. As she signed the drawing, he collected their empties and returned to the bar for another round. When he came back, Clara slid the sketch across the table to him along with his pen.

"Let me tell you about Eliot," he said, as if about to give a lecture. "I don't pretend to be a psychiatrist, but from what people who knew him well in Spokane have told me, the lad's had a great many troubles in life. Mental troubles. Living on a farm and all, he had head lice all the time. You know what they use to kill those buggers?"

Clara had no idea. Her mother used to shave her brothers' heads in the summer and rub baby oil into their scalps. Because she was a girl and didn't run around as much outside, she'd been spared the treatments.

"Lindane," Guy said. "It's what the Army uses. It kills the dreadful little varmints, but too much of the stuff can eat your brains out. It's what's called a neurotoxin. Makes you agitated and hallucinatory. An Army medic I know says he's sent guys to the psyche ward because of the stuff. It's why Eliot's classified F-4."

Clara listened carefully. If what Guy was saying was true, it was terribly sad. She remembered Eliot once talking about having "the cootie frisks" when he was younger, and he often complained that his studio loft was turning into a "cootie trap". His rumpledness was due to the fact that he did laundry two or three times a week and never ironed. Still, none of what Guy told her changed her predicament. Whatever the reason for Eliot's behavior, she could no longer endure it. Once she returned to Seattle, she would stop visiting his studio, stop telephoning him, and let whatever attachment they had wilt away.

After another round of beers, Guy said they should probably get back to the house and see what trouble *the genius* had gotten himself into. "He'll behave himself with me around," he assured Clara.

It was nearly six o'clock as they walked out of the tavern. The sky in the east had turned a deep azure, and in the west, reflecting off the Sound, the sunset burned a dusky orange. As they walked along the road's shoulder, Guy pointed to a boat just beyond the mudflats and said it was an oysterman raking his oysters beds. Feeling mildly drunk, Clara enjoyed walking in the clear air, listening to Guy point things out—the fence-post where the red-winged blackbirds had their nest, the wild rosemary the Indians made marsh tea with, the abandoned shack where a local bootlegger kept his still.

Yet, as they approached the house, she could see even from a distance that the ambulance was gone.

"He's probably out looking for you," Guy offered.

But Clara knew differently, knew that Eliot had fled, and was relieved.

When they entered the house, the battered old gym bag he carried his clothes in was gone. The painting he'd given Guy was also missing. But far worse, Clara's portrait lay in shreds about the main room, the wood frame busted to pieces and fragments of the canvas scattered about like oversized confetti.

"I'm so sorry," Guy said and began to gather the pieces of canvas and place them on the table as if he might try to sew them back together. "I just hope Richard will know what to do with him." Clara knew he meant Dr. Richard

Fuller, the director of the Seattle Art Museum, who was curating Eliot's exhibition.

"I'll paint you another," she said and helped him, but then dropped onto the sofa and placed her forehead into her hands.

Guy finished gathering the pieces of canvas and sat down beside her. He put his arm around her shoulder and kissed the top of her head as she slumped against him. He rested his bristly cheek against her forehead and when she lifted her head to look at him, he kissed her. She put her arms around him and returned the kiss.

For the next three days she stayed with Guy. They collected shells and driftwood on the beach in the morning and in the afternoon drew and painted and took long naps after making love. At night they drank Guy's homemade elderberry wine and made dinner together. When done eating, they lay naked on a tattered Mexican rug in front of the stove's open hatch. Guy was a patient lover, and Clara was content afterward to watch the flames in the stove and twirl her finger through his long gray chest hairs.

They both knew this was an interlude that would have to end soon. Eventually she would have to go back to Seattle, return to work, and resume her life. So on the afternoon of their third day together, when Guy mentioned that a friend was sailing his small sloop down to Seattle the next morning, Clara decided the time to leave had come.

"That's such a bold-faced lie," her friend Jenny at Frederick & Nelson said while she and Clara were taking a coffee break later that week. "You know it is."

Upon her return to work, Clara had had to apologize profusely to Mr. Boykin for missing two full days without calling in. She vowed to work extra long hours over the next several weeks to make up for it, and still he put her on notice that any more shenanigans like that and she'd be let go.

Her co-workers in Ladies Apparel, however, didn't let her off so easy. They insisted she tell them every juicy detail of her mysterious disappearance. Clara downplayed it, though, explaining that she'd gone on a road trip with some friends and gotten stranded when their car broke down. Yet none of the girls bought this, especially not Jenny, who already knew of her involvement with Eliot.

"Come on," Jenny pleaded. "You can tell me. We're old pals, remember?"

Clara didn't give in, though, and from that point on she began working straight through her coffee breaks to avoid the gossip mill at work.

Two weeks passed before she heard anything from Eliot. She'd made no effort to contact him, and though she'd considered writing him a note to let him know just how hurt she'd been by him, she thought better of it. When he finally did call, she regretted picking up the telephone the moment she heard his voice. He expressed no regret for his behavior in La Conner, as if the entire episode had never happened. Instead he insisted on knowing where she'd been the three days following his departure.

"I went by your apartment every day," he said. "But then I got to wondering . . . maybe she's taken up with that old goat."

Clara was determined not to discuss it with him.

"Just tell me," he implored.

She remained silent, knowing he was fuming.

"I just need to know so we can go on. It won't mean anything."

At that Clara had to speak up. "We're *not* going on, Eliot," she told him and tried not to cry.

"He fucked you, didn't he?"

She slammed the phone down. When it rang a few seconds later, she picked it up and dropped it straight back down again. When it rang again, she pulled the black cord from the wall socket.

Well into the spring and early summer, Eliot continued to try to contact her by telephone and letter, yet she stayed resolute and refused to speak to him or reply. What she feared most was that he might waylay her at work or appear some evening at her apartment, though fortunately he never did.

When V-E Day was declared on May 8—less than a month after President Roosevelt tragically died—Clara thought that was it, everything would be different now. The war in Europe was over and the boys would be coming home. She'd see her brothers once again, and a whole new era in their lives would commence. Ken wrote that he was stationed in Reims, France, headquarters of the Supreme Allied Expeditionary Force, yet since he'd been promoted to sergeant major and was being billeted to Germany, he didn't know when he might get to come home. Clara worried more about Freddy, though. Since the D-Day invasion, he'd written home only twice, the long letter she received in October and a briefer one to the entire family at Christmas. Since then there hadn't been a single word from him. Clara tried to reassure her mother that he was okay. "That's just how Freddy is," she told her and wanted badly to believe it herself.

But two weeks later, a staff officer knocked on the front door of the house in West Seattle just as her parents were getting up from the dinner table.

Freddy was dead.

He'd been killed two months earlier taking the bridge at Remagen over the Rhine River. The staff officer could give no reason why it had taken the Army so long to inform the family, though he did emphasize how important Private First-Class Hamilton's sacrifice was to the Army's march on Berlin and the eventual German surrender.

Clara learned all this when she received a phone call from her mother a short while after. Even as she broke down over the news, her mother insisted on reading Mary Baker Eddy's definition of God to her over the phone—*The Great I AM; the all-knowing, all-seeing, all-acting, all-wise, all-loving, and eternal; Principle; Mind; Soul; Spirit; Life; Truth; Love; all substance; intelligence.*

Clara wanted to make her stop but couldn't, and then her mother said, "Freddy understood." She wanted to shout at her mother—*Freddy did not understand!*—but she couldn't do this either. She knew that Freddy was not a believer, and never had been. But none of that mattered now.

She agreed to recite the Lord's Prayer aloud with her mother and share in a silent prayer, following which her mother said her father was going to come to pick her up.

But Clara said no, she didn't want to come home just yet. She needed more time, she said, and then explained how she thought she might go down to the Servicemen's Club first—to talk to the boys—and then come home.

BOOK TWO

Then Kiss Me Once Again

Seattle Waterfront - 1934

On May 9, more than 12,000 members of the International Longshoremen's Association on the West Coast walked off the job, effectively shutting down every port from Bellingham to San Pedro, California. When the clock struck 8:00, the men laid down their cargo hooks, picks and shovels, scows and hook bridles, nets and sling boards, and formed picket lines in front of the piers up and down the length of the waterfront. Once assembled, their first act was to burn the blue books the company hiring hall required of them to work anywhere on the docks. In Seattle, the longshoremen were supported by the Masters, Mates, and Pilots union as well as a handful of unaffiliated seamen's groups.

"All we want's a fair shake," shouted Edgar Ricou, one of the strike committee leaders from the Seattle local. He stood atop a flatbed car on the rail tracks that led down to Piers 40 and 41 at Smith Cove Terminal. "That means first and foremost recognition. If the employers get to have their association, the workingman deserves his union!" The three score men assembled twenty feet from the piers let out a roar of support.

The waterfront employers, though, had readied themselves for the strike. They immediately opened hiring halls to recruit strikebreakers, and began a massive publicity campaign against the union. They secured police protection for the scabs and coerced local government officials into backing them. Seattle Mayor John Dore asked Washington Governor Clarence Martin to send in the homeguard to force open the port, and two days after the strike started, Dore was quoted in the newspapers saying that "The city government of Seattle has been replaced by a Soviet of longshoremen which is destroying private property." He talked Dave Beck, the Teamster boss, into ordering his drivers back to work, even as local Teamster delegate Frank Olsen vowed no member of his union would haul hot cargo. In the end, the Teamster rank-and-file bucked Beck's orders and refused to cross the longshoremen's picket lines, though a few Beck loyalists from other locals in the area weren't so obliging—which led to several skirmishes.

Within three days, many of the employers had strikebreakers discharging cargo on various docks. They had ships anchored in the bay where the strikebreakers could sleep and eat before they were ferried to the waterfront to work the few freighters still coming in. They also hauled university students—

footballers mostly—on tugboats from a dock in Portage Bay to the piers on Lake Union. All of which riled the longshoremen to no end.

On day four of the strike, Carl volunteered for one of the flying squads that patrolled the port on scab-clearing missions where several docks had been reopened. Five days into the strike, after assembling three dozen men in the union hall, Carl led the volunteer crew down the hill and across Railroad Avenue to Pier 1. Longshoremen from Everett and Tacoma had caravanned in to bolster their Seattle brethren and were already at the pier harassing the scabs—most of whom, seeing what they were up against, quickly smartened up and went home. From there the column of longshoremen moved down the waterfront. At Pier 6, a small faction of stubborn strikebreakers from a company gang refused to clear out.

"You can walk off the pier or you can swim," Carl yelled down to them.

Several of the company men held cargo hooks, but when Carl gave the word, his crew moved in with log-rolling peavies. They charged the scabs, who were outnumbered four to one, and chased them to the end of the pier. Of the eight men cornered, four dropped their cargo hooks and were escorted off the pier, while two tried to take a swing at the union men and were clocked on the head by the long reach of a peavy-welding longshoreman named "Pylon" Paul Bivens, a six-foot-six fellow with arms like steel pylons. Two other scabs escaped the charge by jumping off the pier into the drink, where they thrashed about in the frigid water before finding a barnacle-encrusted piling with a boat ladder to haul themselves up on.

By nightfall the strikebreakers at every pier on the waterfront had been sent packing. Carl didn't go home that evening but remained on the picket line to make sure the company scab-herders didn't attempt to sneak in any more strikebreakers. Throughout the night, the longshoremen were jubilant, recounting the rousting they'd given the scabs and predicting a swift end to the strike. They lit drum fires the length of Railroad Avenue and passed around thermoses of coffee and pint bottles of whiskey. Around midnight, as an extra precaution against cargo moving onto or off the piers, they pulled up several sections of rail track.

The next morning Carl was back at the union hall telephoning Glenora to tell her to make sandwiches for the men on his picket line. Someone from the strike relief committee would come by to pick them up, he told her. She begged him to stay out of harm's way and remember how much she and the children loved him. "We're all praying," she added, and Carl was grateful for her support, though he knew she didn't understand the reasons behind the strike and most likely disapproved of it.

By the second week, he had been home only twice. The first time he was ordered home by Patrick Morris, chairman of the strike committee. "You look like hell, Hamilton," Pat told him one morning. "Go home and take a bath, hug her wife and kids, and get a good night's sleep." The second time, he brought Glenora the $50 he'd received from the strike relief fund and put several hours in at the print shop in West Seattle where he picked up part-time work. The journeyman printer who owned the shop was an old pal from White Center where they'd grown up together. To show his support for the striking longshoremen, he offered to print 200 placards for the union at no cost—a hundred that read *Fair Wages + Fair Hiring = Union*, and another hundred that read *Support Strong Unions, Support the ILA!*

By week three of the strike, all the talk in Seattle had turned to the "starving Alaskans." With the Alaska shipping companies shut down by the strike, food was not being shipped to the northland territory. Yet by late May, the delegates from the Joint Northwest Strike Committee agreed to load ships bound for Alaska as proof of the union's goodwill and humanity. Other than that, the strike lingered on. And somehow, to everyone's bewilderment, Dave Beck of the Teamsters again wheedled himself into the on-going negotiations. Worse yet, he was out front in the newspaper calling the ILA strike leaders all sorts of dirty names. Carl couldn't figure Beck's angle, although it began to make more sense when he went after Harry Bridges down in San Francisco, who'd persuaded most of the ILA locals on the West Coast not to concede to the wishy-washy agreements Joe Ryan, the ILA president from back East, was working out with the employers association. From Beck's perspective, as quoted in the papers, the longshoremen's actions were nothing more than a series of wildcat strikes. This remark led Carl to vow that if Beck ever showed his face on the waterfront, which everyone knew he was too yellow to do, he'd be the first to take a swing at him.

TWELVE
Clara, Summer 1945

Clara had never had to fabricate her Wednesday evening testimonies for the sole reason that she always kept them so vague. Unlike other church members, she never testified to specific physical healings because frankly she'd never had one—though her mother insisted she had, and cited the three weeks the year before Clara had been bedridden, recovering only after the church practitioner visited her.

Her mother, on the other hand, testified frequently to healings that struck Clara as quite trivial. A head cold, a touch of thrombosis, her father's piles. She didn't dispute these testimonies, nor would she vouch for them. She was grateful for her mother's healings, yet she often wondered whether her mother and other church members weren't overly vigilant in detecting symptoms that, once identified, they could then dutifully overcome through prayer and scientific healing. Furthermore, it seemed often that the goal of such dedicated prayer was not the healing itself so much as the opportunity to voice one's testimony of it at the regular Wednesday evening meetings.

Clara knew she ought to be ashamed of herself for such cynical thinking. The folks in the church—ladies mostly—were all good, well-meaning people. So she preferred to reserve her harshest criticism for the church practitioners, those Christian Science energumen who in their earnest efforts to restore the sick to God's perfection often reminded her of witchdoctors and old-timey praise healers. It seemed downright venal the way they sought out the sick to pad their healing credentials. When she recalled the handful of practitioners she knew personally, she found it harder than ever to accept the fundamental church creed that sickness was merely an expression of mortal thinking. Try as she might—and truly she had tried—she was incapable of regarding every sore muscle or case of the sniffles as a spiritual shortfall. Rather she preferred to believe her sore muscles and sniffles were just another part of God's divine order. No more illusory than the flowers in the field or the stars in the sky. So when she became sick with a cough and headache, as she seemed to regularly these days, she accepted the physical fact of her condition and waited it out until she was better.

The same held true for mourning Freddy's death. She refused to deny her grief, as her mother did. Just the same, after receiving the wrenching news, Clara made every effort to spend more time at home with her parents. In July, the family's sorrow was softened when they received a letter from Ken announcing he would be home for Thanksgiving and that he looked forward to eating their mother's famous crab stuffing and roasted turkey. He also said in his letter that he hoped his father, who now ran the print shop fulltime yet remained active in the longshoremen's union, could help find him a job on the waterfront. He said he wanted to get involved in the union as well, just as Freddy had before the war.

So despite their sorrow, life was moving on. She worked her job at Frederick & Nelson and kept up with her drawing and painting at night and on weekends. Though she went home regularly, she also spent more time alone, finding comfort in the solitude. Occasionally Jenny would ask her out to see a movie, but she drew the line when her friend tried to set her up on a blind date.

"I really think I prefer being a single working girl," she said the last time Jenny recommended someone.

"But this one's a once-in-a-lifetime catch," Jenny insisted. "He's related to the banking Greens. His great-grandfather or uncle or somebody was Joshua Green. You know, the one the building's named after."

Clara knew the building. It was two blocks from the department store. She'd once stepped into its lobby just to look at its pretty green marble floors and brass moldings. All the same, she wasn't interested. After her episode with Eliot, followed by her fling with Guy, she needed a break from men.

On the night of Tuesday, August 14, as the buzz spread throughout the city that Japan was on the brink of surrendering, Clara went back to West Seattle to be with her parents. The atomic bombs dropped on the two Japanese cities the previous week had left Japanese imperial leaders stunned and demoralized. No one believed they could withstand another such attack, and so Clara wanted to be with her mother and father when the news broke.

When she came down to the kitchen early the following morning, the morning paper had still not been retrieved. Her father sat at the breakfast table eating toast and drinking Postum while her mother stood at the kitchen counter shaking bread crumbs from the electric toaster onto a dishrag. Clara kissed her mother on the cheek, the soft scent of her mother's rose water fragrance combining with the astringent smell of Ajax cleanser, and then kissed her father on the top of the head.

"I'll be right back," she said and ducked out the back door and past the family's small garden. She made her way around the side of the house and across the front yard to the mailbox. The folded *P-I* was crammed into the box the same as it was every morning. She pulled the newspaper out, unfolded it, and stood staring at the towering headline:

PEACE!

And then she read the sub-heading:

Jap Surrender Ends War
'Cease Fire' Order Issued
M'Arthur Given Command

Unexpectedly, Clara's fist thoughts flashed to Merritt, the sailor who had taken her dancing and then shipped out during her three-week illness. She wondered whether he'd survived. Would he go home to Vermont now? Would he ever pass through Seattle again? If he had survived, she hoped he would find happiness now. The war was over. There would be no more young men dying, no more senseless slaughter, no more mayhem and devastation. The world would soon find solace for its terrible grief.

She stood beside the newspaper box and began softly crying. She didn't know how long she remained there, relief and elation sweeping over her in alternating waves, before Mr. Pollard from down the block drove up in his big Hudson automobile honking the horn and waving frenziedly out the driver's side window.

"Come on, honey, hop in!" His shirtsleeves were rolled up past his elbows and he banged the roof of his car with one hand while pressing down on the horn with the other. "The party's going strong downtown. I'm headed that way right now. We won, sister! The goddamn war is over!"

Clara wiped her eyes, thrilled to see Mr. Pollard so jubilant. She couldn't help herself from running up to him and giving him a big hug through the open window. He kissed her face and she kissed him right back, and they cheered as he honked the horn several times more. When her father appeared on the front stoop with her mother standing behind him, Mr. Pollard shouted, "How'bout it, Carl? The squint-eyed bastards surrendered!"

Clara ran up to the front stoop with the newspaper held over her head. She handed it to her father and watched him read. "Thank God," he said and embraced her, and then turned to her mother and embraced her. He strode down to Mr. Pollard's car while Clara hugged her mother, who dabbed her eyes with the corner of her apron. She and her mother both laughed, giddy with the great good news, as her father and Mr. Pollard stood beside his car, shaking hands and slapping one another on the back.

"Why don't you all pile in and hustle downtown with me," Mr. Pollard called up to Clara and her mother as they came down the walkway. "Everyone's gathering at Victory Square for the big celebration."

Clara could hear more car horns blaring, pots being banged, people hooting and hollering throughout the neighborhood as they woke up to the news. She even heard church bells ringing. For as long as she could remember, people in West Seattle celebrated every holiday and major occasion their own way, from the Fourth of July with its parades and fireworks to Christmas with its pageants and lights, separating themselves from the rest of Seattle, and she realized today would probably be no different. Yet one look at her father told Clara he was fighting the urge to jump in Mr. Pollard's car and join in the revelry downtown.

"There'll be a lot of recovery work to get done," he said, as if to squelch the urge to let loose and celebrate.

"For cryinoutloud, Carl, give it a rest," said Mr. Pollard, who worked as a bargeman in Puget Sound. "Here," he said and handed her father a cigar.

"Thanks, Len," her father said and shook Mr. Pollard's hand again. "It's a great day for the country all right. We can all take pride in that."

"All right, Carl," said Mr. Pollard, seeing how it was going to be with his neighbor. "God bless America." He again kissed Clara and her mother and hopped back into his car. "Greatest damn country in the world," he shouted and honked the horn with renewed vigor as he drove off.

Clara's mother let out a sigh and led the way back into the house. Once they were all inside, she asked that they hold hands and share in a silent prayer. *The war was over*, Clara kept thinking to herself, waiting for her mother to say *Amen* and anticipating how she would get downtown to join in the big celebration.

THIRTEEN
Merritt, Fall 1945

It was a rainy September evening when Merritt left the Exchange Building after processing more than fifty seaman out of the United States Navy and back into civilian life. The line officer who'd signed off on his transfer in June had been right about V-J Day being just around the corner and the deluge of discharges that would follow. Yet the task of issuing so many discharges every day made Merritt that much more eager for his own. He had no interest in being a 30-year man. He wanted out. Unfortunately, he and his officemates figured they would have to see every blasted bluejacket in the Navy doff his work blues and dress whites and reenter civvy life—snagging all the good-paying jobs and good-looking women—before they had their crack at freedom.

It was well past 8:00 p.m. by the time he got back to the Hotel Commodore. The room, which included a detached bath down the hall, cost $1.50 a night. Most of the residents in the SRO were either recently discharged servicemen or merchant marines waiting for the next outbound vessel. Merritt didn't find any of these folks particularly good company, though there was always someone to tie one on with. And that's what he had in mind for tonight. He'd drawn his pay the day before and didn't want to stay holed up in his room reading, or go to the movies again, or drink coffee all night in the Unique Diner around the block, or take another long, lonely walk on the waterfront to clear his head. He'd had enough of being a goody two-shoes. He wanted to get tight. So he changed out of his well-worn service whites and into his freshly pressed service blues and headed down to the lobby to see if he could find any takers.

The night manager, a flabby man named Ernie, waved to Merritt from behind the front desk as he entered the wallpapered lobby. A few guys typically would be loitering about reading newspapers, smoking, maybe sharing a flask, but not tonight. When he'd passed through the lobby just half an hour ago, two swabbies he'd mustered out last week were doing a crossword puzzle on the leatherette couch beneath the wall mirror. They gave him a mock salute as he walked past and let out an "*AttENhut!*"

Sea scum, Merritt thought and paused just long enough to threaten to rescind their papers. "It's not too late," he told them, which shut them up. Now, with no one else around, he would settle for a couple of bums like that to share a drink with. He'd even buy.

"Heya, Ernie," he said and flipped through a month-old *Time* magazine that lay on the front desk. The cover displayed a full-color portrait of Chiang Kai Shek. "Where is everyone?"

"Damned if I know," said Ernie. "Maybe it's spaghetti night over at the Catholic Seamen's Club." As night manager, Ernie never felt obliged to shave or wear clean clothes. The man looked a mess, his hair all catawampus, his stained shirt half-untucked, and his gut hanging over his belt. "Can a fella bum a cig," he asked Merritt with rheumy eyes.

Merritt put the magazine down and reached into the inside pocket of his peacoat for his pack of Chesterfields. He shuffled the pack until one came loose. Ernie pulled the cigarette out and put it between his lips.

"Light?" he mumbled.

Merritt flipped open the Zippo lighter his father had sent him as a birthday gift two years ago—*No respectable seaman went without one*—and lit Ernie's cigarette.

"Thanks," said Ernie and puffed away.

Merritt pocketed the lighter and cigarettes and walked out of the lobby and onto Second Avenue. A drizzle that had begun that afternoon still seeped from the sky. He turned the corner, heading for the quarter-schooner taverns along First Avenue. First, he stopped in front of a pawn shop with an iron grate over its front window. It had all kinds of Jap paraphernalia on display, from a Rising Sun flag to a bayonet off an Arisaka rifle, a whole regiment's worth of contraband war booty. First Avenue was full of such places. In three blocks he passed another pawn shop, a greasy diner, a gun shop, a chop suey counter, a couple of clip joints with nickel girlie reels, and a penny arcade with slot machines, Test-Your-Strength games, and a guy named Slim Lewis in the backroom who owned a chimpanzee and would give you a tattoo for just a few bits.

At the corner of First and Union, he pushed through the door of the 'Tween Decks Tavern and took a seat at the bar. The usual-usuals crowded the joint—merchant marine pensioners, dockworkers, assorted slouchers, and half a dozen Navy seamen in their casual whites playing snooker in the back. He'd been in the 'Tween Decks a few times before, so when he slapped a dollar on the bar, the barkeep knew to bring him a schooner glass of beer and three wood beer chips, each redeemable for another schooner. Merritt downed the warm, flat beer in two takes, then slid the chips into his pocket and made a bee-line back out to the street. Now he wanted a real drink. So two blocks farther down, at the corner of Seneca and First (not far from the Hollywood Dance Studio, he thought, remembering his first real date with Clara), he went into the High-End Lounge, a classy, leather-upholstered establishment that served food and hard liquor. He gave his peacoat and seaman's cap to the coat-check girl near the front door and angled his way past the candle-topped tables to the brass-plated bar. He ordered a Rob Roy, and with the tentative first sip of the scotch and vermouth, a sophisticated note registered in his head and he leaned back comfortably in his bar seat.

If not for seeing himself reflected in the mirror behind the bar, dressed in his regulation service blues and looking like every other bluejacket in the world, he might fancy himself a regular swag. What he ought to do, he thought, is buy that old yellow Underwood in the pawnshop window and write a novel. Truly, he thought—why not? It would be based on his life, his adventures, and so on and so forth for a few hundred pages. Yet as he ordered another drink, a single question wilted this fanciful line of thinking. How honest would he be? Would he write about his incident with Ensign Rivard? Or the blackmail letter? Would he include Clara?

He downed his drink and glanced over his shoulder at the sharp-looking gal being talked up by some guy in a serge suit at the table behind him. Her legs were crossed so that the slit in her satin blue dress fell away from her thigh. For just an instant he imagined she resembled Clara, or at least his memory of her. Clara, too, had worn blue the night they went dancing. The sight of the couple made him light-headed. He surveyed the woman's curves until the man leaned into his line of vision and gave him a look that said back off, and as he turned around, Merritt wondered if he would ever be with a woman like that.

"Set you up again, sailor?" asked the barkeep.

Merritt shook his head, sucked down the ice from his glass, and spun off the bar seat. He tipped the coat-check girl, a real looker, a dollar and walked back out onto First Avenue. A heavier rain was falling now and the wind had picked up. He'd grown accustomed to the miserable Seattle weather and no longer gave it a second thought. He was still picturing his hand sliding up the thigh of the woman in the High-End Lounge when he stopped in front of the Va Va Voom Club near Cherry Street and locked his eyes on the poster of the voluptuous bubble dancer gazing down at him.

"You look like a broad-minded fella," the barker called out as he stepped from the doorway of the theater. "And let me tell ya, fella, we've got the broads!"

Merritt rolled his eyes and smirked. What kind of rube did this guy take him for?

"Lookee here," the barker went on and pointed to another poster just inside the doorway, a life-size photo of a busty lady draped in Arabian scarves, her long arms crossed above her head and her bare midriff torqued sensuously in mid-dance.

"That's Nubella the Persian Temptress," he said. "Tonight only we have the seaman special. Free hanky with price of admission."

Merritt shook his head and moved on down the sidewalk.

"Don't be shy," the barker shouted after him. "Remember, new show every half hour."

Two blocks farther along, across the street from the totem pole and cast-iron pergola at the heart of Pioneer Square, he descended the outside stairs next to the old Pioneer Building and entered the basement-level Hole in the Floor Tavern. His first stop was the head. He then made his way to the bar, ordered a schooner, drank it down, and ordered another. The Hole in the Floor catered to an even less savory clientele than the 'Tween Decks. Flophouse down-and-outs and skid row tramps mostly. Guys who, when not lined up for soup at the Bread of Life Mission down the block or passed out on flattened cardboard in doorways, were slamming wine shooters at dive joints like the Hole in the Floor. The Pioneer Square district was full of them.

Merritt smoked a cigarette, downed his second schooner, then slapped his cap back on his head and bound up the stairs to the street. He'd made up his mind, and hurried back up First Avenue and without a word slipped right past the barker and straight into the Va Va Voom Club.

"That's the American way," the barker bellowed, slapping him on the back and directing him to the cashier's window. He pulled back a black velvet curtain and waved Merritt inside. "Show's just started," he said. "Take a seat anywhere, sailor. If you have a bottle, paper cups are on the tables."

Merritt took a seat at a small table near the back. A smattering of men sat at the dozen or so tables. A band—saxophone, drums, bass—were squeezed onto the edge of the stage at the front of the room. They played a sultry number with a heavy bass line while center stage, just above the footlights, a dancer slowly gyrated her hips. She was squeezed into a sequined corset and toted a feathery pink boa that she slid back and forth between her legs and around her waist. Her thighs and arms jiggled as she unsnapped the corset and sashayed out of it, leaving only gartered stockings, lacy underpants, and a pair of nipple tassels to contain her. As the band reached its lazy crescendo, she spread her high-heeled feet and bent forward, letting her bosom drop down and dangle in front of the audience. There were several sharp whistles and a hoot or two, and as the show announcer, who doubled as the band's drummer, exhorted the men in the room to give Princess Pizzazz a big round of applause, the princess exited stage right.

Merritt clapped along with the rest and lit a cigarette. He'd been to all sorts of strip clubs, chippy joints, and B-girl bars in Hawaii while on liberty with his fellow enlisted men. Those were always rowdy affairs, good bawdy fun. But this place . . . this was different. It was sleazier and not quite as fun.

"Now let's hear it for the exotic jiggulations of Bottoms-Up Betsy," the announcer shouted from behind his drums as the next girl strutted out in a black lace bra and black G-string. Straight away she presented her bare behind

104

to the audience as the announcer/drummer beat out a boom-boom-boom with the foot pedal of his bass drum and hit the cymbal each time Betsy reached back around to gave her fleshy derriere a roundhouse slap. Just then the announcer stepped from behind his drum trap and came forward to give Betsy the spanking she so dearly desired. As the men in the audience howled, Betsy bent forward, knees locked, and grasped her calves, allowing the announcer to play a rumba on her buttocks with both hands. The saxophonist accompanied the flesh slapping with squeals from his horn while Betsy dropped her head and lavishly swung her black tresses from side to side. When the spanking was over, she placed both hands on her buttocks, looked out at the audience, and gave a big pout.

"Who's gonna kiss it and make it right?" the announcer called from the stage.

Betsy wiggled her bottom. "Pretty please," she called out and put a finger to her pouty red lips.

"Come on, fellas," the announcer cajoled. "Don't be shy. If you're not gonna make it right with a kiss, I'll have to ask the boys in the band to." The saxophonist squawked his horn, which solicited a sudden laugh from Betsy.

"Alright!" hollered a burly guy up front. He leaned over the stage, grabbed hold of Betsy's hips, and gave her right buttocks cheek a big smooch. Betsy flipped her hair back and gave him a thank-you smile.

"One more, fellas. Just a little peck on the other cheek." The bandleader raised his hand to his brow and peered out over the audience. "How 'bout you, sailorboy?"

Merritt shook his head and waved him off, but the bandleader kept at him, badgering him to come forward. Then the barker, standing by the curtain, egged him on as well. Merritt kept shaking his head, but they wouldn't let up, and so finally he got up, wound his way up to the stage and then, to everyone's applause, reached out and gave Betsy's other buttocks cheek a quick brush with his lips. But before he could retreat, Betsy twirled about, seized his head in both hands, and landed a big wet one on his mouth.

With that, the announcer returned to his drums and led Bottoms-Up Betsy off stage with a ripping solo while Merritt plied his way back toward his table. Yet rather than sit down, he decided he'd gotten his money's worth and headed straight past the velvet curtain and into the lobby.

"Come again, sailor," the barker called after him as he pushed his way through the doors and back out onto the street. "And bring your shipmates with you next time."

Merritt walked as fast as he could up First Avenue, the rain coming hard now. The sidewalk was slick, and oily rivulets cascaded down the gutter. He yanked his collar up and made it as far as the 'Tween Decks Tavern, where he ducked inside and slapped his three beer chips onto the bar. As he drank his beer and stared at the framed photos of the USS *Washington*, USS *Missouri* and USS *Lexington* that hung above the back bar, he knew the night was a bust and he should call it quits. But something else had gotten into him now. Especially after remembering his ensign incident and thinking about Clara and being unable to shake either, he knew he wasn't through.

He knocked off his third beer just as the barkeep came around with a fourth and rapped his knuckles on the bar. "On the house," he said and asked, "Where'd you serve, sailor. If you don't mind my asking."

"Right there," Merritt said and pointed to the photo of the *Washington*. "The Mighty W, most battle stars of any ship in the fleet."

The boast was half-mocking, of course. While he'd shot down a Jap fighter plane and helped put out a couple above-decks fires, he could hardly consider himself a battle-hardened Navy man. He'd been the gunner's mate's second. Even at sea, he'd mostly done clerical work, keeping the boatswain's log and working on the *Cougar Scream*. He calculated that when it came right down to it, he'd typed his way through most of the war.

"No foolin'?" the barkeep said. "You saw some action then, did ya?" He topped Merritt's glass off at the tap.

Merritt shrugged and drank. "Thanks," he said, and stood up and left.

He stumbled into the nearest alley and relieved himself. He already knew where he was going next. For months he'd heard the rumors that the La Salle Hotel was a ten-dollar house. The story went that a woman named Nellie Curtis had bought it after the *Nisei* couple who owned the place and ran it as a legitimate hotel were sent packing to the relocation camp at Tule Lake under Executive Order 9066. Shortly after taking over, Miss Nellie turned the La Salle into a whorehouse. Now, Merritt told himself, it was time to put the rumors to the test.

The hotel stood adjacent to the farmer's market, just south of Pike Street. It was a four-story building with bay windows, a mansard roof, and iron fire escapes. The main entrance was on Western Avenue, but most of the clientele, or so he'd been told, entered and exited through a side door that let out onto Post Alley. When Merritt stepped inside and made his way to the lobby, he was surprised to find how much the interior resembled an old English manor, with an ornately carved front desk, leather chairs, and Tiffany-style lamps. A desk clerk in a suit and tie greeted him and explained that there were two rates, the sleeper's rate and the insomniac's. The latter cost a ten spot and got you a room for one hour.

"Not a minute more," the desk clerk said and took the two fives Merritt handed him. He gave Merritt a key and directed him to Room 317 on the third floor. "Give the housekeeper this when she comes in." He handed Merritt a playing card—the five of diamonds—which apparently served as some kind of chit.

Room 317 was as spare as a room could be—a bed with a beaded bedspread, a small table and lamp, a straight-back chair, and heavy draperies over the window. That was it. No dresser, no sink, not even a rug on the bare linoleum floor. Merritt opened the draperies and looked out at the wet alley below. When a knock came at the door, he pulled the draperies closed, tried to catch his breath, and croaked out, "Come in."

The door opened and a woman wearing a chiffon robe and slippers came in. She was ten, maybe fifteen years older than him, her hennaed hair in shoulder-length rolls and her lips heavily rouged. "Hiya," she said and locked the door behind her. "I'm Camilla." Her voice sounded nice and she had a relaxed, sloe-eyed way about her. "What's your name?"

Merritt couldn't find enough breath to speak. He stammered out his name and added, "How do you do?"

Camilla laughed. "Just fine. How do *you* do?" She crossed the room. "Take off that wet coat." He promptly slipped his arms out of the sleeves of his peacoat and tossed it on the floor. "I never liked these get-ups they make you boys wear," she said. "Too many buttons. Take it off."

Merritt pulled his jumper over his head and fumbled with the buttons of his pants. When he stood in nothing but his skivvies, she looked him over. "You're a tall, skinny drink, aren't you?" She then tugged his underpants down and taking his member in her hand told him she had to inspect for sores. "And anything else I might find."

He looked down and wanted to run his hands through her hair, but didn't dare.

"You're clean," she said and pushed him onto the bed. As she straddled him, she spread open her robe to reveal a slight paunch and small breasts with round, flat nipples. "Nervous?" she asked and started massaging him. "Blink twice for yes."

Merritt didn't know if he appreciated her wisecracks or not. When he tried to sit up and kiss her, she pushed him back down. "None of that," she said. So he reached up and cupped her breasts. He closed his eyes and pictured the woman from the High-End Lounge, then Bottoms-Up Betsy, then Rita Hayworth. He refused to let himself think of Clara. He could feel himself coming to attention, and when he opened his eyes to peer down the length of his own pale torso, he could see Camilla unfurling a prophylactic rubber onto him. She shifted her hips and guided him into her. The pressure made him drop his head back and sigh heavily. She leaned over him, letting her small breasts fall to his chest. He grasped the back of her fleshy thighs and stroked her ass as she slowly rocked forward and back. He furtively touched the slickness and warmth where he entered her. She pushed his hair back from his face and looked down at him. "Do you like?" she murmured, and in answer he reared up his pelvis and seemed to surprise her. "Yes," he said, "I like," then squeezed her ass hard, arched his back, and let out a deep, low groan.

He hardly noticed as she lifted herself off him, removed the rubber, and flicked it into a wastebasket beneath the bedside table. As she stood over him and cinched her robe, he propped himself onto one elbow and asked, "That's it?"

She leaned over and kissed his forehead. "Remember, lover, just ask for Camilla." She picked up the five of diamonds from the table where he'd laid it and walked to the door. "You can take a nap, but Billy wants everyone out by the end of the hour." She unlocked the door and left, her business done.

Alone in the room, Merritt pulled the beaded bedspread over his naked body and stared dumbly at the ceiling, feeling more sober than he had all night.

FOURTEEN
Clara, Fall 1945

Classes at the Cornish School of Allied Arts resumed in September, and in October Clara learned that Guy Anderson would be visiting her studio painting class the following week as a guest speaker. On the evening of his visit, she and her fellow students joined him in the President's Dining Room for dinner, during which Guy was thoroughly cordial, putting Clara at ease about any awkwardness between them. Afterward, in his talk to her painting class, he spoke about various techniques, the increased use of acrylics, and mixed-media works, which he himself had begun to explore. He even allowed himself to muse on the post-war world and the role of the artist in light of the annihilating power of the atomic bomb. He didn't offer any scenarios, but did make clear his conviction that the world, and most especially art, could never return to a pre-war mindset. The talk was well received, and following it a reception for Guy was held in the main lobby.

Only toward the end of the long evening did Clara have the chance to speak to him privately in a corner of the room, away from the other students and faculty. He avoided any mention of their time together in La Conner and instead inquired after her work. She told him it was going well, and then she asked if he'd heard anything about the preparations for Eliot's exhibition at the Seattle Art Museum.

"It's been postponed," he told her. "I'm surprised you hadn't heard."

"No," she said, "I haven't heard a thing." With all that had happened since July—the news of Freddy's death, the end of the war—she'd managed to put Eliot almost entirely out of mind and had only recently begun to wonder if she'd been too severe with him. She even let herself believe she might be missing him.

Guy glanced about the room to make sure he wasn't overheard. "He just became too difficult," he explained. "He kept arguing with Richard until finally Richard had no other choice than to postpone the exhibition."

Though saddened by this development, Clara was not surprised by it. The news carried a measure of justification for her in breaking up with Eliot. She wasn't the only one for whom his obstinacy and temper were too much. Guy told her that he'd seen Eliot only yesterday and that his behavior was worse than ever. "He kicked me out of his studio. With denunciations left and right."

At that moment the dean approached to shake Guy's hand and thank him for his talk, giving Clara the opportunity to say goodnight and, shortly after, excuse herself from the reception. As she left, she remembered what Guy had told her about Lindane and hoped her brother Ken, who was due home in a few short weeks, had been spared such treatments during his three-and-a-half year stint in the Army.

Yet, even while looking forward to Ken's return, Clara continued to grieve for Freddy, carrying on as best she could. Her mother's faith gave her the strength to persevere, while her father kept his nose to the grindstone and lined up a job for Ken on the waterfront. Her father also began fawning on her more, the way he did when she was a little girl, especially after he learned she'd stopped seeing Eliot.

Despite the family's quiet suffering throughout the autumn, and the heavy sorrow in her own heart, Clara could look about as she walked home from the reception for Guy and appreciate the change of seasons. The trees flashed yellow and russet, and soon the autumn rains would come, pasting the colorful foliage to the streets and sidewalk. Summer was gone, and the long, terrible war was over. Though broken and sad—especially as the photos of the German death camps began to appear in the weekly news magazines—the world held forth hope. Ken's imminent return gave the family something to look forward to, and she even let herself wonder whether one day she might have a family of her own, as strange and improbable as the prospect seemed at that moment.

After a year and a half as a clerk in Ladies Apparel, she finally received the chance to present her portfolio to Maximillian Lundquist, head of the Frederick & Nelson staff of in-store illustrators. Max, as he was known, was not nearly the prima dona Mrs. Evans in Personnel had said he was. To the contrary, he was a rather sweet man, though someone who obviously didn't suffer fools lightly. After requesting to see Clara's portfolio, he met with her in the store's Tea Room to discuss the position.

She found him sitting at a table in the corner—*his* table—in the blue and yellow Tea Room. He sat straight and poised, a trim man in his fifties, dressed to the nines in a pin-striped suit with a red silk scarf in the breast pocket and a gold tie-pin holding down his red silk tie. He was freshly shaven, and his uncommonly dark hair was heavily pomaded and combed straight back from his forehead. Clara had been told by one of the illustrators on his staff that he was a disciple of Cristobal Balenciaga, the daring Spanish couturier in whose Paris showroom he had worked as an assistant prior to the war.

"Ah, Clara." Max pulled a chair out from the table for her. "Would you like a glass of port?" The Tea Room did not serve alcohol, but Max had a special arrangement with the manager to keep a private bottle on hand for him. Clara declined and ordered a cup of tea.

"Shall we?" he said and opened her portfolio.

Clara had included a variety of pencil, charcoal, and watercolor portraits she'd made in the past year. Some were just sketches, others more detailed likenesses. She tried to demonstrate her range as an artist and show that she was capable of both expressive and precise renderings.

"You're very talented," began Max. "And I like what I see. But you must know that the task of a fashion illustrator differs significantly from that of a portraitist." Clara acknowledged the point with a nod and sat up straight, the better to receive whatever came next. "You must understand the fashions you are drawing. Your charge is to represent the clothes, not the model. This is a crucial distinction. Never compromise the designer's vision. Do you understand?"

Clara's tea arrived, yet she ignored it to maintain eye contact with Max and convince him how thoroughly she understood what he was saying. "Yes," she said. "Absolutely."

"Good," he went on. "I'll admit that I'm a fashion purist. I find a sophisticated gown to be almost architectural. To me, a smart, well-designed jacket resembles a piece of sculpture. I love a clean silhouette. And yet there must always be harmony and elegance throughout. Even a certain effervescence. And all of this must come through in the illustration. So what are your thoughts on Dior?"

Clara had taken pains in recent months to school herself on the most current fashions and designers. She knew all about Christian Dior's New Look. His lavish use of fabric for the swishing, full-cut skirt, his broad, sloped shoulders, his up-lifting bodice and nipped-in waistline. It had its appeal, but it also seemed like an overreaction to the "siren suits" from the war, the unflattering dressing gowns women wore in Europe so they could run from house to bomb shelter whenever the air raid sirens sounded.

"I prefer Coco Chanel," she said, knowing that he was testing her. "I favor her more relaxed fit to Dior's restrictive Bar suit."

"Indeed," replied Max, though Clara couldn't tell whether he agreed with her or not. She took a sip of tea and waited. "I would like to place you on our staff," he continued, "but on a probationary basis, you understand, to give you a chance to do some drawings for the team . . . beginning with tomorrow's show."

Two months before Frederick & Nelson had begun staging fashion shows every other week to showcase the new styles coming out of Paris and New York. The shows were orchestrated by Max, of course, using a team of models he also supervised.

"You can come backstage and have five minutes with each model," he informed her. "Tomorrow's theme is leisure wear. With a few Digby Morton luncheon dresses thrown in. Make your sketches and bring me your illustrations the next morning."

"Thank you," was all Clara could think to say, thrilled at the opportunity but also wondering what she'd gotten herself into. "This means so much to me."

"Yes," replied Max. "Now let's talk about other matters." He closed Clara's portfolio and slid it back across the table to her. For the rest of their meeting, he expounded on how he'd made it his personal mission to bring fashion sense to the hinterlands of the Pacific Northwest. He remarked on the tan tunic dress Clara wore and was impressed when she told him she'd applied the green piping herself. When he declared his abhorrence of rayon, Clara made a note to herself to dress only in cotton and wool from now on, at least while at work.

The next day Clara attended the fashion show, made her preliminary sketches backstage, and that evening filled them in with charcoal and pastels, and in the morning delivered her work to Max's office. Two days later, giving her illustrations his approval, he hired her fulltime. She said her goodbyes to the girls in Ladies Apparel and was assigned to one of the half dozen drafting tables on the fourth floor where she would now be working. Her initial assignments were strictly contract work for the store's catalogs and circulars, the type of work the veteran illustrators abhorred, which they found below even *prêt-a-porter*. Her best work in this vein, she believed, was an extended series of illustrations of undergarments—brassieres, panties, briefs, girdles, garter belts, and dress shields. "Intimate apparel," as the catalog listed them. She'd been instructed to draw figures cross-legged to avoid any hint of immodesty. On the other hand, she had to make the bosoms as high and pointed as humanly possible to achieve the "flattering uplift" touted by the catalog copy. As for color, the undergarments were strictly limited to herring bone white, powder blue, midnight black, and pale flesh pink. She figured she was paying her dues. But no matter. It was still drawing, and that was the important thing.

The second week of November, Clara caught a cold that dragged her down horribly. She went to work and attended her classes at Cornish, but afterward headed straight home where in the quiet of her apartment she sipped hot tea and ate dry toast (*shingles*, Ken called toast in his most recent letter home). She swallowed Hill's quinine cold tablets before getting into bed and drew in her sketchbook until dropping off to sleep. When her mother phoned, Clara tried to conceal her nasally voice and pretend she was perfectly well. She knew that at any hint of illness her mother would begin praying in earnest, a church practitioner would be called in, and she herself (out of sheer habit) would feel guilty for the error of her material thinking in letting herself become sick at all.

After six tiring days of coughing and congestion, she felt well enough to agree to go to a movie with Jenny, who said she wanted to see *Spellbound*, with Ingrid Bergman and Gregory Peck. She'd been friends with Jenny since her first day at Frederick & Nelson and remained so even after she left Ladies Apparel. Jenny told Clara she had to go out with her that night because she couldn't possibly watch such a scary movie by herself. She said she could see *The Bells of St. Mary's*, but then who wanted to see that la-la boy from Tacoma, Bing Crosby, crooning away in a priest's collar? So Clara went with Jenny to see *Spellbound* and after the movie, even though her energy was waning, they went to Bob Murray's Doghouse on Seventh Avenue, Jenny's favorite spot for her favorite foods—cheeseburger, French fries, and Coca-Cola—and, go figure, for meeting eligible men.

"No one too high class, mind you," Jenny remarked as they scooted into a booth, "but 'spectable enough."

The waitress knew Jenny and brought her a Coke before even taking their orders. Jenny latched her lips onto the straw and sized up the half dozen men seated at the counter, deeming them slim pickin's. The restaurant was dark, though, and it was hard to see very well. The walls were brown and the booths and counter seats were covered in black Naugahyde. Yellowed photographs of sportsmen adorned the walls—two men crouched beside a Roosevelt elk, holding up the massive head by its antlers, a man showing off the 30-pound King salmon he'd caught, grinning at the camera—that kind of thing. A mural of Mount Rainier in the WPA style stretched the length of the wall above the counter. Back in the kitchen, the cook worked furiously, sliding orders beneath three heat lamps suspended above the back counter.

When their food came and was set before them, the first thing Clara did was drag a French fry through a glob of ketchup on her plate and dangle it into her mouth. When she looked about again, someone was standing beside the table, not their waitress, looking down at her. It took Clara an instant to recognize the person as Callie Porter.

"I thought that was you," Callie said. "How's my favorite West Seattle artist?" Callie had grown heavier since Clara saw her last about a year before. She was probably topping 200 pounds now, though she didn't seem fat so much as just plain solid. She wore a long peasant skirt and a tan canvas jacket over a gray sweatshirt, and she had on the same leather work boots she'd worn the last time they met. Her hair was short over her ears in a kind of frizzy pageboy cut. Clara knew Jenny was staring.

"I'm fine," Clara answered and without the least hesitation pushed free from the booth and gave Callie a hug. "It's great to see you."

"I was sitting over there in the corner with Bernadette when I saw you come in," Callie explained, adding, "Here she comes now. We were just finishing."

Bernadette, a short, rather diminutive woman, came up to Callie and put her arm around her expansive waist. She was dressed in boys denim pants, the cuffs folded up, and a red-and-black hunting jacket, as if she'd just come from a mountain camp. Callie introduced her to Clara, and Clara in turn introduced them both to Jenny.

"I don't know if you've heard," Callie began in a more somber tone, "but Eliot's been admitted to the hospital. The psyche ward actually. They're giving him insulin shock treatment, which everyone says is better than being hit with the juice."

Clara sat back in the booth stunned by the news. Poor Eliot, she thought. How had it come to this? She thanked Callie for telling her and asked if she thought Eliot was going to be all right.

"We hope so," Callie said and reached out and patted Clara's hand. "You did the right thing." Then changing the subject and sounding more enthusiastic, she said she wanted to see what Clara had been working on lately.

"I'm mostly doing illustrations for Frederick & Nelson these days," Clara said proudly. "Though none of them have appeared in the paper yet. Just catalog stuff so far."

A worried look came over Callie's face. "You haven't given up painting, have you?"

"No," Clara insisted. "I still paint." She'd never liked talking about her own artwork, and now was no different. "I'll call you," she said. "We'll get together and catch up."

Callie slung her arm over Bernadette's shoulder. "Let's do that," she said and winked at Clara.

After Callie and Bernadette said their goodbyes and left, Clara turned to find a look of utter astonishment on Jenny's face. She resumed eating her French fries and waited for what was to come.

"Who—were—*they*?" Jenny demanded to know, and added, "Are they . . . *you know*?"

Clara glanced up to see Jenny crossing her eyes.

"Cross-eyed?"

"You know what I mean," Jenny protested. She leaned over the table toward Clara. "Are they funny," she whispered conspiratorially. "You know. Lesbians."

Clara was becoming exasperated. Show a little sophistication, she wanted to tell her friend. "Maybe," she answered and shrugged. "I really don't know. I never asked. All I know is that Callie is an incredibly talented artist and a good friend."

"What about Eliot?" Jenny went on. "He's the boy you were seeing, right? The one involved in your mysterious disappearance last summer?"

"I didn't disappear."

"It's because he's crazy then, isn't it? *Gawd*, Clara, you live in a whole 'nother world. That's kinda strange, don't you think? It's almost like a double life."

Clara wiped her fingers on her paper napkin and tossed it onto her plate. "This isn't the movies, Jenny." One of the men at the counter swiveled about to gawk at them, but when Clara stared him down he did an about-face. "I live a very full life. Or rather I used to. Now I go to work and school and that's it. A very dull, very tedious, and *very* exhausting existence." In fact, she felt slightly woozy right now and put both hands to her head and pressed her fingers to her temples. "I think I might still be a bit sick," she said "Can we go now?"

Jenny apologized for grilling her and said how she was just an ol' gossip hound and didn't know any better. "You look a little pale," she told Clara.

Jenny paid the check at the front register and without any further discussion of Callie and Bernadette drove Clara back to her apartment.

The next morning, a wet, dreary Sunday, Clara awoke with a fever, along with a cough that wouldn't let her rest. In the afternoon, Jenny came over and brought with her a bottle of Creomulsion. Clara read the label, which explained how the medicine was good for "coughs and bronchial irritations due to colds."

"That sounds about right," Clara said weakly. But when she choked down a tablespoonful of the wretched, pine-tinctured emulsion, she regretted having ever lapsed from the Christian Science disdain for such material remedies.

By early evening, her fever broke and her cough subsided enough for her to sit up in bed and make a drawing of Callie and Bernadette. When Jenny went home after making a can of chicken noodle soup and opening a box of Saltines for her dinner, Clara recalled the stark account of her life she'd given Jenny the day before. She realized that not only was she working inordinately hard these days, but, without even knowing it, she'd become terribly lonely in her day-to-day existence—which was all the more reason to look forward to meeting with Callie once she felt better. In the meanwhile, she figured, she should be well enough by morning to throw herself into another long week of work and classes.

FIFTEEN
Merritt, Winter-Spring 1946

The day Merritt mustered out of the Navy, five months after V-J Day, was a glorious day. Though shy of the points needed for an official discharge, he managed to finagle one for himself by signing up for the Naval Reserves. This arrangement meant he would remain in Seattle for the foreseeable future, an option that, he felt, was far better than sticking it out indefinitely in the service. The day after his discharge, he followed up on his officemate's offer and landed a job driving a refrigerated truck for Vitamilk Dairy, making deliveries five days a week between 4:00 a.m. and noon. As promised, it was a union job—with the Teamsters. It also left him plenty of time each day to take courses at the University of Washington across town. He packed his classes into his afternoons and spent as much time as he could in the library. At 5:00 each day he walked from campus to University Chicken Pie, at 45th and University, and ate dinner. Then he rushed to the library where he stayed until nine, at which time he rode the bus back downtown to his new apartment in the Charlesgate, a three-story brick building on Fourth Avenue, and went straight to bed. The next morning he was up at 3:30 a.m. and heading into work. It was a exhausting schedule, yet at the same time an efficient one—as well as, he calculated, the only way to meet his goal of graduating in three years.

Ex-servicemen crowded the university classrooms, taking advantage of the G.I. Bill, which provided for tuition and books and a $50-per-week living allowance. By the start of the spring term, he declared himself a Political Science major and was pressing forward. Exempt from the mandatory Military Science and Physical Education requirements, he used the available credits to take classes in British history from Professor Giovanni Costigan, whose reputation as a radical was well established on campus. Ideas mattered to Costigan, whether they were radical or not, and that's what Merritt liked about him. He also took Narrative Writing with Grant Redford, a writer himself, though Merritt quickly abandoned his notion of penning the next Great American Novel. It wasn't in the cards for him, he realized after the first assignment—though if anyone had a shot, it was Dick Hugo, an ex-Army flier who wrote circles around everyone else in the class.

Merritt didn't have a great many friends at the university. In the Navy, especially after his incident with the ensign, he'd learned to keep to himself. And because he didn't reside in the former war housing on campus that had been converted to men's dormitories, he had little occasion to pal around with his classmates, most of whom were younger anyway. The situation left him fairly lonesome, but also gave him time to focus on his studies. From time to time he thought of stopping by the Reading Room downtown—just to see, he told himself—but with his frantic schedule he never found time.

One friendship that did take hold was with John Peter Hughes—or J.P., as his friends called him—who was in nearly every one of his Poli. Sci. classes. They both supported Professor Costigan when he came under fire from university administrators for his method of advocacy teaching. ("Do we not have a right to our opinions?" Costigan asked in an open letter to the school newspaper. "So, too, do we not have the right to challenge the opinions of others? To me, this is the essence of a university education.")

J.P. had served in Africa and Italy and liked to say how the Army had radicalized him far more than Rommel or Mussolini. He urged Merritt to read Marx (beyond Costigan's requirements), Max Weber, and Thorstein Veblen. He spoke Spanish, too, and after touring Mexico and Central America over the holidays had come back to declare Latin America ripe for the next great peasant uprising. Having grown up in Seattle—Mercer Island actually, in the middle of Lake Washington—J.P. was also a devoted outdoorsman. He took Merritt hiking and rock climbing in the Cascades. He also skied, which sparked a rivalry between them to prove which state, Vermont or Washington, produced the best skiers.

It was his weekend skiing with J.P. that led Merritt one afternoon to go to the Frederick & Nelson sporting goods department to buy a new pair of ski boots. As he quickly discovered, though, he couldn't afford the expensive boots and had to settle for buying a tin of the store's famous Frango mints to send home to his mother. He also strolled through the men's department looking at hats, since he still wore the fedora he'd found in the lobby of the Hotel Commodore months ago. He wore the ratty hat with his old Navy peacoat, so while he was at it he also tried on several new overcoats. Yet when a store clerk asked if he needed assistance, Merritt replied that he was just looking and moved on, embarrassed at being so down-at-the-heels broke.

He was leaving the store, walking past Ladies Apparel, when a face among the evening wear caught the corner of his eye. It was a full two years since he'd seen her last, but he still recognized her. He took another look and there was no question. It was Clara. She held a sketchbook and pencil and was drawing one of the mannequins. He instantly recalled their first encounter that rainy morning when he held the door open for her, her arms full of sketchbooks, and the way she came after him on the sidewalk. He'd never imagined he might happen upon her like this, out of the blue, and wondered what he should do. If he approached and said something to her, she might not recognize him. Even though they'd gone out twice, to a movie and dancing, that was a long time ago. A lot had happened since then. People changed. They moved on. Plus, the last thing he wanted to do was make her feel uncomfortable. At any rate she appeared busy and probably wouldn't want to be bothered.

He kept looking at her all the same and finally let himself sidle past the display case of muffs and gloves, past a rack of house dresses, and close enough to the evening wear to make sure it was her—and decided he had to say something. He removed his hat and stepped forward to greet her.

She made a final quick mark with her pencil and looked up.

"Do you remember me?" he asked.

She squinted at him, a hint of befuddlement on her face, and then said, "Merritt?"

"It was a while ago," he said. "We took a dance lesson together."

She looked at him incredulously. "Don't be ridiculous," she came back. "Of course I remember you. Step one, slide two, and turn."

"That's right," he said and laughed. He was about to ask what had happened to her, how she'd come to disappear on him—but stopped himself, knowing only a fool would bring up such a thing.

"Gosh," she said and put a hand on her hip. "You're the last person I expected to see. What are you doing?"

He glanced nervously about Ladies Apparel. "I was down in Sporting Goods and I . . . ."

"No," she laughed. "I mean, I assume you're not in the service anymore. What've you been doing since the war?"

"Oh!" he came back, feeling his face flush. "I'm enrolled at the university. And I drive a dairy truck, if you can believe that." A moment passed during which she seemed to mull over this information. He figured she was picturing him in a white milkman's uniform and cap, carrying clinking milk bottles about and collecting money from housewives. The fact was his deliveries were strictly to restaurants and small mom-and-pop markets throughout the city, and his uniform was grey. "Are you still at the Reading Room?" he asked.

"No," she said. "Not for a while now."

"I see."

"I work here at Frederick's."

"How 'bout that!" The uncertain look on her face told him he was blowing it—his just desserts, he supposed, for all the ways he'd botched his first chance with her. When he asked what she did at Frederick's, she tucked her sketchbook beneath her arm and glanced at her wristwatch. He anticipated her excusing herself to go back to work.

"Actually," she answered, "I'm on break right now. Maybe, if you like, we could talk someplace else." She indicated the rack of evening wear they stood next to. "There's a lunch counter in the basement."

As Clara, the girl from the Christian Science Reading Room, the girl he'd obsessed over since their parting kiss so long ago, the girl he'd tortured himself over imagining how he'd lost her, the girl he'd dwelled upon when believing his ship was going down in the South Pacific typhoon, the girl he longed to be with again more than anything else in the world and yet had shamefully feared ever encountering again . . . as this very same girl led the way through the department store, he could hardly believe his extraordinary good fortune. He noticed again how tall she was. He himself was six-foot-one and she wasn't more than two or three inches shy of that. Shoppers in the store seemed to take notice as well. As Merritt quickly realized, it wasn't just her height they gawked at. All her features were incredibly fetching. Her face was smooth and clear, her body broad and firm . . . and yet there was something else, too, a certain grace and confidence in the way she walked, in the way she carried herself, that made her appear thoroughly unassuming and at ease with herself, that gave her that inexplicable quality people called *presence*. Everything about her that had made her so appealing to him so long ago—none of which he'd ever forgotten—was right here before him again.

As the hostess led them to a table and the waitress brought menus, he pulled the tin of Frango mints from the pocket of his peacoat and twisted off the lid. "Care for a mint?" he asked.

She laughed. "I eat these all the time," she replied and took one. "They're one of the perils of working here."

As she ordered tea and a tea cake and he ordered coffee, it struck him how remarkably easy it was to be in her company. She seemed genuinely pleased to be sitting with him, and so he doubted she could be troubled with all the pestering questions about their last meeting that plagued him still. Right away he was convinced she knew nothing of his ensign incident—which, like so much else since the end of the war, belonged now to another time and another life.

They talked about her job as a fashion illustrator at Frederick & Nelson and her classes at Cornish. They also talked about his job at Vitamilk and his classes at the UW. The small talk flowed smoothly between them, and she clearly felt at ease, but that changed when the war came up and Clara told him how she'd lost her brother Freddy in Germany. Merritt expressed his deepest condolences, and for several moments they remained silent.

It wasn't until Merritt offered her another mint and she shook her head to say no that Clara looked at him and broached the subject that—revealing his error—was apparently on her mind as much as his.

"Why didn't I hear from you again?" she asked. She was not the kind

119

of person to dice her words, this much was clear. "I never understood what happened. I'm so sorry you were called away, but I thought I still might hear from you. A letter at least."

Merritt replaced the lid on the tin of mints. He couldn't tell if her question was a reproach, a condemnation, or simply a plea for understanding. The manner in which they had parted had undoubtedly left her bothered, just as it had him.

"I wish I knew," he said after a too-long pause. "I went by the Reading Room almost every day, and I tried to call. The evening we spent together was one of the most enjoyable of my life. It really was."

It seemed to occur to her at that moment how her disappearance from the Reading Room must have looked to him, because she immediately went into a long and apologetic explanation of how she'd become ill over the weekend following their dancing date and in fact had become so sick that she'd lost all track of the days—and that by the time she'd recovered enough to phone him at the Recruitment Station, he'd already shipped out.

Merritt was dumbstruck by this explanation, and all he could think to say was, "I didn't know," and they both fell silent again.

After a while, though, he said, "I just got it into my head to see some action. Sitting out the war in the Recruitment Station was driving me nuts." He knew this was only the partial truth, that he wasn't coming perfectly clean with her, and that the line he was feeding her cast a far better light on him than he'd seen himself in prior to shipping out when he felt about as low as a person could. He also knew his statement didn't fully account for his conduct toward her. "But you're right," he added. "I should have written, and I'm sorry I didn't."

He noticed for the first time that there were no rings on her hands and concluded she was still unmarried. He wanted to ask her why she no longer worked at the Reading Room, but he knew that what she'd done after he shipped out was none of his business.

"Well," she said and reached for the tin of mints, "I'm glad we settled that, more or less."

"Me too," he said, but couldn't think of what next to say, knowing they couldn't return to their earlier small talk, not at this point.

"I'm also glad we saw each other again," she added, and glanced at her wristwatch, which made Merritt realize time was running out.

"Maybe," he offered, "we should try to go dancing again sometime."

She began to unwrap the mint she'd taken from the tin, but paused and looked at him. The look she gave him was not encouraging, and Merritt was convinced he'd overstepped some boundary. The suggestion of another date obviously offended her . He'd betrayed her trust once, so how could he possibly think he deserved another chance?

120

"Do you think that's a good idea?" she asked.

The question, posed the way a school teacher might ask the square root of nine, puzzled him, and at first he didn't know how to respond. Was she being facetious? Or just cautious? He chose to play it straight, and replied, "Yes, I do."

"In that case," she said more buoyantly, resuming her effort to unwrap the mint. "Let's."

SIXTEEN
Clara, Winter-Spring 1946

Ken's return the week before Thanksgiving was a joyful and heartbreaking occasion. Broad in the shoulders and touting a well-trimmed moustache, he'd become a full-grown, deep-voiced man since they'd seen him last. He'd survived the war and returned a sergeant major decorated with a Distinguished Service Cross. After their tearful reunion at the King Street train station, the family climbed into her father's old Model A and drove back to West Seattle. As they pulled up to the house, they all noticed the two flags that hung in the front windows—a blue star flag for Ken's safe return and a gold star flag honoring Freddy's sacrifice. Once inside, Ken took a moment to consider Freddy's Silver Star medal, awarded posthumously by the Army and now displayed on the living room mantel. He then asked to lead the family in a reading from the Bible and *Science and Health*, the two volumes he credited with seeing him through the war.

The following week after their big Thanksgiving dinner, Ken lazed about the house eating leftovers and going fishing in the evening with their father. Nonetheless he rose each morning to join their mother in studying the daily lessons. Then, that first Monday in December, he donned a new set of work clothes and accompanied their father down to the ILWU hiring hall, where he was promptly assigned to a work crew. By Christmas, Ken had been issued his official union card and was working the waterfront, which was busier than ever following the war.

At first it felt odd to Clara to have Ken living at home with their parents while she had her own apartment. It went to show that she'd grown up too. Yet when Ken began grilling her about not attending church—something Freddy would never have done—she gave the excuse that she was too busy with her new job and art classes. Eventually, he stopped pestering her, though he continued to express his displeasure and even had a subscription to *Christian Science Journal*, with its "instructive articles" and verified reports of Christian healings, delivered to her apartment. She knew her brother meant well, but she couldn't help but feel he was overly judgmental. He wouldn't dare take such a lofty attitude toward their father, who'd never converted and therefore couldn't fall away. Instead her brother became increasingly involved in the union—fervently so—and it became the focus, along with fishing, of every conversation between him and their father.

When Ken asked Clara one day whether she had a beau, she said flat-out no, she had enough to keep her busy. Yet she could tell what her brother was after. He wanted to know when she was going to marry and settle down.

"You're going to be turning twenty-one in July, aren't you?" he said.

"And I expect an armful of presents from you," she answered.

Yet when he ventured to ask whether she'd been kissed yet, she drew the line and made a face that let him know it was none of his business—and meant it. This was one reason she refused to say anything to him or her parents about her forthcoming date with Merritt.

The date was set for the Saturday following their encounter at Frederick's, and when Merritt picked her up after work that evening, he was driving a shiny new Buick Century. She was shocked, thinking he was one well-healed milkman, until he informed her the car was a loaner from his college chum J.P., whose father had bought it for him after the war.

"It's good to see you," he said once he'd closed her door, trotted around the front end of the large car, and gotten in behind the wheel.

"You too," she said, and noted how he was dressed far better than when they dated last. Gone was the plaid-'n'-plain, and in its place was a smart new blue suit with a simple red tie.

She was still not over the fact that they had run into one another the way they had. In some ways it was as if only a few days had gone by since their last evening out, and she had to admit it felt strange. So much had happened to her in that time—but undoubtedly to him as well. They were no longer the same people, though fortunately, she supposed, they'd never had much of a chance to get to know one another in the first place.

Like her brother, Merritt had also grown into manhood during the war. He wasn't as ruggedly built as Ken—was still rather skinny, in fact—but his face had matured and he no longer looked like the awkward boy she remembered. His dark hair had begun to recede, giving him a high and shiny forehead, and there was also a trace of crows feet around his brown-gray eyes. Oddly enough, he still wore the same round spectacles he'd had on when she first saw him in the doorway of the Reading Room. In all, she concluded, he was not a bad looking fellow.

Merritt drove through downtown and pulled up to the new seafood restaurant opened by the local radio personality Ivar Haglund. A sign above the entrance read *Keep Clam*, which she thought rather corny, but inside the restaurant appeared much more classy than this initial impression led her to believe it would be. She removed her coat and handed it to the coat-check girl, revealing the simple green dress she'd pulled off the rack at Frederick's that afternoon. As they were being seated, everything seemed to be going well, yet once they had looked over the menu, placed their orders, and for the first time looked directly across the table at one another, a certain awkwardness set in. They made a few jokes about V. Markum Lerner and Miss Jeannie Northrup, the dance instructors at the Hollywood Dance Studio, and talked about different movies they'd each seen. Yet it seemed as if they were trying too hard to recover something they'd either lost or, more likely, never really possessed.

When their food came, they ate in relative silence, and after the waiter had cleared their plates, the awkwardness became even more acute, until finally Clara could stand it no longer. The question of their falling away remained unresolved, and this was where the problem lay.

"Honestly, Merritt," she began. "Why *didn't* you write?"

He looked up at her, so she knew he'd heard the question. She felt bad for being so direct, but it was best to clear the air now and have done with it.

"I wish I knew," he answered, glancing down at the table and then up again. "I guess I was just scared. I went by the Reading Room I can't tell you how many times, and when you weren't there I didn't know what to think. At first I figured you might be sick, but then as the days went by I thought maybe you just didn't want to see me again. Then other things happened . . . "

"What other things?" she asked.

"Nothing important. Not any longer at least." He reached for his water glass and took a sip. "The point is I didn't know what I was doing or what to think, and so shipping out seemed like the best bet."

She knew it wouldn't be right to press him further. He seemed genuinely regretful about what had happened. In the end, it seemed, circumstances had simply conspired against them, and she could no more hold that against him than she could hold herself responsible for what had happened. It was what it was, and if they were to get through this evening they would have to accept that fact.

When the waiter returned to their table, she ordered dessert and Merritt asked for coffee. When the waiter left, she decided it was her turn to make amends and began recounting how sick she'd become following their last date.

"By the time I was well again, I didn't know if three days or three weeks had passed," she explained. She laughed at the memory of her bedridden situation and added, "And of course there was no calling a doctor."

"Ah," Merritt let out.

"Though I wish I had."

She told him about falling away from the church since he'd last seen her, how she'd stopped working at the Reading Room some time ago and no longer attended Sunday services. "I just need to think about something else for a while," she said.

"I know what you mean," Merritt replied.

They then looked at one another and she reached across the table and placed a hand on his.

"That's alright," she said as the dessert and coffee arrived. "I don't suppose it was an easy time for either of us."

The conversation took on a much lighter note after this and their dinner stretched out another hour. After paying the bill, Merritt helped her on with her coat and they drove several blocks to the High-End Lounge on First Avenue, where, Merritt told her, a seven-piece band played every Saturday night. They took a center table and Merritt lit a cigarette from the candle on the table. The place seemed rather hoity-toity to Clara, and she wondered whether Merritt was one of those types who regularly patronized such places, sipping martinis and chain-smoking cigarettes. She was asking herself what she really knew about him when the band started into a slow Duke Ellington number and she decided to give him the benefit of the doubt.

When the waitress came around to take their drink orders, he asked Clara if drinking was against her religion.

"It is," she confessed. "But I've gotten good at breaking the rules."

"Will they still let you into heaven?"

"I'll have to two-step my way in," she said

She ordered a glass of rosé and he ordered a scotch on the rocks. Then, shortly after their drinks came and they'd each taken a few sips, he put his glass down and asked her to dance. She said of course, and being a gentleman, he took her hand and guided her out to the dance floor. As they faced one another, he put his hand on her lower back and she leaned in close, taking in his scent of cigarettes, scotch, and new clothes.

The next afternoon Merritt telephoned Clara to tell her what a fine time he'd had. After two more dances and another drink each, they'd left the High-End Lounge and stopped at Prospect Park on Queen Anne Hill to take in the view of the city spread out below them. Since the lifting of the blackout order following V-J Day, the city had let itself light up brighter than ever and sparkled now with a new radiance. They then drove the short distance back to her apartment and Merritt saw her to the front door of her building, where he gave her a goodnight kiss and asked if he could see her again. She suggested they meet during the week at the Frederick & Nelson lunch counter, and a day and time were set.

This began their routine of meeting every Wednesday afternoon for lunch and every Saturday evening for dinner and dancing. On their second Saturday, because J.P.'s car wasn't available, they walked to a restaurant downtown and from there walked to the High-End Lounge. Around 11:00, they took a bus to lower Queen Anne Hill and strolled the rest of the way up the hill to Clara's apartment building. She knew it wouldn't be right to invite him in—not yet at least—and so they tarried by the front entrance, kissed several times, and finally said goodnight. The next weekend Merritt picked her up from work in the used car he'd bought three days earlier, and for two weeks in a row they went to the rooftop ballroom at the Camlin Hotel. Then their routine was disrupted suddenly when Clara had to join her parents in driving down to Kelso, a milltown on the Columbia River, to visit her "Grandpa Kelso," as the family called him, who'd been ill for a long time.

During their lunch on the Wednesday prior, when she told Merritt she would have to go to Kelso, she also took the opportunity to fill him in more on her family. She told him about the loss of baby May when she was just five, followed by her mother turning to Christian Science; about her father who worked hard all his life, was a staunch union man, and loved to go fishing; about her oldest brother Freddy and how much she missed him (and how she knew he would have gotten along with Merritt); and about her other brother Ken, who worked on the waterfront, was studying to become a church practitioner, and was basically a very serious sort of guy. When Merritt looked at her quizzically at the mention of church practitioners, she explained that this was the designation given church-sanctioned healers. "The closest thing Christian Scientists have to a pastor," she said.

When Merritt next asked what her father did, she explained how he used to work on the waterfront but now ran a print shop in West Seattle, adding, "But he'll always be a union man—through and through."

Merritt then mentioned that Vitamilk Dairy was a union shop and that he belonged to the Teamsters. This took Clara aback, and she explained how longshoremen, including her father and brother, had a longstanding beef against Teamsters. She didn't know all the details of the feud, but whenever there was mention of Teamsters in her house, one or the other of the men in her family would give a snort and cuss under his breath for several minutes. This information hung a frown on Merritt's face, so she placed her hand on his arm and told him not to worry. To herself, though, she hoped it wouldn't be a problem.

The next Saturday she again had to skip their dancing date, this time to attend her Grandpa Kelso's funeral. Merritt sent a card to the family and when he saw her on Wednesday he expressed his condolences for her loss. She informed him that Christian Scientists didn't mourn a person's passing since the corporeal body was viewed as little more than a piece of luggage on the spiritual journey to Truth. "Still," she said, "I loved my Grandpa Kelso, and I'm going to miss him."

She sympathized when Merritt admitted he didn't always get what she was saying about Christian Science matters. Who could blame him? Without the usual hierarchy or liturgy or ritual most churches partook of, the faith could be hard to grasp. She knew this, and so she tried to go easy on him whenever she brought up church-related topics.

When she asked him when she might be able to meet his friend J.P., Merritt lit up. "How could I forget," he said, and told her that J.P. had invited them to join him and his girl on a weekend camping trip. Now that spring had sprung, he said, it was the perfect time to drive over Stevens Pass to Lake Chelan. They would leave two weeks from this Saturday. They'd drive over in the morning and then drive back on Sunday. He and J.P. would be in one tent and the girls in another. "What do you think?" he asked, looking eagerly at her.

The invitation reminded her of her first trip with Eliot, when they'd visited La Conner, and how excited she'd been leading up to it—and how, without her even knowing it, it portended the disaster that would become their second trip. So she was reluctant to show too much enthusiasm over another get-away with a guy who, when it came right down to it, she hardly knew. Yet she reminded herself that this was Merritt, not Eliot, and said, "That would be wonderful," and pictured herself sketching the group of friends as they sat around the campfire beside the mountain lake.

SEVENTEEN
Merritt, Summer-Fall 1946

As spring came on, Merritt knew he had a superb dance partner in Clara and thought of her now as his regular sweetheart. His fear that she knew about Ensign Rivard had obviously been unfounded. Each week now, with few exceptions, he and Clara kept to their Wednesday and Saturday routine. Their dance circuit included the High-End Lounge, the Camlin Hotel, the Olympic Bowl, and the Trianon Ballroom. Each Saturday at the Trianon, the bandleader—Curt Sykes of the Curt Sykes Orchestra—dedicated a number to his favorite dance couple, awarding the couple exclusive rights to the floor for that dance. On the night the bandleader dedicated a number to Merritt and Clara, Merritt knew they'd come a long ways. On some Saturday nights, though, to give their feet a rest, they would skip the dancing and catch a picture instead. They liked to go to the Orpheum and afterward get dinner. Most of all, Merritt enjoyed being with Clara no matter how they spent their time. She was about the truest girl in the world—just as he'd always imagined her.

So much steady dating was only possible, of course, after he bought his car. It was a white, bulbous, four-door '38 Plymouth DeLuxe Sedan with baloney-skin tires, rusted undercarriage, and torn upholstery, which nonetheless ran like a charm. He bought it off a tank-trunk driver from his Teamster local. Since the Office of Price Administration in D.C. still regulated prices and supply, filling the tank with gas wasn't cheap. In all, though, owning the car made Merritt feel like a kid again tooling about the yard in the Roadster peddle-car his parents gave him one Christmas. Only now he tooled about Seattle with a tall, good-looking gal beside him.

The camping trip to Lake Chelan unfortunately was cancelled after J.P. broke up with his girl. Yet Merritt figured the cancellation was probably for the best. With summer classes having commenced, he had less free time than ever, and it was all he could do to put his early morning hours in at Vitamilk and keep up with his course work. In fact, to help with one of his classes—European Philosophy—he started meeting once a week with a classmate to review class notes.

Sid, who was three years younger, had graduated from Roosevelt High the previous June, and because the Germans had already surrendered and the

Japs were on the ropes, he went straight into college. Sid was smart, and also a real talker. He liked to tell how he wasn't such a good student in high school and his parents, contrary to people's notion of Jewish parents, never got on his case about it. He'd skip school and go down to Garlic Gulch, around Rainier Avenue, and buy pignoli cookies from the Italian bakery. On weekends he and his friend Benny, a Filipino kid, rode the trolleys all over town. Sid recounted how before the war started he and Benny would go out onto the split-log booms in Salmon Bay, pitch a pup tent, and camp overnight on the floating island. Then something really grisly happened. Not long after the attack on Pearl Harbor, they came upon the decapitated body of a Japanese man beneath the wooden bridge that spanned the Interbay. It was in all the papers, and his footloose days abruptly ended when his parents wised up fast and sent him to Hebrew School at Temple de Hirsch on Capitol Hill. "Just as well, too," he said. "That beheaded guy scared the bejesus out of me."

The next time they met at the coffee shop where they liked to meet, Sid was too excited to review Professor Phillips' lecture on Cartesian logic. He fidgeted so much Merritt wanted to tell the waitress to cut off his coffee.

"I met a girl," he announced, leaning over the table of the booth where they sat. "Man oh man, have I ever met a girl." He leaned back with a punch-drunk look on his face, then poured milk into his coffee and looked about for the sugar, which was still scarce from war rationing. He finally gave up, sat up straight, and took on a serious demeanor. "For starters," he said, "she's Orthodox."

Merritt figured this meant she was Jewish. Growing up in Lyndonville, Vermont, he hadn't known a single Jew. It was only with the rise of Hitler—and then of course the nightmarish photographs from the death camps—that he even became aware of how persecuted Jews were throughout the world. Oddly, Sid never talked about any of this.

"I met her at Hillel," he said. Merritt knew this was the Jewish version of chapel on campus. Sid also belonged to the university's only Jewish fraternity, Sigma Alpha Mu. "She's gorgeous."

"I'm happy for you, Sid. What's her name? Are you going to take her out?"

"Amy," he said and slurped his coffee.

Merritt then got a brilliant idea. "What say you and Amy and me and Clara go to a picture this Saturday at the Orpheum."

Sid ordered a piece of coconut cake from the waitress. "That's the thing," he replied. "She's Orthodox, which means she observes the Sabbath, which means she can't do anything until sundown on Saturday, and around here that's not until eight o'clock or so, which is too late to catch a show. So many *mitzvah*! Thank God we Reform Jews aren't so observant.

"This is all news to me, Sid," said Merritt. When he'd told Sid last week that

Clara's family was Christian Scientists, Sid looked utterly befuddled and asked, "They're the ones with the Reading Rooms, right?" That's all anyone ever knew about them. That and their gripe with doctors. "Maybe getting them together isn't such a good idea," Merritt said now, thinking it over. "What if they start talking about religion?"

"We should go to a ball game instead," Sid suggested. "There's one this Sunday."

Since the start of the baseball season, he and Merritt had twice taken the bus down to Sick Stadium to watch the Rainiers play. Sid, a huge fan, told Merritt that before the war the team had dominated the Pacific Coast League. But these days, they were dead last in the standings.

He and Sid agreed to the double-date and arranged to meet that Sunday at the ball park, half an hour before the first ball was thrown out. It would be his and Clara's first occasion in public with people one of them knew personally—which, by Merritt's reckoning, would make them an official item.

A big crowd filled the 14,000-seat stadium that bright, warm Sunday afternoon in South Seattle. Merritt bought 50-cent tickets for the left field bleachers where Sid said all the loudmouths, boozers, and baseball reprobates congregated.

"Ah," said Merritt. "The Holy Church of Baseball."

"Temple Beth el Baseball," Sid shot back.

The girls got along splendidly. Not once did they bring up religion. Clara looked sharp in her red-checkered halter dress, her wide shoulders and long arms ravishingly bare. Amy was much shorter than Clara and dressed more conservatively, yet she was a lightning wit and matched Sid's every quip.

The stadium outfield was plastered with billboards for Sick's Rainier Brewing Company, and a legion of beer guys worked the stadium aisles. The sun was making its summer debut, heating up the wood bleachers, and as soon as Merritt sat down he shouted to the beerman to bring him a couple of cold ones—one for him and one for Clara. Sid and Amy, he already knew, didn't drink.

When the players from the Rainiers sprinted out onto the field to start the game, the fans cheered wildly for them, and after three quick outs to retire the side, the Hollywood Stars took the field and the fans jeered the California visitors just as wildly. As the game wound on, Clara became less talkative and at the top of the fourth inning Merritt turned to ask her something and saw that she was nodding off. He figured the beer and sun were too much for her, and decided to let her doze. He then turned his attention to Sid, the de facto team statistician for the Rainiers. He knew every player's name and position as well as the player's season and career batting averages, his offensive and defensive quirks, his most telling personality trait, the various teams he'd played for, and the name of his hometown, usually some podunk burg in Idaho or Montana.

"Kirby Wilbur can't hit low and away," he apprised Merritt. "Watch as the pitcher throws him outside sinkers. If he gets any wood on it, he'll ground out to third or blooper to left. If he'd step into the plate more, he could hit 300. He's got a nice swing. He just doesn't know how to use it."

As if on cue, Kirby Wilbur went fishing for a slider on the outside of the plate and the third baseman for the Hollywood Stars scooped up the slow grounder and tossed Wilbur out at first before he could make it half-way down the baseline.

"What I tell ya?" said Sid. "The third baseman saw that coming last week when he checked the schedule and saw the Rainiers on deck."

The announcer urged the crowd then to give a loud round of applause for Edo Vannini, next up to bat. Instead of applause, though, the crowd let out whoops of derision and shouts for Edo to "get the leado out." Clara was roused awake by the ruckus and when she apologized for nodding off, Merritt kissed her forehead, her hair glistening yellow in the sun.

"That announcer's a real wise guy," said Sid and explained how Edo Vannini was the Rainiers' worst player—maybe the worst player in the whole Pacific Coast League.

Vannini stepped to the plate and on the first pitch swung and missed. The crowd doubled its heckling. With the next pitch, though, he made contact. The ball looped over the second baseman's outreached glove for an easy single, but as the right fielder scooped it up, Vannini rounded first base heading for second. The crowd shouted at him to go back, but Vannini was determined to stretch the single into an unearned double. Surprised by the move, the right fielder hurled the ball to the infield where it skidded on the dirt, bounced past the shortstop's glove, and ricocheted across the infield and straight into the visiting team's dugout. Vannini came into second base standing up, spotted the infield error, and with a jig in his step trotted down to third base. The crowd went into a paroxysm of cheers and hilarity at the hapless Edo Vannini's good fortune.

The next batter up was Earl Tatter, whom everyone called "The Earl of Snohomish" because he hailed from the small town of Snohomish north of Seattle. The Earl was a crowd favorite, and when he singled to center and Edo Vannini sauntered down to homeplate to score the first run of the game, the crowd was beside itself. Merritt kissed Clara again and slapped Sid on the back, but Sid didn't share in the delight, warning that it was still early in the game.

By the seventh inning stretch, Clara was resting her head on Merritt's shoulder and he was feeling pretty drowsy himself—and the Rainiers were down by five runs. When he nudged Clara and suggested they head out before the score turned any worse, Clara, half-asleep, agreed, and they said their so-long's to Sid and Amy, who were determined to stick it out.

Outside the stadium, Merritt could see how red Clara's face, neck, and shoulders were from being in the sun. He said he should have known better and asked her if it hurt. She told him she was fine, that it wasn't bad at all. Yet he persisted in blaming himself for her sunburn until finally, as they reached the car, she said she had some Pond's Cold Cream back at her apartment and if he liked, he could come over and put some on her shoulders.

Over the course of the next few weeks as Merritt was figuring out whether he was in love—and he was almost certain he was—he came down with a toothache that became so painful he was forced to go down to the Teamsters Hall on Denny Way and Taylor Street to inquire about union-approved dentists. While there, looking over one of the union hall bulletin boards, he spotted a posting for an office clerk job with Joint Council 28, the affiliation made up of all the Teamster locals in Washington State and the Alaska Territory. The position paid sixty cents an hour more than his job with Vitamilk. Plus, he thought, if he was ever going to propose to Clara, he needed to start making something of himself. So sore tooth and all, he entered the Joint Council office, showed the secretary his union card, filled out an application form, and was told to take a seat. Ten minutes later a sinewy, middle-aged fellow in short sleeves and a thin, black tie stepped out of a side office and introduced himself as Leo Reinke, secretary of Joint Council 28. He led Merritt into his office and told him to take a seat. The interview lasted all of ten minutes. Merritt explained how he'd worked in the Navy recruitment and discharge offices and served on the USS *Washington* during the war and how he was now enrolled at the UW studying political science. He even added, off the cuff, that he'd always been interested in union issues.

"That's fine," said Reinke. "We need young men like yourself. Let me introduce you to Mr. Olsen, head of the Western Conference, and Mr. Beck, our vice president."

An hour later the job was offered to Merritt and he accepted it on the spot. The next morning he gave his two weeks' notice to Vitamilk, but they told him he could leave anytime, and so by the end of the week he was seated at his own desk in the Joint Council offices in the Teamsters Hall.

He worked harder than ever at his new job and over the next couple of months moved from sorting mail and filing membership records to corresponding with various locals, coordinating Joint Council membership drives, and drafting routine policy statements that he would hand off to Leo to double-check before they were passed on to Frank Olsen and then Dave Beck for final approval.

As a matter of course, Merritt did become more interested in labor issues. Within a year of the war's end, strikes were breaking out all over the country. One of Merritt's professors told the class that more strikes had taken place in 1946 already than in all of '34, the landmark year the National Industrial Recovery Act gave workers the right to collective bargaining. Of course there were a lot more unions now, unions such as the International Longshore and Warehouse Union—the one Clara's father and brother belonged to—that knew how to wield the strike to their advantage and weren't afraid to do so. (No one was surprised, therefore, when the ILWU began threatening in August to close down the waterfront again.) In all, you couldn't take a cross-town bus without seeing two or three picket lines by the boilermakers, pipefitters, joiners, welders, carpenters, plumbers, elevator operators, garbage collectors, telephone linemen, you name it. If they had a union charter, they would eventually picket. Sometimes a particular union struck on its own, targeting a specific employer. But more often than not, the unions formed alliances to support one another's strikes and went after an entire industry. It all depended on whether they were AFL or CIO, or unaffiliated. Whatever the case, Merritt always sided with the striking union, and even more so as he began to consider himself a dedicated union man. He recognized that the general disruptions that strikes and lockouts caused were an unfortunate side effect of such actions, but that such disruptions were just as much management's fault as they were the union's. The strike was every union's right and prerogative, and the threat of one resembled a great big game of chicken between labor and management. Unlike most other unions, though, it was a game the Teamsters didn't play.

The reason was simple: Dave Beck. He was one of the most powerful men in the most powerful union in the country, the International Brotherhood of Teamsters, Chauffeurs, Warehousemen and Helpers. Even though strikes in and around Seattle gave the lie to the argument that Beck held most of the city's unions under thumb, it was true he wielded tremendous local influence. Overall, Seattle experienced far fewer strikes than either San Francisco or Portland, owing in great part to Beck, who stridently opposed strikes as a labor tactic. He touted himself a friend to businessmen and an ally of city officials and worked his deals behind the scenes. The more time Merritt spent at the Teamsters Hall—"The Building Beck Built," the two-story yellow-brick structure that was headquarters to Local 174 of Seattle, Joint Council 28, *and* the entire Western Conference of the IBT—the more he came to understand how Beck operated.

When he saw his boss in the tan-tiled hallways of the union hall, Beck would greet him cordially. Now and then Merritt was summoned by Beck's devoted secretary, Ann Watkins Kotin, to his office to review some task or another Leo had assigned him. As the months passed, Merritt saw that nothing slipped Beck's notice. Whether you worked for the Seattle local, the Joint Council, the

Western Conference, or the International Brotherhood itself, he knew *who* you were and *what* you did. When Merritt was promoted to "executive assistant" to the secretary of the Joint Council, he believed he'd received Beck's blessing, and from then on let himself believe there might be a real future for him with the Teamsters.

The only problem was that his new job worried Clara to no end. Already her brother Ken was giving her trouble about her dating a Teamster. She tried to downplay the situation, but Merritt could tell it was causing no small measure of strife for her with her family.

"First the church and now this," she said to him one afternoon during their regular lunch date at the Frederick & Nelson lunchcounter. "I don't think you and Ken should meet."

"Ever?" he asked.

"It's like some kind of blood feud," she replied. "It just goes on and on. I've never understood it."

Merritt didn't know what to say. Should he quit his job just to placate her irrational brother? Weren't union men supposed to stick together? Weren't they one big union in the end, as he'd always heard? Apparently not. Which left him feeling bad for Clara, who was stuck in the middle. He tried to reassure her that he would do everything in his power to minimize the tension his job caused her with her family, and with nothing else to say, she seemed to accept this.

It was in his new position as executive assistant that he accompanied Leo Reinke one afternoon to Beck's office after being summoned that morning by Mrs. Kotin. When they arrived, she asked them to wait outside while Mr. Beck finished a long distance call to Indianapolis, which everyone knew was where Daniel Tobin, the Teamsters' General President, ran the union's national headquarters.

When Mrs. Kotin gave them the go-ahead to enter, Beck stood up from behind his immaculate mahogany desk and greeted them both with a firm handshake. As usual he was dressed to the nines, as if he might be asked to pose for a photograph with the governor or mayor at any moment. His short, bulldog frame was packed into a custom-tailored blue suit, a pressed white handkerchief folded in the left breast pocket. The starched collar of his white dress shirt rose high and tight around his stump-like neck, held there by the perfect Windsor knot in his red-and-gold striped tie. Beck's head and hands, Merritt noted each time he saw him, were something to behold. They were thick and rough—though clean—and told you that here was a true working man. Except for a well-trimmed tonsure around the sides and back of his head, he was bald. His head and face created a fleshy oval that led people behind his back to refer to him as "Baby Beck." This baby-faced appearance was enhanced by a pair of pale blue eyes. At the same time, his face was that of a real bruiser, someone who could take a punch square in the kisser. The weighty gold watch and gold wedding band on his left hand highlighted his thick wrist and fingers. On his right hand, he wore a ring with the Teamsters emblem—two percheron horse heads over a wagon wheel—the same emblem that adorned the billboard on the roof of the Teamsters Hall, the building's cast-iron front gate, and the union letterhead.

Beck signaled Leo and Merritt to take the two chairs in front of his desk, then sat down in his own leather saddle-seat chair. He dropped both hands on the wood armrests of his chair and looked across the desk at them.

"Leo, how're things faring in your territory?" Being a man who neither smoked nor drank, Beck possessed a smooth, almost high-pitched voice. The sound of it was always unexpected coming from a man with such a burly build. "What're the roll numbers looking like?"

Leo sat forward. "They're improving every day, Dave. The locals are really doing their part. The Coke-Cola distributor over in Yakima finally came around. I don't know what he was thinking. The organizers at Local 760 stepped up and got him on board." Leo turned to Merritt and asked, "How many drivers was that?"

Merritt thought a moment. "A dozen at least," he answered. He had checked the rolls of the Eastern Washington locals just that morning. "That one Coke-Cola distribution center covers the whole central district from Okanogan to Pasco. They have more drivers than most Seattle distributors."

Leo nodded. "I have Merritt calling the business agents at each local to check their roll numbers and make sure someone is covering every district. So let's say 760 in Yakima has their beverage division covered, we want to make sure they're not letting laundry fall through the cracks."

Beck listened to this report and then piped up with, "You know I want them to be especially vigilant with laundry," and laughed.

Every Teamster west of the Mississippi knew that Beck got his start driving a laundry truck in Seattle before the First World War, just around the time Seattle Local 174 was chartered, which put him on the ground floor. It was also common knowledge that no matter how wrapped up in contract negotiations for health benefits or other such matters the union became, the bottom-line for Beck was always organizing. It wasn't enough to be a stern shepherd. You had to go out and grow the flock. That meant signing men up. Putting them on the roll call. That's how Beck had tripled Teamster membership in the West to nearly a million strong since the early 1930s.

"You're doing a good job, Leo," Beck said and turned to Merritt. He lifted both hands from the armrests of his chair and dropped them down again. "You too, Merritt." He took a deep breath and sat forward, looking across the desk at Merritt. "So tell me, how're your studies going? Leo's not working you too hard, is he? You don't want to fall behind."

Now it was Merritt's turn to sit forward. This kind of solicitousness was not uncommon with Beck. He liked it to be known that he was looking out for his members. "They're going fine, Mr. Beck."

"You can call me Dave," Beck interjected.

"Yes, sir.

"You were saying."

"My courses are going just fine. They're a lot of work, of course. A lot of reading, a lot of writing, the usual stuff. But that's why I'm there. This job makes the whole deal possible."

"Union wages!" Beck declared proudly.

True enough, the dollar-sixty-three an hour Merritt now earned was a third more than what he made driving the Vitamilk truck. The hours were a lot better, too, especially since Leo let him schedule his work around his class times.

"It's interesting work as well," Merritt went on. "That makes a big difference. For a while I thought I might take the civil service exam, go into government, but I'm not so sure anymore." Even though he knew it sounded like he was sucking up, he meant what he said. He liked his job.

"Listen," Beck said. "It's a good thing you're in college. The union needs college-educated men, people with smarts who can get things done, figure things out. Our muscle is in the rank-and-file, but the brains of this organization aren't going to be your average Joe hauling crates of apples across the mountains or bedroom suites for Bon Marché. You follow me?"

Merritt nodded, even though Beck's words seemed rather harsh, perhaps even insulting to someone like Leo who wasn't college-educated but who'd driven a truck most of his life, remained committed to the union, and worked his way up through the administrative ranks.

"Eventually," Beck went on, raising a hand and pointing a blunt index finger out the window, "this whole operation's going to have to get out of Indianapolis and set up in D.C. You know why? Because that's where things *really* get done. That's what I was telling Old Man Dan just now on the telephone."

Merritt and Leo didn't move or say a word. They let Beck take the conversation wherever he was going to take it. Merritt was just relieved he wasn't being called onto the carpet for mishandling something or another, because word about the union hall was you didn't want to get on Baby Beck's wrong side.

"I read your article in the newsletter about inflation," Beck said to Merritt. "It had a lot of smarts to it."

"Thank you," Merritt replied. His short piece in the Local 174 newsletter about wages keeping pace with post-war inflation was something the treasurer of the Seattle local had asked him to do. It took him two nights to research the issue and write up the article.

"You should do more like it," Beck went on. "It's good for the members to know what's happening in the world, to give them something other than funny books to read."

Merritt was flattered. "I'll do that, sir," he said. In fact, the treasurer, who oversaw the newsletter, was already angling to turn the whole undertaking over to him, which Beck probably knew.

Beck studied Merritt as if sizing him up for a new suit. "This is why I called you in," he said. "You're up on the university campus a lot for your school work, right?"

"Seven days a week. Either in class or the library."

"You've heard the longshoremen are probably going to go out again, right?"

"Yes," he said, wondering if Beck knew about Clara and her family of longshoremen. The last thing he wanted the Teamster boss to know was that he was dating the daughter and sister of two die-hard ILWU members—or that he was having his first Sunday dinner with them this weekend.

"Well, it doesn't take a genius to know that if the moon's full, Harry Bridges will be calling a strike."

"Sonuvabitch," Leo said. "It's like clockwork. It's in his Commie blood."

Beck let Leo have his say and went on. "Bridges is coming to town in a few weeks to give a talk at the university. I'd like you to go and hear what he has to say. The papers will be there, but I want one of our own to hear him talk. Then write up what he says like you would for the newsletter and give it to Mrs. Kotin. Don't leave anything out. Got it?"

"Yes, sir," Merritt said, thinking this might be the start of something, that in time he could be writing for the *International Teamster*, which was sent to the household of every IBT member in the country.

Beck stood up and reached his meaty paw across the table. "Thanks, Leo. Keep up the good work." He shook Leo's hand. "Same goes for you, Merritt." He shook Merritt's hand too. Then, as he sat back down and the two were departing, he called out to them, "Tell Mrs. Kotin she can put that call through for me now."

EIGHTEEN
Clara, Summer-Fall 1946

When Clara's first illustrations appeared in the Sunday edition of the *Seattle Times*, she phoned Merritt before anyone else. It only made sense. From the start of their re-acquaintance, they'd become steadily more involved. He was smart, courteous, and good-looking, after all. Plus he danced like a dream and was a keen kisser. Whether he was someone she could fall in love with, only the future would tell. But for now she enjoyed taking things in their own sweet time and seeing where it brought them. She knew he would be as thrilled as she was by the publication of her first illustrations.

It was shortly before noon when she phoned him. He sounded almost alarmed to hear her voice, as if she might be in trouble, yet when she explained why she was calling, he congratulated her and said he was going to run out and buy the paper. "I'll call you right back," he said.

Ten minutes later her telephone rang.

"Got it," he said when she picked up.

"Page A-9," she blurted into the receiver. She could hear him rustling the paper open.

"There," he said, and after a short delay added, "It's wonderful, Clara."

She liked how he always said her name like that. She pictured him at his kitchen table—though she hadn't even seen his apartment yet—with the Sunday paper spread out before him, looking down at the half-page Frederick & Nelson advertisement with her illustrations of two women, one wearing a long skirt and bolero jacket, the other in a crepe dress with a bold, leafy pattern.

"It's what Max is pushing for late summer," she said, and when Merritt asked how long it had taken her to draw them she explained that she'd made a dozen sketches before she got them the way she wanted. "The leaf pattern gave me fits."

"This calls for a celebration," he announced and said he would buy her lunch at Charlie's on lower Queen Anne Hill, half-way between her apartment building on the hill and his downtown.

Much later that evening—after getting tipsy on the mimosas they ordered with their lunch and afterward taking an afternoon nap—she ventured to make her first drawing of Merritt, not counting of course the one she'd made of the anonymous sailor who'd strayed into the Reading Room years ago. His face possessed a seriousness that could take a person off guard, and capturing that gave her some difficulty. With his full, almost feminine lips, he appeared rather sullen at times, as if he were pouting. His dark eyes and even darker eyebrows also gave him a pensive cast. She pictured his sloping forehead with the receding hairline, his angular face with the thick-rimmed eyeglasses (gone were the oval spectacles), and his slender neck with its bulging Adam's apple. When she finished the drawing, she couldn't decide whether it was a complimentary portrait or not. Had she missed something, or did he always look so hang-dog? Giving Merritt the benefit of the doubt, she decided she'd missed something and would try again another time.

For the next several weeks she and Merritt continued their routine of meeting for lunch on Wednesdays and dinner and dancing on Saturdays. From the start of their reunion, Clara had resolved not to hurry matters. She didn't want another episode like the one she'd had with Eliot. Fortunately, Merritt seemed satisfied with their pace, but far more important—and so unlike Eliot— he seemed to genuinely enjoy doing things with her.

In early September, as the leaves on the alders fluttered yellow and yet the days remained sunlit and warm, Clara talked him into going salmon fishing with her. She hadn't gone fishing since before the war when her father took her to his union's salmon derby. She landed a 25-pounder that day. As the fish had pulled her into the river, her father seized the pole from her and wrestled it down river until another longshoreman waded in with a net and scooped it up. The salmon took third place in the derby and the family ate salmon steaks and salmon loaf for the next two weeks. And Clara had wanted to go fishing again ever since. So with directions to the exact spot on the Carbon River where she'd landed the Silver that day, she borrowed rod, reel, and tackle from her father and set off with her beau.

They drove south down the Kent-Auburn Highway to the small railroad town of Orting at the confluence of the Carbon and Puyallup rivers. At the general store there, they bought fishing licenses along with several hardboiled eggs, cheese, baloney, bread, and several bottles of Oly. From town, they followed her father's directions until they came to a dead-end road where they found the trailhead that led down to the river. According to her father, they needed to walk another quarter mile up-river to a bend where a 100-foot cliff rose above the opposite bank. The salmon often rested at the base of the cliff, he told her, where the river ran deepest, before pushing farther upstream to spawn.

Clara and Merritt found the bend in the river and clambered down the embankment to the sand bars and river rocks. "Here we are," she exclaimed. "This is it. This is where I caught that enormous fish."

As Merritt anchored the beer in the river to keep it cold, Clara cast her line in one smooth motion just short of the cliff on the opposite bank. Her father had tied a lure onto the line of each rod and shown her how to make the four-loop knot in case she or Merritt lost a lure. With her line in the water, she looked over her shoulder at Merritt to find him struggling with his rod and reel. "Let it sink with the current and slowly reel it back in," she advised.

"Okay," he answered, having never fished before in his life. When he threw his line out, the lure plopped into the water three feet in front of him.

"You'll get the hang of it," she said.

In no time he was casting out to midstream. The opposite bank was made up of exposed dirt for fifteen feet or so, indicating the high-water mark, above which clumps of hemlock and alder clung to the rocky cliff. As the sun rose higher and the beach warmed, Merritt removed his jacket. They kept casting and reeling in, casting and reeling in, and fell into a comfortable silence. Clara kept an eye on him to see how he was doing, yet she was also thinking how he was someone she could trust, someone with a real sense of commitment—even if it did make him rather predictable at times.

As she watched him, he ripped his rod through the air and gave a shout that echoed off the opposite bank. "I've got one," he yelled, and sure enough a fish jumped mid-stream, thrashing at the end of his line.

Clara dropped her pole and ran up to him. "Reel him in slowly and get him onto the bank," she instructed.

"Praise the Lord and pass the ammunition," he yelped as the fish leapt again. He stumbled on the river rocks, nearly falling over, and pulled the fish up onto the sandy beach.

"Bring it up onto the rocks," she shouted. She then took hold of his line and held the fish up by its gills. It was a Pink, maybe seven or eight pounds.

"Will you look at that," Merritt let out, breathing hard and sounding as excited as a young boy on his first big adventure in the great outdoors.

"I'll say," said Clara and beamed at him, thinking, *How could she not love such a man?*

"What do we do now?"

"We kill it," she answered. She pried the hook from the salmon's mouth. "Here," she said and handed the slippery fish over to him. "Lay it on a rock and take another rock and give its head a good, hard whack."

"Are you sure?" he asked.

"Yes," she said. "If you want to keep it."

"Of course I want to keep it. It's tonight's dinner, right?"

"Okay then. That means you have to kill it first."

Merritt picked up a fist-size rock and lined the salmon's head up against another rock. "Like this?"

"Now give it a good, hard whack."

He brought the rock down on the salmon's head. Blood smeared the rock and splattered his pants leg, and the fish went limp.

"Now for the gory part," she said and retrieved a knife from her father's tackle box.

Merritt handed the dead salmon over to her. "You show me," he said.

She snickered at him for being so squeamish and took the fish to the river's edge. She knelt with it over the water and after inserting the tip of the knife into its rear hole splayed it open. She then ran her fingers inside the length of the salmon's belly and pulled out its innards. "It's a female," she said and held up a slimy string of pink roe for him to see before tossing it into the river. She finished by hooking the salmon onto the stringer line and laying it in the stream. She rinsed her hands off in the river and stood up and gave Merritt a big kiss on the mouth.

"Congratulations," she said. "It's a beauty."

"That was great," he said. "I want to catch another."

Clara retrieved her own pole and glanced at Merritt standing on the bank, casting his line now like an expert fisherman. Sure, I've caught a man, she thought, but I want to land another Silver, and sighting a spot on the river, cast her line.

Perhaps Clara's only concern about her increasing attachment to Merritt was the time it took away from her painting—time every artist knew was precious. After each excursion with him, she would return to her apartment and see her easel standing neglected near the front window and want to cancel their next date so she could stay in and paint. At Cornish, she was enrolled in a color theory class that left her eager to test various color scales and explore the subtle shifts in hue, intensity, and tone value of each. She now recognized how much chemistry was involved in making colors, and told Merritt he ought to take a chemistry class at the UW to help her better understand the chemical compounds of the infinite number of pigments she had to memorize.

At least twice a week during her work breaks at Frederick & Nelson, she went to Seattle Art Supply to stock up on palette paper or indulge in the purchase of a new brush or two. That's where she again ran into Callie. Whereas her friend Jenny only ever wanted to talk about men and movies, Callie had no interest in either. She was only interested in art, and naturally wanted to know what Clara was working on.

"Color," Clara responded.

The dimples in Callie's fleshy cheeks deepened as she smiled. "Fascinating," she said.

"I think so," Clara replied, pleased to have impressed the woman who'd become in many ways her unofficial mentor for what she came to think of, in Callie's own words, as *la vie artiste*.

"Tell me more," Callie came right back.

Clara felt put on the spot, so she rehearsed her instructor's lesson on the six common ways of achieving color harmony and balance, beginning with analogous and ending with triadic. And to Clara's relief, Callie seemed impressed.

"So what's your favorite color?" Callie asked her.

Clara looked about the store and saw Mr. Abbott eavesdropping on their conversation. If anyone knew more than Callie Porter about the Seattle art scene—or art in general—it was Mr. Abbott. Callie had once told her that before the war, and long before opening Seattle Art Supply, he had been involved in the Federal Art Project in Seattle and taught art classes at the university. He knew just about everyone, and just about everyone knew him. So for this reason, Clara didn't mind him listening in on their conversation.

"Anything alizarin," she said in answer to Callie's question. "My friend Mary Beth says a dab of alizarin crimson makes any painting better, and I agree."

Callie seemed satisfied with this answer, as did Mr. Abbott, who resumed reading his newspaper.

Yet when Callie took hold of Clara's elbow and leaned in close so Mr. Abbott couldn't overhear, Clara feared she was going to ask her about Eliot or maybe even Guy. Since reuniting with Merritt, she hadn't given either a thought, preferring to let what had passed between them both fade into the unspoken past. So when she heard Callie whisper how she and Bernadette were forming a new organization of women painters and wanted her to join, Clara was relieved.

"Sign me up," she said.

NINETEEN
Merritt, Fall 1946

"How can you work for that strikebreaker?" Clara's brother demanded of Merritt. Though he and Clara had been dating for several months already, she had only recently invited him to Sunday dinner to meet her family.

Merritt could tell that Clara's brother treated her rather severely. He commended her for the relief work she'd done during the war, even showing off the certificate she'd received from the American Red Cross for knitting more servicemen's socks than anyone in all Seattle. But he also dismissed her artwork and frowned on her job at Frederick & Nelson. Worst of all, he nagged her about neglecting the teachings of the Mother Church and not attending Sunday services.

Clara had just stepped into the kitchen, leaving Merritt alone with him for the first time since they'd arrived at the family's West Seattle house. To this point, Ken had been a paragon of civility, but after hearing Clara mention again that Merritt was a Teamster, he dropped all pretense of welcoming him. He said he was just grateful their father wasn't home yet, explaining how Mr. Hamilton had worked most of his life on the waterfront and had always been a loyal, active unionist—International Longshore and Warehouse Union—despite years of Teamster opposition to the ILWU. He went on to tell Merritt how their father had purchased the modest two-story house they sat in with his hard-earned union wages and had eventually saved enough to buy the print shop where he'd worked as a printer's devil since the big strike year of '34.

Merritt remarked on how admirable this was and iterated that he shared Ken and Mr. Hamilton's belief in a strong union.

"What of it," Ken pressed him. "Do you even know who you're working for? Beck has sold more working men down river than all the big-time employers put together."

"Those are strong words," Merritt replied, wishing to avoid a confrontation with Clara's hard-nosed brother, but also unwilling to stand by and let him hurl insults at him. "The union does right by its members. Dave Beck sees to that. He's always gotten the workingman a square deal."

Ken glowered at him, and Merritt could see what he was thinking—that he didn't even drive a truck but was just some lowly desk jockey. It didn't help Merritt's case either that he'd been a swabby in the Navy. He remained seated on the living room sofa as Ken stood up and paced the room.

"See," Ken said, pointing his finger at Merritt, "that's where you're all twisted up. Sure, Beck takes care of his own. He's the big papa bear. Mess with his cubs and he'll maul you to death. But step outta line, maybe call a wildcat strike if your local's getting screwed over, and he'll eat his own, too. God forbid the boys down at the Chamber of Commerce get their feathers ruffled."

"It's a big union," was Merritt's only response, growing anxious as Clara's brother turned more livid. "Someone's got to be in charge."

"It's the sweetheart deals he makes with the employer associations that's the trouble," Ken said. "He doesn't leave the workingman any leverage."

Everyone knew Beck opposed the use of strikes to settle labor disputes, which was the exact opposite of Harry Bridges, leader of the ILWU, who believed the strike was the employees' primary means in forcing concessions from management. In all honestly, though, pro-strike or not, Merritt didn't want to have this debate with Ken—not now at least, when he wanted to show Clara how well he could get along with her family.

When she finally returned from the kitchen, she seemed to size up the situation and shot her brother a sharp glance to warn him off, then came up to Merritt and gave him a kiss on the forehead.

"Can I help in the kitchen?" he asked, reaching out for her hand.

"Don't be silly," she said and patted his forearm. "I'll call when dinner's ready. I just came in to see if Father was home yet."

When she went back to the kitchen, Ken sat down in his father's armchair beside the Philco radio—the identical radio, Merritt noted, to the one his own family had sat around when the news of the attack on Pearl Harbor broke.

"Where were you in the war?" he asked Merritt. "I was 3rd Infantry Division. Africa, Italy, and France."

"Seaman First-Class, aboard the USS *Washington*, BB-56," Merritt replied.

"The Pacific?"

"Saipan, Leyte, Okinawa," he said. "The Emperor's backdoor."

Ken eyed him as if wondering how much action he'd really seen or whether he was just boasting. "I was with Patton in the desert before we landed in Sicily and fought our way up the boot," he went on.

Merritt just nodded. "I hear the Chianti over there is choice," he said with a note of sarcasm that made him think Ken might jump up and punch him in the nose.

"I don't drink," he replied. "And I don't go around chasing skirts either."

Merritt took offense at this and sat forward on the sofa. "Listen," he came back, "I admire Clara very much. You don't have to go questioning my motives."

Ken bit his lower lip and said, "I'm her big brother, the only one she's got."

Merritt said he appreciated that fact and repeated that his intentions toward Clara were honorable. "At any rate," he added and looked Ken straight in the eye, "you might have noticed she's not the kind of girl to have the wool pulled over her eyes—not by me, you, or any other fellow."

"And don't try your luck," Ken said. "I've seen what you bluejackets are like once you start combing the beach. That's all good and fine for shore leave in Manila, but it's different here at home."

"Look here—" Merritt shot back, feeling his temper rise.

Yet before he could go on the front door opened and Clara's father walked in. He appeared tired as he removed his canvas coat and wool cap and hung them on the coat rack by the door. He then stepped into the living room, and Ken and Merritt both stood up to greet him.

Merritt reached out his hand. "Merritt Driscoll, sir."

Clara's father shook his hand. "Glad to meet you, Merritt." He wore a blue work shirt and work pants. His hands, hardened by his many years on the docks and in cargo holds, were ink-stained, the knuckles like black drawer knobs. He had a full head of gray hair that was quite shaggy about the ears and the scruff of his neck.

Clara came into the dining room with silverware and glasses, set them on the table, and entered the living room to give her father a kiss on the cheek. When she asked if he and Merritt had been introduced, her father nodded. "Good," she said. "Dinner's almost ready."

Ten minutes later they were all sitting down to Mrs. Hamilton's pot roast. The dinner included browned potatoes, boiled peas and carrots, and Hawaiian sweet rolls. When a pitcher of ice water was passed around, Clara's mother asked Merritt if he would rather have a glass of milk.

"Water suits me fine," he answered, and added, "'The only drink for a wise man,' as Henry David Thoreau said," and instantly regretted the comment, knowing how egg-headed it probably sounded to Clara's father and brother.

Clara went on to tell the table about the baseball game she and Merritt had gone to earlier in the summer. Throughout the dinner, everyone kept the conversation on polite subjects: the weather, Merritt's parents in Vermont, his classes at the UW, Clara's classes at Cornish, Ken's bowling league, the quilt her mother had begun now that scraps were no longer needed for war relief, the small motorboat her father planned to buy so he and Ken could go out fishing on the Sound.

At the mention of fishing, Clara bragged about the salmon Merritt had caught on the Carbon River. This made Merritt remember what he'd been planning to tell Clara and announced that the Teamsters were going to hold their annual salmon derby next Sunday and he wanted Clara to join him. "A fellow Teamster promised me a couple of spots on his boat," he said.

Yet the mere mention of Teamsters dampened the mood at the table and no one said anything further about fishing. To everyone's relief, though, the meal was almost over, and the three men waited in silence as Clara and her mother served them all rhubarb betty and vanilla ice cream for dessert.

After everyone had had a second serving on the dessert, Merritt thanked Mrs. Hamilton for the delicious dinner and offered to help with the dishes, but she just shooed him away. Then, as she and Clara cleared the table, the three men retired to the living room.

After filling his father in on a resolution recently drafted by the ILWU's Puget Sound Sub-District Council, Ken turned to Merritt and said, "I'm the council rep for Local 19. My father was one of the local's founders—back in '36. Isn't that right, Dad?"

"Ten years already," his father replied, "and still going strong. Best move we ever made, breaking with the ILA." For whatever reason, Mr. Hamilton didn't seem to have the same level of animosity toward the Teamsters that Clara's brother did. But maybe it was just his age. Merritt figured he was well into his fifties.

"The resolution renews those founding values, Dad," Ken said. "Right there in the second paragraph, it lets every new member know about our tradition of militancy and our struggle on behalf of the workingman. It also reasserts our determination to stand strong against attacks by the shipowners—" and here he paused, it seemed, to make sure Merritt heard him —"and sell-out labor leaders."

"That's good, Kenny," said his father.

"Like I said," Ken continued, "it reasserts the union's values and puts the rank and file on notice of their responsibility as dues-paying members. You know, Dad, we'll be hitting the bricks before the year's out, and it's not going to be pretty."

A wince flickered over his father's face, perhaps as he remembered past strikes and all that he'd gone through in his many waterfront battles against the maritime companies.

"We'll have to draft up demands and a strike program in the next week or two," Ken said more somberly. "Dad, we both know the shipowners won't give us a contract worth the paper it's printed on. Not unless we go out."

Merritt remained careful to stay out of this conversation. But right then, as if to let him know his Teamster presence hadn't been forgotten, Ken added, "We'll be fighting for our jobs and livelihoods while other folks are out salmon fishing."

Merritt, however, didn't take the bait. He held his tongue and waited for Clara to finish helping her mother in the kitchen.

* * *

As Ken had predicted, the waterfront strike began in October. It involved several unions under an umbrella organization called the Committee for Maritime Unity, with the largest union, the one driving the strike, being the ILWU. It was a straightforward economic strike, with the unions demanding a 15-cent-per-hour wage increase to keep up with the rampant inflation hitting the country since the end of the war. The increase seemed fair enough, but a *Seattle Times* columnist who condemned all union activity insisted these kinds of wage demands had sent the country's economy into a price-wage spiral. The economy would never get back on track, the columnist railed, until employers held their ground against the radical element in unions such as the ILWU.

Merritt summarized this argument to his friend J.P. as they walked across the campus toward the auditorium where Harry Bridges would be appearing that evening. J.P. knew all about Bridges. His talk was sponsored by the Student Progressive League, a campus group J.P. belonged to. A cold rain sliced across their path as they made their way. Merritt turned up the collar of his overcoat and pulled the brim of his new felt hat down over his brow. He walked with one hand stuffed in his coat pocket, the other clutching his canvas book bag, and angled himself into the wind and pelting rain.

"It's demagoguery like that that's going to get the Republicans elected next month," J.P. barked. He didn't wear a hat, but the rain rolled right off his well-combed, oiled hair. The sleek capeskin jacket he wore didn't fare so well. It was splotched by every drop that hit it. "And then we're going to see a backlash against the unions the likes of which we've never seen before. Why isn't this guy at the *Times* telling employers to cut back on profits? What about the price-profit spiral?"

J.P had a good point. All the same, it disheartened Merritt that little more than a year after the war had ended the country was ripping itself apart over these issues. Where was the national unity that had whipped Hitler and broken Hirohito? Where was the good will and civility that followed V-J Day? After laying waste to the Axis powers, it seemed that all we wanted to do now was tear at each other's throats. Shouldn't there be some kind of moratorium on such acrimony? Two years, say—just half the time it took to win the war?

"You're full of shit," J.P. told him as he offered up this idea. "The struggle never ends. The war was just another part of it."

They reached Meany Hall on the edge of campus. As they approached the entrance, they crossed in front of a dozen students carrying placards denouncing Bridges as a Communist and calling for his deportation back to Australia where he came from. J.P. was familiar with all the campus groups and told Merritt this bunch called themselves the Student Freedom Alliance. "Student Fascist

147

Alliance is more like it," he added loud enough for one of the protesters to hear.

"We should deport you, too, Hughes," the student-protestor shouted at him. "You and Bridges can sit at Stalin's feet in Russia where you belong."

"Go to hell, Brinkley," J.P. answered as he and Merritt entered the hall.

Inside, Merritt removed his hat and coat and shook off the rain. A half hour remained before Bridges' talk and the auditorium was less than half full. He wanted to use the time to read—there was always more reading than he could keep up with—but J.P. insisted on passing the time bad-mouthing groups like the Student Freedom Alliance. He told Merritt that Brinkley had been in his History of Politics class last term and would never shut up. "Kept saying how Communism was the oldest threat to the world, no matter if the prof was talking about ancient Greece or feudal China. The guy's a fanatic. And worse still, his old man's running for the state legislature."

The 300 or so seats in the auditorium gradually filled with a mix of students, professors, and weathered-looking men Merritt figured were longshoremen and ILWU officers. When he took a notebook from his book bag, J.P. asked what he was doing and Merritt told him about the assignment Beck had given him.

J.P. shook his head. "So he has you spying for him now?"

"I'm writing an article for the newsletter," Merritt retorted, though he wasn't sure his write-up on Bridges' talk was actually meant for the newsletter since Beck wanted him to give it straight to Mrs. Kotin, his secretary. "Whatever happened to your 'one big union' talk? Don't you think chauffeurs and helpers care about what a leader like Bridges has to say?"

"Do what you have to, brother," was all J.P. said and turned his attention to surveying the crowd.

J.P.'s dismissal of him reminded Merritt why he was often of two minds about his friend. While he admired J.P.'s commitment to progressive causes, this same commitment often came across as fanatical as Brinkley's out there in the rain. It seemed J.P. rarely bothered to scrutinize his own positions, just those of others. The fact that he hailed from the family of a prominent Seattle physician didn't help either. Although such a privileged family background in and of itself didn't compromise or contradict J.P.'s political views, Merritt couldn't help but sneer every time J.P. climbed onto his soapbox. Of course, J.P. was a good-hearted sort, and Merritt knew this, which is why he sometimes thought of him like Hal from Shakespeare's *Henry IV*. J.P. was the handsome, conflicted prince of the Northwest.

The auditorium had nearly reached capacity when Merritt spotted Ken Hamilton and his father walk in and take a seat about ten rows below where he and J.P. sat. Their being such stalwart members of the union that Bridges had founded, it only made sense they would come out for his talk. No doubt Bridges would also be visiting all the ILWU locals in the region as well. For an instant Merritt wondered if he should have invited Clara along, too, but thought better of it. He was here on business, and if he knew Clara's brother at all—which he felt he did after their Sunday dinner together—she already got an earful of union talk every time she went home.

Eventually three men walked onto the stage from the wings and the audience settled down. There were three chairs to one side and a podium center stage. Two of the men sat down while the third stepped to the podium. He introduced himself as Professor Anderson from the Department of Political Science, someone Merritt knew of but had never taken a class with. On behalf of the Union of University Faculty, he welcomed everyone to that evening's talk. He then introduced Mr. Kyle Schays from the C.I.O.—"That's Congress of Industrial Organizations," he added as an aside and the audience laughed—who would introduce the evening's speaker. Mr. Schays came to the podium, thanked Professor Anderson, and recounted his long association with the ILWU in Washington State. Then, without further delay, he introduced Harry Bridges, president of the International Longshore and Warehouse Union.

Bridges sprang from his chair, strode to the podium, and shook Kyle Schays' hand as the audience applauded the union leader. He was a gaunt-looking man in a ten-dollar suit that hung on him like excess drapery. His large beaked nose dominated his narrow face. Of average height, he struck Merritt as a very unimposing man. Yet he was full of energy, and his eyes were sharp and intense.

Just as Bridges faced the audience and the applause subsided, a man jumped into the center aisle below where Merritt and J.P. sat and began cussing Bridges, calling him a Commie stool. Everyone's attention was directed to the outburst and several of the longshoremen types in the audience—including Ken Hamilton—leapt from their seats, collared the man, and hustled him out of the auditorium.

Bridges leaned over the podium. "That's alright," he said into the large microphone. "I get that all the time. But the Supreme Court of the United States, on which Washington State's own William O. Douglas serves as Associate Justice, doesn't buy it."

The statement brought cheers and thunderous applause from the audience, and Bridges smiled and raised a hand to settle everyone down. The reference, as Merritt understood it, was to the Supreme Court's recent decision to overturn a lower court's ruling to deport Bridges as a confirmed Communist, which he denied he ever was.

"But I'm not here to talk about me," he went on. "I'm here to talk about the hardworking people of all races, creeds, religions, and yes, political persuasions who make this country what it is—a land of liberty, opportunity, and justice for every man, woman, and child. A land where a fair day's work earns a fair day's pay." His voice went up with this last phrase, and again he had to settle the audience down. Merritt soon felt as if he'd come to a political rally rather than a university talk. Bridges' charisma was undeniable, enhanced by the trace of an Aussie accent.

Bridges thanked Professor Anderson for inviting him to the University of Washington. He also thanked Kyle Schays and joked about how they'd had their differences in the past. "And probably will again tomorrow when we sit down at our new building on—I'm not making this up, folks—Union Street." He commended the Committee for Maritime Unity for holding firm during the current lockout. "The Committee was formed on the fundamental principle that all maritime workers, irrespective of craft or affiliation, must unite and work together to protect themselves against the growing power of the shipowners' organizations. That's what's at stake, and that's why the CMU will prevail."

Bridges then turned his talk from the on-going turmoil on the waterfront to broader political issues. He remarked how President Roosevelt once said the Department of Labor should be called "the Department *for* Labor" and castigated President Truman for weakening worker protections implemented under his predecessor. He condemned the Department of Justice for kowtowing to the red-baiters and accused J. Edgar Hoover of being the greatest enemy that free-speech and justice-loving citizens of this country ever faced. He concluded by slapping his palm down on the podium and declaring, "Whereas Roosevelt lived and led, Truman concedes and cowers! Yet if workingmen stand by their union—as we're seeing done this very day by the brave maritime workers on Puget Sound—we won't ever go back to those dark days of slavish exploitation, but will continue the march forward, into the future, toward what's rightful and just."

Most of the audience, including J.P., rose to their feet to give Bridges a standing ovation, while Merritt remained seated, transcribing Bridges' remarks into his notebook. Bridges acknowledged the applause with a smile and a nod, waved to the audience, and walked off the stage followed by Anderson and Schays. As soon as he was gone, the audience members began to gather their hats and coats from off their seats and disperse. Then, when Merritt stood up, he saw Ken Hamilton standing in the aisle, looking up at him. Carl Hamilton was already half way out the hall, being pushed along by everyone making their way to the exit. Merritt raised a hand to wave to Clara's brother, but as he did so, Ken turned about and pushed his way through the crowd toward his father.

Two days after Bridges' talk, Merritt handed his typed account to Mrs. Kotin to give to Dave Beck. He didn't know whether he would hear anything back on it or not. J.P.'s remark about spying for Beck stuck in the back of his mind, but he tried to dismiss it. It was a public event after all, and he would have gone whether Beck asked him to or not.

In any case, when he returned to his apartment building that evening he didn't want to think any further about labor unions or employer association, longshoremen or Teamsters, C.I.O. or A.F.L. He only wanted to think about Clara. He was more and more weighing the prospect of marriage—and sex—and whether these two events might be in the near future for them. This is where his mind was when he opened the brass door to his mailbox in the lobby of his building and found a hand-addressed letter to him. He thought it might be from his mother or father at first, or maybe his older sister, but he didn't recognize the handwriting. Then he recalled the last time he'd received a letter that didn't have a return address on it and his breath shortened.

He waited until he was upstairs, behind his apartment door, before opening it. He tore open the envelope, unfolded the letter, and read the five short sentences of the unsigned letter.

> *We never figured you for a traitor to the union. Why else would you be sitting up there writing down everything the Commie bastard said? We know about your girlfriend and her longshore brother. The father too. The ensign sends his regards.*

Merritt was stricken sick. It was the same sonuvabitch who'd come after him almost three years ago. Now, whoever the person was, it appeared he belonged to the same union as Merritt and again had it in for him. He tried to remember all the Teamsters he'd processed into the Navy that one particular day back at the Recruitment Station. It could well be one of those fellows, though that seemed hard to imagine. For a moment, he thought it might even be the guy from the Pre-Sep Center who'd set him up with his job at Vitamilk. But nothing he knew of the guy would lead him to believe he was the blackmailing type. It was someone else, he was certain of it—which meant it could be almost anyone.

Although he'd put the incident with Ensign Rivard far behind him, he knew it would not go well for him if people found out about it. Admitting to such a transgression would be worse than declaring himself a card-carrying member of the Communist Party. That's just how it was. And if found out, he might as well leave the country. Mr. and Mrs. Hamilton, Clara's brother Ken, his friends J.P. and Sid, his professors, other union members, even Beck . . . he wouldn't be able to face any of them again. And as for Clara, what woman could bear to know such a thing about the man she was dating, the man who hoped to marry her? It would be too much for her. His only recourse would be to call everything off, just as he had the first time, and slink back to Vermont hoping his parents never learned about it.

He found the pint of Irish whiskey he kept in a bottom kitchen drawer, poured several fingers into a water glass, and threw it back. His thoughts focused on Clara still. He was convinced that what he felt for her was the genuine article. I'm in love, he thought. None of the rest mattered. He would quit his job and the union tomorrow if it would preserve what they had. They could move to California and never look back.

He threw the letter into the wastebasket, changed into his pajamas, and sat down with pen and paper to write Clara a letter expressing once and for all his true feelings to her. Shakespeare still stirred around in his head from his English 300 class, so he tried quoting from Sonnet 43—*All days are nights to see till I see thee, /And nights bright days when dreams do show thee me*— and added to this—quite boldly, he thought—a quote from Emily Dickinson's most racy poem—*Wild Nights – Wild Nights / Were I with thee / Wild Nights should be / Our Luxury!*

Yet it sounded all so pretentious. So he tried again, this time in his own words. But nothing came out right. Everything sounded too goopy. He tried to keep it simple and just describe Clara's beauty . . . her skin so soft and fine, the gentle plane of her forehead, the subtle slope of her cheeks, her moist and tender lips, the sweet fragrance of her hair. This seemed to work better, so he endeavored to be a bit more risqué. He described the supple hollow at the base of her neck, the full and inviting curve of her bosom, the thrill to his fingers as he caressed her forearm, the thrill to his lips when he kissed her . . . and then crossed this out too.

He put his pen down, flopped into his reading chair, and picked up the hefty Frederick & Nelson catalog that sat on the floor. Clara had brought one with her last Wednesday to their meeting at the basement lunch counter. She'd leafed through it showing him her illustrations, without the least embarrassment pointing out the nightgowns and undergarments she'd illustrated. Then, after she took the elevator back to the fourth floor and he was leaving the store, he stopped at the customer service counter and picked up a copy of the catalog to take home with him.

Perusing her illustrations now, it was easy for him to imagine Clara as one of the fine-figured ladies she'd drawn. He could sense the warmth of her body beneath the long cotton nightgown of the brunette on page 278. With a pull of the ties that formed the pretty little bow at the neck, the delicate knot came undone, and as he gave each string a gentle tug, the neckline fell away. He reached down and slipped his hand beneath the hem of the nightgown, slid his palm over her ankle and calf, then farther up to that most tender recess just behind her knee, then farther up still to her silky inner thigh, and just as she cooed her acceptance of his caresses, he stepped back and pulled the long, blue-and-white nightgown up over her head, mussing her hair and exposing her splendidly bare body and . . . .

He let the catalog drop to the floor, and, after crumpling the letter he'd been writing to Clara and tossing it into the wastebasket, climbed into bed and buried his anger, shame, and frustration into his pillow.

TWENTY
Clara, Fall 1946-Winter 1947

When Clara won the Juried Art Competition at Cornish for Best Portrait—a bright and boldly outlined rendering of Guy Anderson seated on a piece of driftwood in front of his home in La Conner—Merritt took her to a restaurant to celebrate. She dolled herself up special for the occasion. She wore a powder-pink satin dress with rounded shoulders, the waist cinched with a black leather belt that complemented her pair of black open-toe heels with ankle straps. She also donned a pair of wide gold earrings and applied a glistened crimson lipstick. The whole outfit made her feel like one of her own illustrations.

All Merritt kept saying was how stunning she looked. He also apologized for bringing her to such an unclassy place, a seafood restaurant called Skipper's where the windows were portholes, lanyards hung from the ceiling, scale models of sailing ships adorned the shelves, and the tabletops were hand-painted sea charts. Yet Clara told him she loved it.

They ordered a plate of oysters to start them off, and when their drinks arrived Merritt raised his glass. "To Best Portrait," he toasted. "And the most beautiful artist ever."

Clara accepted the toast and they clinked glasses

When their entrees came, she dug right in. As Merritt asked about the Cornish competition, she gave short, neutral answers and kept eating. However, when he came around to asking about her prize-winning portrait, his tone shifted and his voice sounded almost quivering. "Do you know Guy Anderson through your art classes?"

Thrown off guard by the question, she avoided eye contact and took a sip of wine. "A friend introduced us two years ago," she said. "He's quite well known. Maybe one of the most famous painters around. He also visited my studio class once."

Merritt wanted to know more, though. For the past week, Clara noticed, something had gotten into him that made him more insistent toward her, yet at the same time more rueful and apologetic. The change was not pleasant, and tonight was no different. He wanted to know how well she knew Guy and why she'd chosen to paint a portrait of him. He also wanted to know why she set it where she did. Clara suspected he only wanted to know, just as Eliot had, whether she'd had sex with Guy.

"Did he pose for the portrait?" he asked.

"I sketched him first," she said. "In my sketchbook, as I always do. Then made the painting from memory." She stared at the stem of her wine glass and wondered how much she should tell him, how much he deserved to know. She liked Merritt—maybe even loved him—but how much of one's past was a person obliged to divulge? She had never regretted her affair with Guy and she wasn't going to start now. Nor did she believe admitting it before Merritt would do either of them any good.

"It's a wonderful painting," he said.

"Thank you."

"La Conner looks like a beautiful area."

"It is."

"Do you think I'll ever meet him?"

"*Merritt*," she exclaimed, becoming fed up with him.

"I'm sorry," he said. "I guess I'm just jealous."

"You needn't be," she said, trying hard not to sound peeved at him, which she was. "Would you like me to paint your portrait?"

"And ruin your reputation? Never."

They laughed at this and she could see it was going to be okay between them. She reached across the table and took his hand. "I care for *you*," she said, and then asked him if they were going to have dessert.

They each ordered the Key lime pie and the conversation moved on to other subjects. Clara told him how Frederick & Nelson was planning a huge holiday bash for the unveiling of their Christmas window display. "I want you to come. It'll be great fun."

Merritt scowled at the suggestion. "There may be something in the Teamster contract about socializing with window dressers."

Clara slapped his wrist. "They're called 'designers,'" she corrected him. She then asked if instead of dancing they might go to a late show at the Fifth Avenue Theater after dinner. She wanted to see the new Ingrid Bergman and Cary Grant movie. There was just something about Ingrid Bergman, she said. She didn't know what it was, but she really liked the actress.

Clara invited Merritt to her family's house in West Seattle for Thanksgiving dinner three weeks later. Both her mother and father accepted him now as a regular feature in her life, though her brother was another story. Ken harped on Merritt about his job with the Teamsters, pestering him about Dave Beck's condemnation of the recent ILWU strike, which had ended after two short weeks. In turn, Merritt frustrated Ken by insisting he didn't have an opinion

155

on the matter, that he was just a paper pusher and didn't get involved in policy decisions.

Clara was disappointed when Merritt told her he was returning to Vermont to spend the Christmas holiday with his parents. She forgave him, though, when he explained how his parents wanted him to move back East and the trip was just to placate them. Before he left, however, Clara made him go to Frederick & Nelson with her to have their picture taken with Santa Claus, one of the store's long-standing traditions, and he promised to hurry back in time to spend New Year's Eve with her.

Over the holiday they spoke long-distance on the telephone only once, yet Merritt kept his promise and returned the day before New Year's Eve. That evening he picked her up at 7:00 and took her to Skipper's for dinner, after which they went dancing at the Palomar Ballroom. Then, an hour before midnight, they picked up a bottle of champagne from his apartment, drove to Lake Washington, and wrapped themselves in a blanket on the grassy shore as the clamor of the New Year's celebration crescendoed throughout the city.

Clara was beginning to feel everything was right in the world until three weeks later she received the devastating news of Eliot's death. It was Callie who phoned to tell her. He'd committed suicide just days earlier, Callie explained. She was reluctant to give many more details, yet Clara insisted, saying she needed to know, to have the finality of it. Callie replied that she knew only what a mutual friend from Spokane had told her. Eliot had been released from the hospital in the fall and was living back home with his parents just outside of Spokane. He'd set up a studio space for himself in a back shed and seemed to be doing okay until the holidays rolled around, at which time he started drinking heavily and arguing with everyone again. Then earlier that week, he went to the shed and—who knows why—ingested a whole bottle of varnish remover. He followed it with a canister of bromide sulfate that he found stored in the shed. The bromide sulfate dissolved his insides and choked him as it fomented back up into his throat. After he ran out of the shed in a panic, his mother saw him from the kitchen window writhing in the yard and ran out to help him, but there was nothing she could do. He was dead by the time his parents got him to the hospital.

"His folks are Catholic and don't look kindly on suicide," Callie finished. "So they buried him yesterday without any kind of service."

Clara thanked her, hung up the telephone, and crumpled to the floor. She knew she couldn't have done anything to help Eliot, that he would have continued down his self-destructive path with or without her. Yet this knowledge did nothing to relieve her sorrow.

She didn't know how long she'd been on the floor when the telephone rang. She picked it up and heard Merritt's voice on the other end. She tried to sound composed, yet when he asked whether something was wrong, she told him how she'd just learned an old friend had died. She'd never spoken to him about Eliot. While she might refer to him now and then in casual conversation, she never told him who Eliot was, figuring he was smart enough to figure it out. Now she told him everything, and when she finished he sounded confused and even a little hurt, but then told her he would be right over.

A half hour later Clara met him outside in front of her building. "Thank you for coming," she said. She was bundled in her wool overcoat, a scarf tied around her head. "Can we just drive somewhere?"

Merritt opened the car door for her, and after they'd both gotten in, he asked where she wanted to go.

"I don't know," she said and looked across the dark seat at him.

"Are you hungry?" He sounded subdued, and she could tell he was uncertain how to respond to the whole situation. She had probably pulled him away from his studies, and maybe he just wasn't keen on comforting her over the loss of an ex-boyfriend.

"No, are you?"

He shook his head and put the car in gear. "Let's just drive then," he said.

They remained quiet as Merritt drove over the top of Queen Anne Hill and took the on-ramp to the new George Washington Bridge spanning the canal. In the six months since the bridge had opened, three people had jumped to their deaths from it. She looked down at the Fremont neighborhood to the left, remembering Eliot's garage studio, and thought how if he'd been living in Seattle he might have been one of those jumpers.

They drove up Aurora Avenue and circled Green Lake. The mile-round lake had a thick layer of fog rising from its surface. Streetlamps emitting a diffuse yellow glow ringed its parameter. On sunny days people fed the ducks, sat on benches, and strolled about the grass-lined neighborhood lake. At this midnight hour, in late January, the area was deserted.

When Merritt pulled into the field house parking lot and turned off the engine, Clara slid across the seat and held his arm. She kissed his cheek, which was coarse with whiskers, and he removed his glasses and rubbed his eyes. They both looked out through the windshield at the placid water until Merritt put his glasses back on and asked, "Do you want to drive some more?"

"Do you mind?"

It was approaching 1:00 a.m., yet he drove around the north end of the lake and returned to Aurora Avenue, which near Greenwood, north of the city limits, turned into U.S. Highway 99, the route she and Eliot had taken to La Conner. The recollection held no sentimental value for her now, and just made her sad.

When they were nearly to Edmonds, she asked Merritt if they could stop.

"There's a diner up here somewhere," he said.

When they passed the Pine Lodge Motel, advertising "Tourist Cabins," Clara turned to him and said, "We could get a room if you like." She didn't know if this was right or not, and she certainly didn't know how Merritt would respond.

He glanced at her and turned his eyes back to the road, driving past the motel. At the next traffic light, he leaned toward her and said, "Coffee would be a better idea, don't you think?"

"Okay," was all she could say in response, and as the traffic light turned green and they drove on, she stared out her window at the passing businesses—Camden Used Tires, Triple-X Root Beer Drive-In, a Union 76 service station, Chubby-Tubby War Surplus—until they came to an all-night roadside diner and Merritt pulled into the parking lot.

For the next hour or more they sat side-by-side in a booth in the front window and ate blackberry pie and ice cream and drank coffee that Merritt said tasted like "axle grease." With her head hung low, Clara apologized for what she'd said earlier about getting a room, but Merritt just laughed it off. He appreciated the thought, he told her, and ordered seconds on the pie and ice cream.

BOOK THREE

Crazy Kind of Daze

Seattle Waterfront, 1934

When the newly elected mayor, Charlie Smith, came into office at the end of May, he started talking tough right off and set a June 14 deadline for settling the longshoremen's strike or else. He then put the entire Seattle police force at the ready to protect the strikebreakers. When President Roosevelt appointed an arbitration board that was thrown into the mix of the coast-wide negotiations, Mayor Smith delayed sending in his troops for a few days longer. But on June 20, he changed his mind and decided it was time to force open the city's port. The showdown, he told the Seattle newspapers, would come at Piers 40 and 41—the two piers Carl worked.

It was a mild morning when the Police Chief moved his men in, 300 uniformed bluecoats along with several dozen of what the newspapers called "special deputies," all toting riot clubs, shotguns, tear gas grenades, and the usual arsenal of sidearms. A squad of twenty mounted coppers was also trucked in. With 200 strikers looking on, the police formed a perimeter in front of the two piers, behind which they set up a camp of cots in the warehouses and cook tents and shower stalls beside the tracks. They also took up rear positions, placing gunny bales on the Garfield Street Bridge overlooking the entrance to the terminal and positioning themselves behind the bales with Tommy guns. Motorcycle and sidecar units patrolled the roads leading to and from Smith Cove. Within two hours after the police brigades secured the Smith Cove piers, scores of strikebreakers started being ferried in on tugboats.

Carl joined the chorus of the union loyal shouting them down. A few men hurled rocks over the police lines at the scabs clambering off the tugboats and onto the piers.

"Do yeh wanna know how Webster's Dictionary defines a scab?" asked Marty Cole, a hatchtender whose gang Carl had worked on in the past. He liked Marty, who was smart and kept a good sense of humor about the struggle.

"You bet," Carl answered.

"I'll tell yeh," Marty said. "According to Webster's, a scab is, and I quote, 'a mean, dirty, paltry fellow.' I looked it up last night."

"That sounds right to me," said Carl.

That night the ranks of picketers swelled to more than 1,000 longshoremen and strike supporters as reports got around of the stand-off at Smith Cove. They lit bonfires on the tracks, greased the rails, and jimmied the switching gear, all to keep railcars from reaching the piers. They also cut power and telephone lines, and near the on-ramp to the Garfield Street Bridge leading into Smith Cove they turned back cars and trucks. The one truck they did allow through carried a crate of a hundred baseball bats, which the strikers swiftly distributed among their ranks. Word went out that for every striker injured, three strikebreakers would get a free ambulance ride courtesy of the union.

It was a long, tense night that followed. Morning found Carl squatting on the rails with a row of other tired strikers. While a fellow might take the opportunity to lean back against the cyclone fence and doze a few minutes, no one really slept. By daylight, everyone was cold and jittery. The women on the Strike Relief Committee had been ordered away from the terminal at midnight, so no one ate. As the morning fog lifted, the strikers knew the day did not bode well. Everyone was on edge, nerves taut. The strikebreakers had been discharging a freighter all night along the brightly-lit pier, which enraged the strikers more. They expected a string of rail cars to pull away from the pier at some point during the day, and if the picket line was going to hold, they would have to stop that train.

The sunless sky remained a steady gray as noon approached. When Carl and the other men squatting along the rail lines saw a phalanx of club-wielding policemen coming down the tracks, they were told by their strike leaders to clear out and let them pass. The policemen guarded a crew of scabies repairing the tracks. Carl watched as one policeman, in his gold-buttoned blue coat and black-visored cap, swung an ornately carved billystick about his hand and wrist like some kind of parade twirler. When the copper saw Carl watching him, he grabbed the handle of his billystick, raised it shoulder height, and looked at Carl with a smirk that said this was for him if he tried anything.

Having always been a law-abiding man who respected the men in blue—many of whom, he knew for a fact, supported the striking longshoremen—Carl wanted to pick up one of the bricks lying at his feet and hurl it at the smug sonuvabich. That's when Marty stepped forward.

"Go home and polish your night stick, why dontcha, yeh jack-happy shamus," he shouted and made an obscene gesture toward the bluecoat.

By noon, the strikers numbered 2,000 or more. When the gates to the piers opened, Carl heard someone say, "Get ready, boys, 'cause there's going to be hell to pay." A switch engine could be heard powering up. With the strikers along the tracks now outnumbering the police who had originally walked down the rail line, the mounted police moved in, side-stepping down the tracks and moving men aside with the powerful flanks of their mounts.

When the switch engine on the pier lurched forward and began to pull out of the terminal, a roar went up from the strikers. They charged the gates and within moments broke through the police lines. The foot police and mounteds swung their riot clubs at the strikers. A gang of strikebreakers counter-charged the strikers who were swarming the switch engine, pulling the engineer away from the controls, and yanking out the coupling links to pry the rail cars loose from one another. Carl joined the men from one of his old shoveling gangs overturning a freight car on one of the side tracks and trying to drag it onto the main track. They managed to overturn the car but couldn't budge it once it lay there.

With the train stopped and fighting taking place at the edge of the pier, Carl suddenly heard a series of streaming whistles overhead and looked up to see the white contrails from tear gas grenades being launched into the fray from atop the Garfield Street Bridge. The policemen retreated into the terminal as the gas erupted into plumes across the rail yard, rose into the air, and merged into a cloud above the heads of the strikers. Several longshoremen with scarves pressed to their faces and wearing leather work gloves ran into the gas plumes, seized the canisters, and lobbed them back onto the bridge.

As Carl choked on the eye-singeing gas, he heard the first gun shots. He tried to see where they were coming from and heard a dozen more shots in rapid succession. Men were yelling to take cover.

The police fell back from the worst of the rioting while the strikebreakers retreated onto the piers, where they took protection behind the police lines reforming at the gates. The strikers had kept the switch engine and rail cars from leaving the terminal and were now trying to regroup through the noxious haze of tear gas while their wounded were carried to the longshoremen's encampment beneath the bridge.

As the gas cleared, Carl recovered himself long enough to see where he was and, staggering back from the pier, spotted Marty lying on his side near the cyclone fence.

"Marty," he called and crouched beside his friend, expecting he'd been clubbed on the noggin and needed to be brought to. He put his hand on Marty's shoulder and shook him. "Hey pally, you're gonna be all right. Come on." Yet when Carl rolled Marty onto his back, his head flopped to the side and a black-red hole in the side of Marty's throat stared up at him, slow-leaking blood like a dark spring burbling over. Carl looked down the length of Marty's body and saw that he lay in a slick halo of his own blood. In an instant he took hold of Marty's left arm and hefted his body over his shoulder as if packing a 3-and-1 flour sack onto the dock and trotted with him toward the encampment.

Marty was dead weight, he could tell. One of the goon squad coppers had shot his friend in the neck, and he'd choked to death on his own blood. Beneath the bridge, Carl went down on one knee and leaned Marty's slumped body against a concrete pillar. For the first time since his infant daughter had died, he stilled himself enough to pray. He bowed his head over the rumpled, bloodied figure, closed his eyes, and said the Lord's Prayer. He then removed his canvas jacket and draped it over his friend's head, shoulders, and torso. He sat down next to the body and rubbed his still-burning eyes.

Several minutes passed before anyone came up to Carl and noticed the body lying beside him. As word spread that a man had been killed, the strikers rallied again. They threw rocks, bricks, pipes, anything they could lay their hands on at the police lined up on the bridge and behind the terminal gates. They also resumed tearing up the rail tracks until finally, climbing atop a rail car, two members of the strike committee, waving a union banner between them, managed to quail the strikers and bring the picket lines back under control.

Eventually several longshoremen came and hauled Marty's body away in a canvas sling. Carl looked down at the blood on his jacket and knew he would have to discard it before returning home to Glenora and the children.

TWENTY-ONE
Clara, Spring 1947

Clara was convinced she and Merritt had experienced something special the night of their long drive up Aurora Avenue. From that point on they were more relaxed with one another, as if they'd come to a new understanding about themselves, and so as spring returned and the weather warmed they spent more time together—at least as much as their hectic schedules would allow. One day after they drove up to Snoqualmie Falls and witnessed a wedding party coming out of the lodge there, Clara even let herself silently speculate on her own marriage prospects.

The spring season brought a torrent of activities at work that she needed to attend to. The biggest was Frederick & Nelson's plan to host twenty-five of the world's leading fashion designers and writers for six days in April to debut the '47 spring collections. The event would put Seattle on the fashion map. For the store's buyers, models, window designers, illustrators, and even floor clerks, the weeks leading up to the extravaganza turned into sheer frenzy. The store scheduled ads for every major fashion magazine in the country, which meant the illustrators were cranking out illustrations night and day. Beginning in March, Clara worked twelve-hour days. As for Merritt, he was just as busy. In addition to his overload of classes at the university, he was putting in more hours than ever at the Teamsters Hall as his responsibilities there increased. Come Saturday of each week, they were both too tired to go dancing, so Merritt would come by in his car, pick her up, and take her to a restaurant, and maybe they would see a movie afterwards. But that was it.

During the six-day fashion bonanza in late April, Clara attended more fashion shows in the Frederick & Nelson Tea Room, encountered more high-end designers, and met more associates and sycophants from the fashion industry than she'd imagined possible. She heard French and Italian spoken on the floor of the store. Seattle sidewalks bustled with the most beautifully accoutered men and women, as if the illustrations and photographs from the glossy fashion magazines had leapt off the page and onto Pine and Fourth. The window designers went all out, creating elaborate sets, with themes that included Springtime in Paris, Midsummer's Night Dream, Neptune and his Mermaids, and New York's Fifth Avenue and the Plaza Hotel. Twice each afternoon, Max staged fashion shows in the main front window, and as word got out, the shows drew more and more people from the surrounding office buildings until the sidewalks were packed and policemen had to direct traffic so that no one would get run over.

At the height of the extravaganza, a purchaser with Bloomingdale's asked Clara, strictly on the Q.T., whether she would be interested in coming to New York to work for them. "We would pay you handsomely. Double what you're making now, I'm sure of it." The woman handed Clara her business card with the phone number of her Seattle hotel on the back and asked that Clara let her know before she flew back East.

During her lunch break, Clara telephoned Merritt at the Teamsters Hall, something she'd never done before, to tell him what had happened. He must have thought she was seriously considering the job offer because after sounding pleased for her, his voice went low and somber.

"I would never take it," she promised him, and the instant the words were out of her mouth she experienced a dash of disappointment. It was Bloomingdale's after all! New York City! Fashion capital of the world! *Art* capital of the world!

Merritt said she shouldn't be so quick to make up her mind and suggested she sleep on it. But she pooh-poohed him and said she was a small-town Seattle girl and that's all there was to it.

She forgot all about the Bloomingdale's job the next day when an assignment manager from *LIFE* magazine approached her about participating in a shoot he was doing on Pacific Northwest fashions.

"You want the girls in modeling, don't you?" she asked him.

"Not at all," he told her. He'd heard she was a fisherman and they wanted someone who would look the part standing in a stream in rubber waders with a rod and reel in her hand and a wicker tackle basket slung about her neck.

Clara confirmed that she knew how to fish and so four days later—one day after the fashion extravaganza concluded—a photography crew from *LIFE* picked her up from the store and they drove down to the White River near Black Diamond to photograph her fishing. She didn't tell them that it wasn't salmon season. They wanted a *look*, authentic or not, and they got it. Two weeks later, the May issue of *LIFE* came out. It contained a half-page photo of Clara in waders standing ankle-deep in water, casting a line out into the stream. The spread also included photos of a girl on skis at Snoqualmie Pass, three girls on a motorboat on Puget Sound, and another girl holding a salmon at the Public Market.

* * *

Clara appreciated her work at Frederick & Nelson more than ever. The sewing she'd done during the war years for the Relief Committee, her understanding of fabrics and thread, her knowledge of patterns and stitching, she'd never regarded as anything other than a practical set of skills handed down to her from her mother and the other church ladies to demonstrate what a self-sufficient lot they were—and during the war how helpful they could be. In their minds the skill had nothing to do with fashion; it was solely about clothing oneself and others in as discrete and utilitarian a manner as possible. Personal expression through one's attire was anathema to the entire Christian Science enterprise. But in the world of Frederick & Nelson and beyond, fashion meant something. It was art! Clara appreciated the colors and patterns and textures of fabrics as never before. Fabric attained an aesthetic value for her. Fabric and thread were their own medium, like pastels or oils. When she sketched a new line of dresses, it was never enough for her just to view the garment being modeled in one of the store's fashion shows—though this was vital to understanding how a dress hung, how it moved, how it expressed itself. She needed to go to the back changing room after everything had been modeled and the models had all gone home and handle each dress, each skirt and each blouse, each jacket. She needed to feel the fabrics. And not just with her hands. She would slide the fabric over the soft underside of her forearms, then raise her own skirt and slide it over her calf and knee. She liked to bring it to her cheek and let it caress her skin and hold it to her nose and breath in the fabric's smell. Silk, cotton, wool, and all the new synthetics, each had a different scent and tactically left a distinct impression depending on the weave and finish. She would hold each garment at arms' length and examine its pattern, and next bring it up close and scrutinize its stitching. And the colors! It seemed as if overnight the world was making up for the drab uniformity of browns and grays it had endured during the war years. Colors and patterns appeared everywhere, in every combination.

None of the other illustrators went to the trouble she did to appreciate the fashions they drew. They made their sketches of the runway girls, colored them in back at their drawing tables, and filed them with Max. But for Clara, venturing into the apparel room became a secret quest. She anticipated it like a romantic tryst. There seemed something almost illicit in the faint thrill she experienced in giving herself over to the new garments. It seemed even mildly lewd.

This tinge of shame, of course, was the result of her Christian Science upbringing, even though a Christian Scientist would never cast shame on one for such tactile, even sensual apprehension of the material world—because shame meant acknowledging that world existed. Rather, a good Christian Scientist preferred to ignore the world's materiality as the illusory error of our unfortunate misunderstanding of God's pure, spiritual nature. Yet such notions, Clara saw plainly now, never promoted good fashion sense.

She found herself paying more mind to her own wardrobe as well. She dressed more *vividly*, as her mother said whenever she saw her in a new dress. She no longer cared what the smart set was wearing. She was determined to dress to suit herself. Her wardrobe was not extensive, yet she mastered the art of mix-and-match and would redesign pieces that had grown dull.

"You hemmed that skirt, didn't you?" her mother would remark, the question itself a form of censure.

"Be careful," Max would warn, "or next you'll be showing knee."

When on this particular morning she put on a pair of her brother Freddy's old blue dungarees (rescued from the basement) and rolled the cuffs up about mid-calf, she knew people would take notice. Anyone would recognize they were boys pants, which was no big deal, but to wear a sheer white blouse, untucked, on top.... Well, people could say what they would, she didn't care. She liked the look. She also liked wearing with it her favorite pair of white crochet gloves and, draped over her shoulder, the drab olive Army sweater she bought last month at the surplus store.

"You look great," Merritt said after pulling up to the curb and pushing open the passenger side door for her. Of course, he always said she looked great, no matter what she wore. As she scooted onto the front seat and folded her sweater in her lap, he placed a hand on her knee, leaned over, and gave her a kiss.

Merritt himself was a rather plain dresser. He always appeared neat and well groomed, paying some mind to what he wore, but not a lot. For instance, he liked to shop at Appleton Men's Wear at Second and Cherry. It's where he'd gotten the tan jacket he wore—the same tan jacket he wore every weekend—and probably those god-awful brown gabardines he wore as well. Today, though, he happened to be wearing a tie with his starched Oxford shirt, almost as if he planned to don a suit jacket and go into the office as soon as their afternoon drive was over.

"You look nice, too," she returned as he pulled into traffic and headed down the steep slope of Queen Anne Hill.

In the distance, Harbor Island where her brother worked appeared busier than ever. Every time she stepped out of her building and looked out toward the waterfront, she thought of Ken down there longshoring just as their father had for so many years (and just as Freddy had once he graduated high school) and wondered how it could be she had fallen so head-over-heals for a fashion-dim, dues-paying Teamster.

Regrettably, Ken still made clear that he did not approve of her association with Merritt and told her he would be happy to set her up with someone from the church or one of his longshore buddies. His enmity toward Merritt was wearing thin with her, and sooner or later she would tell him so.

She eyed Merritt's tie. "Are we going some place? Should I have dressed up more?"

"You look great," he repeated. He seemed tense, both hands locked onto the steering wheel, his eyes riveted to the road. Sometimes Merritt behaved just odd enough to make her think that maybe her brother was right, maybe she was making a mistake and Merritt was not the the prize her girlfriend co-workers at Frederick's said he was.

He turned onto Alaska Way heading south along the waterfront. Across the Sound, the Olympic Mountains appeared bright blue against an even brighter blue sky. Sunlight dappled the stretch of water between the waterfront and the West Seattle bluffs. As they approached the Colman Ferry Terminal, she asked, "Are we taking a ferry ride?"

"It would be a nice day for it," he answered and drove straight past the ferry terminal.

He didn't say anything more and so Clara gave up on him. She looked out at the Port of Seattle piers along the East Waterway. Before long they crossed the Spokane Street Bridge and drove down Harbor Avenue, at which point she figured he was taking her to Alki Beach. Silly as it was, every time she crossed the bridge to West Seattle, passing the Bethlehem Steel plant, it felt like a homecoming of sorts. It felt that way now as they passed the grain elevator and made their way toward Duwamish Head.

She rolled down her window and let the strong breeze swirl her hair about her head. She slung her arm across the door frame and laid her chin on her forearm. The view of the skyline across the bay never failed to fascinate her. As a young girl she liked to imagine The Smith Tower with its pyramidal crown atop the white terra cotta campanile as the residence of the Queen City princess, whom she had befriended. Together they would sail on the princess's royal yacht to Victoria, British Columbia, and have high tea with Princess Elizabeth and Princess Margaret at the Empress Hotel while their father, King George VI, visited with the Canadian governor-general. Then they would sail back to Seattle for a slumber party at the top of the Smith Tower.

The car rounded Duwamish Head and the view of the skyline was replaced by the Olympics across the Sound. She lifted her head and noticed the small bungalows tucked beneath the sandy bluff on the opposite side of the road. She pictured hunkering down with Merritt in one of them as a storm roared in from the Pacific. They would huddle before the stone fireplace and when the storm had passed they would comb the beach to see what the waves had washed up.

At Alki, Merritt made a sharp left turn away from the beach and they began winding their way up the West Seattle bluff.

"I thought we were going to the beach," she let out, becoming rather annoyed at this point.

"I want to see something first," he said. "It'll just take a minute." He must have guessed at her annoyance because the next thing he said was, "There's a park up here. At the top of the bluff. It's supposed to have a beautiful view."

"I know," she said flatly. "I've been there."

She inclined her head out the window again, closed her eyes, and let the sun warm her face. She stared into the luminescence behind her eyelids and followed the red spots that slid in and out of view, letting her head lull to one side and then the other. When she opened her eyes, Merritt was pulling up to the park. As he turned off the engine and looked away from her, she thought he appeared somewhat sad—more so than usual—and feared he was going to tell her he'd found someone else and they were through. Without saying anything, he put on his hat and came around to open the door for her. She pushed back the mass of tangles the wind had made of her hair as she stepped out of the car. A shiver came over her as soon as she stood up straight.

"Do you want your sweater?" he asked and reached across the front seat to retrieve it for her. "It's chilly up here."

She took it from him and put it on, trying to determine the right degree of outrage to express when he broke the news to her. They then walked across the grass toward the edge of the bluff. No matter what happened, she resolved, she would keep her composure.

To the west lay the open Sound with the snowy blue Olympics on the horizon, while to the east across the bay stood the growing city with the Cascade Mountains stretched out behind it. Mount Rainier reared up just to the south, and toward the north Mount Baker poked over the horizon. Out in Elliott Bay, a ferry heading toward the Coleman terminal crossed in front of a freighter making its way toward Harbor Island. As she looked about, Clara found herself excited to be here. Belevedere Park had always been one of her favorite parks in all Seattle, and it had been years since she'd been here. She took a deep breath and raced forward.

"Look," she shouted. She forgot about the pout she was working herself into and pointed to the totem pole at the crest of the park. "I remember staring at these for the longest time," she said, indicating the figures carved into the 25-foot pole. "Bear, raven, salmon, man, and otter," she recited and read aloud the plaque at the base of the pole. "Carved by the Bella Bella Indians on Vancouver Island in 1901."

Yet when she turned toward Merritt, he wasn't looking at the totem pole. Instead he stared straight at her in a way that was quite unnerving. He seemed almost catatonic. Yet before she could say anything he opened his mouth and muttered, "Clara, I've never . . . ." He then halted, and stared at her a moment longer. "I wanted to come up here," he managed to get out, "because I know how beautiful it is and because, well, just being over here, in West Seattle, where you grew up, I wanted to come up here with you . . . ."

When he removed his hat, she could see that he was perspiring. He took something from his jacket pocket, reached out to take her gloved hand in his, and dropped to one knee. "Clara Evelyn Hamilton," he said, "I want to do everything that's right by you to make you happy, and I want you to know how much I love you, so, well, I'm asking . . . will you marry me?"

Clara's first thought was what a beautiful spring day it was, perfect for flying a kite. She recovered her senses, though, saw Merritt on his knee, holding her hand, and realized she was being proposed to. She blinked several times and saw that he was still kneeling before her. The grass was wet and she worried his pants leg would get stained. Her answer to his question passed through her mind—*Yes*—and then she squeezed his hand and managed to say it—"Yes."—prompting him to look instantly relieved. He stood up and hugged her harder than he ever had.

"Are you sure,? he asked, pulling back and putting his hands on her shoulders.

"Yes," she said, and removed her glove so he could place the engagement ring on her finger.

"It goes on the left hand, right?"

"I believe so," she answered. "Between the middle and pinkie fingers."

Once the ring was on her hand, they hugged again, and Clara almost started crying. She was the first to say *I love you*, and then did cry.

"I love you, too," he said and took a handkerchief from his pants pocket to wipe her cheeks dry.

It took them a while to settle down, and at last they took a seat on a nearby bench. For a while, they just held hands. She told him how she thought he might be breaking up with her, and he said he'd never been so nervous in his life and didn't think she'd say yes.

Eventually they strolled about the grounds, joking about Merritt's tie and shirt and her faded blue denims and Army-issue sweater. Clara said she wished they had a camera so they could take a picture, and Merritt picked her a bouquet of pink rhododendron blossoms. He then turned playful, wrestling her to the damp grass and kissing her neck, ears, and nose until she couldn't stop laughing. When they brushed themselves off and returned to the bench, she held her hand up and gazed at the engagement ring, a modest diamond in a silver setting, and said it was the most beautiful ring she'd ever seen.

As the afternoon receded, she was reluctant to leave. They agreed not to talk about wedding plans just yet, that there was plenty of time for that, and Clara rested her head on his shoulder.

When the sun dropped below the horizon and they finally returned to the car, she had to remind herself she was now somebody's fiancée. The man whose hand she held was no longer the guy she was simply dating. He was the person she was engaged to be married to, and as she watched him open the car door for her, the whole notion took on a strange and inviting aura.

The next day when they announced their engagement to her parents at Sunday dinner, her mother cried and kissed them both, and her father embraced Clara and shook Merritt's hand. Her brother Ken was not there. They also made a long-distance call that same afternoon to Merritt's parents in Vermont. Clara was pleased to hear their voices, and afterwards she thought she better understood where Merritt had gotten his reticent ways.

Three weeks later, with their engagement an established fact and summer advancing fast, they ventured out of the city on their first road trip together. They called it a pre-honeymoon trip. First they drove across the mountains on the Snoqualmie Highway to Ellensburg, a stockyard town in central Washington, and headed down Highway 97 through the steep canyons formed by the Yakima River. Just outside of Yakima, they ate a picnic lunch in an orchard where the white apple blossoms blanketed the ground, then continued south through the Yakima Indian Reservation until they reached The Dalles Dam on the Columbia River. After finding a secluded spot down river from the dam, they pitched a pup tent that night, rolled out their sleeping bags, and made love for the first time.

The next morning they drove along the Columbia, stopping to look upon the massive Bonneville Dam. They continued west until they reached Willapa Bay, where they took 101 due West to the Long Beach Peninsula and ran smack into the Pacific Ocean. They drove the length of the peninsula to the rundown village of Oysterville, where they met a gray-bearded local named Nyls Sidney, who invited them to dig littleneck clams with him in the low-tide mudflats. That evening they pitched their tent just this side of the sand dunes, away from the wind, and after dark built a driftwood fire on the beach—and again made love.

The next morning, as they drove back to Seattle, they discussed the wedding and agreed that Saturday, September 6, would be the big day. They also agreed to keep the whole affair very simple. They even talked about having a family one day. Merritt said he wanted two children, a boy and a girl, and Clara joked she would like to have a third. "One I can dote on more than the rest," she said.

"We'll see," Merritt responded, and they agreed that no matter how many children they had, starting a family would have to wait until he finished his university degree and they could afford for Clara to quit her job at Frederick & Nelson.

Over the course of the three-day trip, Clara kept her sketchbook out at all times, drawing the people they met as well as the changing landscape. When she could, she brought out her watercolors and filled in her sketches—the abandoned tractor in the field near Ellensburg, the orchards outside of Yakima, the green iron bridge across the Columbia River, Nyls in the backyard of his whitewashed house, the terns and pelicans skimming the breakers that rolled in off the Pacific. Her drawing helped fill some of the long silences between them as they drove. With the windows rolled down, the cool air whipping through the car, she appreciated that neither felt compelled to speak at every turn. They both understood they had the rest of their lives for talking.

TWENTY-TWO
Merritt, Fall 1947

The anonymous letter—so threatening, even though it didn't qualify as overt blackmail—haunted Merritt for several weeks more. He became brooding and irritable. When Clara asked him if anything was the matter, if she'd done something to upset him, he realized the letter was affecting their relationship, gnawing at his ease with Clara, eroding their companionability. He imagined himself buying a handgun from one of the pawnshops on First Avenue, tracking down the bastard, and making sure he never sent another letter again—if only he knew who the person was. Plainly it was someone who saw him about town and maybe even tailed him. Knowing this made Merritt crazy with suspicion as he scrutinized everyone in the union office, just as he'd done at the Recruitment Station long ago, and tried to guess who among his fellow Teamsters had been in the Navy. Eventually he could no longer sleep for all the worry.

It was after the late-night drive he took with Clara that his thinking turned around about his predicament. Perhaps for the first time, he could see that Clara needed him, just as much as he did her. He couldn't let some two-bit blackmailer scare him into losing her again. Besides that, there was nothing he could do to respond to the threat. So his only recourse, he decided, was to ignore it. Even though he knew whoever was behind the letter would not relent—the person had already proven that—he could show the bastard he wasn't going to be intimidated. He could also show Clara how much she meant to him.

In April when Frederick & Nelson was having its big fashion brouhaha, the Penney's and Rhodes department stores in town launched their "Bag It and Bring It Home!" campaign, aimed at convincing shoppers to carrying their purchases home rather than have them delivered. This reduced each store's delivery costs, but also cut into their drivers' hours, which hurt the Teamsters who drove trucks for Penney's and Rhodes. So Merritt went to Leo to suggest the union start its own campaign: "Just Say *Deliver It!*" Reinke took the idea to Olsen, who took it to Beck, and within two weeks every truck in the city had a placard on its side panels trumpeting the slogan "Just Say *Deliver It!*" along with the Teamster emblem in the corner.

A week later Merritt received a 25-cent-an-hour raise, and this was when he knew he could finally buy Clara a proper engagement ring. He recalled how, during the war, neighborhood patrol wardens would shout, *Clara, Clara!* to give the all-clear after air raid warnings, and the all-clear call was reverberating in his head when he made his way to Pioneer Loans on First Avenue to borrow the $500 he needed for the ring. He had no collateral other than his honorable discharge—what guys called their "big ticket"—and his affiliation with the Teamsters. When the loan shark asked if he knew Dave Beck and he said, "Heck yeah, I work for Dave. He's a good man." he got his loan on the spot, no questions asked. As the saying went, if you worked in Seattle, you worked for Beck. He bought the ring from Friedlander Jewelers—a 2-karat diamond set in a sterling silver band—with a guarantee from the salesman that he could return it within two weeks with only a minor surcharge. That Sunday, though, when he went down on one knee in the park in West Seattle, Clara accepted his marriage proposal and the jewelry store's return policy was null and void.

Unfortunately, other than weekends together and their road trip in June, he and Clara hardly saw one another after that since they were both so busy. Back in February, Mrs. Kotin hand-delivered a memo to Merritt from Dave Beck requesting he contact a Professor Allen K. Feinsinger at the Wharton School of Finance and Commerce in Philadelphia who'd been contracted to do a report on collective bargaining in the trucking industry for the Labor Relations Council. "You're going to be his research assistant at this end," the memo said, and for the next several months he received Professor Feinsinger's requests, researched them, cleared his findings with Beck (via Mrs. Kotin), and sent them off to Philly.

This was just the start of all the work he had to do on top of attending classes at the university. He'd never seen people in the Teamsters Hall as frantic as they were these days. Everyone in labor was worried after the Republicans wiped the floor with the Dems the previous November in the first national election since the end of the war. The GOP took control of the House and Senate in D.C., as well as the state legislature in Olympia. J.P. blamed the red-baiting, fear-mongering newspaper columnists. Throughout the fall campaign, Republicans had promised to crack down on what they called out-of-control union radicals driving a wedge between American business and American workers, and after being sworn in they went to work.

"Labor *is* business," Dave Beck pronounced in March at the convention of the Western Conference of Teamsters. One week prior, Beck had called Merritt into his office, without Leo this time, to read a draft of his convention speech while Beck looked on from behind his desk. One sentence in particular showed Merritt that Beck was responding to Bridges' talk last November at the UW. "Some men in Labor have felt that when Franklin D. Roosevelt passed on to his reward, everything he fought for would go to wreck and ruin," wrote Beck, "but that, of course, is pure foolishness." For the most part, the speech addressed how labor and capital benefited equally from the prosperity of industry, and how, whether on the part of labor or management, power carried responsibility. Aside from a few jabs at the "crackpots of Communism," it was a measured speech, Merritt thought, and told Beck so. But when he ventured to ask whether the anti-Communist parts fit with the overall message, Beck rebuked him.

"There's nothing gratuitous about the threat of Communism," he said to Merritt. "And it's not just a one-sided threat either. Business may think itself the bulwark against the rising tide of Communism, but they promote socialism as much as Bridges and his ilk when they start leveraging government to regulate labor. The government should stay out of industry and let labor and management sort out their differences. As far as the Communists go, Mr. Driscoll, vigilance is the watchword, whatever else your professors at the university tell you."

Merritt wasn't going to argue the point with him, so he offered a handful of line edits to the speech and left it at that.

As soon as Merritt returned from his road trip with Clara, Beck had him working double-time to get ready for the big national convention set for mid-July in San Francisco—the union's first in seven years. To make more time for his job at the Teamsters Hall, he enrolled in three correspondence courses for the summer term (rather than drive to campus and attend classes), and still he could barely keep up with the work Leo and Beck piled on him. They had him researching every facet of the Taft-Hartley Act, enacted by Congress in January, so he could get word out on the new law to the entire Western Conference membership. President Truman had vetoed the legislation, calling it "a slave-labor bill," but the Republican-led Congress overrode his veto, which sent the bill into law, rescinding or compromising most of the gains made by labor since the 1930s.

Merritt wrote up bulletins on Taft-Hartley that he sent to the locals throughout the western states. He also posted updates in the monthly newsletter. Even the most disputatious unions—namely the Teamsters and ILWU—agreed the new law was a vicious attack on labor. And among the nation's labor leaders, no one railed against it more than Dave Beck. Merritt had never seen him so single-minded and driven. His florid face and undiverting eyes reminded him of Captain Ahab at the helm of the *Pequod*. He was finally seeing the hard-nosed SOB people always said Beck was, the testy, intolerant labor boss who through force of will (and muscle when necessary) strong-armed people into doing his bidding, the kind of leader who compelled people's unflinching loyalty to both himself and his cause—the two being indistinguishable—and God help you if you stood in his way.

As Beck strode down the hallway or entered a room, his compact build reinforced his imposing presence. He took on an ever more commanding role in the union hall as the date of the IBT convention approached. He kept fit by riding a stationary bicycle an hour every day in the union hall basement and lifting dumbbells in his shirtsleeves in his office. He took deep, fierce breaths through his nose, expanding his barrel chest until his pin-striped vest strained to contain him. His whole person swelled when he became angry, his round face and thick neck turning red, constricted by the starched white collar and silk tie he always wore. When he met with his confederates in his second-floor office, he took off his jacket, hung it over the back of his saddle-seat chair, and rolled up his shirtsleeves as if he were preparing to load a truck. When he stepped out of the office, even for just a word with Mrs. Kotin, he rolled his shirtsleeves down and donned his jacket.

Merritt routinely spotted city councilmen and business leaders waiting in the front office until Mrs. Kotin admitted them in to see Beck. He was the city's very own Genghis Kan, Napoleon Bonaparte, Ulysses S. Grant, and General Patton rolled into one. Even those who reviled him acknowledged he brought major contracts to Seattle that would otherwise have gone to San Francisco or LA. When it came right down to it, Beck ran Seattle. In fact, as chairman of the Western Conference, he ran the entire West, from Seattle to San Diego, Albuquerque to Billings. Though a newspaper reporter might squawk about racketeering or collusion, the reporter was drowned out by the chorus of praise, led by the Seattle City Council and Chamber of Commerce, for "our man Beck."

The more closely Merritt worked with him, the more clearly he saw how it was. Cronyism was not a dirty word with Beck. It signaled loyalty and trust. Yet since Merritt believed in the ideals of trade unionism, and because the Teamsters union did right by its members, he chalked up Beck's ethical shortcuts to the cost of doing business in the hardball world of labor politics, and asked himself, *Would I rather work for a weak union or a strong one?*

When Alec Gossett came down sick and no one stepped forward to take his place as an alternate delegate at the IBT convention, Merritt was appointed to the spot by Leo—with Beck's blessing, of course. They seemed to believe Merritt had the smarts, as well as the mettle, to go far in the union ranks. Beck's top-down approach to management welcomed college-educated talent. The boss knew that his beef squad days were over and that he needed to put the real power brokers—the lawyers and bureaucrats—to work for him, especially as he set his sights on the Teamsters general presidency. Everyone said Beck was Tobin's heir apparent, and Beck obviously thought so, too.

Beck's clear interest in grooming Merritt for higher management positions in the union, however, did not always sit well with Merritt himself. It made other guys in the office, union veterans, for instance, wary of him. One afternoon he overheard a crack about his being Beck's cabin boy. Then, the next time he saw

Alec Gossett in the basement coffee room, Alec hardly seemed sick at all and Merritt wondered why he'd withdrawn as an alternate. He even acted glad that Merritt had replaced him.

"Congrats, college, the boss thinks you have real potential," Alec said as he stirred sugar into his coffee. Alec was an intra-city hauler who'd risen from shop steward to business agent over the past half dozen years. He'd been the natural choice to serve as the Seattle local's main delegate at the convention, but the vote had gone instead to Ben Holmes, whom everyone knew was Beck's pick, even though Ben didn't have half the experience Alec did. So when Alec was named as Ben's alternate, that's when Alec came down sick. It all made sense now.

"It's quite a party," he added, sipping his coffee. "The boss spends freely. I was an alternate in '40 and I'm still recovering. Probably just as well I sit this one out."

Merritt snagged a mug from the tray beside the coffee urn. "I don't have to do much, do I? Just be there in case Ben drops out."

"Got that right," said Alec. He wore a blue snap cap pulled low over his brow. When he peered out from beneath it, he looked the way a person would expect a truck driver to look—like someone who knew how to get where he was going. So Merritt figured it must have burned him bad when Beck threw a road block in his way. "Hell, even the delegates don't do anything. It's all taken care of in committee. The delegates rubberstamp what the committees put forward and that's that."

"So you won't miss anything," Merritt said and immediately wished he'd kept his mouth shut. He waited for Alec to respond, and for an instant it looked as though he might do so with his fists. But then he swallowed some coffee and laughed.

"Got that right," he said again and walked away.

Come July, as Merritt prepared to attend the IBT convention, nearly eight months had passed since he'd received the last anonymous letter. He knew his tormentor was not the type to forget. He knew that he would hear from him again, but the more time that elapsed, the better off he was—and the more confident he felt. He was now a man betrothed to the woman he loved, and his position with the Teamsters was becoming more solidified with each passing day. So he again determined to push forward.

Mid-July he joined a group of seventeen delegates, alternates, and guests from Joint Council 28 on a charter bus donated by a Seattle bus company. "In recognition of the contributions made by the International Brotherhood of Teamsters to the City of Seattle," read a letter signed by the company president and pinned to the bulkhead behind the driver's seat. Before the bus reached

Tacoma where it was to pick up half a dozen delegates from that local, a bottle of bourbon was opened and everyone on board held out his coffee mug. Jesse Romer, a veteran delegate from the Port Angeles local, stood at the front of the bus and proposed a toast to the International Brotherhood.

"Under one banner," he declared, quoting from the union's constitution. "To build up and perfect an impregnable labor organization." When he raised his coffee mug, someone from the back of the bus shouted, "Hey Jess, what about the part where it says 'a profitable Teamster must be honest, *sober*, intelligent, and naturally adapted to the business?'"

The bus rocked with laughter as Jesse suspended his toast and shouted back, "Let's see, Roy. I'm the honest one of the bunch. You're naturally adapted to the business. And Merritt here, or so I'm told, is the intelligent one." He reached out to Merritt sitting one row back and pulled his hat down over his eyes. "And our bus driver up here, he sure as hell better be sober. So I guess that covers all the bases."

"Hear, hear!" Roy yelled, and everyone joined in and tipped back his mug.

When the bus arrived in San Francisco the following morning, Merritt and the other reps from the Joint Council checked into the Clearview Hotel south of Market Street. Beck had flown to Indianapolis two days earlier to meet with Dan Tobin and then fly straight to San Francisco. This being Merritt's first time in the beautiful city by the bay (other than being anchored offshore when aboard the USS *Washington*), he kept thinking it a shame he was here with 8,000 Teamsters and not Clara, the woman he would marry in less than two months.

At one o'clock that afternoon, General President Daniel J. Tobin gave his opening report to a packed convention hall. A lumbering, jowly man, Tobin commanded the hall. At seventy-two, he'd headed up the Teamsters for almost forty years. He reported on the tremendous growth in the union's membership and treasury. He condemned the Taft-Hartley Act and vowed the union would work night and day to run out of office every congressman and senator who'd voted for it. He excoriated the press for its deceitful and unjust reporting of union matters.

"It's because you have done things and are going to continue to do things that the press hates you," he rumbled with an upswing of his fist.

The crowd in the hall rose to its feet and cheered. Merritt sat with the Western Conference delegates about half way back from the stage. It was one of the biggest contingents there, giving Dave Beck, as everyone well knew, a significant voting block for his agenda. Merritt recognized Earl Warren, the Governor of California, on stage with Tobin, sitting next to someone he guessed was the San Francisco mayor.

Tobin went on to denounce Harry Bridges, calling him a fraud and a menace, endangering the jurisdiction of the Teamsters as well as sound business practices in San Francisco, where Bridges was based, and throughout California. Governor Warren applauded this last bit as Tobin went on to say that the Teamsters would end the interference of labor leaders like Bridges who, he declared, "were possessed of radical and un-American ideas and were dead-set on destroying free enterprise in American industry and business." The delegates booed Harry Bridges—though not as fiercely, Merritt noted, as they'd booed the Taft-Hartley Act.

There were other Opening Day addresses from the president of the AFL, Governor Warren, the San Francisco mayor, and others. There were also reports on union finances from the General Secretary-Treasurer and various Trustees, including James R. Hoffa, a Midwesterner who Merritt once heard Beck say was someone with real grit, someone who'd go far in the union. By this time, though, the delegates on the floor were dozing in their chairs or else wandering off to the nearest bar. When Jesse Romer strayed by and offered Merritt a snort from his hip flask, Merritt accepted.

"Why're you sticking around?" Jesse prodded him as someone at the podium spoke about surety bonds.

"I don't honestly know," Merritt said. "They brought me here, so I figured I should stay."

"Let's go," Jesse ordered him. "A bunch of the fellas are going up the hill to see Miss Dodo shake her bazungas at the Hoochie-Coochie Club." Jesse grabbed Merritt's sport jacket off his chair and tossed it over Merritt's shoulder. "Let's go," he repeated. "There's plenty more convention tomorrow."

By the time Merritt returned to his room that night, he was too drunk to telephone Clara. He also didn't make it to the convention hall the next morning. He slept till noon and barely got himself up in time to make it to a special afternoon session on Taft-Hartley. By the end of the session, one thing was plain in his slowly clearing head. The Teamsters were going to need a legion of lawyers not only to fight Taft-Hartley but advise union officials on how to conduct their business without being sanctioned or thrown in jail. As one lawyer put it, the future of all labor unions would be settled in the courts.

That night at the nearby Majestic Steakhouse, which Teamsters had taken over for the duration of the convention, everyone was exhausted but having a good time. The delegates from Joint Council 28 had commandeered a back room with half a dozen tables and a running tab that Leo would pick up at the end of the week. Merritt ate a ribeye steak and baked potato and even lit one of the Havana cigars from the box laid open in the middle of the table. He'd just ordered a scotch, neat, and was preparing to put his feet up on the table when Dave Beck entered the room. The dozen or so members clapped and huzzahed

179

as someone made a place for Beck at the head of the largest table. He was dressed in a perfectly tailored suit, yet as he sat down, he loosened his tie and unfastened the top button of his shirt.

"You men having a good time?" he asked the room at large, and more cheers went up. "We're really getting to see what this union's made of. This Taft-Hartley horsecrap"—This was the first time Merritt had ever heard Beck cuss—"isn't going to do us in, nosirree. We're not going to slink away or run scared with our tail between our legs. We just need to be smart is all."

The waiter came in and set Merritt's drink in front of him. He asked Mr. Beck what he would like, and Beck ordered a tonic soda with lime. When the waiter returned with his drink, Beck stood to offer a toast. "To the greatest union in the greatest nation." Everyone rose and raised his glass. "But also," Beck went on, "here's to the locals of Joint Council 28. The best this union's got."

Everyone gave a rousing "Hear, Hear!" and drank up.

"By the next convention in '52," Beck predicated, "headquarters will be in Washington, D.C."

Anyone in the room who kept an ear to the ground and followed Teamster politics knew what this meant. To wrest control from Dan Tobin, Beck needed to get the headquarters out of Tobin's home turf of Indianapolis and into the country's power center, which, if accomplished, would mean Beck would be elected General President at the next convention, slated for Los Angeles, the city that everyone had said couldn't be organized—that is, until Beck rolled into town back in the '30s with his brass-knuckled membership drive.

One of the older delegates in the room who understood the import of Beck's prediction raised his glass. "To Dave Beck," he saluted, "who made this union what it is today."

Everyone stood again and toasted, and, to Merritt's eye, Baby Beck looked positively beatific in the dark, smoke-filled backroom of the Majestic Steakhouse.

"You give all us laundry truck drivers hope, Dave," someone shouted out good-heartedly, and everyone laughed, knowing well the legend of Beck's humble beginnings.

Beck laughed right along with the rest, and still standing, he said, "I'll tell you what gives me the most pleasure," and looked around the room with a proud yet almost sinister glint in his eye. "It's that we're having this little gathering of some 8,000 Teamsters right here in that Red bastard Harry Bridges' living room." A round of hoots and howls and Bronx cheers filled the room at the mention of Bridges' name. "I'll never forget the balls of that SOB to come up to Seattle and declare his queer little union of Commie sympathizers was going to start their 'march inland' for control of our warehousemen."

Merritt, thinking of his future in-laws, refrained from booing along with

180

the rest and crouched over his drink as Beck warmed up to the subject of his arch-rival.

"Well, you know what I did?" Beck asked.

"Tell us, Dave," came a shout from one of the tables.

"I came straight down here and announced to the City Club of San Francisco that the Teamsters were launching their own 'march seaward' for control not only of the warehousemen but the dockers as well."

"Give 'em hell, Brother Dave."

"The biggest mistake the Supreme Court ever made," he went on, "was not to throw his Aussie ass out of this country when they had the chance. From what I hear, even the boys over at the CIO are wising up to him. The man can't sleep unless he's calling a strike and trying to bring down American industry. I figure some of them longshoremen would just rather not work, just let the employers give 'em their paychecks and send 'em home. And that's when unions are in trouble, my friends. It's not how this country became great. It's not how we beat the Fascists in Europe or the ruthless Japs in the Pacific."

Heads nodded at this pontifical declaration. Merritt thought again of Clara's father and brother—Carl Hamilton and Ken, both hardworking men, both longshoremen and members of ILWU, the union Harry Bridges had founded and led. Even if Clara's brother Ken was a touch crazy, and a true hothead when it came to union politics, he wasn't a radical or a Communist or anything other than a guy who stuck by his union so he could earn a decent wage and have safe working conditions. Nothing more than what the average Teamster wanted for himself.

Merritt murmured something beneath his breath and wasn't sure himself what it was until Beck looked over at him and ordered him to speak up. Merritt peered up from his drink, shocked by the attention he'd drawn to himself, as Beck watched him, waiting, along with everyone else in the room. Merritt sat up and tried to think.

"I know a coupla longshoremen," he said, "and they're all right fellas."

Beck put the fingers of his right hand to his chin, reminding Merritt of magazine photos he'd seen of Il Duce. He seemed to ponder Merritt's words and then said in a very measured manner, "Of course they are, son. They're honest workingmen, and all honest workingmen need to stick together." Beck nodded then as if to acknowledge Merritt's willingness to gainsay him.

"It's their leadership that's the problem," he went on. "Bridges believes the strike is the only way to get things done. And it's not. Were any of you old-timers here around for the General Strike in 1919?"

A couple of the older men in the room spoke up and said, sure, they'd been in Seattle for the strike in 1919 and seen it all.

"What a disaster," Beck called out. "The whole city shut down and everyone scared out of their wits. Mothers wouldn't open the front door, much less take their babies for a walk in their carriages. And it was all because of a few firebrand radicals among the I Won't Workers."

Merritt picked up on Beck's shot at the Wobblies and downed the rest of his Scotch. He wondered sometimes if Beck ever talked about anything other than the union. Did he ever go to a Rainiers' game? Or the movies? Was he like this at home with Dorothy, the wife to whom he was reportedly so faithful? Or with his dear old mams, Mrs. Mary Beck, whom he looked after as the devoted son he was?

Beck finished off his tonic in one gulp and banged the glass down on the table.

"Gentlemen," he declared, "the night's young and there're a helluva lot more Teamsters like yourself out there I need to congratulate for conducting such a successful convention."

Again, anyone with an ear to the ground knew this meant Beck had to get out and do more glad-handing. He was the lead horse for the top spot in the union, but the race had just begun.

Beck went around the room shaking everyone's hand, and when he came to Merritt, Merritt stood up and thanked him for inviting him to the convention. "I've learned a lot," he said.

"Sure you have," Beck replied, looking him hard in the eye. "You can learn as much from these men here as from any of those fancy-talking professors of yours," and with that Beck made his exit.

Over the next two days Merritt did his best to make himself sit through all the convention proceedings. There were reports and debates on everything from officers' salaries and pension plans to rules of order and pending litigation. On the third day when it came time to revise Article VI of the union constitution, cited as Duties and Powers of the General President, the Western Conference contingent came to life. This is what they'd been waiting for. Tobin was appointing "Brother Beck" to Executive Vice-President, a newly created position with direct access to the Office of the General President, elevating him above the other regional vice presidents. Once the appointment was confirmed by a floor vote, Tobin spoke. "I know that Dave Beck could double his salary in industry," he intoned, "but he's not in the labor game for dollars," and proceeded to recommend a salary increase for the new Executive Vice- President, which the Committee on the Constitution, chaired by Beck, promptly approved.

By day's end, Merritt sorely needed a break from his fellow Teamsters. He walked down Market Street to the Embarcadero, strolled along the waterfront, and then climbed the hill to Coit Tower to take in the view of the bay, including the Golden Gate Bridge, just barely visible through the in-coming fog. It was well past nightfall when he made his way down to North Beach and the intersection of Columbus and Broadway, where the blinking marquee lights, neon signs, and backlit billboards dazzled the eye. He was still chagrined at himself for going to the Hoochie-Coochie Club two nights earlier. What would Clara think if she knew? It felt like he was cheating on her. He'd never told Clara about the Va Va Voom Room in Seattle or the LaSalle Hotel or, of course, his incident with Ensign Rivard—and this would be no different.

He was angling down Columbus Avenue, headed downtown, when he passed a nondescript bar set back from the street in a small alcove. Having had nothing to drink all day, he ducked into it, took a stool at the bar, and ordered a pint of Steamer beer. A warm, yellowish light gave the place a comfortable atmosphere. Photos of boxers and baseball players hung on the back wall. He was happy just to sit and drink his beer, which tasted good, and after a trip to the head he told the bartender to pour him another.

That's when an older fellow, about the same age as Clara's father, sat down at the bar next to him. He had on a skull cap and a grey wool mackinaw, which seemed odd for July, even in chilly San Francisco. Merritt pegged him for a merchant marine, and when he caught a side view of him he saw that the man's face had a thick, grey stubble and his hands were chapped. He ordered a double gin on the rocks, which he downed in one swig, then spun about on his bar stool to face Merritt.

"You're Driscoll, right?"

Merritt turned and tried to make out if he knew the man.

"Local 174, right?"

"That's right," Merritt said, now that he knew the guy was a Teamster.

"Down for the convention, are ya?"

"Right again."

"Local 38," the man said. "Everett."

"Good to meet you." Merritt put his hand out and they shook. "You didn't come down on the bus with the Everett delegates."

"I drove down with my son. He's in the Seattle local too. Also a former Navy man."

The way the man eyed Merritt made him uneasy. He was almost smirking, and there was something oddly insinuating about him. Merritt figured the fellow knew his name from the Joint Council newsletter, or maybe recognized him from the Majestic Steakhouse. Even though the man's son was also in Local 174, Merritt likely didn't know him since the local had more than 500 members. But how, Merritt wondered, did the guy know he'd been Navy?

"Listen, Driscoll," the fellow went on, leaning in closer. "I've heard some things." He tilted back to see how Merritt took this and then leaned in close again. "Things maybe you don't want people to know about. You know, if you're wanting to be an officer in the union or, let's say, marry a nice Seattle girl. Things some people might find questionable. Know what I mean?"

Merritt stared hard at the man. Who was this guy? He didn't know if the fellow was stewed, just plain nuts, or what. Was he referring to Clara, for christsake? Because if he was . . .

"What the hell are you talking about?" Merritt said to him.

"Hey, don't get riled up," the man replied and put both hands up defensively. "I've been to the La Salle a few times myself. A man has his needs. I ain't arguing with you there, pal."

Is that what this was about? thought Merritt, for an instant having believed it might be going in a different direction. His visit to the Seattle whorehouse had been almost two years ago. It was his one and only time, out of all the opportunities he'd had while in the service, passing up on the stream of V-girls and patriotutes he'd watched other bluejackets stroll off with while on shore leave. Besides, who was this old coot to bring up his private business? It ticked him off. And then he also remembered the blackmail notes. . .

"I don't know who you are, mister—"

"Arda Smitson," the fellow answered. "Like I said, Local 38, Everett."

"—but I don't like the way you're talking." Merritt downed the rest of his pint and slammed the glass on the bar. When the bartender asked if he wanted another, he waved him off.

Smitson raised his own glass to his mouth, looked surprised to find it empty, and said, "Now why's that? We're both Teamsters, right? It's not like I'm one of Harry Bridges stoolies. So whaddaya say you buy me a drink?"

Merritt pushed away from the bar and headed for the door. It couldn't be, he told himself, and just wanted to get outside, maybe walk around the block, and then decide how he'd confront this guy.

"You know what they say in the Navy," Smitson called out to him, sneering. "If ya can't find a woman, a yeoman will do."

Merritt barely caught the remark as he pushed his way out the door, and he was half a block down Columbus before the man's meaning hit him. He stumbled to the curb, doubled over, and heaved into the gutter. Then as he straightened up and wiped his chin, he cussed himself and ran back up to the bar. But the old man was already gone.

TWENTY-THREE
Clara, Summer 1947

Clara had never seen Merritt so tired and bedraggled as when he returned from the Teamsters convention in San Francisco. It was plain to see he'd been drinking too much. A thin bloodshot line ending in a tiny red speck marred his right eye, which made her worry the stigma might burst and, as her mother used to say when her father worked the waterfront, leave her listed as "wid." in *Polk's Directory*. There was something else as well since he'd come back. He seemed beset by something. Yet if she asked about it, he said it was nothing and he was fine, just overworked. She couldn't help but attribute his moodiness to regret over their impending nuptials, stirred in him by the junket to San Francisco. Just the same, she told herself it was only temporary, something every man went through as he realized his bachelor days were numbered.

Since her engagement to Merritt, something had also come over her. She was experiencing a burst of creative energy, producing some of the best work she ever had as an artist. After returning from her road trip with Merritt, she cut back her hours at Frederick & Nelson, telling Max that she needed to prepare for the wedding, but then using all her time to paint. The Dean at Cornish gave her a larger studio space as well as a key to the building so she could work at any hour of the day or night. In May she launched a project that quickly grew into something she could not fully grasp. She started painting random portraits, but after six or seven canvases it struck her what she needed to do. She would paint everyone she'd ever known—*Everyone!*—and create a portrait gallery of her life, from her most tender years forward. And she wouldn't fuss over who she painted either. If a person's face came to her, she would paint it.

She worked fast, starting with her family, her mom and dad, her two brothers, and both sets of grandparents. She then moved on to Merritt and his parents, using photographs of them. Then she worked her way down the street from her parents' home in West Seattle. She painted Mr. Pollard, Mrs. Holmquist, and all the other neighbors she could recall. She made portraits of everyone she'd known in church, including Mrs. Berner from the Reading Room. She painted the people she knew from her apartment building, including the manager and his cranky wife. In time she started on her classmates from her years of schooling in West Seattle, painting the kids whose names she could remember as well as those she couldn't. She also painted her teachers from first grade on through high school. She painted Adel, at whose apartment in the U District she'd met Eliot. She painted Eliot, and also Don Oschner, who'd been killed in the war reporting on the Ardennes Offensive, the same campaign Freddy had died in. She painted the people she worked with at Frederick & Nelson, starting with Mr. Boykin and Jenny and Max and working out from there, and the people she knew at Cornish, including Mark Tobey and the Dean. She painted her favorite vendors down at the Pike Place Market, such as the Italian butcher who broke into song every time she approached his counter to buy a small pork chop or minute steak for dinner. (To her dismay, the Seattle City Council had recently passed an ordinance banning vendors from singing in the market and now, in protest, the butcher only mouthed the words.) She also painted Mr. Abbott from Seattle Art Supply, who continued to give her generous discounts. She painted friends of her father, guys he knew from the waterfront who'd been like uncles to her when she was growing up. She painted Merritt's friends J.P. and Sid, and even his boss, Leo Reinke, whom she'd met one day after walking from Frederick's all the way up Fifth Avenue to the Teamsters Hall to have lunch with Merritt.

The canvases were standard-size for the most part, three-by-two, with some smaller and some larger. Her approach to the portraits was by no means uniform. She approached each one on its own terms. Some paintings had a subtle chiaroscuro quality and took her days to complete. With these she would apply coat after coat of glaze, and each afternoon after the glaze had dried she would add another layer of shading. With other paintings, she relied on an impasto approach in which she laid the color on heavy with thick brushstrokes, using inordinate amounts of paint, that gave the dried canvas a pronounced toothiness. Some of the portraits were so flat and mannered they looked like Russian icons, while others attained a near-photographic likeness. She even experimented with camaïeu, the monochromatic technique favored by Mark Tobey, and scumbling, patting wet paint onto dry in the intimate fashion of Chardin, the French still-life artist. Her favorite paintings, though, the ones she dashed off in just a few hours, were those she infused with impressionistic brightness. In painting these, she indulged her uninhibited, lifelong passion for rich, saturated color.

Throughout the summer she painted feverishly, in a state that at times was wonderfully energizing and at others absolutely enervating. She used what little savings she had to buy supplies and even paid a cash-strapped student at Cornish to stretch canvas for her. She owned exactly eleven brushes of various lengths and diameters, made of white bristle and imitation sable hair, which she took scrupulous care of. Because of the volume of paints she bought, Mr. Abbott gave her a more than usually generous discount on hi-test oils. Although she mixed many of her own colors, she also loved the array that he carried: burnt sienna, yellow ochre, zinc yellow, raw umber, terre verte, burnt umber, ivory black, ultramarine blue, permanent blue, permanent green light, mars violet, crimson, viridian, cerulean blue, cobalt blue, cobalt violet, several alizarins and all the cadmiums (red light, red deep, yellow light, yellow deep, orange), and of course zinc white in giant-size tubes. She also used an ample amount of linseed oil (for reducing paint) and rectified turpentine (for cutting gloss) from the gallon vats available in the Cornish studios.

Clara even tried her hand at encaustic painting, which Callie had recommended to her, and was seduced by the smell of the warm beeswax on top of the electric hotplate. Mixing the assorted pigments into the wax was like witnessing the creation of color itself. She became enraptured by the thick vibrancy of each new color. Applying the mixture to the canvas reminded her of sculpting as she maneuvered the wax about with an offset spatula borrowed from her mother's kitchen. The finished surface often had the texture and appearance of flesh, a kind of multi-color epidermis, which was both strange and alluring. Yet, the materials for encaustic painting were so expensive and prepping them so painstaking that after half a dozen portraits she returned to painting with oils.

Before long the portraits cluttered the extra studio space she'd been allotted at Cornish, and when the Dean politely asked how much further she planned to take the project, she answered quite honestly that she didn't know. She would talk about the project with Merritt, but refused to let him up to the studio to see it. She didn't want him to know how obsessed she'd become. At times she wondered if she hadn't stepped over some invisible line, and if that's what had happened to Eliot? How would one know when the line had been crossed? In the end she didn't really care, because whatever portrait she was working on at that moment was always the one that mattered most, and she never kept count of how many she'd done. In July when Merritt went to San Francisco, she spent four straight days in the studio, sleeping on a couch in the foyer and avoiding having to change her clothes by never removing her smock.

Increasingly she got each portrait right on the first or second try. She stopped sketching the face first and began painting free-form onto the canvas. This allowed her to pick up her pace, yet more important it freed her to be more expressive with the lines and contours of the face. She also began applying the paint much thicker and using more saturated colors. By late summer, forty or so portraits of family, friends, and acquaintances watched over her as she painted the next one, and the next after that.

When the dean strolled into the studio one evening, he commended her on her extraordinary output, but informed her that she would have to store some of the paintings elsewhere. That's when Clara enlisted Merritt's help in transporting half of the portraits to her parents' basement. Yet rather than admit him to her studio space, she carried select canvases down to the first floor for him to bring out to his car. It took them two runs to West Seattle since she refused to let him place any of the portraits in the trunk and he could only fit ten at a time in the backseat.

"Is that all of them?" he inquired after the second trip.

"For now," she said, knowing that just as many paintings remained up in the studio.

She wasn't sure why she was so reluctant to show her project in its entirety to Merritt. He was the very soul of encouragement, always saying how proud he was to be marrying a real artist. Last week he'd even given her an autographed copy of Ben Shahn's book *The Shape of Content* that he'd found at Shorey's Bookstore. (She kept it in her studio space right next to the Helmi Eckenson book Callie had given her.) She finally had to admit that the source of her reluctance was entirely herself. The project had become so engrossing and all-consuming that she was abashed by it, almost as if she'd compromised herself and broken faith with him. She understood, too, that once they were married everything would change and that marriage might very well spell the end of such artistic endeavors.

Nevertheless, by mid-August she began asking herself whether there was no end in sight to the project. It could conceivably go on forever since she met new people whom she could paint all the time. It was this unsettling prospect that inspired her to solicit Callie's opinion on the whole crazy undertaking. Callie's idea of an organization of women artists had never materialized, yet she remained as avid as ever in her promotion of her female compatriots. This became evident when she met Clara for breakfast on Capitol Hill, with the plan to inspect Clara's portraits afterward.

As soon as they sat down in the diner, Callie began venting about how two weeks ago *LIFE* magazine put Mark Tobey on its cover with an accompanying article extolling the so-called "Mystic Painters of the Northwest," describing "the numinous use of muted colors and abstract designs" in the works of Tobey, Morris Graves, Kenneth Callahan, and Guy Anderson—the four horsemen of the Northwest art scene—concluding that the artists had been inspired by the region's misty, ethereal landscape.

"All men," Callie fumed as she poured ketchup over her western omelet and hash browns and doused both with salt and pepper. "Not a single woman artist mentioned. *Mystic* my great big behind. The only women named in the article are the gallery owners, Marian and Zoë, the admiring patronesses."

Clara had only recently heard about the *LIFE* article, which was generating a great deal of buzz at Cornish since many of the artists named in it had taught there at one time or another. Mark Tobey remained the headliner among the group, of course, and though Clara admired him as a teacher, she still failed to see the appeal of his work. She was sympathetic to Callie's gripe about all the attention going only to men. Even at Cornish—founded by Nellie C. Cornish—the male students received the overwhelming favor and support of the teachers. The assumption persisted that women were better suited for the decorative arts such as interior design, or crafts such as ceramics, or the professional arts . . . such as fashion illustration. Since Callie had been in the art racket so long, Clara could only imagine the level of her friend's frustration.

"Bernadette and I are planning an all-woman show," Callie announced between forkfuls of omelet. "A kind of Salon des Refusés *des femmes*."

"That's a great idea," Clara said. She had always admired Callie's dedication to her own art as well as the art of her friends and associates.

"We thought so," she replied and wiped her mouth with a napkin, "except that no gallery owners, not even *les madames patroness*, are willing to sponsor it. And the museums are out of the question."

"Maybe Frederick & Nelson would sponsor it," Clara offered, brightening to the idea. "They have the Little Gallery there." In fact, as Clara knew, a group of women artists already held its annual show there every February. It was dominated each year by still-lifes of flowers in decorative vases, but still, the artists displayed ample talent. And during the war years, as Clara recalled, they auctioned off their paintings to buy war bonds.

Callie held her coffee cup to her mouth. "Hmmm," she let out and took a sip, then said, "I'm not talking about a show of the Ladies Watercolor Auxiliary—no disrespect to my watercoloring sisters. I'm thinking of the very best and most daring women artists in the Northwest. A bold counter-statement to that magazine's refusal to acknowledge *our* work and—" She must have seen the look of dejection on Clara's face because she caught herself up short and said, "It's worth a try, dear," upon which Clara instantly volunteered to make inquiries, despite the apparent snootiness of her friend's initial response.

"Now let's go see which of your paintings we'll include in the show," Callie concluded and pushed away from the table.

They walked down Broadway to Roy Street where Clara escorted Callie into the terra cotta building that housed the Cornish School. As they made their way up the stairs to the artists' studios, Callie remarked that she'd never been inside the school before this moment, which surprised Clara.

They crossed to her corner of the large studio and Clara announced, "There they are," indicating the thirty or so portraits scattered about her area, leaning three or four deep against the partitions and on either side of her work table and easel. "This is about half of them. The other half are in West Seattle."

While Clara stood next to her worktable fidgeting with her brushes, Callie made her way to the various stacks and inspected each and every painting. She took her time and didn't speak, though at one point Clara heard her murmur something that she couldn't make out. When she did finally say something, it was to commend Clara on keeping herself so busy over the past several months.

Unable to stand it any longer, Clara excused herself to go down the hall to the ladies' room, yet when she returned Callie was still sorting through the paintings, lifting them out one at a time and holding it at eye-level so she was face-to-face with the portrait. When she put the last painting down, she glanced about at the stacks one more time as if to take inventory of the entire lot and then looked over Clara's easel and worktable.

"Superlatives don't do it justice," she said at last, turning to Clara. "I believe these are more than just portraits. They're like some kind of remarkable gathering that I feel I've been invited to." Her eyebrows rose and an incredulous expression came over her face. "And you say you have just as many at home?"

"About this many, yes," Clara said, letting out the breath she'd been holding in since Callie finished her appraisal. "I don't really keep count."

"I would like Bernadette to see them," Callie said. "All of them. These and the other ones as well. There's something here that's very intimate, on the one hand, and yet monumental on the other, and that—"

"I'm not finished yet either," Clara interjected.

A rather cross look came over Callie's face at this interruption, and then she grinned and reached into her jacket pocket for her cigarettes.

"As I was saying," she went on, lighting up. "I admire how you've achieved a balance of the figurative and expressionistic. Catch words, I know. But these are very individual works and I'm at a loss, offhand, how to articulate my response. And that, my *chère amie*, is a rare experience for me."

Overcome by Callie's endorsement, Clara hugged her friend. She'd been painting so incessantly, so instinctually for the past several months that she had no perspective on the project and, what's more, had lost sight of her life beyond the paintings. With no small measure of relief, as well as regret, she saw now that this was about to change—and that the project would soon be coming to an end.

TWENTY-FOUR
Carl Hamilton, Summer 1947

When Clara and Merritt told him and Glenora they were engaged, Carl wanted to be happy for them, he truly did. But his daughter was marrying a Teamster. What's more he worked directly for Dave Beck, the scourge of the ILWU and Harry Bridge's sworn foe. It was a long established fact that longshoremen and Teamsters did not get along. Not in Seattle at any rate. Not since Beck tried to break the longshoremen's strike back in '34.

Carl was also disappointed the young man hadn't come to him first to seek permission to ask for his daughter's hand in marriage, as Carl had gone to Glenora's father in January 1919. He'd been discharged from the Army three months earlier, after spending twelve weeks in the trenches in no-man's land on the Western Front and later going over the top with the 79th Infantry Division in the attack on the Hindenburg Line. It was a muddy, maggot-infested mess of a war, and toward the end he came down with a case of the bloody flux that almost did him in. By the time he recuperated in one of the tent hospitals in France, the Armistice had been signed and he was being sent home. That's when he set his heart on marrying his sweetheart back in Seattle, but knew he first had to see her father.

But times had changed and now people conducted themselves differently. Young people did things their own way.

Carl figured what was needed was a good sit-down talk with this Driscoll fellow to clear the air. Other than a few Sunday suppers and Thanksgiving dinner last November, he hadn't had much time to speak with the young man. Yet, to his future son-in-law's credit, Merritt beat him to it, in early August telephoning Carl to ask if they could meet for coffee some morning. Carl appreciated the gesture and offered to meet that Saturday morning at 6:00 a.m. at Clarks 'Round the Clock Restaurant, which was where he'd gotten his morning coffee all the years he worked on the waterfront and where he still ate breakfast twice a week with his old union buddies.

Carl was already seated in his usual booth when Merritt walked in. He was drinking coffee, black, and when Merritt sat down he ordered the same. The waitress, who'd worked there as long as Carl could remember, asked Merritt if he wanted anything else and he told her he'd take a bearclaw.

"How 'bout you, Carl. What'll you have?"

"Just coffee, Peg."

The waitress planted her hand on her hip and gave him a disgruntled look.

"Okay," he relented. "Bring me an English muffin. Yeh happy?"

Peg walked away, writing down the order.

First off Carl wanted to make clear to Merritt how much Clara meant to him and her mother, especially after the loss of little May so long ago and then their son Freddy in the war. He wanted Merritt also to understand what a special girl Clara was and that he couldn't bear to see any harm come to her. But before he could open his mouth, Merritt started talking. The young fellow went on about how much he loved Clara and wanted to take care of her. He said he knew how lucky he was that she'd accepted his proposal, and that he would work hard to be a good husband to her and, in due time, a good father to their children. He said also he hoped to be a good son-in-law.

Peg set the English muffin and bearclaw on the table and after she'd topped off their coffee, Carl told Merritt he appreciated him saying that. "Clara means everything to me and her mother. She's always been my sidekick. And her brother . . . well, you've seen how protective he is of her."

Merritt nodded.

"She's always been very independent," he went on, "and you have to know that about her. It hasn't always been easy for us, especially her mother, but that's how she is." Carl then asked Merritt what his plans were after he and Clara were married, and Merritt answered that he expected to graduate from the university in about a year and perhaps go on to law school. He also said he would likely stay on with the Teamsters for a while longer.

Carl glowered at him when he said this, and Merritt must have noticed because right away he put his fork down and asked straight out what the big beef was between the two unions.

"Why all the bad blood?" he asked. Sure, labor politics were involved, he added, maybe even some territorial disputes, but there must be more to it than that. "Plus I'm sick and tired of Ken climbing on my back about it all the time."

It was clear he was bothered. And who could blame him? He just wanted to do his job, Carl figured. And he was right. It was a shame so much contention had to exist between the two unions. Until Merritt had come into their lives, Carl hadn't thought about it all that much. It seemed the divide had always been there. IBT or ILWU. AFL or CIO. Beck or Bridges. In Seattle at least, you were either on one side or the other.

The best he could do was to tell Merritt what he'd gone through himself— and so that's what he did. He started all the way back in '34, right after passage of the Recovery Act, when unions were making their move, fighting for members' rights, demanding a seat at the table right beside management. He recounted his own organizing efforts on behalf of the ILA, before the ILWU was formed. He told about the hatchtender who tried to kill him and the maritime companies' using UW students as strikebreakers. He praised Harry Bridges' tough stand against Joe Ryan, head of the ILA, who with Beck tried to sell out the longshoremen. He cussed Beck for ordering Teamsters to cross the longshoremen's picket lines and said, "That's where the bad blood really started," and described the scab-clearing squads along the waterfront he'd participated in. He even told him about his pal Marty taking a bullet in the neck. By the time he finished filling Merritt in on the longshoremen's longstanding grudge with the Teamsters, it was well-nigh 8 o'clock and no longer dark outside.

After walking out to the parking lot, they shook hands and were about to part ways when Carl asked Merritt if he would like to go over to the ILWU hall with him. He could show him around and they could talk some more. Merritt agreed and they left his car in the Clark's parking lot and took Carl's car. As they drove in the "family flivver," as Carl called his old spoke-wheeled Model A, he asked Merritt if he'd ever boxed and Merritt said no, never, though he'd had some hand-to-hand training in boot camp. Carl then reminisced about his days as a tournament fighter in Seattle in the early '20s when he needed to earn a few extra dollars after marrying Clara's mother. His own father—Clara's Grandpa Kelso—had taught him the pugilistic arts growing up. And he did pretty well in the ring until he lost the Seattle bantamweight championship bout to an upstart Filipino with lightening jabs and feet like a dancer. The Filipino, a fellow named Von Binuia, with the nickname Kid Cebu, went on to win the West Coast title. "The guy trained on my chin," Carl boasted. "I figured that was my contribution to his success."

He fought for another year after that, Carl said, and eventually hung up his gloves and turned to training young kids, continuing to spar now and then at the local gym. In '38, he talked the Local 19 membership into chipping in to equip a gym in the union hall basement, complete with a roped-off ring, body bag, speed bag, several pairs of gloves, jump ropes, medicine balls, and dumbbells. When one member griped that he got all the exercise he needed working on the docks, Carl replied it wasn't the same as keeping in fighting shape. "I told him, 'You never know when those bulls on the force or Beck and his boys will try to break us again,'" Carl repeated for Merritt's benefit, and went on to explain how he liked the finesse of the sport. "That's why Binuia was so good. He knew how to move." Yet during the war, the basement gym fell into disuse, and now he was thinking he might have to dismantle it and donate the equipment to the local boys club.

As they parked in front of the two-story brick union hall, Carl turned to Merritt and said he ought to know how to defend himself if he was going to take care of his daughter. He then asked if Merritt thought he could take on a

54-year-old man like himself and, you know, see what he's got. "You look plenty fit," he told Merritt.

Merritt was dumbfounded by this suggestion, blinked several times, and finally said, sure, why not, as long as no one got hurt. Carl jumped out of the car. "We don't want that," he said, leaning over the ragtop. Yet as he led Merritt around back to the alley entrance, he felt bad for setting the young guy up like that and knew Glenora and Clara would give him hell when they found out.

After unlocking the back door, he punched the light switch and went down the stairwell into the basement gym where four bare bulbs hung from the low ceiling. The cinderblock walls were damp and the room smelled of mildew and old sweat. Although it was August, the sub-level basement was cool. Carl thought how in his many years as a union member he'd probably spent more time down here than in the meeting room or offices upstairs.

"A few calisthenics will warm us right up," he said, tossing aside his jacket and rolling up his sleeves and nodding to Merritt to do the same. He started in on jumping jacks and Merritt followed his lead with Carl counting out loud. "One-two, one-three, one-four . . . ." He then swung into a series of alternate toe-touches and next dropped to the floor for sit-ups and push-ups. His breathing was steady but not too labored as he finished with a series of leg lifts. Maybe, he thought, he could even talk Ken into coming back down to the gym with him sometime. Of the two boys, Freddy had been the real boxer, but Ken had bulked up during the war and might fare pretty well now as a welterweight.

"We'll do some bag work first," he said and handed Merritt a pair of training gloves and told him to begin with the speed bag that hung from a square of plywood in the corner. "Keep count in your head," he instructed. "One-two, one-two. And pick up speed as you go."

The lad did okay and Carl moved him on to the body bag, a large Army duffel bag packed with saw dust and hung from a chain in the ceiling.

"You're a goddamn southpaw," Carl barked, watching Merritt take his first swing at the bag. "I'll have to watch my starboard." Carl laughed and as he held the bag told Merritt to move his feet and bob. He knew he was tiring the young fellow out, softening him up for the ring, but what of it? He let go of the bag and told him to take a blow.

Merritt removed the training gloves, dug in his jacket pocket for a pack of cigarettes, and lit up. When he offered Carl one, Carl declined. While Merritt smoked, Carl found an old jar of trainer's grease that had long ago turned yellow. When Merritt was ready, he smeared the goop on Merritt's forehead, nose, cheeks, and chin. He applied a healthy coat to his own face and explained that it would keep them from getting cut if either happened to land a punch. Carl then handed him a pair of 16-ounce leather gloves and told him to put them on. The boy's shirt was stained with sweat.

194

Carl tied Merritt's gloves and put his own on, tying the first with one hand and the second with his teeth—a trick his old man had taught him.

"Let's go," he said.

Two thick dock ropes wrapped about four iron posts sunk into the concrete floor served as the ring. Gymnastic mats, sown together, cushioned the floor inside the makeshift ring. Carl climbed in first and held the ropes for Merritt. Once inside the ring, he felt like he was twenty-five again and threw a flurry of dummy punches. Carl looked at Merritt and remembered his first bout against an Irish shaver named Tim Gilhooley. The kid had looked somewhat like Merritt—tall, trim, and dark-haired—and was a pistol with his hands. But when Carl got Gilhooley on the ropes in the second round and drilled his midsection, he doubled him up and the ref jumped in and called the fight. It was the first of several TKO's in his short boxing career.

"No blows below the belt," Carl instructed, tapping his gloves to Merritt's, "and we'll go half strength."

Merritt raised his gloves and tried not to appear nervous, though Carl could see that he was. The first few punches they exchanged landed on the other man's gloves or arms and were easily deflected. As they paced about the ring, Carl could sense Merritt was reluctant to throw anything very hard. When he told him to take his best shot, Merritt shuffled in closer and threw a few half-hearted right jabs, which Carl blocked. Then, probably thinking he would catch Carl off guard, he threw a roundhouse left at his head. Carl dodged it and counterpunched with a swift jab of his own to the boy's forehead, which he followed with a quick one-two to his midsection, the way he'd done Gilhooley. While the head blow had surprised the boy, it was the combo to the body that walloped the wind out of him. Merritt turned away and dropped his forearms onto the top rope to catch his breath.

"Sorry 'bout that, kid," Carl said and placed an arm across Merritt's shoulder. He was sorry and he wasn't. Who was this hotshot anyhow to come into his home and steal his little girl from him? Just maybe he needed to be taught a lesson. "Instinct took over," he said. "You hurt bad?"

Merritt pushed himself off the ropes and raised his dukes. "I'm fine," he said with a trace of anger in his voice. "Let's go again."

That's the spirit, Carl thought, and they picked up the tempo. Merritt used his feet to avoid Carl's steady trudge toward him. When Carl crowded him into a corner, Merritt pushed him off and ducked out and back to the center of the ring. At one point when Carl turned to pursue him, the young turk was waiting for him. Merritt connected with a right jab to Carl's nose and then clocked him on the jaw with the same left hook he'd thrown earlier. Carl stumbled backwards, but far worse than this was the fact that when he glanced up, Merritt was grinning at him.

He quickly recovered himself. "That the best you got, college boy?" he taunted and crouching low went at him again.

Merritt had sharp reflexes and fended off Carl's uppercuts by sidestepping to his right. Carl kept after him, though, thinking how the kid had received darn good training in the Navy. After a few more times around the ring, he found Merritt's weakness. Like most southpaws, he couldn't move to his left. So Carl came at him from his right. Yet as he was about to unload his big guns—to hell with half strength—Merritt sent a fast jab past his gloves and tagged him square to the forehead. This one stung and Carl stood back a moment, mildly dazed.

Merritt apologized and said he didn't mean to hit him so hard, but Carl just snorted and said it was nothing. "I've been hit a lot worse," he said. But that was it, he thought, he'd had enough of this Teamster punk. "You move around like a goddamn *chauffeur*. Beck's boys never could stand and fight."

The boy seemed to chortle at this, as if he couldn't believe what he'd just heard.

"Teamster bastards," Carl added for good measure and threw a right hook that landed full force on the side of Merritt's brow, snapping his head and spinning his body about until his legs buckled and he went down.

The boy was out.

Yet, an instant later, as Carl bent over him, he came to. He helped Merritt sit up, threw off his own gloves, and then unlaced Merritt's and tossed both pairs out of the ring.

"At least we know you can take a punch," Carl commended him and checked his pupils just to be sure. "That's just what Kid Cebu did to me. Except I was stupid. I let him knock me down twice more. Turned me into a certified canvas inspector."

He helped Merritt to his feet and out of the ring. The boy looked pale and, when he bent over Carl slid a bucket in front of him in case he puked.

"You all right, son?"

Merritt nodded vaguely.

Carl led him to a chair and told him to put his head between his knees. "You held your own pretty well for a first-timer," he said.

"For someone with a head made of glass," Merritt replied.

That was a good one, Carl thought, relieved the boy wasn't badly hurt or even very sore at him. When it came right down to it, the Driscoll lad was an all right sort. He could trust him to take good care of Clara. He looked at the clock on the wall—almost noon—and told Merritt he'd buy him a beer at the corner tavern.

196

TWENTY-FIVE
Merritt, Summer-Fall 1947

Merritt returned from San Francisco distraught from his encounter with Arda Smitson. Though Smitson's words were vague, his drift was plain enough, at least in hindsight, and Merritt had to ask himself if this was his guy. Despite the two letters he'd received over the course of three years, it sometimes seemed his incident with the ensign had never really happened—or else had happened to someone else, someone he was only remotely acquainted with. Like everything that had taken place during the war years, the whole incident seemed past and over with. Those times weren't even worth talking about, much less stewing over. To hell with joining the VFW or American Legion or any other veterans group, Merritt had thought after he mustered out of the Navy. He wanted to get on with his life, not memorialize it. And that's what he'd been doing, or so he believed, until he received the second letter and then ran into Smitson his final night in San Francisco. For a time he tried to tell himself it was nothing, that he'd overreacted, but he kept fretting over it until finally he decided to find out who this Smitson fellow was. So a couple of weeks after his return from the Teamsters convention, he looked up the rolls for Local 38 in Everett in the Joint Council office and sure enough, there he was, Arda Smitson, a union member since 1936, an over-the-road driver for the Weyerhaeuser Lumber Company.

Yet this didn't explain how he knew who Merritt was, or knew that he'd visited the LaSalle, or knew about Ensign Rivard. So he considered tracking Smitson down up in Everett and calling his bluff. He would confront him *mano-a-mano* and bring the whole situation to a head. But again as the weeks passed and the San Francisco trip receded, he thought better of it and tried to write Smitson off as just another oddball Teamster tight on gin who didn't know his own ass from a hole in the ground. If and when the matter came up again, he told himself, he would deal with it then. If Smitson tried to hold something over him, he would deny everything and put the screws to him for trying to blackmail a fellow Teamster. After all, he worked for the top honcho, the big boss, the toughest Teamster of them all. He might even enlist some Seattle muscle to set Brother Smitson straight.

With the exception of letting Carl Hamilton knock him out cold in the basement of the ILWU union hall, Merritt spent the rest of the summer focused on his studies and his job. The job, though, was starting to get to him. The red hysteria poisoning the country was now contaminating the labor movement. Three weeks after the national convention, a memo went out to Teamster union officers and organizers instructing them that initiation fees and monthly dues were not to be collected from any known affiliate of the Communist Party, past or present, and if a Teamster knew of a member who was or ever had been tied to the Communist Party, it was beholden upon that Teamster to report said member to a union officer. The memo was signed *Dave Beck, Executive Vice-President.*

Shortly after circulation of the memo, Merritt ran into Beck in the second-floor men's room. Beck used the occasion to let Merritt know that the newspapers the next morning would be announcing his appointment by Governor Mon Wallgren to the University of Washington's Board of Trustees.

Merritt quickly zipped up and stepped over to a sink. "That's quite an honor, Mr. Beck," he said as he washed his hands. He'd long ago given up trying to call him Dave.

"Yes, it is," Beck replied, apparently pleased by Merritt's acknowledgement of the fact. "It's a great institution, the University."

"Topnotch," said Merritt.

"I hope to advance the standards and uphold the reputation that have brought it so far in its short history," said Beck, sounding as he often did, like he were making a speech or public statement.

Merritt didn't know what else to say. He wondered what a university trustee did exactly, but didn't dare ask. "The U-Dub's a great place all right. I'll have to do some bragging next time I'm on campus."

Beck smiled at this. "Go right ahead," he told Merritt, obviously pleased with himself. "Just wait till tomorrow's papers come out is all." And with that, Beck adjusted his tie in the mirror and walked out of the men's room.

As the day of his marriage neared, Merritt wanted to contact Clara's brother Ken to clear the air with him, much as he had her father. Admittedly, he was more anxious about approaching the brother than he had been the father, so as the weeks passed he put it off until one pre-dawn morning, without any warning, Ken happened to show up outside Merritt's apartment building.

He heard someone calling his name—"Hey, Driscoll"—followed by something hitting the window. "Wake up. I need to talk to you." Merritt crawled out of bed and opened the window that looked out over the alley one story below.

"What is it?" Merritt called down, thinking it might be J.P. come to drag him off for an unannounced trek through the woods.

"I need to talk to you about my sister. Get dressed."

Then he realized it was Ken Hamilton. Clara's brother had somehow learned which apartment was his and now stood in the foggy dark of the alley. Merritt couldn't figure out what he was up to. Was he there to get him to call off his engagement with Clara? To intimidate him?

He leaned out the window. "Wait a minute," he called out. "I'll be right down," and closed the window. He pulled on his pants and shoes, found an old shirt, and looked about the dark apartment for his hat and overcoat. He had no idea what Ken was capable of, and, as he put his keys and wallet in his coat pocket, he wasn't eager to find out. He walked down the back stairwell and before opening the back doorway lit a cigarette.

Ken was leaning against the opposite brick wall when Merritt entered the alley. His Nash Rambler was parked at the alley entrance, the engine idling.

"Forchistsake," Merritt said to him. "It's five a.m. What is it?" He jammed his hands into the pockets of his overcoat.

"That's right," Ken said and came up to him. "Listen, Driscoll, we need to talk."

"You can't call me on the telephone?"

"I like talking in person."

"Fine for you," Merritt said and dropped his cigarette into an oily puddle. He decided to downplay the whole situation, crazy as it was, and asked, "You want to come up? I'll heat some coffee. I want to talk to you, too."

"Let's go for a drive," Ken replied. "I think better that way."

"Whatever you say," Merritt answered and shrugged. First Clara's old man tries to knock him out in the basement of the longshoremen's union hall and now this. What kind of family was he marrying into, he asked himself as they walked to Ken's car.

As Ken drove south through the downtown, neither spoke. He kept driving, and Merritt couldn't tell where they were until they passed through the Mount Baker Park tunnel heading toward Lake Washington. As they emerged from the dark tunnel, Ken continued across the new pontoon bridge, which reminded Merritt of something the Seabees might construct.

"Where the hell we going?" he said.

"There's a thermos with tea on the backseat," Ken answered.

Merritt looked over his shoulder. In addition to the thermos and a lunch pail, there were two canvas gun cases. "Where're we going hunting?" he asked facetiously.

"Lake Sammamish," Ken said. "Northeast side of the lake. There's a good cove tucked away there." He told Merritt he had an extra pair of hip boots in the trunk that Merritt could wear. "They let you handle firearms in that pissant Navy?"

Merritt ignored the wisecrack. "I'm a coffee drinker," he said. "Tea's for women."

The pale morning light had turned the waters of Lake Washington a deep indigo. Looking south, he could see dock lights along the Mercer Island shoreline. "I've got class at eight-ten this morning," he informed Ken as they crossed the island and then the short truss bridge connecting it to the Eastside.

"Skip it," was all Ken said, the light from the dashboard making his smirk look rather sinister. Only now did Merritt notice that Ken was wearing a shell vest beneath his canvas coat.

They headed east on Highway 10 into the Cascade foothills. At Issaquah, a small town near Lake Sammamish, Ken pulled into the parking lot of a roadside diner, told Merritt to wait, and went inside. Merritt rolled down his window, took in the cool morning air, and lit a cigarette. When Ken came back, he handed Merritt a cup of coffee in a paper cup and a bacon and egg sandwich wrapped in wax paper.

"I don't have a license, you know," Merritt said, biting into the sandwich and wondering when they were going to get around to talking about Clara.

"No matter," said Ken. "The game warden never comes around to this part of the lake."

They wound their way along the north end of the lake on a narrow paved road. At an opening in the thicket of alders and larch that only he saw, Ken drove the Nash Rambler straight into the underbrush and the next instant they were bouncing down a dirt track. When the track ended, he stopped the car and told Merritt to get the guns from the backseat.

Ken hauled two pairs of rubber hip boots from the trunk, tossed one pair at Merritt's feet, and began putting on his own. Merritt placed the shotguns and his cup of coffee on the hood of the car.

"They're some wool socks and a jacket in there," Ken instructed, pointing to the trunk. "It's going to be cold."

It was cold already, thought Merritt, and pulled on the wool socks and hip boots and traded his overcoat for the musty old stag coat in the trunk. The coat fit fine in the chest but was short in the sleeves, which led him to guess it belonged to Carl Hamilton.

Ken took the guns from their cases and began checking them. One was a double-barrel shotgun, which he said had belonged to his older brother. The other was a six-shot slide-action that he'd bought from Ben Paris Sporting Goods when he got back from Europe.

"My father used to take Freddy and me out here," he said, handing Merritt the double-barrel shotgun, slamming the trunk closed, and trudging off through a stand of alders without another word.

Merritt grabbed his cup of coffee and followed, tromping over the thick floor-covering of crowberry and salal and hacking back the thorny salmonberry branches that snagged at his coat. A few minutes later they came into an opening about ten yards from the grassy shoreline. Ken signaled Merritt to keep hush. He went into a crouch and crept toward the shoreline until he located the blind, a waist-high crosshatching of branches that faced the water. He dropped to one knee, set the butt of his shotgun on the ground, and looked out over the cove.

"Nothing," he said and kept looking. "But they'll come. Geese. Canada mostly, but sometimes snow, too. They're just starting to migrate south."

Merritt cleared a patch of ground of its layer of moldy leaves and sat down.

Ken sat back on his haunches and said, "Maybe Dad can look past your being a Teamster, but I don't know that I can. Beck tried to break the waterfront strike in '34, told his men to deliver to the piers. But they wouldn't do it. They honored the longshoremen's picket lines. Back then he had the muscle but not the might. Even with his beef squads, the rank-and-file weren't about to do his bidding. But now he's got the might and doesn't need the muscle. Just look what he did to the clerk's union down in California."

Merritt didn't know much about the California situation. He knew the store clerks' union down there had gone on strike after voting against affiliating with the Teamsters. In turn, Beck had refused to honor their picket lines and sent Teamsters in to replace the clerks. In less than a week the clerks union called off its strike and were now negotiating for terms with the AFL. It was rough-'n'-tumble jurisdictional politics—and Beck had won.

"I can't defend every action the Teamsters make," Merritt said, "just as I can't control them. It's a big organization. Maybe they don't always play pretty, but I can tell you what the membership polls say, especially about the leadership. They're all for it. One hundred percent. They know the union's looking out for them."

Ken shook his head in disgust. "You just don't get it, do you? There's nothing worse than being a strikebreaker. *Nothing.* And like I said, Dad might look past you're being one of them"—Merritt wasn't so sure of this—"but as far as I'm concerned, anyone associated with Beck is either a past scab or a soon-to-be scab."

Merritt didn't say anything. What could he? He wasn't going to quit his job, and certainly wasn't going to give up Clara—especially not over some asinine union turf war. He finished off his coffee, crushed the cup in his hand, and tossed it into the underbrush behind him. He'd had enough of this bullying and decided to tell Clara's brother so.

"I don't give a horse's ass," he said. "I've heard about all I want to hear about who gets to sign up the warehousemen and every other petty dispute between the two unions. I've heard enough, too, about what happened a dozen years ago. What do you want from me?"

Ken glowered at him, then rose to one knee and peered over the blind. "We may have to settle for mallards," was all he said in response to Merritt's tirade, then turned about just enough to eye Merritt and added, "There's bad blood on both sides, so don't kid yourself. Plenty of spilled blood, too."

Ken turned back around and abruptly let out a loud shout, sending half a dozen mallards into the air, angling away from the water toward the shoreline. Ken raised his shotgun, slid the breech and shot, slid it again and shot, then slid it a third time and shot. On the third shot he was firing straight over Merritt's head, the blasts cracking his eardrums.

"Missed," he said angrily and sat back down. "It'll be a good long while before any return. They're some more sandwiches in the lunch pail back in the car."

"Well goddamn it all to hell," Merritt said.

The rest of the morning thankfully was uneventful. Merritt took a wild shot at a goose and missed, the shotgun's recoil leaving his shoulder bruised and sore. They remained relatively quiet as the hours passed, not once mentioning union matters again and bringing up Clara only occasionally. They spoke briefly about their war service, complaining about rations and commanding officers. Their talk strayed once or twice onto politics, and they agreed the next two years under the Republicans didn't bode well for labor—longshoremen or Teamsters. At 10:30, Ken declared that if they hadn't bagged one by now they wouldn't bag one at all, and they walked back to the car.

By the time Ken dropped Merritt back off in the city, it was too late for him to make his morning classes, but he no longer cared. He was just glad, as he kept telling himself, that Ken hadn't blasted his head off.

As summer wound down and autumn came on, it seemed to Merritt the whole world was coming undone. Clara was on a painting jag that left him utterly confounded, and because of that he rarely saw her any more. Then he goes out for coffee with her father and they end up punching the crap out of one another in the basement of the longshoremen's union hall, and a couple of weeks after that, as if all the Hamilton men were allowed one free potshot at him, Ken shows up at his apartment before dawn and takes him to Lake Sammamish to go duck hunting and "talk" about his sister. They spend three hours hunkered down in a wet, marshy blind with loaded shotguns, all the while Merritt thinking how at any moment Ken's going to shoot him dead and call it a hunting accident.

Then later that same week while making a mailroom run to send off ballots on several Joint Council initiatives, he passes the union pharmacy on the first floor and thinks he recognizes the guy that's standing at the counter. He delivers the ballots to the mailroom and when he passes by the pharmacy again on his way back to his office, the guy's just coming out. This time Merritt gets a good look at him, and it's him all right, the jerk who caused all the ruckus at the Harry Bridges talk at the university back in November, the very same guy Ken Hamilton and a few other longshoremen had hustled out of the auditorium. He's a fairly young guy, roughly Merritt's same age, and obviously a Teamster or else why would he be there, which leads Merritt to wonder whether Beck sent him to Bridges' talk as well. The notion doesn't seem as farfetched as it might have nine months ago, before he'd received the second letter or had his encounter with Arda Smitson in San Francisco. Now almost anything seems possible.

And that's just the craziness in his own life. Outside his little world, the entire planet seems like it's coming unhinged. To read the morning newspaper is to watch the global map shifting before one's very eyes. At the start of one week, India declares its independence, and by the end of the next week, Pakistan, also once part of the subaltern British Raj, partitions from India and immediately Muslims and Hindus are at each other's throats. Meanwhile, in Southeast Asia, Burma and Ceylon get set to break from colonial rule as well. In the Middle East, Jewish refugees from war-ravaged Europe pour into Palestine and prepare to declare a Jewish homeland (making Merritt wonder if Sid and Amy, who wed last fall, will join the great exodus). And all the while the U.S. and Soviet Union begin facing each other down like the world is one great big OK Corral with Truman and Stalin at twenty paces, pistols cocked and loaded. The U.S. rushes aid to Greece to keep it from falling to the Communists, and the Soviets install puppet governments in Poland and Hungary and threaten to roll their tanks into Czechoslovakia at the least provocation. Each week the United States tests bigger, more powerful A-bombs, and one radio commentator says the Russians will have the bomb any day and that before long the two countries will possess an arsenal of atomic weaponry capable of annihilating all humanity. The widely released photographs showing the unthinkable devastation to Hiroshima and Nagasaki only confirm such a scenario, and suddenly people are building blast shelters in their backyards, farm fields, and orchards.

Meanwhile, demagoguery grips the nation's capital. The hysteria over Communist infiltration brings the federal government in D.C. to a virtual standstill. Congress starts investigating stage actors, high school teachers, building janitors, you name it. A local version of the House Un-American Activities Committee starts up in Olympia, headed by State Senator Albert F. Canwell from Spokane, who begins bullying his way across Washington State. To top it all off, nutjobs of every stripe begin spotting UFOs in the skies above America more regularly than anyone can keep track of. One of the first sightings takes place near Mount Rainier a few days after Merritt and J.P. go hiking up there. A nice, ordinary couple enjoying the great outdoors tell the newspapers of seeing four enormous saucers, each radiating a bright greenish light, circle the mountain, hover near its summit, widen their circle, and then disperse in all four directions—north, south, east, and west—in a simultaneous flash. The newspapers quote conspiracy theorists who speculate the incident is top-secret Air Force tests out of McChord Air Base near Tacoma. (One of the mailroom clerks in the basement of the Teamsters Hall, a real wiseacre, tells Merritt, "Leave it to Tacoma. Everyone knows those smelter stacks down there are really Martian radio transmitters. They guide their spaceships by the stench.") Another brilliant mind interviewed on the radio theorizes the lights are generated by accumulations of plutonium isotopes escaping from the Hanford atomic energy facility east of the mountains. The theory goes that since Mount Rainier has a highly charged magnetic field, the isotopes are drawn to the mountain by its gravitational pull, creating distinct isotopic clusters that orbit the snowy dome until they lose their ionic charge, at which point they're expelled from the mountain in oppositely-charged, mutually-opposing directions. ("Who came up with that theory?" another mailroom clerk inquires. "Buck Rogers?") When Merritt asks J.P. his opinion of the UFO sightings near Mount Rainier, J.P. confesses he's had similar experiences in the pastures up there while sampling the fungi known as *psilocybe semilanceata*, a small mushroom locals call liberty caps. "The woods are full of strange and inexplicable phenomena," J.P says knowingly and asks Merritt if he wants to go to the Blue Moon Tavern—where all the poets, painters, and university professors hang out—to get a pitcher or two of beer.

"Why not," Merritt says, and the next morning he wakes up in the backseat of his Plymouth DeLuxe near the Seattle Gas Works on Lake Union, asking himself what the hell's happened and where are my shoes.

TWENTY-SIX
Clara, Fall 1947

It was regrettable how little she and Merritt saw each other as the summer waned. Just enough to remind themselves they were engaged—and still in love. All the same, she sometimes had difficulty imagining herself a married woman, and it was at such moments that she wanted to scratch their wedding plans and simply elope.

After Callie had viewed the portraits, Clara worked on half a dozen more and spent the first two weeks in August touching up earlier ones. The director of the Little Gallery at Frederick & Nelson declined to host Callie's Northwest women's art show, citing an already crowded schedule for the gallery, including the annual exhibition of the Women Painters of Washington, the group Callie had previously disdained (and which Clara now thought of joining), and so Callie and Bernadette continued to search for a venue to stage their exhibition. Callie kept insisting Clara needed a one-woman show to exhibit her entire portrait series. She also insisted Clara catalog all of the paintings. Yet while the idea of a one-woman show intrigued Clara, she couldn't find the drive to pursue it, especially as the project wound down and her attention turned to her wedding less than a month away.

The news that she and Merritt would not be married in the Church of Christ, Scientist greatly disturbed Clara's mother. She feared she would lose her only daughter to "hardened disbelief," as she put it, just as she'd lost her eldest son, implying that Freddy had died because of a lack of faith—which infuriated Clara.

"That's an insult to Freddy's memory, Mother. How can you say such a thing?" Clara shot back when she heard her mother's words.

Her mother immediately looked chastened—and rightly so, Clara thought—and later in the day mollified her objections to Clara's wedding plans, asking only that wherever the service was to be held it be conducted in accordance with divine Principle. "It would mean so much to me," she said with such wistfulness that Clara had to bite her tongue to keep from snapping at her again.

Fortunately for her and Merritt, whose lives were already overwrought with their hectic schedules, the wedding required minimal planning. They decided to hold the ceremony at a small church in West Seattle that had once belonged to the Presbyterians but was now an ecumenical chapel maintained by Unitarians. Merritt's friend J.P., who was to serve as best man, had recommended Reverend Alan P. Shelton, a minister in the Emersonian Unitarian tradition. "They don't come any less doctrinaire," he'd told Merritt. And surprisingly, their choice of minister satisfied Clara's mother. As for her bridesmaid, Clara thought of asking Callie but in the end chose Jenny, who was just as dear to her and would create less of a stir with her parents. She nonetheless invited Callie, whom Merritt had never met. As for the wedding gown, she kept it simple and chose a white satin dress with a Juliet waistline that a designer at Frederick's, a former student of renowned designer Claire McCardell, had made. The dress did not have a wedding train, which pleased Clara, since the last thing she wanted to do on her wedding day was bustle yards of excess fabric. Finally, the one issue that required no discussion whatsoever was their decision not to invite any Teamsters or ILWU members to the wedding. Firstly, they wanted to keep the guest list short, and secondly, they didn't want any fights to break out.

Two days before the wedding, Merritt's mother and father arrived. They had driven from Vermont to Boston and from there flown to Chicago and then on to Seattle. She and Merritt went out to Boeing Field to wait in the United Air Lines terminal for their plane's arrival. It had taken two weeks for Merritt to convince his parents that the only way they could attend the wedding was to board an airplane. Clara, who'd never been on one herself, understood their reluctance, but Merritt, who'd flown twice before, assured them that it was safe and that people flew all the time these days. Plus, they lived too far away to take the train. He and Clara would have to postpone the wedding to October unless they flew in.

It was a cool, sunny morning on the day his parents were to arrive, yet by the time their plane landed in the afternoon, the sky had turned overcast and the region's famous misty rain begun to fall. She and Merritt watched as his parents stepped gingerly down the boarding stairs and walked across the tarmac. Both parents had put on their Sunday best. Mr. Driscoll, a coal distributor throughout Vermont's Northeast Kingdom, had on a brown woolen suit and wool-knit necktie, a slightly crumpled beige hat, and polished brown brogans. Clinging to his arm, Mrs. Driscoll wore a tan dress, the hem of which dropped below her wool overcoat, a calot hat with a veil draped over her face, and white gloves. A large corsage adorned the lapel of her overcoat. Clara noticed that neither parent possessed Merritt's height, and both appeared more fragile and elderly than she remembered them from the single photograph Merritt had shown her. As parents go, Merritt once told her, his were on the older side since they'd had him rather late.

As they entered the terminal, Merritt greeted his mother with a gentle hug and his father with a two-fisted handshake. "Mom, Dad, welcome to the Great Northwest," he said, summoning all his cheerfulness on their behalf. Clara knew he was nervous about his parents' visit. They were both rural people who rarely ventured beyond the stateline. "A drive to St. Johnsbury is a big deal," he'd explained while they waited in the terminal. "It's the county seat for Caledonia County, so if you need a license or permit for anything, that's where you have to go. And in winter there's four feet of snow on the ground."

Then Clara stepped forward and gave them each a warm hug. Mrs. Driscoll declared she was as pretty as she'd imagined her. "And so tall," Mr. Driscoll added. Mrs. Driscoll then apologized that Merritt's sister and her husband could not attend the wedding. "The children, you know."

Then Merritt stepped in. "How'd you like that Boeing 377?" he asked his father.

"Not so much," his mother replied for both of them. "It was terribly bumpy."

"I'm sorry to hear that, Mom," Merritt said dejectedly and a moment later dashed off to retrieve the single suitcase his parents' had brought with them. Left alone with Mr. and Mrs. Driscoll, Clara fumbled for something to say, then told them how much her own parents were looking forward to meeting them and how she knew they would all get along splendidly.

On the drive downtown, Merritt's parents sat in the backseat and commented on how much water there was everywhere and how tall the trees were. Merritt did most of the talking, though, saying how it was a shame they couldn't see the mountains today. By the time they'd delivered his parents safely to their room at the Olympic Hotel, the finest hotel in the city, Clara had concluded they were both very sweet but very reserved people, just as she figured they'd be.

"They're both from hardy New England stock," Merritt said after leaving them off, bragging how his father used to race cutters in the winter and trotters in the summer and how his mother raised hens and grew roses that were the envy of all Caledonia County.

The next two days went by breathlessly and by the morning of her wedding day, Clara was ready for all of the hullabaloo to be over. Her parents drove her and Jenny to the church where Merritt, his mother and father, J.P., Callie, and Ken were already waiting. (Sid and Amy were unable to make it.) Standing in the foyer in his best gray suit and red silk tie, with a white boutonnière pinned to his lapel, Merritt looked more handsome than she'd ever seen him, and she almost teared up right then and there. As they accompanied one another to the front of the church, she held a small wedding bouquet of creamy white roses. With each step forward, she recalled her and Merritt's first encounter in the doorway of the Reading Room on that rainy autumn morning so long ago, and the sketch she'd made of him that evening, which she planned to have matted and framed and hung on their bedroom wall when they returned from their honeymoon.

At the front of the church—there was no alter—she handed her bouquet to Jenny and took Merritt's hands in hers as Reverend Shelton welcomed them all to this very blessed ceremony, adding how it is well for a man and woman to enter into the sacred bonds of marriage and that every new marriage was cause for celebration.

To further appease her mother—and because it was the right thing to do—Clara had asked Ken, now a church-certified practitioner, to read a passage from *Science and Health* prior to the exchange of vows. After clearing his throat, Ken stepped forward, stood next to Reverend Shelton, and paraphrased Chapter III from *Science and Health* on how marriage is a concession to material methods intended to achieve spiritual good, how completeness is found in the union of masculine and feminine virtues, and how marriage reminds us that happiness is ultimately spiritual. He then opened his well-worn copy of the book and read a passage that, curious as the words were, brought tears to Clara's eyes.

"Love enriches the nature," he read, "enlarging, purifying, and elevating it . . . Marriage is unblest or blest, according to the disappointments it involves or the hopes it fulfills. To happify existence by constant intercourse with those adapted to elevate it, should be the motive of society. Unity of spirit gives new pinions to joy, or else joy's drooping wings trail in the dust." He then carefully closed the book, kissed his sister on the cheek, and resumed his position beside their father, who was to give Clara away.

From there Reverend Shelton, smiling benignly the whole while, proceeded with the exchange of vows. Clara looked into Merritt's eyes and said, "I do," and then Merritt followed with his own "I do." There was the exchange of wedding bands and the reverend declared them man and wife and told them they could now seal their vows with a kiss. At the same time, a woman enlisted from the Unitarian Church played *Ode to Joy* on the upright piano in the front corner. Merritt then shook hands with Reverend Shelton and Clara pressed her cheek to his, and they both turned to face their family and friends, exchanging hugs and kisses and hearty handshakes all around.

After all of the congratulations were said and the party moved back down the aisle toward the church doors, Clara could hear J.P remark how it was a short but effective ceremony. "Right to the point," he said, "just as it should be."

Clara held Merritt's hand and twice asked him to show her the wedding band on his finger. His earlier nervousness was gone and he seemed as giddy as she. The whole group exited the church and tarried on the front steps for a short while longer. Jenny produced a camera and took photographs of everyone, beginning with Clara and Merritt by themselves, then the newlyweds with each set of parents, then with Reverend Shelton, and finally, once she'd shown the church pianist how to operate the camera, the entire wedding party. Eventually everyone, including Reverend Shelton, piled into three separate cars to drive downtown to the Olympic Hotel for the wedding dinner.

The lavish dinner in the hotel's stately dining room was something Clara's father had insisted upon. He wanted to send off his only daughter in high style, he'd told her when he first announced his plan. Knowing her dear and generous father as she did, she also figured he wanted to impress the Driscolls. And indeed the candle-lit table spread with a lace tablecloth and floral-pattern china was something to behold. Once everyone was seated, J.P. rose to offer a toast to the newlyweds and even Clara's teetotaling mother joined in raising a glass of champagne to wish them the very best. Callie, wearing a long black skirt and black waistcoat with tails that made her look like a stout penguin, also rose to propose a toast. "To love everlasting," she said simply, "and may your hearts always be one," and sat down as everyone nodded appreciatively.

As each course was wheeled to the table on a linen-draped cart, Mrs. Driscoll sucked in her breath and exclaimed over the extravagance. The feast included appetizers of oysters Rockefeller and crab cocktail, followed by salmon bisque and a main course of sirloin steak with scalloped potatoes and young asparagus. When the meal concluded with a blazing baked Alaska that was nearly as large as the table, Clara could see that everyone's *oohs* and *ahhs* delighted her father.

Throughout the meal she and Merritt kept pressing their legs together beneath the table. She had one glass of champagne and Merritt had two, yet their friends J.P. and Jenny drank several. Eventually Mr. Driscoll leaned back in his chair, patted his stomach with both hands, and announced he couldn't eat another bite. Shortly after that, Reverend Shelton excused himself, again congratulating the happy couple, and on his way out Clara watched as J.P. followed the reverend and discretely handed him the envelope containing his fee. Merritt's mother and father looked tired, too, and when they finally excused themselves from the table, they each kissed Clara on the cheek, said their *thank-you*'s to her parents, and wished everyone goodnight. Callie was next to call it quits, giving Clara and Merritt each a big hug and signaling the maitre d' to call her a cab. Then Jenny and J.P., both a bit tipsy, gave their heartiest well-wishes to Clara and Merritt and departed (as Clara noted) in tandem. Finally, it was her parents and brother's turn, and Clara cried and laughed as she said goodnight to them and thanked Ken again for giving such a moving reading.

At last she and Merritt were alone, and a moment of awkwardness came over them as they remained seated at the table. This passed, though, as the server came around asking if they wished for anything else, and in unison they replied no. Then as the band in the dance pavilion down the hallway struck up a number, Merritt turned to her and said, "May I have this dance?"

"It would be an honor," she replied.

Merritt held her chair as she rose from the table, and after facing one another, she let him glide her about the empty dining room for several turns and then out across the marble-floor of the lobby and straight to the brass doors of the elevator, which they rode to the fourth-floor newlywed suite.

It was well past ten the next morning when they hurried down to find Merritt's parents in the hotel restaurant sipping their morning coffee and waiting patiently for them. The plan had been to meet his parents for breakfast at nine-thirty before departing on their honeymoon. Mr. and Mrs. Driscoll had one more day in Seattle and then Clara's father would take them to the airport for their return flight home. Clara and Merritt apologized as they greeted his parents, who didn't seem the least put out by their tardiness. After eating a hearty breakfast, everyone put on a brave face to say farewell. Merritt embraced his father this time, and holding his mother's hands in his assured her they would visit *very* soon and gave her a long hug.

She and Merritt then dashed to load their luggage into the trunk of the Plymouth and rush down to the ferry terminal to catch the 12:10 sailing to Bremerton. From there their plan was to drive to Lake Quinault on the Olympic Peninsula, where they would stay at the famous lodge where Franklin Roosevelt had stayed when he toured the peninsula in '38.

For the next four days, she and Merritt—*my husband*, as she kept referring to him—lounged about on the lawn that led down to the lake, canoed on its peaceful waters, strolled through the nearby rain forest, drove to the coast for a long walk on the beach, and in the evening sat snugly before the large stone fireplace in the expansive common room. Clara could not fathom being happier, and in their spacious corner room at the lodge they made love every night and most mornings, as well as once in the woods when they found a luxurious bed of moss to lie down on.

When their four days were through and they returned to Seattle, they moved into the married student apartments near Portage Bay. The three-room apartment with kitchen nook came mostly furnished and took very little settling into. Yet before Clara could even arrange her clothes in the bedroom closet, she became sick and was hardly able to get out of bed. Either she'd caught a chill at the lake, they figured, or else an early flu bug was going around. In either case, she apologized for being such a poor wife and companion to Merritt the first week in their new home. She struggled through two days at work, but finally the fever and rasping cough were too much for her, and she was laid up for four days straight. She was reluctant to see a doctor, having done so only twice before in her life—after slicing a finger while cooking in her apartment, for which she received eight stitches at the medical clinic on Queen Anne Hill, and when

Jenny recommended her to the physician who dispersed contraceptives. On her fourth day home, however, Merritt insisted on taking her to the University Health Clinic, where the on-duty doctor read her temperature (a slight fever), took her pulse (normal), peered into her eyes and ears (all clear), and listened to her breathing with a stethoscope (some congestion). He determined she had a minor viral infection and that aspirin for the fever and plenty of rest would have her back on her feet in no time. "But go easy," he advised her. "It's best to let these things run their course."

Back at their apartment, lying in bed, Clara accepted the two aspirin and glass of water Merritt brought her. "Mother would be so disappointed," she said. "You can't tell her I saw that man today."

"Do you mean the doctor?"

"Yes!"

"Because mind governs body?"

Clara rolled her eyes at him, but before she could come back with a quip of her own, a harsh cough caught her up short. As she leaned forward with the force of it, Merritt patted her back.

"That's right," she replied hoarsely as the cough subsided and she recovered her breath. "Material body is a mental conceit—and never forget it."

"Then take these material aspirin and get some mental sleep," he advised and kissed her warm forehead. "I have to go to class and the library, but I'll come straight back after that."

Yet before Merritt left for campus, she asked him to bring her sketchbook and pencils and set them on the bedside table. Once he was gone, though, she remained too weak to draw. As a child whenever she had a cold or fever, she would lie in bed and sort through her thoughts to ferret out the fears and mistaken beliefs that might be causing the illness. Her problem had always been she didn't really fear that much, other than the usual stuff like bad storms and mean dogs. Could such simple fears cause her to sneeze and have a runny nose? And as for mistaken beliefs, how did one tell between true beliefs and mistaken ones? Beliefs were just that—*beliefs*. If they could be proven true or false, they would be something other than beliefs. So she would eventually abandon this mental endeavor and focus her thoughts on pure Mind and ever-present Love— capital *M*, capital *L*, as the words appeared in *Science and Health*, since both were synonymous for capital-*G* God. She found this approach much easier, setting her thoughts on pure light, limitless space, unending time, absolute emptiness, which usually calmed her down enough to sleep. And trying it now, she soon dozed off.

Before long, though, another coughing fit woke her. She was just recovering from it when she heard the apartment door open and Merritt appeared in the bedroom doorway.

"Did you sleep?" he asked.

"Some," she said and lay back with relief that her chest had finally quieted down.

"I'll run to the pharmacy and buy a bottle of cough syrup."

"Don't," she said. "It's vile."

"Then I'll get a Benzedrine inhaler. It'll help your breathing."

"I doubt it," she said. "The doctor said rest. He didn't say anything about inhalers."

""How about Vick's Vap-o-Rub?" he persisted. "It might help you rest."

Clara sat up in bed and looked at him sternly. "You've already gotten all those things, haven't you?" His sheepish look told her he had.

"I went to the pharmacy for more aspirin," he said in his defense. "The druggist recommended the inhaler. Then I remembered how my mother used to rub Vick's on me as a kid. The stuff's like a stiff drink. It knocks you right out."

Clara pulled the covers back and swung her feet over the side of the bed. "I'm feeling much better," she declared as she found her slippers beneath the bed, "and would really prefer to have something to eat right now. Did my husband bring home any food?"

"Wait right here," he said, putting on his hat and taking his keys from his pocket. "I'll run up to Manny's and bring back some soup. What else would you like? A club sandwich?"

"Soup will be fine," she said.

Half an hour later, Merritt returned with a container of soup and a turkey club sandwich, and after eating she felt better. She even felt strong enough to draw and arranged several objects on the dresser bureau into a still-life: a Japanese glass float she and Merritt had found on the beach near Oysterville, an inlaid hair brush and hand mirror, a tapered bottle of Gemey perfume, and the dried white roses she'd kept from her bridal bouquet. She wished she had her watercolors but knew they were buried in one of the boxes still in the living room and had neither the strength to hunt for them nor the heart to ask Merritt to do so for her. Whenever she felt a cough coming on, she closed her eyes and tried to calm herself to let the urge pass. This worked fine the first few times, but eventually the cough won out, erupting from her chest. She leaned over the side of the bed gasping for breath, and when she finally sat up, she told Merritt to bring her the cough syrup and in quick succession swallowed three tablespoons of the viscous green liquid.

TWENTY-SEVEN
Merritt, Fall 1947-Winter 1948

The wedding in September was a welcome distraction from everything weighing on Merritt's mind. The honeymoon was even more welcome—the luxury of lying in bed with Clara late into the morning, legs interlocked, stroking her hair, kissing her fragrant neck, nuzzling her warm bosom. Yet the bliss came to an end and worry set in again when Clara fell ill shortly after their return from Lake Quinault. Because her cough was especially persistent, he had to insist finally on taking her to the university clinic. Even though she no longer considered herself a Christian Scientist, the cracked religion still held sway over her, as evidenced by her stubborn reluctance to see the doctor. Nevertheless, she did go and before long regained her health, and as autumn came on he began to relish the domestic routine they gradually settled into. They even looked ahead to the day when they might have children, though they both knew that day remained a good ways off. While they understood that starting a family was the next logical step for them, they also recognized there was no hurry. For now they just wanted to enjoy their new life together.

Down at the Teamsters Hall, there was far less to be content about given the turmoil on the national labor front. Under the harsh chafing of the Taft-Hartley Act, disputes between labor and management flared up regularly. Somehow the Teamsters managed to keep above the fray while continuing to condemn the new law. In November, Dave Beck asked Merritt to review a draft of a statement he planned to run in *The Argus*, a Seattle opinion paper. The statement argued that Taft-Hartley eroded industrial peace by not allowing unions to regulate and discipline their own members, thus permitting "Communist troublemakers" into their midst. It was a deft argument, Merritt thought, however skewed its claims and warrants, and he strongly agreed with Beck's closing assertion that "Industry cannot long remain free if Labor also is not free." Even Harry Bridges would sign on to that.

What really came as a surprise to Merritt was Carl Hamilton's invitation to him in early January to attend a meeting of the ILWU Seattle local. Ken protested, saying flat-out that it would be an insult to the membership to bring a Teamster to a meeting, going so far as to suggest Merritt might divulge union business. All the same, Carl's invitation held, and Merritt accepted it, partly to spite his brother-in-law.

"Let him see how a democratic union operates," Carl told Ken, a comment Merritt viewed as a slap at Teamster leadership, which didn't pester the rank-and-file with the nitpicky details of every business agreement it signed. According to Beck, the workingman wanted to do his job and go home. He didn't want to sit through tedious policy meetings. The union paid its officers a respectable salary to handle the day-to-day operations, and the members didn't care how their breaks were negotiated as long as they got them.

Two weeks later Carl cleared the visit with the president of the ILWU local. The meeting was scheduled for that Wednesday night, but Carl told Merritt that before the meeting began he wanted to take him down to the Lander Street Freight Docks on the East Waterway, across from Harbor Island, to show him how things were done. So that Wednesday afternoon Merritt left the Teamsters Hall early and accompanied Carl to the waterfront. As they walked down the first pier, longshoremen and dockers greeted Carl like some kind of returning hero. He introduced Merritt as "my son-in-law" to the men and bragged that Merritt was studying to be a labor lawyer, which was a stretch. He didn't let on that Merritt was a Teamster.

Carl lit up when he introduced Merritt to Pete Bolotof, a longshoreman from the days when the ILWU was just forming back in '36.

"That's right," Pete confirmed after Carl recounted a bit of their history together. Pete had a kind of Popeye smile that turned up at one side of his creviced face. The quill-like hairs of his eyebrows arched up over a pair of sharp, squinty eyes, and a watch cap that was far too small for his head was cocked to one side of his white-haired head. "Longshore Registration Number 5881, Union Book Number 5046, Local 10, ILWU," Pete rattled off. "I worked lumber for five years and general cargo as a hold man for the past nine."

"No one can discharge a freighter faster than Pete," said Carl.

"And I still got all my arms and legs," Pete bragged. "Fingers, too."

A freighter from Formosa had just come in loaded with sacks of raw sugar, and Pete had to haul his 4-wheeler, a kind of flat-bed wagon, aboard the ship and get it lowered into the main hold. His job was to move palettes loaded with sugar sacks from the fore and aft holds to beneath the hatch of the main hold for discharging. He shook Carl's hand, then shook Merritt's hand and said, "Nice to meetcha," and pushed his 4-wheeler toward one of the booms to be hoisted aboard the freighter.

As they moved along to the next dock, Carl explained how Pete's job, and most of the manual labor jobs down here, would eventually be mechanized, and that men like Pete would be out of work before too long. Freighter companies were more and more using cargo containers, which would eventually change how everything was done. "Ken will have to see the union through that," he said with resignation.

As they reached the next dock, an argument broke out between the dock supervisor and two men who had just delivered two truckloads of lumber from the Weyerhaeuser mill in Everett. Apparently the two men, both Teamsters, had been told in Everett that the lumber was to go straight onto the longshore cargo boards for loading into the hold of the Philippine freighter tied to the end of the dock. But the dock supervisor said no, he wanted double-handling, which Carl told Merritt meant unloading the lumber onto the floor of the dock and having longshoremen restack it onto the cargo boards.

"You see, the man in the ship's hold who's standing beneath the hook, he'll only work under a load that's been stacked by a docker. He doesn't trust anyone else." Carl seemed to enjoy the altercation, as if he were watching a boxing match. "This means those two Teamsters there, rather than having the lumber taken off their trucks by a docker and placed directly onto the cargo boards, have to unload it onto the dock themselves. Then a docker, an ILWU man, will load it onto the cargo boards. Those're the rules."

"Why not go straight to the hold with it?" Merritt asked, sympathetic to the Teamsters, who'd been told one thing at the lumberyard and something else at the point of delivery. Yet, even though they had a legitimate gripe, they weren't going to find any satisfaction down here unless they forced the issue and refused to unload the lumber at all.

"Chances are," said Carl, pointing to the two flatbed trucks, "each of those loads are over the sling load weight limit, especially if it's not come out of one of our warehouses—which it hasn't. So it's dangerous if you're that guy in the hold trying to maneuver the sling load into place. Once it's on the dock, the gang boss will have his men skim the load down to size as it's put on cargo boards. The supervisor up in Everett, if he's not in a ILWU warehouse, wants to ship what he's got as fast as he can. He's not beholden to union rules, even if they're right there on his clipboard."

Merritt heard one of the Teamsters call the dock supervisor a bastard as he affixed a sling to the manual crane at the front end of his flatbed and prepared to unload the lumber. Carl and Merritt watched as he operated the crane and the other man brought each stack of lumber to rest on the dock. The dock supervisor left one of his dockers on the scene to witness the unloading and went about his business.

"Gotta play by the rules," Carl said as they walked away, "or someone gets hurt." He turned to Merritt. "Your two Teamster buddies back there should file a complaint against the Weyerhaeuser yard. Maybe get Beck to go up there and make it right himself."

Despite his father-in-law's sarcasm, Merritt knew Beck was the kind of guy who just might do that. Beck liked to take matters into his own hands, large or small, which was how he let people know they couldn't pull something over on him. If someone cheated a Teamster, they were cheating *him*—and would have to answer for it. In the case of Weyerhaeuser, this could mean the next shipment out of the Everett yard sat in the rain for a month and missed the next ten freighters to the Philippines or Japan or wherever it was headed. In fact, Merritt had half a mind to file a complaint himself, with a follow-up memo to Beck.

Next he and Carl watched a cargo of green coffee in burlap sacks being discharged from a ship from Guatemala, then bales of jute from a Brazilian ship—the longshoremen stabbing their cargo hooks into the jute bales and leveraging them into place—and finally a load of furniture that a local antiques dealer had shipped over from cash-strapped Europe. Finally, they swung by the Dispatch Hall, where Carl explained that twice a day, at 6 a.m. and 6 p.m., the union dispatcher checked the plug board to assign men to their proper shift rotations. By the time they drove over to Harbor Island to pick up Ken, who worked as a ship clerk there, it was already dark.

The three drove to a diner on East Marginal Way for a bite to eat, and by then it was time to get to the union hall for the meeting. On the drive over, Ken, sitting up front, turned around and looked at Merritt in the back.

"You're my sister's husband," he said, "so when I tell you not to repeat anything you hear tonight, I know you'll keep your mouth shut."

"Right," said Merritt, knowing that no amount of assurance would be enough for Ken.

More than a hundred men were in attendance at the meeting of ILWU Local 19. Merritt and Carl sat in the back of the smoky hall while Ken, who was a union organizer, sat near the front. The president of the local called the meeting to order, and the last meeting's minutes were approved. The secretary of the local then read through a list of notices. Men were warned to keep lunchrooms clean at their respective piers or else have them closed. Any hatchtender overseeing more than one set of winches at a time, they were told, would be fined $10. The local would loan $1,000 to Local 7 in Bellingham to help in its legal battle against the maritime employers association, which was seeking access to the local's financial records. Eagle Transfer had agreed to use drivers from the 19 hiring hall rather than Teamsters, Merritt noted. Night business agent Vern Sevenson had reported that working long steel at night at the Ames Steel dock did not appear safe and so the local was going to send an investigator to look into it. The local would donate $50 to the annual charity drive by The Millionair Club. And finally, the hat was passed around for Benny Lands, who came down ill last month and had a wife and four kids to support.

After the notices were read, the floor was opened to discussion of that evening's announced topic: the prospect of the union losing control of its hiring halls under Taft-Hartley. One by one, men stood from their folding chairs, lined up before the microphone set in the middle the floor, and had their say.

"Brother Holmstrom is recognized," the secretary said from the podium at the front.

"I've known this law was rotten from the start," Brother Holmstrom shouted into the floor mike, sending a screech of feedback from the floor speakers. "They're trying to go back to a company union with this thing. Probably bring back Blue Books, too. Before you know it we're back to shape-ups and speed-ups and no sling load limits and all hell's busted loose again on the docks and men are out work, getting hurt, or worse." He paused and when the secretary asked him if that was all, he leaned into the mike and said, "For now, Chuck," and sat back down to the guffaws of the membership.

Next Brother Redfield stepped to the microphone, thanked the secretary for recognizing him, and succinctly said that the Seattle local, and all the locals up and down the West Coast, had better prepare to do what needed to be done to get this law turned around. "That's all," he said, and the membership applauded vigorously.

Merritt had never seen this level of participation in a union local before—certainly not at the meetings of Local 174 of the Brotherhood of Teamsters, which were dull as dust. Whether anything was being accomplished here was hard to say, but members certainly had the freedom to speak their piece. When he heard Brother Hamilton being recognized, he looked around to see Ken stepping up to the microphone.

"The shipowners are waiting for the current agreement to expire so they can test this law out and see what kind of teeth it has," he said authoritatively. He was all business. "I don't think we can wait. Elsewise we'll be caught flatfooted. The Executive Board talked this through last night and came to the conclusion to recommend starting up a strike fund this very night—without delay. Therefore, I move the membership accept the Board's recommendation."

After asking Ken to repeat the motion, the secretary called for a second and Carl stood to second the motion. The vote that followed was unanimous, and it was furthermore agreed that each member would pay $20 into the strike fund no later than March 1, 1948, with the stipulation that, in the event no strike or lockout occurred on June 15 when the current agreement expired, each member would be refunded his prorated portion of the strike fund.

After that, another half dozen votes took place on matters ranging from strike preparations to pension funds. Nothing of cost or consequence to the local occurred without the rank-and-file's approval. This meant the meeting went well into the night, lasting more than three hours, and that it was well past 11:00 p.m. by the time it was adjourned.

Carl then drove Merritt back to his car, which he'd left parked near the

East Waterway. During the drive, Ken slung his arm across the front seat again, looked back at Merritt, and reminded him to keep his trap shut about what he'd heard that night. Merritt told him not to worry and thanked Carl for letting him tag along. When they pulled up next to his car, he shook hands with both men and got out.

"Give Clara my love," his father-in-law said as Merritt fished in his pocket for his keys.

He said he would, and as he got into his car, he pictured Clara asleep back at their apartment in the University District—his wife, he thought, the longshoreman's daughter.

BOOK FOUR

Only When I Dance With You

Seattle, 1934

More than fifteen hundred longshoremen and maritime workers marched four abreast behind the hearse that carried Marty Cole's casket. Men held banners and placards and sang union songs as the funeral cortege made its way from the union hall, across the top of Capitol Hill, to Lakeview Cemetery. The procession was led by Shannon Creeley, a jitney driver who'd been on the picket lines in '21 before the longshoremen's union was first busted up. He walked beside Marty's widow, who was cloaked in black, a woman just a few years older than Carl's oldest son, Freddy. Also at the head of the procession were Frank Jenkins and Shaun Maloney, both members of the strike committee. Farther back, Carl marched alongside three men from his most recent pick-and-shovel gang. Some men in the procession wore black suits, as Carl did, while just as many wore their work clothes, prepared to return to the picket lines once the burial service ended.

As they proceeded down Broadway Avenue, bluecoats on motorcycles and in sidecars sped ahead to block traffic. Before the procession had left the union hall, a warning went out about agitators, company agents who might want to disrupt the funeral proceedings and keep the union faithful from paying their last respects to a fallen brother. For this reason everyone was on their best behavior.

So when a young roughneck tried to start something by shouting down one of the coppers and calling him a coward and a murderer, several older longshoremen interceded. The upstart was pulled back into line while one of the wiser, more level-headed men started singing. When he came to the chorus, half the procession joined in:

Solidarity forever, solidarity forever
Solidarity forever
For the Union makes us strong.

After reaching the gravesite, the men from Marty's last gang lifted the casket from the open hearse and lowered it into the earth as if it were a sling board they were lowering into the hold of a freighter. The Methodist Episcopal minister from Marty's church offered a short benediction, and then Shannon Creeley stepped forward to give the eulogy.

"Marty was a man who loved the waterfront," he began. "But Marty Cole was no common wage laborer. Hell no . . ." And here he paused, as if embarrassed at having cussed in front of Marty's widow and the minister. "No," he went on, louder and more forcefully, looking out across the rank-and-file that encircled the gravesite. "Marty Cole was a union man through and through!"

At this a hurrah went up from the throng of longshoremen. A cargo hook was passed forward and when it reached the gravesite, it came to Carl, who handed it to Shannon.

Shannon raised the hook above his head.

"How committed was Marty to the cause of his union?" he shouted hoarsely. The throng quieted down to hear the answer, and lowering his voice Shannon declared, "He was willing to die for it," and bent over the open grave and placed the cargo hook on top of the casket. When he straightened up, he looked once more over the crowd. "For Marty," he shouted, "and for every man who's made the final sacrifice for his union—We shall prevail!"

The policemen who stood on the parameter of the service shuffled their feet and looked nervous as the longshoremen roared their approval.

A few minutes later when a representative from the ILA National Council, speaking on behalf of Joe Ryan, stepped forward to read a statement of condolences to the family, the crowd jeered him. Carl feared the guy might be assaulted, but then another union rep, this one from the ILA Local in San Francisco, came forward to read a statement from Harry Bridges on behalf of the West Coast Strike Committee. The statement reiterated the principles of trade unionism and ended with a quote from 1 *Corinthians*: "Every man's work shall be made manifest: for the day shall declare it, because it shall be revealed by fire; and the fire shall try every man's work of what sort it is."

Everyone seemed moved by the Scriptural passage, and then, after a sheet of lyrics to a hymn were passed around, Shannon Creeley started everyone off with his raspy Irish tenor:

> *If I walk in the pathway of duty,*
> *If I work till the close of the day;*
> *I shall see the great King in His beauty,*
> *When I've gone the last mile of the way.*

Following the hymn, nearly every man in attendance walked past the gravesite to toss a fist-full of dirt onto the coffin of Marty Cole and express his sympathies to Marty's widow. Before the cortege had set off from the union hall, Shannon had informed everyone that she would receive Marty's full pension—at the very level for which they were fighting and not a penny less!

As the service came to a close, Carl drifted away from the crowd, exited the cemetery through the side gates, and made his way downtown to catch the trolley back to West Seattle.

For supper that evening Glenora served beef stew—potatoes and turnips mostly—and afterward sat Clara and Kenneth down on the living room floor to review the day's lesson from the Bible and *Science and Health*, while Freddy ducked out the backdoor. With a belly full of stew, Carl dozed off in his armchair. Yet when he woke a few hours later, the house was quiet, darkness had fallen, and it was time to get back to the picket lines.

TWENTY-EIGHT
Clara, Winter 1948

Clara and Merritt had their first quarrel not long after the holidays when Merritt unexpectedly raised the subject of children again. They had agreed they wanted to have children—at least two, maybe three—yet the plan was to wait a year or two. Merritt still needed to finish school. Plus, though she'd only ever been enrolled part-time at Cornish, she now wanted to take her degree. Then there were their jobs. Between the two of them they earned enough to support themselves—nearly $80 a week—and were even able to start a savings account. But a baby would bring added expenses and mean Clara would have to quit her job at Frederick & Nelson, which she didn't want to do, at least not yet. So she told Merritt they ought to hold off, as they'd planned, until they got their feet more firmly planted.

"That's just selfish" was his curt and rather hurtful response. It was probably the harshest thing he'd ever said to her, and she didn't know what to make of it. They'd squabbled in the past, but always over inconsequential matters such as Merritt's refusal to buy a new suit or Clara's over-tipping the waiter at Skipper's. In five months of marriage, they'd not once bickered about the usual things married couples bickered about: visiting their in-laws, keeping the house tidy, telephoning when one was going to be late for dinner, that kind of thing—which only made Merritt's outburst that much more confusing.

"Why's it selfish?" she asked. They sat in the living room, she on the velour-covered sofa, he in the armchair. The walls were hung with a painting of mixed flowers Clara had done and a woodcut print of the lodge at Lake Quinault they'd purchased on their honeymoon. "Just because I don't want to hurry into something, that's selfish?"

Merritt tapped the end of his cigarette into the ashtray stand next to his armchair. She didn't mind his cigarettes, but two weeks ago he set a box of White Owl cigars beside the armchair and now every evening after dinner he lit one up as if he were Winston Churchill in a wartime newsreel, stoking away at it until the tip burned bright orange and rancid cigar smoke clouded the air, smelling like scorched leather.

"Because we're ready," he said and exhaled a stream of cigarette smoke through his nose. "I am at least."

Clara gave him a hurt look. "Don't say that," she said. "I want to have children as much as you do."

Did she? she wondered as soon as the words left her mouth, and told herself, *Yes, she did . . . Just not right now.* She rose from the sofa, walked around the back of the armchair where Merritt sat, and wrapped her arms around his chest.

"We should practice more first," she said and kissed his whiskered neck. "As they say, practice makes perfect."

Merritt crushed his cigarette out in the ashtray and stood up, breaking free from her arms. "I'm serious, Clara." He looked back at her. "I'm going to graduate this summer and I already have a good job. My sister had her first child when she was still in her teens. We're not getting any younger, you know."

This was true. She'd never imagined herself turning twenty-three, but she was going to in three short months. She pictured herself holding a swaddled baby in her arms, sitting on the sofa while Merritt smoked one of his cigars in the armchair. It wasn't an especially appealing scenario to her. She thought of the letter she'd received recently from her old friend Adel, who was living in Paris with a Romanian composer she'd fallen in love with. They weren't even married, yet they lived together in a large apartment with a balcony overlooking the Rue de Sévigné. Clara was embarrassed to write back saying she lived in university housing just off Pacific Street in the U District. She couldn't possibly imagine telling Adel that she no longer painted, no longer did illustrations for Frederick's, had married a Teamster, and was pregnant to boot. She would come off as a regular West Seattle *hausfrau*.

Three weeks later, however, and equally to her surprise, Merritt announced that he was taking her on a weekend retreat to a lodge in the Cascades. She didn't know how or why, but this generous gesture changed her mind and overnight she decided the time *was* right to have children. Merritt was a fine husband and would be a wonderful father and they would raise happy, intelligent children together. So for two days she and Merritt stowed themselves away in the rustic room of the mountain lodge and rarely left their high platform bed. Beneath the heavy wool blankets, they watched snow form drifts along the window ledge, thought of names for the baby (both boy and girl), and copulated to their hearts' content.

In six weeks' time, right on schedule, her menses stopped, the morning queasiness began, and when she went to the University Health Center, the obstetrician confirmed she was pregnant. Because she was now one of the senior illustrators at Frederick & Nelson, of which there were only three, she was able to arrange with Max—whom Merritt liked to poke fun at for being so fey—to work primarily from home. In her first trimester when she came down sick again with a fever and cough, the doctor attributed it to increased susceptibility as her body adjusted to the hormonal changes and suggested she consider lying up as her due date approached.

When Clara told her parents she was pregnant, her mother advised her to rest often and remember to heed spirit over physiology by praying daily. "A child is a divine idea, sweetie, and God in his goodness plans only good for you and your baby," she told Clara. Meanwhile, Merritt was as solicitous as any husband and father-to-be could be. He placed damp washcloths on her forehead and neck, messaged her aching back and feet, and when she lost weight rather than gained, he prepared meat and potatoes for her every night. From the start of the pregnancy, her body seemed to take on a will of its own. She became thirsty, hungry, itchy, achy, and nauseated at the most inopportune times. Out and about in public, she often had to excuse herself to rush to the ladies' room to urinate or vomit.

She had only just begun adjusting to the physical turmoil of being pregnant when she experienced severe cramps one afternoon, and later that evening found brownish-red spots on her underpants. She was reluctant to call the doctor or go to the health center, not wanting to overreact to every minor agony her body put her through, and instead remained in bed that evening as Merritt cooked minute steaks, fried potatoes, and canned cream corn for dinner. She tried to detach herself from her material frame, as the church had taught her to, and dwell instead on mental anatomy, and eventually the cramps subsided and she was able to fall asleep.

She slept fitfully through the night and woke early the next morning feeling a warm and unpleasant wetness in her pajama bottoms. When a sharp pain stabbed at her abdomen, she hurried into the bathroom and instantly felt a rush of thick fluid come from her. She sat on the toilet and started whimpering as the discharge continued. Merritt knocked lightly at the bathroom door to ask if she was okay, but before answering she looked into the toilet to see the clots of blood and mucus and turned away and flushed. She was crying when she came out of the bathroom and told Merritt she thought she might have just had a miscarriage.

Later that morning the doctor at the clinic said it sounded very likely that she had miscarried, but that they would only know for sure in a day or two if Clara stopped experiencing the usual effects of the pregnancy. She and Merritt went home confused and distraught, wondering what had gone wrong. Was she simply incapable of bearing a child, as some women were? The doctor had assured them that she was perfectly capable, and that an incident such as this did not equate to infertility. It was not unusual, he told them, for miscarriages to occur in first-time mothers, but that at her age and being in good health, they should not be too concerned. He advised them to wait six months and try again.

"I'm not *even* a first-time mother," Clara said and collapsed onto the sofa and cried as Merritt held her. Why had her body betrayed her so? Or was the betrayal really her own—a betrayal of Spirit born in God? Had she erred so terribly in fruitless worship of material over spiritual science that this was the tragic result? Would Merritt come to think that she never really wanted a baby in the first place, that this was her retaliation for his insistence on starting a family so soon? *No*, she told herself. It was not her fault—nor her intention. It just happened. They would do as the doctor advised and try again in six months. The second pregnancy, the doctor had told them, almost always succeeded.

After their visit to the clinic, Merritt coaxed her into drinking a cup of tea and eating two of the ginger cookies her mother had sent over the day before. He helped her into bed and she laughed at him for treating her like an invalid. When she held his forearms and asked if he was going to be all right, he kissed her on the forehead and told her not to worry about him.

Losing her own baby reminded Clara of the loss of her baby sister May. Five years old at the time, she couldn't comprehend why her little sister had gone away. The baby was there in the house, just as her precious baby had been inside of her, and then was gone. You try to bring a child forth into the world, she thought, but sometime they part from it before you can convince them with your love to stay. As she endured this latest grief, it made sense that a woman in her circumstances, as her mother had been seventeen years ago, would turn to the spiritual healing advocated by someone like Mary Baker Eddy, someone who offered spiritual nurturance and promised her followers eternal health.

Clara turned instead to her art. She painted with a level of interest she'd not had since completing her portrait series. She also found relief at her drawing table at Frederick & Nelson, working fulltime again and illustrating the soon-to-be-released designs from France and New York and even Milan. It was almost April, a month since her miscarriage, when Merritt suggested they go dancing again. He took her to the Cloud Room, which had recently opened atop the Camlin Hotel downtown. They dressed up, Merritt in his standard blue suit and red tie, she in the new outfit that he'd insisted she purchase after she described to him its swooping neckline. ("Have it delivered," he reminded her.) The ensemble included a pink pleated top, the revealing neckline edged with black lace, and a black rayon skirt that fell just below the knee. The combination accentuated her shoulders and long legs, and with the black heel-and-strap espadrilles and black silk gloves, she looked more fetching than any one of Max's silly Tea Room models.

The Cloud Room had overnight become one of Seattle's hottest night spots. When they stepped off the elevator into the large open room, Merritt gave the maitre d' his name and they were escorted to a window table. The entire room was enclosed in floor-to-ceiling windows that looked out in all four directions—toward Puget Sound, Lake Union, Capitol Hill, and the downtown. The interior had soft russet lighting, enhanced by a single tapered candle on each table, which the maitre d' lit as they seated themselves. Everything about the new club was elegant and suave, and Clara imagined herself sitting in the famous Cloud Room atop Rockefeller Center in midtown Manhattan. It seemed Seattle had finally reached the pinnacle of refinement and sophistication.

Merritt ordered champagne, and they toasted to their evening on the town. The French on the menu gave them some difficulty until the waiter came to their aid. For her entrée, Clara ordered coq au vin and for dessert crème brulé. Merritt ordered the beef bourguignon with celery remoularde, followed by a chocolate tart. Merritt also ordered a bottle of Bordeaux wine without even asking the price, and after the main meal they had coffee and sipped an after-dinner liqueur.

Clara was more than a little tipsy when Merritt set his napkin down, stood up from the table, and asked her to dance. As they made their way to the dance floor, the band played a slow rendition of Glenn Miller's "Body & Soul." They hadn't danced since their honeymoon, when Merritt twirled her across the windswept deck of the Kalakala ferry as it plied its way across the Sound. It seemed dreamlike now to be dancing so high above the city, to feel Merritt's hand pressing the small of her back, to slide-step-and-turn, to nod politely to the other handsomely dressed couples, to admire the band in their black tie and tails, to hear the brassy horns followed by the clarinet's playful trill, to glide across the polished parquet floor. All Clara could do was close her eyes, lean in close to Merritt, and breathe in the spicy scent of his freshly-shaved cheek.

When the number ended, they stepped outside onto the balcony for some fresh air, and as Merritt lit a cigarette and loosened his tie, Clara leaned on the railing. The cool night air made her lightheaded. She looked out at the dark patch of Lake Union and the lights climbing Queen Anne Hill, then took a deep breath and abruptly started coughing as if she'd swallowed wrong and was choking on something. Merritt stomped out his cigarette and came to her side.

"Let's go back in," he said as she recovered.

"In a moment," she answered and touched his arm. "I'm okay." She felt another cough coming on, swallowed hard, and crossed her arms.

"It's too cold out here," he insisted and standing behind her wrapped his arms about her torso. The warmth of his body, combined with the breeze on her face and bare arms, made her almost swoon.

"One more dance," she said, "and then we'll go home."

TWENTY-NINE
Merritt, Spring 1948

Merritt had never known death's cold presence in his life. Not directly at least, as he did now with the loss of their baby. Even in the war he hadn't actually seen men die. The USS *Washington* had miraculously escaped having a single casualty while he served on her. There were men he heard about being killed in battle elsewhere—including his high school friend Archie—but that was different. Both his parents and his sister were alive, and his grandparents had all passed away before he was born. So until this moment he had effectively been spared the sudden and irrevocable experience of loss, grief, and mortality that death imparted.

In the weeks following the miscarriage, he mostly wished to comfort Clara any way he could. She stayed in bed three days straight after it happened and even had Merritt retrieve for her a copy of *Science and Health* from the downtown Reading Room, which he hadn't entered since he first met Clara there. But then she started to draw again and eventually brought out her watercolors and oil paints, and he turned the guest bedroom into a studio for her She also returned to her job at Frederick's, and two weeks after that he took her to the Cloud Room, after which it seemed everything would return to normal.

At the university, his advisor told him he ought to apply for "internship credit" for his job with the Teamsters, and Merritt also made up his mind to write his senior thesis on the history of the International Brotherhood of Teamsters in Washington State. He was given full access to the Joint Council and Western Conference archives and conducted a dozen interviews with Teamster old-timers, including Beck himself, who coyly stepped around discussing details of his early brass-knuckle days as an organizer. Merritt's advisor eventually approved the thesis, describing him as "Ph.D. material," and he was one step closer to graduation.

Everything seemed to be back on track until he received another letter, this one signed:

> *Being a fairy is one thing, but we never took you for a stoolie too. I guess you're family now though. Our Everett boys saw you at the Lander dock with that commie-loving father-in-*

228

law of yours. They radioed in and had you tailed to their hall. You must be a big hero down there, being an insider on Denny Way and all. Imagine, a regular quisling right there in our very own headquarters. Beck would love finding that out, wouldn't he? Watch yourself sisterboy. We're done sweet talking. — A. Smitson

The letter came straight to the apartment, without a return address. Merritt read it in the living room while Clara painted in the guestroom. After reading it twice through, he was too ashamed—and furious—to face her, so he called out that he was going for a walk, grabbed his jacket and hat from the front closet, and drove up the street to the College Inn Pub.

He slid into a back booth with a pitcher of beer and tried to figure this thing out all over again. It was obvious Smitson had something on him, as he had all along. He probably got it through his son, who Smitson said had been in the Navy and was also a Teamster. After the one incident in the Exeter Hotel, already four years ago, Merritt had never seen or heard from Ensign Rivard again. Even after he received the first letter, he expected the matter would just go away if he ignored it. Though he couldn't remember anybody by the name of Smitson ever coming through the Recruitment Station, that didn't mean a thing. More than a hundred men had been processed through the office every day. If the Pre-Separation Center hadn't closed up shop at the end of the previous year, he could have gone down and found out more about Smitson Jr.'s service in the Navy. Maybe he'd even been aboard the USS *Washington* with him. With a crew of over a thousand seamen, he'd known at most a handful of his shipmates. If he went out to the Sand Point Naval Air Station, he thought, maybe he could find a copy of the ship's manifest.

But honestly, what good would it do? Smitson apparently had him dead to center on this thing and that's all that mattered. Which brought him back to thinking he could always just deny it. Unless Rivard himself was involved in the blackmailing, which he doubted, it was his word against Smitson's. On the other hand, he was a terrible liar and knew it. It was one thing to keep a secret, but another to maintain a boldface lie. Besides, once word of something like this spread, denying it would be pointless. If people even had a hunch you were funny, you were done for. There was never any benefit of the doubt or leniency toward the weak, much less forgiveness or understanding. It was a smear that would leave him marked for the rest of his life, his humiliation trailing him like a mangy old dog.

Poor Clara, he kept thinking and poured himself another glass of beer. There would have to be a divorce. They would never have another chance to start a family. She would move back in with her parents and he would never see her again. The prospect enraged him, and he cussed the Smitsons under his breath, father and son alike—but especially the father, whom he could put a face to. *Brother Smitson*! He'd have to show the sonuvabitch he had as much Teamster grit as the next fellow. He would drive up to Everett right now and have it out with him. He got up and went to the phone booth at the back of the pub to telephone Clara and tell her he was going down to the union hall to take care of some business that was still on his mind.

"I love you," he said and waited for her to respond in kind.

"I love you, too," she said and added, "Don't stay late."

Before driving the two hours to Everett, he would get Smitson's address from the Joint Council records. He gunned the car across the University Bridge, down Eastlake Avenue, and pulled up to the Teamsters Hall in record time. He'd been given keys to the union hall entrance and Joint Council offices three months before when he started work on his thesis. This after-hours mission, though, had a far different purpose, and so he was tense as he let himself into the darkened union hall. Light from the streetlamps filtered through the iced glass of office doors as he walked down the polished hallway floors. He passed Beck's office, half expecting him to be inside plotting his next move toward Teamster dominance.

The whole situation was unnerving. How long had the Smitsons been keeping tabs on him? At least back before he'd shipped out—which in itself was outrageous. Yet apparently they weren't alone in tracking him. How else could he explain the two Everett Teamsters snitching on him when he was down at the docks with Carl, then having him followed to the ILWU union hall? What the hell was going on? Was some rogue element of the Teamsters conducting its own witch hunt for union infiltrators? Did the Smitsons really take Merritt for an ILWU plant, spying on the Teamsters on behalf of Harry Bridges? Or did they just have it in for longshoremen and anyone associated with them? The hostility between the two unions could not be underestimated. From the way Smitson alluded to his father-in-law in the letter, it seemed he might even know Carl. On the other hand, maybe the Smitsons weren't rogue Teamsters at all, but just two of Beck's own handpicked agents. Like the heckler at Bridges' talk. Or himself, for that matter, acting as recorder of the same talk. He'd become much more privy to Beck's tactics in the past year and almost anything seemed possible now. How different really was Dave Beck today from Dave Beck twenty or thirty years ago?

Merritt turned on the overhead light in the main office of the Joint Council and located the Membership Directory. It listed Arda Smitson as a member of Local 38 in Everett but didn't give a home address, as it did for every other member. So he opened more cabinet drawers, going deeper into the files. Each local was required to submit duplicate initiation cards upon every member's admittance to the union. The entire file contained thousands of cards going back decades, filed numerically by local. When he found the cards for Everett Local 38, he promptly pulled out the one he was looking for. It read:

Arda Smitson. Initiation into membership of the International Brotherhood of Teamsters, Chauffeurs, and Wagoners: 1936. Employer: Weyerhaeuser. Former union memberships: International Longshoremen's Association (ILA), Local 38-12, Seattle—AFL affiliate. Member in good standing.

So Smitson had been an IBT member for the past twelve years, since before the union updated its official name by dropping *Wagoners* and adding *Warehousemen* and *Helpers*. The card listed his address not as Everett, but Seattle, 63rd St. NW, which put him in Ballard, smack dab in the neighborhood some people called the Scandinavian ghetto. While the Seattle address came as a surprise to him, it was Smitson's past membership in the longshoremen's union that really caught Merritt's interest.

He pulled the card from the file and folded it into the inside pocket of his jacket. If information was a blackmailer's lifeblood, he wanted as much on Smitson as he could get.

It was past ten by the time he drove over the Spokane Street Bridge and down 35th Avenue West on his way to the Hamilton house. Before leaving the Teamsters Hall, he'd phoned ahead, apologizing to Carl for rousing him out of bed and asking if he could come over and speak to him in private.

"Is it Clara?" Carl asked. "Is she okay?"

"She's okay," he assured his father-in-law. "She's probably sound asleep by now. It's a union matter."

"At this time of night?"

"It's not official business," Merritt explained. "I want your take on something."

Carl said he'd leave the porch light on and the front door unlocked. "Just come in," he told Merritt "Don't knock or you'll wake the missus."

Fortunately, Ken Hamilton had recently moved into the new government housing at High Point, not far from his parents' house, and was planning to marry a girl he'd met at church. This meant Merritt didn't have to worry about his hardnosed brother-in-law being there when he entered the house to speak to Carl.

As Merritt let himself in the front door, Carl was seated in an armchair waiting for him. He had on a green hunting jacket over his pajamas and was in

231

his bedroom slippers.

"Let's step out onto the stoop," he said and guided Merritt back out the front door.

There was a pungency in the spring air, and Merritt could see Mrs. Hamilton's crocuses and daffodils sprouting in the flower beds along the side of the house. He took out his pack of cigarettes, offered one to Carl, who declined, and lit one for himself.

"What's on your mind?" his father-in-law asked.

Merritt reached into his jacket pocket, pulled out the Teamster initiation card, and handed it to him. "Do you know him? He's drives a truck now, but he used to be a longshoreman. I thought since you were active back then, you might recognize the name."

Carl unfolded the card, held it up to the porch light, and squinted at it. "This is a Teamster initiation card," he said and eyeballed Merritt.

"That's right."

"So what's this fella to you?"

Merritt took a long pull on his cigarette and rubbed it out on the riser of the front stoop. He flicked the butt into the grass.

"He's getting on my case," he replied vaguely. In his excitement to ferret out information on Smitson, he hadn't anticipated Carl asking him questions about his late-night sleuthing.

"Union matters, you say?"

"That's right," said Merritt. Of course he could never mention to Carl or to anyone else Smitson's threatening letters, since to do so would be to reveal the source of the threats. It made him nervous now to have to dance around the issue, and it was clear that Carl knew he was holding something back.

Carl returned the card to him. "I didn't know he was a Teamster," he said. "Once Smitson left the waterfront, I never heard hide nor hair from him again. And good riddance."

Merritt tried to keep a sure and steady posture and not start grilling his father-in-law. "So you knew him?"

"Come to think of it," Carl said, "I remember hearing he tried to get on at one of the exception ports, maybe up at Anacortes. So I figured that's where he'd gone." The so-called exception ports, as Carl had once explained to Merritt, were Anacortes, Aberdeen, and Tacoma, each of which had refused to break with the ILA in 1936 when the ILWU formed on the West Coast.

"What do you know about him?" Merritt asked, trying not to sound too eager.

"I know he was a Joe Ryan man all the way. I know he was a dirty weasel who tried to kill me once by dropping a sling load on my head."

"That was Arda Smitson?" Merritt asked incredulously, remembering Carl's account of the days leading up to the violent '34 strike. He pushed his hat up and rubbed his forehead as a sharp headache came over him.

Carl proceeded to fill in the details of what he knew of Arda Smitson from that period. "He must've sat out the strike, because I can't recall once seeing him on the picket lines," he said and stared into the darkness beyond the front stoop. "But once we won, there he was again."

He recounted how, as a Joe Ryan man, Smitson threw a fit two years later when the West Coast longshoremen voted to break with the ILA and, under Harry Bridges, start up the ILWU—that is, all but the three exception ports. Smitson despised Bridges, thought he was a Soviet agent sent to sabotage the shipping industry by undermining Joe Ryan and the ILA. Plus Smitson was a hothead, and when Seattle longshoremen abandoned Ryan and went with the ILWU, he turned even meaner. He threatened the new local's business agent and everyone else who was active in the union—but especially Carl, since they'd already had their run-in with one another in '34. That meant Smitson made a lot of enemies. "Then as now," Carl added as if to make yet another jab at the Teamsters, "our membership was very active."

Merritt let it pass and asked what else he knew, and Carl went on to say that Smitson stayed on the waterfront for the first few months after the split, but when he stopped paying his ILWU dues, the dispatcher stopped sending him out on jobs. Then one night in the Hatch 'n' Hold Tavern, Smitson said he was going to burn the hiring hall down if he didn't get put on a gang the very next day. Carl was there when he said it and even lent a hand in tossing him out on his head. A couple weeks later, someone said he tried to get on up at Anacortes, or maybe it was Tacoma or Aberdeen—one of the ILA ports at any rate.

"That was the last I heard tell of him," Carl said. "I don't know if he longshored again or not. But I'll tell you this, it makes sense that he ended up a Teamster."

This was another jab, but it didn't matter either. Merritt was still trying to put together all of this new information Carl had given him and reconcile it with Smitson's hounding of him.

"Back then if you were a Joe Ryan man," Carl volunteered, "you were a Dave Beck man, too. They were two of kind. Like that." Carl held two thick fingers side-by-side to demonstrate the close alliance between Ryan and Beck. "Both men were dead set against the '34 strike, and I'll bet you anything Beck blew his top when we broke with the ILA and AFL. He lost any clout he had on the waterfront that day."

It was serious business this, Merritt thought, and the men involved, men like Carl, Ken, Smitson—and Beck—took it all very personally.

"So there it is," Carl concluded. "I don't know if this helps with whatever your business with Smitson is, but I'll give you one bit of advice. Stay clear of him. He's trouble. Maybe he's even got it in for me still. Who knows? You're a straight-up sort, Merritt. You've been a good husband to Clara, so I'll help you anyway I can. But it's best you stay clear of this Smitson fella."

Merritt put his hands in his pockets. The elder Smitson's motivation, his whole character, seemed clear enough at this point. He wanted revenge on Carl and the entire ILWU. But what about the son? Why was he involved? Also, to what extent were other Teamsters helping them? It was questions like these that Merritt could never ask his father-in-law.

"Thanks for talking to me," he said and shook Carl's hand. "It'll probably just blow over."

"Go home to your wife," Carl told him.

"I'll do that," he replied. As for Carl's other advice—about staying clear of Smitson—he only hoped he could.

THIRTY
Clara, Summer 1948

Clara spotted the notice in an insert box on page 6 of the June 12th edition of the morning *Post-Intelligencer*:

Free Chest X-Rays.
Get your chest x-ray at any of the following locations today.

The notice listed twelve locations in Seattle where mobile x-ray machines were set up as part of the drive by the city's Health Department to screen all Seattle residents for tuberculosis. The screening took five minutes, according to Jenny, who'd gotten hers the week before. She told Clara it was painless and urged her to go right away.

The cough that had been nagging her for the past several months had turned more persistent, more rasping, and more worrisome. She tended to suppress it so as not to concern Merritt, and then when he was away from the apartment, she would break out in uncontrollable fits of coughing that would leave her ribs sore and her entire being—mind and body—exhausted. When she went to work, she carried in her handbag a bottle of Pertussin Cough Syrup and a tablespoon, and if she felt a coughing spell coming on she would excuse herself to go to the ladies room and swallow several tablespoons of the foul liquid before the cough erupted. She also began sneaking cod liver oil because she'd heard it was rich in curative properties. She even discovered something called oleum percomophum, several blended fish oils fortified with Viosterol, whatever that was, and convinced herself it made her feel *invigorated*, as promised on the bottle label. For a while, whenever the cough abated for more than a few days, she would let herself believe the snag in her chest had gone away for good. Inevitably, though, it would return, and the whole cycle of coughing and worrying would begin again.

As the coughing fits worsened and began to wake her at night, she could no longer hide the problem from Merritt. When he suggested taking her to the hospital for a chest x-ray, she told him she'd had enough of doctors lately—a reminder to him of her recent miscarriage—and he let the matter drop. But not for long. The very next night, after she'd recovered from one of her fits in bed, he propped himself up on one elbow and challenged her refusal to go to the doctor. "If you're not going to see a doctor, should I just call your mother and have her send over a church practitioner?"

"Stop it," she snapped back at him. She threw off the bed covers and walked across the room. "It's just a cough. Don't get so beside yourself." She went into the bathroom and closed the door.

She felt the cough coming on as she leaned over the bathroom sink. If he said another word, she would order him to stop smoking his damn cigarettes and cigars in the house. Maybe that was the problem, she thought as she angrily washed her face. When she'd composed herself, she came out of the bathroom and apologized for being so brusque.

"Just think about it," he pleaded, and they went back to bed with neither daring, she understood, to express the single thought on both their minds—that she might have TB.

Despite the fund drives each holiday season for Christmas Seals, Clara had all but come to believe that tuberculosis had been eradicated. The disease seemed like something from the past, like small pox, though in truth she knew otherwise. Everyone in Seattle had heard how the celebrated hometown authoress Betty MacDonald had been struck with the disease prior to the war and survived. And that was before all the latest cures. These days the newspapers reported daily on how modern medicine was on the march, inoculating the human race with new vaccines and freeing the world of contagious diseases. Despite such efforts, TB seemed to hang on, and the new mobile x-ray machines signaled only the latest attempt to contain the disease.

When she scrutinized the list of locations for screenings, she saw that there would be machines in the basement of Frederick & Nelson as well as at the Bon Marché and Rhodes department stores. She opted, however, to make her way to the Textile Building, ten blocks away, trusting this would be the least conspicuous location for her to have it done.

As she soon learned, and just as Jenny had told her, the procedure was a simple one. A person stepped behind a painting-size screen that enabled the physician to peer into one's insides and examine the lungs. If the physician detected anything unusual, he directed the person to a private physician for further examination and testing.

And this was just what happened when she took her lunch break to go to the Textile Building. After studying her x-ray and detecting several dark spots on her lungs, the physician listened to her breathing with his stethoscope and tapped her back and chest with two fingers. Her breathing, he told her as she repressed a cough, was extremely labored.

"It could just be congestion," he said, "but you need to have a full examination and sputum test." He then gave her a list of hospitals where she could have these done. "And cover your mouth when you cough."

Clara left the Textile Building that afternoon trying hard not to become alarmed. The physician had informed her that if it was TB, the disease was thoroughly treatable these days and she could be cured within a relatively short period of time. So once back at her desk at Frederick's, she tried to concentrate on her illustrations, deciding she would wait until the evening to tell Merritt, especially since she hadn't even told him she was going for a screening. She would put a drink in his hand, sit him down, and repeat exactly what the doctor had said. In the meanwhile, she allowed herself a silent prayer—*in God's likeness we are all immortal*—and set about illustrating a series of spring hats with names like Feather Puff, Flower Topknot, Glamour Girl, and Halo Cap.

Three days later at the U.S. Marine Hospital on Beacon Hill, she received the official diagnosis. A tuberculin test showed her to be sputum-positive for the tubercle bacillus bacteria, and another more powerful x-ray revealed lesions on both lungs, but especially on her right lung, which, as Dr. Larkin explained, had "an excess of pleural effusion," though her left lung was relatively free of contamination.

Dr. Larkin explained that it appeared she'd been carrying an initial infection for several years, as indicated by the sizable lesion in the upper lobe of her right lung that had calcified over. Clara instantly recalled the terrible episode she'd had four years ago that laid her up in bed for three weeks and led to her losing contact with Merritt. The doctor said the initial infection seemed to have been contained, allowing her to carry on without becoming further ill, but that she'd likely been re-infected in recent months, the new infection reactivating the old one and causing the disease to spread more aggressively through her lungs.

Wearing a flimsy cotton hospital gown and seated on the cold examination table while Merritt held her hand, she didn't cry when the doctor delivered his diagnosis. This seemed different than her miscarriage—which Dr. Larkin confirmed was likely related to the TB—since the loss of their baby was so much more sudden and irrevocable. The miscarriage came with no prognosis, no hope, and brought only grief. With the TB diagnosis, she found herself concerned mostly for Merritt, who would have to endure her prolonged confinement and recovery.

As soon as the doctor left the examination room, Merritt held her in his arms. He let her know everything would be okay and she nodded, but didn't kiss him, understanding that from now on she would need to be extremely cautious not to contaminate him or anyone else. A few minutes later the doctor returned to discuss her treatment options.

"While I wouldn't describe your case as advanced," he opened, sounding very formal, "it's far enough along to concern me, given this is your first diagnosis." Dr. Larkin was a middle-aged man with salt-and-pepper hair, firm hands, and an understated manner, all of which conveyed the impression of a very knowledgeable professional. According to the certificates on the wall, he was a *Phthisiologist* with a degree from Yale University Medical School, as well as a former Navy hospital corpsman. "Some of the most effective measures in fighting this are still rest, good nutrition, good hygiene, and a change of climate—preferably someplace in the mountains since the dry, thin air starves the infection of oxygen. Unfortunately, here in Seattle, we live in a less than hospitable climate for tuberculosis patients."

The doctor's tone remained subdued yet authoritative as he told Clara he was going to start her on the most recently developed bactericide, streptomycin, which had shown remarkable results against her particular strain of pulmonary tuberculosis. "We'll see how you respond," he said, "and after three weeks or so we might combine the streptomycin with other therapies, depending on your progress. We want to be fairly aggressive. First, to avoid surgery, and second, to keep the disease from spreading to other portions of the lungs."

Clara listened calmly, without interrupting. The doctor seemed encouraged, especially in light of the new drug he would give her, though he also warned that the intramuscular injections would not be pleasant. One question on her mind, however, forced her to speak up.

"Will I have to go to a sanatorium?" she asked.

Though she was not even sure sanatoriums still existed, the prospect of quarantine—away from Merritt, from her family, and from her work and art—was what she dreaded more than the disease itself. She glanced at Merritt, who appeared surprised by the question.

Dr. Larkin didn't reply right away but looked thoughtfully at her and Merritt as he weighed his words. "It all depends," he answered finally.

"I can take care of her at home," Merritt interjected before the doctor could say anything more.

"TB is a pernicious disease. It's highly transmissible," the doctor told him. "You'll need to have a skin test yourself."

Merritt scowled as if the doctor were threatening him. He said he would take the skin test first thing in the morning, and then Clara put her hand on his arm to settle him down.

"For now," the doctor went on, addressing Merritt, "I believe Clara would receive the best care at home. As I said, rest, diet, and hygiene are essential. In three weeks we'll do another x-ray, take another sputum sample, and see where she stands."

"So I don't need to go to a sanatorium?"

"No," he answered. "You'll need to adhere to strict home confinement and for the most part remain in bed. And you can't go out in public. You can go outside, but only to parks and other open areas, and only on dry, sunny days." He turned to Merritt. "Mr. Driscoll, you'll have to be exceedingly careful in regard to physical contact with your wife. In fact, I'll consult a colleague about placing you on streptomycin as well, as a precaution." Dr. Larkin then left the examination room again to retrieve instructional literature to send them home with.

Clara set her eyes on Merritt but could think of nothing to say. She apprehended the terrible burden about to be placed on him and wanted to apologize, to tell him she never would have married him if she'd known she was infected. It seemed all she ever did anymore was cause him trouble and worry. First the miscarriage and now this. On top of her already difficult family. It was more than any husband could have bargained for. And yet here he was, steadfast and loving as ever, in sickness and in health, ready to take care of her.

She wanted to spring up and smoother him with kisses, but she was already too weak—and too afraid—to attempt such affection.

The next day Clara wrote two letters, one to Max Lundquist and one to Mr. Boykin, tendering her resignation from Frederick & Nelson, and asked Merritt to hand-deliver both letters directly to the store. She also phoned home to tell her mother and father the regrettable news. To her mother's credit, she refrained from quoting Mary Baker Eddy and offered to bring Clara anything she needed during her recovery—extra linens, bath towels, food stuffs, anything. Yet by the time she hung up, Clara could tell from her mother's strained voice that she was holding back tears, longing for her daughter's spiritual recovery.

Except for a brief visit to the hospital for a skin test, which proved negative, Merritt stayed home the next day to help her get settled into the home confinement. He called the Teamsters Hall and spoke directly to Dave Beck, who, according to Merritt, told him the Teamsters were a family organization, one that looked out for its members when one of them was down, and let Merritt know he could take as much time off from work as he needed.

From that day forward she remained housebound, and suddenly the married student housing seemed like very cramped quarters for only two people. She tried not to let Merritt see her tear up, yet at least once a day, whether out of fear, self-pity, or just plain exhaustion after one of her coughing fits, she fell into a crying spell that usually left her even more exhausted. She waited for the effects of the streptomycin to take hold and resigned herself to her new routine of lying in bed all day. She tried to draw each day, but for the most part she read a lot of books, novels mostly, to wile away the endless hours. She read *Anna Karenina* in one week and then took on the new novel everyone was talking about, *Raintree*

County, which weighed in at over a thousand pages.

Beginning the first week of her confinement, her mother made meals for her and Merritt—soups and stews, various casseroles, bread and muffins—that her father would deliver to their apartment in big steaming pots and towel-draped baskets. Merritt also became a much better cook and even taught himself how to use the pressure cooker he'd given her last Christmas that she refused to go near. He purchased *Cook It Outdoors* by chef James Beard and brought home a charcoal grill which he placed on the walkway leading up to the apartment door. He made a ritual each evening of pouring himself a glass of red wine before commencing the meal preparations, and then allowed Clara to have half a glass of wine with her dinner as well. He also kept the apartment spick and span, scouring the bathroom and kitchen surfaces with Ajax every day and refusing to let Clara lift a finger to help. He stopped smoking inside the apartment and wore a sterile surgical mask whenever they were in the same room, even though she said she should be the one wearing it, not him. Meanwhile, at night he slept on the convertible sofa-bed they bought from Frederick & Nelson with her final employee discount. Sleeping apart like this was the most difficult part of the confinement for Clara. In the seven months they'd been married she'd become accustomed to the warmth and weight of Merritt's slumbering body next to hers, and now it seemed as if the bed were too large, and she would sometimes roll over half-asleep, expecting to drape her arm over his torso, only to embrace the empty space.

By month's end she seemed to be responding well to the combined therapy of streptomycin and strict bed rest. Though her sputum sample still tested positive, the lesions on her right lung had diminished significantly and on her left lung all but disappeared, allowing her to breathe with much less strain. Dr. Larkin now spoke of surgical procedures that might speed her recovery. He described the pneumothorax treatment, whereby air was injected into the lungs with a needle, effecting a partial collapse of the lung and isolating the infected portion. However, the treatment carried only temporary results. Thoracoplasty, on the other hand, involved permanently collapsing the more severely infected lung by removing the ribs that held the lung in place within the chest cavity. By killing the lung tissue in this manner, the infection was also killed. This procedure was highly effective but could only be undertaken if the other lung was free of lesions, which Clara's was not. Yet thoracoplasty was a fairly extreme measure, he advised, and one that resulted in minor disfigurement. As Dr. Larkin went on to explain, many phthisiologists and pulmonologists were increasingly recommending resectioning as an alternative to full thoracoplasty. This procedure involved a limited excision of the diseased pulmonary tissue in the most severely infected lung.

"In your case," he told Clara and Merritt during their weekly visit to the hospital for her injection of streptomycin, "the worse cavitation is in the upper lobe of the right lung, so we would excise the tissue there. This would not eliminate the infection entirely, but it would save the lung and allow your body to fight the remaining infected areas more vigorously."

The prospect of any sort of surgery gripped Clara with the worst kind of dread. It wasn't only that such extreme *materia medica* violated the Christian Science precepts on Divine Authority, which meant succumbing to the lie of the material self. It was more the plain and simple fact that, in her mind at least, modern medical science overestimated its own efficacy and was far more fraught with uncertainty than it owned up to. When Merritt asked the doctor for figures on the success rate of the pulmonary excisions, the doctor replied that he didn't have exact figures on hand, but that his colleagues throughout the Seattle medical community were convinced of the procedure's merits. As Merritt commented in the car as they drove home, he generally trusted medical men, having seen what shipboard medics could do to keep a burned and mangled seamen alive, but he didn't appreciate the doc's dodge about showing them the figures. And Clara agreed. In Christian Science terms, she wanted "a demonstration" from the doctor, just as she would from a church practitioner, before submitting to his healing practices.

Furthermore, she didn't like how the doctor had stopped speaking of Clara's tuberculosis as "eradicable," a term he'd used frequently in his earlier consultations with her. Now he spoke only of "arresting the disease." It seemed to Clara that he was hedging his bets, which left her perplexed at best, and at worst dejected. He increased her dosage of "strep" and prescribed continued rest, and because of her weight loss in the past two months—almost 20 pounds—he urged her to eat more red meat and fish. The strong and hearty woman she'd been just half a year earlier now appeared winnowy and frail in the mirror. Her long arms looked boney, her collar bone craggy, and her high cheeks hollow. By all appearances it looked as though she were becoming a bona fide consumptive, a term no one used any longer but one she increasingly identified with, as if her body were being consumed before her very eyes.

Dr. Larkin also encouraged her to take some exercise in moderation—"A walk around the block," he said, "or to the park. Nothing strenuous. Just enough to get the blood flowing."—advice that he said was based on recent studies of the body's immune system. And Clara welcomed this opportunity to escape the apartment—that is, whenever the sun appeared—and stopped complaining to Merritt so much about cabin fever and becoming stir-crazy. She would make her way down to Portage Bay to stroll along the banks and feed the ducks, and twice she walked across Montlake Bridge all the way to the University Arboretum and back. Yet each time she returned to the tomb-like quiet of the apartment, she realized anew how lonely and frustrated she was without the casual companionship that came with work and school, and wondered how much more of this existence she could endure. She thought how when it came right down to it only two scenarios existed, and to recognize one—that her health would improve—meant to recognize the other—that it would only worsen.

THIRTY-ONE
Merritt, Summer 1948

Until the diagnosis, Merritt had been contemplating confessing his ensign incident to Clara—to clear the decks and save their marriage. But the circumstances of her confinement, the physical demands and emotional strain that it imposed on both of them, squelched that idea. Instead he strived to be as good a husband and caregiver as he could, in penance perhaps for the shame he knew she would suffer if his secret ever came out, but also out of devotion to his one and only love and the fear that he might lose her. When he decided to skip the graduation ceremony at the university, Clara protested, but he insisted if he couldn't attend the ceremony with her, he wouldn't go at all.

As for the Smitson dilemma, he heeded Carl's advice and tried yet again to put it out of mind. He burned the last letter he received and flushed the ashes down the toilet. To respond would only strengthen the Smitsons' conviction that they had something on him. And besides, he had too much pressing upon him at work and at home to be bothering with some two-bit blackmailing scheme.

All the news in Seattle these days was focused on the machinists strike against Boeing Airplane Company, whose production of the B-17 bomber during the war had, to many people's thinking, made victory possible. After a brief post-war lull in its manufacture of aircraft, Boeing had again become the military's primary supplier of bombers and fighter planes. The company was also developing a new line of commercial airplanes. Yet despite this expansion, the mechanics and machinists, the very men who assembled the planes, hadn't seen a single pay raise since the war ended. Their contract had expired and their union, the International Aero Mechanics, wanted to renegotiate. Three months ago, under authority of a provision in Taft-Hartley, President Truman had ordered a mandatory 90-day cooling off period, but contract negotiations kept stalling as Boeing President William Allen refused even to recognize the IAM, much less sit down at the bargaining table with them. So in late spring, members of Seattle Local 751 of the International Aero Mechanics union walked out.

Teamster rank-and-file might have been divided over the strike, yet one thing was certain, and that was that Dave Beck condemned it—forcefully and in no uncertain terms. In a public address at the National Association of

Manufacturers' meeting in Seattle that July, he vowed to restore the integrity of Boeing's production line by any means, even if it meant bringing down the entire International Aero Mechanics union. He was so fervently involved in opposing the strike that Merritt rarely saw him in the Teamsters Hall anymore. He was either locked away in his office, the door guarded by a vigilant Mrs. Kotin, or else running about town meeting with the mayor, the City Council, or William Allen.

For his part, Merritt backed the striking Boeing workers. So one afternoon, wanting to see for himself what they were up against, he left the Teamsters Hall, drove across the Spokane Street Bridge into West Seattle, and headed down West Marginal Way along the Duwamish Waterway toward Boeing Aircraft Plant Number 1. This part of the city had always been a mystery to him, the shores of the waterway part marshland, part industry—an old wooden pier with a fishing shack perched at the end of it right next to a large gravel pit with dump trucks coming and going, a swampy stretch of ditch grass, cattails, and alders beside a quicklime plant from which a cloud of white dust arose. The waterway itself was busy with ship traffic. Two freighters made their way upstream to the turning basin while a Foss tug towing a garbage barge headed in the opposite direction, past Harbor Island and out into the Sound. Closer to shore, a couple of shirtless boys sat on a scow with a dozen trot lines hung over the side.

At West Front Street, Merritt hung a right that put him directly in front of the gates of the Boeing plant. Right away a score of men on the picket lines, all wearing *STRIKE* banners across their chests, began shouting as he idled past, yelling at him to turn back. It took only an instant for him to realize they thought he might be trying to sneak past their lines and into the plant. He heard someone shout out, "Scab!" as a rock dinged the side of his car. He thought of rolling his window down to tell them he had just taken a wrong turn, but before he reached the road that would take him to the First Avenue Bridge and back across the waterway, a line of men blocked his way, and, pounding their hands on the front hood and roof of his car, they ordered him to stop. He rolled his window down as one of the men came up to the driver's side door.

"You don't want to be a strikebreaker, brother," the man said to him. He wore a crumpled ball cap and toted a canvas satchel. He reached into the satchel and handed Merritt a copy of the Aero Mechanics newsletter. "It says it all right there, brother. What we're fighting for."

"Thanks," Merritt said and took the newsletter, relieved he wasn't going to be dragged from his car by the picketers. The line of men parted, and he edged forward. They cheered as he made the next turn and headed away from the plant and toward the bridge.

As he drove north back toward downtown, he glanced at the newsletter beside him on the car seat. The headline read *Teamsters Organize Scabs In Try to Make Strikebreaking Appear to Be "Legal" Act*, and it dawned on him that if he'd been fingered as a Teamster back there, he would be a dead man right now. He pulled to the side of the road to read the rest of the article, which began, "The money-hungry and power-thirsty officials of the Teamsters union, who never allow their sense of fair play to interfere with their love of collecting dues, are up to their old tricks of playing hand-in-glove with employers in trying to raid members from other unions." It went on to describe Teamsters' efforts to officially organize the strikebreakers at the various Boeing plants in a jurisdictional *coup d'etat* that would oust the aero mechanics union. Nothing less than control of the entire work force of aircraft machinists and mechanics— 14,000 strong—was at stake. The article ended by reprinting a letter from IAM President Harvey Brown to Teamster President Dan Tobin asking him to adopt a "hands-off policy" in respect to the strike. Below the article were photographs of six men and two women who had crossed the picket lines. The faces in the photographs appeared grim and shifty, and the caption beneath the photos gave notice that photographers were stationed at each Boeing plant to snap a picture of all scabs, followed by an additional warning that "Once a man is labeled a 'strikebreaker' he carries that brand forever." Merritt immediately wondered if his picture had been taken back at the plant, and whether it might appear in the next issue of the IAM newsletter.

The short but nerve-jarring encounter with the strikers—along with Beck's role in trying to break the strike—left him sickened. The last place he wanted to go was back to the Teamsters Hall. If this was Beck's response to the aero mechanics, what would he do to thwart the longshoremen if they went on strike, as everyone expected them to do in the next month or two? Could he face Ken Hamilton, much less his father-in-law, if his own union tried to bust theirs again? He couldn't figure it. The Teamsters were the largest, most powerful union in the nation, so how come their policies and practices were so goddamn anti-union?

As he drove back along the waterfront, it seemed to him that the labor movement was caught in some kind of twisted, self-defeating impasse, pitting union against union, worker against worker, and likely leaving management tickled-pink over their internecine feuding. He knew he should go back to the office and finish the piece he was writing for the newsletter, updating the Teamster membership on the union's opposition to Taft-Hartley. Yet just the thought of the task made him feel duplicitous, knowing how Beck was manipulating the weakened rules on shop elections under Taft-Hartley to undermine the aero mechanics' strike. Beck's divisive maneuvering to stamp out the IAM made it next to impossible, now that Merritt really thought about it, for him to reconcile his work for the Teamsters with what he'd always believed to be labor's bulwark principle—union solidarity.

So he went straight home and made sure Clara was okay back at the apartment and later that afternoon snuck off to the Blue Moon Tavern to meet J.P. The smoky, beery atmosphere, the clack of pool balls, the loud jukebox, the noisy mix of workers and students, poets and artists, deadbeats and louts, helped Merritt relax. As usual, he and J.P. sat in one of the plywood booths at the back, and for the first time ever in J.P.'s company Merritt began grousing about his boss. "Did you know," he said after their first pitcher of beer, "that the Executive Vice President of the International Brotherhood of Teamsters is the reason we're drinking Rainier Beer right now and not Schlitz or Schaeffer?"

J.P. looked thoroughly disinterested, perhaps expecting some kind of tribute to Dave Beck to follow. "Is that so," he said.

"That's right," Merritt went on. "The Midwest brewers union delivers the Midwest brewers' beer, and Beck won't let any beer that's not delivered by Teamsters into his territory. It's that simple." It was as if Merritt now kept a checklist in his head of all the ways Beck ruled Seattle, from street sweepers to city hall. Two days ago, he'd met a window washer at Rhodes department store, a fellow who complained that he earned 45 cents an hour and out of that measly wage had to pay a nickel-an-hour in dues to the Teamsters. And for what? So he could carry a union card in his back pocket and keep his job.

"Good thing I like Rainier Beer," J.P. said, unimpressed, and picked up his schooner. He emptied the rest of the pitcher into his glass, drained the glass, and brought the pitcher up to the bar for a refill.

"Listen," J.P. blustered when he came back to their booth carrying their second pitcher of beer, "I don't give a horse's ass about Dave Beck. We're going back down to protest the Canwell hearings tomorrow and you need to come."

The Canwell Committee had finished going after union leaders in the state—steering clear of Beck, of course, but forcing the presidents of the IAM and ILWU locals to testify, as well as Harry Bridges' ex-wife, who now lived in Seattle—and had turned its anti-Communist zeal on university and college faculty throughout the area. A dozen professors from the University of Washington were accused of being Communist Party members by the committee. One of those, Dr. Joseph Butterworth, had been Merritt's English professor for Shakespeare. Most of the professors had declared their refusal to cooperate with the committee and now faced contempt charges. The hearings, which were being held at the brick-and-concrete armory building belonging to the 146th Field Artillery at the base of Queen Anne Hill, had begun to draw loud protests, especially from UW students and faculty. Two days ago, J.P. had joined a group of protestors ordered out of the building by Senator Canwell after they disrupted the hearings with catcalls of witch-hunt and red-baiting.

"I can't," Merritt replied. He lit a cigarette.

J.P. was quiet a moment as it dawned on him why Merritt couldn't join the protests. "That's all right, sport," he said sympathetically and asked, "How's Clara doing?"

Merritt stared down into his beer. He wanted to get tight, and not just on beer, and smoke until his lungs burned as bad as Clara's must when she had one of her coughing fits "Not well," he answered. "She's having night sweats, and the aspirin she's taking for the fever upsets her stomach so bad she has to throw up all the time." He looked up at his friend. "I don't think she's getting any better."

J.P. lifted the pitcher of beer and filled Merritt's glass. "That's rough," he said. "We all know what a great gal she is." And shortly after that they called it a night.

The next afternoon, though, Merritt received a phone call from J.P. at his office in the Teamsters Hall. He and three other students had been arrested after bolting past the policemen stationed at the Armory entrance and barging into the hearings. They were now sitting in the King County jail downtown. J.P.'s father, the prominent physician, citing the need to teach his heedless son a lesson, had refused to post bail, so now J.P. was calling on Merritt for help. Merritt told his friend absolutely, and immediately telephoned Sid, who was a newly minted attorney. Sid agreed on the spot to represent all four students *pro bono* because, as he put it, "This Canwell's a nutjob and a half," and said he'd have the students sprung from the clink by nightfall.

When Merritt drove home later that evening, he was pleased with his role in helping out the four students. When he entered the apartment and called out to Clara, though, he heard only a feeble groan from the back bedroom and his good cheer instantly dissolved.

He found Clara sprawled across the bed, sweating through her pajamas, the bedcovers tossed to the floor. Her suffering was too much for her to pretend otherwise, as she often did when he entered the bedroom. He went about helping her change out of her sweat-soaked pajamas and into a loose-fitting nightgown. He also changed the bed sheets and gave her a damp washcloth to place over her forehead as she lay back in the bed. Yet every few minutes, another coughing fit seized her, leaving blood-specked clots of phlegm in the handkerchief he held to her mouth. He opened the windows throughout the apartment to get a breeze circulating through the stuffy rooms, and after she had sipped some ice water, she finally settled down. He took the now-warm washcloth from her and replaced it with another cool one, then sat in the chair beside the bed and watched as she closed her eyes and tried to breathe without bringing on another attack.

THIRTY-TWO
Clara, Summer-Fall 1948

She knew she was suffocating. Even gasping as she was, she could not take in enough air. She implored the atmosphere for relief, a single inhalation, and tried not to panic. Her body wrenched off the bed as her lungs strained to expand, and she had neither the breath nor strength to move or speak.

When Merritt arrived home, he held her in his arms to calm her, and after she collapsed back onto the pillows, her pajamas damp with sweat, he changed her out of them and into a nightgown. Her head burned as the airless room pressed in upon her. Then another coughing spasm seized her, tearing at her rib cage until her chest felt as though it was being pried open with massive hooks. If death had appeared disguised at that moment as a cool, unrestricted breath of air, she would have welcomed it as life itself. Eventually, though, the convulsions subsided and she collapsed back onto the bed and closed her eyes in relief.

When she awoke in the middle of the night, her blood was hammering away in her ears and another coughing spell took hold, gripping her body and not letting go this time. She didn't know when she lost consciousness, but the next time she came to, she didn't recognize where she was. The small white room seemed familiar, the metal bed with white sheets where she lay oddly comforting, almost like her childhood bed. The head of the bed was raised and she could see the opposite wall.

She was in a hospital room, she understood, but couldn't remember how or when she'd gotten there. When she focused her eyes enough to make out the rest of the room, she discovered Merritt across the room, slumped in a chair, his tie loosened, his arms crossed, sound asleep. The wan light in the room told her it was morning. A weight on her chest pinned her to the bed, and she allowed only her eyes to move as she scanned the sparse room. If she tried to adjust her body, she sensed that there would be more pain than she could endure, so she remained motionless, paralyzed by the fear of another coughing fit. She wanted to whisper to Merritt, to call his name, but was afraid the effort would require more breath than she could marshal. So she remained perfectly still and watched him, his steady, unlabored breathing, and tried to match her own to his.

As he stirred in his chair, she continued watching him. When she'd read *Anna Karenina* several weeks ago, it amused her to think of Merritt as Lévin, the intelligent, caring, well-intentioned, yet utterly befuddled aristocrat-farmer. And she? Was she his Kitty, the princess who denies Lévin and only later, heartbroken and humiliated, admits to the fullness of her love for him? Or was she Nicholái, Levin's dissipate, consumptive brother, sweating and coughing the night away as he calls on God and devil, without distinction, to save him, leaving poor Lévin to ponder his own mortality and the insoluble fact of death?

Merritt stretched his arms and legs, opened his eyes, and saw Clara looking at him. He gave her a weak smile, scooted his chair to her bedside, and leaned forward. "You're awake," he said.

"Back from the dead."

"Now, now," he scolded her. "None of that." He brushed her hair away from her face and off her forehead. His hand felt cool and soothing.

"Your fever's gone," he said.

"Umm." She closed her eyes as he stroked her forehead as if petting a cat.

"Would you like some water?"

She rolled her head to one side and then the other.

"It's right here on the tray if you do."

She opened her eyes. "Okay," she said and tried to sit up, letting Merritt adjust the pillows behind her back and hand her the glass. Once the water touched her lips, her tremendous thirst became apparent. She could hardly believe how parched she was, and as she took several more gulps, Merritt had to tell her to slow down. She drank half the glass of water before he took it from her and placed it back on the bedside tray.

"I told your mother I'd phone when you woke up."

"Not yet, Kóstya," said Clara and squeezed his hand.

Merritt looked at her as if she might be hallucinating. "Are we speaking Russian now?"

"Yes," she said, smiling at him, yet knowing that if she laughed it might trigger more coughing. "This happens sometimes after a fever. The passionate Russian soul in me breaks forth."

"Should I call the nurse to bring us a bottle of vodka?"

Even this little bit of banter wore her out, though, and she closed her eyes without responding. She knew Merritt continued to watch her and pictured the concern on his face. She wanted to pull him down to her, kiss his lips, rub her cheek against his whiskers, nuzzle his ear, smell the warmth of his neck. But none of this was possible.

"You should put a mask on," she told him, her eyes still closed.

Merritt patted the back of her hand. "I'll go phone your mother," he said, and she heard him move toward the door, not wanting him to leave but unable to summon the strength to tell him so.

The room fell silent, while outside a truck ground its gears and a car honked its horn. She drifted away, her thoughts turning blurry, and when she opened her eyes again she was standing barefoot on a pebbly shore somewhere along Puget Sound. She turned around, saw the wave-washed cliff behind her and immediately recognized the spot. She was at Fauntleroy Cove, just below Lincoln Park in West Seattle, where she used to come as a child with her two brothers. Freddy and Ken would fish from the nearby public pier while she combed the beach. Never before, though, had she seen the tide so low. A large, jet-black crow with shimmers of blue on its head hopped among the wet rocks pecking at barnacles. She bent down, touched the center of a small orange sea anemone and watched it retract into itself. As she straightened up, she noticed the sky void of color, a uniform blankness, erasing any view of the mountains across the Sound. She stood in a hospital nightgown, looking out at the calm, pale-blue waters, wondering where all the ferries and other boats had gone.

"I detest crows," said Ingrid Bergman, standing beside her. The actress threw a stone at the crow on the beach. It arched its wings, lifted into the air with a raucous screech, and landed about fifty yards away. "And priests."

Did she say priests or police, Clara wondered. She'd never heard Ingrid Bergman speak so harshly. Her clear, gentle voice sounded stern and contempt-filled. Clara was momentarily fearful of her until, watching her more closely, she saw the familiar look of compassion come over the actress's lovely face, and Clara thought how flawless she was.

"Do you live near here?" Clara asked her.

Ingrid Bergman pointed across the Sound like an explorer, a hint of laughter in her eyes. "I live on that island. But I like to come over here and look back at where I live."

Clara puzzled over this. She let it pass, though, and took a tentative breath. Then she filled her lungs with abandon and felt them expand—*Such capacity!*—and knew the sea air would sustain her, that the sea was the source of all life, that she could survive on air and water alone.

"And look how beautiful," Ingrid Bergman said, gazing past Clara at the curving shoreline, and Clara thought, *I'll go home and paint her.*

After the re-sectioning surgery at the Marine Hospital, Clara was admitted to Firland Sanatorium in North Seattle where she could receive around-the-clock care. The pulmonary re-sectioning removed nearly a half of her right lung, which gave her relief from her coughing but left her extremely weak. Nonetheless, despite this setback, she promised Merritt she would get well now and told him she hoped to be home in time for Christmas, even though the doctor said she would require a minimum of six months to recover.

Merritt visited her at Firland every Tuesday, Thursday, and Sunday, the sanatorium's designated visiting days. Visiting hours were limited to 4:00 p.m. to 6:00 p.m., yet on Tuesday and Thursdays when he had to work he could only make it to the sanatorium by 4:30. The facility was a converted Navy hospital that now housed several hundred TB patients. Clara's bed was one of ten in a ward designated for female post-op patients. Five beds were lined against one wall, five against the other, barracks-style. Flimsy roll-away curtains separated each bed, giving patients minimum privacy. Most of the women pushed the curtains aside so they could chat with one another or listen to the single radio allowed on the ward. To a person, the women were confined to strict bed rest. They took their meals in bed, made use of the metal chamber pots that slid beneath the bed frames, received sponge baths every other day from an attendant, and were allowed to escape in a wheelchair to the nearby common room only when they were receiving visitors. Clara found it difficult to comprehend the convalescent advantages of such restrictions, yet the floor nurse made it clear that patients had little choice in the matter. The sanatorium was officially authorized by the Health Department to quarantine the city's most severe tubercular cases and its rules were nonnegotiable.

For Clara, the long, tedious days in bed turned into extended waiting periods between visiting days when she knew she would see Merritt again. In anticipating his arrival, she would have an attendant wheel her down to the common room a few minutes early so she could wait for him. When he entered the large, nondescript room, he wore the sterile white facemask all visitors were required to wear. He and Clara would try to find a quiet corner to themselves, yet sound traveled in the stark room so they had to keep their voices low. Clara reported on the doctor's wry bedside manners and the peccadilloes of each nurse and attendant, while Merritt gave her a rundown of his job at the union hall. Because patients were not allowed to read the daily newspapers for fear national and world events might unsettle them, he caught Clara up on all the goings-on. He rattled on about the national campaigns gearing up for the fall presidential election, the first since the end of the war. Former Vice President Henry Wallace was running as the Progressive Party candidate, he told her, and the yellow dog bigot from South Carolina, Senator Strom Thurman, had broken with the Dems to form his States Rights Party. People figured that after sixteen years of Roosevelt and Truman, the Republicans would finally take the White House, but Merritt was sticking by Truman. "As much as he gets my goat," he added and said how J.P. had joined the Progressives and was organizing a rally for Wallace at the university. The Teamsters, though, were throwing their support behind Truman, and this, he said, could make all the difference in the November election.

None of this really mattered much to Clara, but she enjoyed hearing him speak, even when he got riled up over politics. "*You* should run for president," she told him, her eyelids getting droopy.

Merritt brought her art books and fashion magazines to look at since she no longer had the stamina to read novels. He also brought her sketchbooks, pencils, and charcoals, though she rarely had the energy to draw. Now and then during visiting hours, he would give her a cup of her favorite wine, chilled Grenache-rosé, which he would sneak into the sanatorium in a coffee thermos. Yet every time he prepared to leave, it was all she could do to keep from breaking down in tears. Merritt would eventually have to go, and an attendant would wheel her back to her bed on the post-op ward. She would pretend to sleep the rest of the evening, and eventually she *would* fall asleep, but when she woke again it would be dark outside the tall sanatorium windows, and she would be unable to recall what day it was or whether it was evening or morning—*Was Merritt coming today?*—and she would begin to cry.

The first time her parents visited her at the sanatorium, her mother said very little, and when she did speak it was to recount a rather peculiar, and worrisome, accident that had befallen her father. Just the week before, her mother explained, her father had left the print shop late at night when a car hit him as he crossed the street. He came home limping and complained of a back ache, yet after she had prayed all night, he woke up the next morning as spry as ever.

Clara's father nodded as her mother related this demonstration of mental healing, but instead of acknowledging her evident power of prayer, Clara looked at her father in astonishment and asked if he was all right.

"The driver should have seen me," he replied. "I tried to get out of the way, but I guess I wasn't fast enough. He hit me right where I live," and with that he slapped his buttocks. "I rolled right off his front fender."

Her mother changed the subject then by asking Clara if she was getting enough to eat, and Clara said she was. Her father told her the salmon were running and he wanted to take her fishing again as soon as she got well. Next her mother removed a Bible and a copy of *Science and Health* from her handbag and set them on Clara's bedside table, along with a schedule of the daily lessons. Clara thanked her, but after her parents said their goodbyes and left, she dropped the two books into the cardboard box beneath her bed with her other things.

Regrettably, her brother Ken continued in his refusal to visit her. He said in a letter to her that his "absolute reliance on truth" prevented him from acknowledging her illness. To become a practitioner, Ken had had to demonstrate his healing prowess to local church members as well as to representatives of the Mother Church in Boston. His confirmed healings through spiritual science so far included a woman with severe allergies, another with a case of shingles, and young man who suffered from migraine headaches. According to her mother, whose pride in Ken was plain to see, church members called upon him routinely for healings, understandings, and spiritual guidance. In his letter to Clara, he told her he would seek to bring her thoughts into accord with spiritual law through *absent treatment*, but that he couldn't do it alone, that ultimately she herself must bring her thoughts back in line with true Principle.

The Tuesday after she received Ken's letter, Merritt related to her how he'd gone to her parents' house that past Sunday for dinner and gotten into another argument with her brother. He urged Ken to visit Clara at the sanatorium, citing how even their mother had gone, which only made Ken mad. He called Merritt a pointy-headed agnostic and accused Clara of indulging her *disease* through her own deliberate misunderstandings. At this, Merritt said, "I almost slugged him," and when her father jumped in between them, Merritt gave Ken a good cussing and left the house.

It came as a surprise to Clara, therefore, when the next Sunday toward the end of visiting hours Ken showed up at the sanatorium. Merritt was already there, but when Ken arrived he excused himself to have a smoke outside. This left Clara alone with her brother, who looked as somber as ever in the same gray suit jacket and black pants he wore to church each week. All the same, she was thrilled to see him.

Since Ken believed that in God's perfect creation infectious disease didn't exist, he removed his facemask the moment the attendant left the room. He embraced Clara and kissed her on the cheek. She cleared the tears from her eyes and asked him about his wife, Cynthia, whom he'd married last month right after she was admitted to Firland.

"Merritt showed me the wedding photos," she said. "Her dress was so beautiful." Yet she couldn't help herself from teasing her overly serious brother and added, "You looked quite handsome yourself. For a wharf rat."

During the entire time of Ken's visit, she strained to suppress her coughing, always careful to reach for a Kleenex when she did cough and then carefully placing it in the brown paper bag provided to patients for that purpose. When Ken commented on how thin she was and asked if they were feeding her enough, just as her mother had, she told him they were fed three square meals a day and that she'd actually gained two pounds in the past week. Ken then told her how he and Cynthia had applied for a G.I. loan to buy a house in Burien and expected to move in within a couple of weeks. They wanted to have kids soon, he said, and needed more room. Clara must have flinched when he mentioned children because he looked chagrined and changed the subject to his union activities, telling her about the impending strike.

"There's going to be another strike?" she asked.

With the exception of the three and a half years during the war, she couldn't remember a time when the men of her family weren't embroiled in either a strike or preparations for a strike. The labor unions seemed to her sometimes like so many unruly boys playing at club house, and whenever she heard talk of yet another strike, she just wanted to shout at them, *Enough! Behave yourselves!*

"It'll be over quickly," Ken assured her. "We're old hats at this, you know that."

When Clara grew fatigued from all the catching up she and her brother had to do, Merritt returned and suggested he and Ken probably ought to leave. Merritt asked if she wanted him to bring her anything on Tuesday when he visited next, and she said she had everything she needed. She then added jokingly, "Everything but my health."

"Health is yours in God," Ken said upon hearing this and came to her bedside to ask if she would take a moment to pray with him.

Clara could see that Merritt was about to grab him by the collar and pull him away from her, so she took her brother's hand, thanked him again for coming, and politely answered no. "I'm just happy to see you," she said. "You be sure to bring Cynthia with you next time"

She released Ken's hand and as he walked away, she winked at Merritt and told him to be patient with Ken and try not to come to blows with him. Merritt grumbled some but consented.

"Solidarity," he said.

"For the union makes us strong," Clara replied.

THIRTY-THREE
Merritt, Fall 1948

Everyone knew there were sissy boys among the seamen corps and midshipmen ranks. You would hear stories of someone being caught *in flagrante delicto*—or, *in fellatio delighto*, as a lot of guys called it. Merritt never paid the talk much mind, even after what took place between him and Ensign Rivard. He had better ways to occupy his time. Besides, what happened happened. He'd been drunk and hardly knew what was taking place. Plus, Rivard had been a commissioned officer and Merritt an enlisted man—his subordinate. Every time Merritt found himself thinking back on it now, he caught himself shaking his head, not so much out of shame but simple incredulity that the incident still nagged at him, and that Arda Smitson and his son were the main source of that nagging. Then after Clara told him how her father had been hit by a car and the driver had driven off, he couldn't help but wonder . . . . Was Smitson involved in this, too?

The summer wore on and hints of autumn appeared in the cool morning air, the colorful tops of trees, and the increased rains. Merritt visited Clara, went to work, and did little else. The labor situation in Seattle was about to boil over. Beck threw all his efforts into breaking the machinist strike at Boeing, even going so far as to charter a new Teamster local—Local 451—to rival the International Aero Mechanics local. The new local, sanctioned by Boeing, gave union cover to strikebreakers and IAM defectors. It was union raiding, pure and simple. While Seattle businessmen praised Beck as a "labor statesman" for trying to save the city from economic disaster, the city's labor leaders— those few not under Beck's thumb—condemned him as a "labor racketeer" hell-bent on ruling the city's labor force. It seemed to Merritt that more than ever Beck believed that might equaled right, and that he was determined to exercise that might.

Under such unprecedented pressure, the International Aero Mechanics union eventually called off its strike against Boeing, and its members returned to work without a contract. Merritt had never seen Beck as satisfied with himself as he was that week, striding through the hallways flashing his baby-faced smile, greeting one and all with hearty hello's, and shaking hands with anyone who stopped to speak with him. Toward the end of the week, it was announced he would host a Saturday afternoon reception at his home for the combined staff of the Western Conference and Joint Council to honor the leaders of the newly formed Local 451. Though Beck had never been one to gloat, the end of the machinist strike against Boeing clearly marked a sweet victory for him. And though Merritt was disinclined to share in the celebration, he knew Beck would take notice if he didn't show up.

When Saturday rolled around, he donned a tweed jacket and headed out to the Ravenna Park neighborhood where Beck had recently built a new home. Word around the union hall was that Beck possessed numerous properties throughout the city and was regularly buying more under the auspices of the Teamsters, ostensibly as pension fund investments. He would then transfer the titles of select properties into his name in lieu of the periodic cash bonuses outlined in his contract. Since many of the properties were just empty lots downtown, Beck liked to brag about becoming a parking lot attendant and sitting around all day collecting people's quarters to park in his lots after he retired.

Despite the season's incessant rains, on the afternoon of the reception at Beck's house the skies cleared and the sun looked brand new. At first Merritt considered walking, but then remembered he was a Teamster and that Teamsters always drove. In front of the large red-brick house in the lush Ravenna neighborhood, a line of cars waited as three valets working the reception scurried about to park each vehicle. As Merritt crept forward in his reliable old Plymouth, he recognized two of the valets as guys from his local, one a cement truck driver, the other a carrier for a medical supply company. The third valet was also someone he recognized. It was the guy who'd heckled Harry Bridges on the UW campus almost two years earlier, the same one he'd spotted some time back coming out of the pharmacy in the union hall. He caught Merritt's eye and there seemed to be a moment of recognition between them, but when the guy opened the driver's side door, waited for Merritt to climb out, and then slid in behind the wheel, he didn't acknowledge Merritt at all. The encounter once more sparked Merritt's suspicion, paranoid as it might be, that certain Teamsters were keeping tabs on him.

Just outside the entrance to Beck's house, people formed a receiving line, waiting to be greeted by Beck and his wife Dorothy, who stood inside the front foyer welcoming their guests. Since his appointment to Executive Vice-President, Beck had become much more willing to participate in such ceremonial duties, preparing himself for the social trappings of higher office and eventually life in Washington, D.C. Merritt stepped across the front threshold and reached out his hand to Dorothy, who greeted him with a stiff smile, and then to Beck, who gave him an uncommonly firm handshake.

"Tell me," he said to Merritt, sounding quite somber, "how is your wife, Clara?"

It always astounded Merritt how well Beck remembered peoples' names. It was the *in loco parentis* side of him. He probably knew the name of every Teamster in Seattle, if not the entire Western Conference.

"She's doing better since the operation," Merritt answered. "Thank you for asking." He glanced at Dorothy, who conveyed her sympathies with plaintive eyes.

"You let me know what we can do to help. Time off, a driver, you name it," Beck said.

"I appreciate that very much, Mr. Beck," Merritt replied in all earnestness. Beck was a master at making people under him feel appreciative. "I think we'll get through it all right."

Beck nodded affirmatively and gave Merritt one of the tight-lipped grins that let a person know he was going to tough it out right beside you. "That's the spirit," he said and shook his hand again. "Go on in now and enjoy yourself."

Merritt moved forward into the big house, feeling mildly sycophantic, as if he'd traded on Clara's illness to gain sympathy from the boss, though he knew this wasn't the case. In the front hallway, a life-size portrait of Dave and Dorothy Beck—she seated, he standing behind her—adorned the right-hand wall. The house was decorated in a combination of modern furnishings and antiques, a sectional sofa and matching ottoman next to an ornate French china case with beveled glass. Teamster officials and their wives crowded the den and living room and spilled out onto the back patio. Merritt glanced out the back door and saw a canvas canopy erected in the center of a well-manicured lawn, under which a table was set up with chafing trays of food. At another table in a corner of the yard, children pressed forward for ice cream served by a Negro woman in a housekeeper's uniform. Merritt walked past the back door and quickly angled his way into the kitchen to the makeshift bar.

"Rye highball," he told the bartender, who wore a black bowtie and black apron over a crisp white shirt. You have to hand it to the bastard, Merritt mused as he savored the first sip of the rather strong drink, the man knows how to cater a party.

He wandered about the premises, greeting people from the union hall, all of whom solicitously asked after Clara's health. Each time he answered that she was doing fine, he felt more phony, more dissembling, as he smiled and thanked the person for asking. Finally, when he went back into the kitchen for another drink, he thought that the next time someone asked him how Clara was doing he would come right out and say, *My wife is dying, okay? Next week's our first-year anniversary and we're going to spend it in the goddamn sanatorium. I don't know if she'll live past Christmas, if that long. That's how my wife's doing.* This would be closer to the truth, and certainly closer to how he felt.

At the steam table, he loaded a paper plate with Swedish meatballs, German potato salad, and pickled beets. When he sat in one of the metal lawn chairs, a waiter came by and asked if he would like another drink. With two ryes under his belt already, he decided to switch to beer. "An Oly," he told the waiter and a moment later was brought an ice-cold bottle of beer wrapped in a damp cocktail napkin.

Then, as he held his plate in his lap and the beer in his hand, an overwhelming wave of grief swept over him. It overcame him like nothing he'd experienced since Clara's diagnosis or her admission to the sanatorium. He set his plate on the grass, pressed two fingers to the bridge of his nose, and checked himself from breaking into sobs. Clara should be here with him, he realized, by his side. Not because it was some fabulous event she was missing out on, but because she was his wife, like the other wives who had accompanied their husbands to the reception, and because she was a bright, beautiful woman who should be seen and listened to instead of wasting away on a barren TB ward surrounded by sickly strangers who didn't know her from Eve. He needed her here and she needed to be here with him—and yet she wasn't. Why was *he* even here, he wanted to know? Why was he sitting in this chair in the backyard of some bully he held little—if any—respect for any more?

Before Merritt could dwell very long on such questions, Beck stepped out of the house accompanied by a tall, silver-haired man in a blue blazer who looked more like an Ivy League scullsman than any Teamster he'd ever known. Beck clinked his glass with a fork to summon everyone's attention and then introduced the new president of Local 451, Hoyt Bennett. He told the crowd that Hoyt was a man who had served as a trustee of the Los Angeles local for two years and who would now lead Local 451 to victory in next month's election to determine which union, the Teamsters or IAM, would represent the machinists at Boeing. There was polite applause and Bennett thanked everyone for the warm, though rather rainy, welcome he'd received in Seattle. "This is the first real sunshine I've seen since I arrived two weeks ago," he said, soliciting bemused smiles from everyone. He then looked down and took on a more serious demeanor. "When we're done with this thing," he said, looking up again, "Local 451 will be one of the largest Teamster locals around. And the kind of catastrophe that has befallen Bill Boeing's company, the industrial pride of this magnificent city, will never happen again." There was applause following this statement, and Dave Beck raised his glass of tonic water and called for a toast to Local 451.

Merritt, however, was unimpressed. He knew that Bennett was essentially a hit man in a suit. Trustees had long been Beck's method of bringing wildcat locals into line. With Dan Tobin's blessing, Beck had license to remove any local's recalcitrant—though duly-elected—president, business agent, or organizer, and replace that official with his own hand-picked trustee. If the remaining officers didn't fall in line and abide by the new arrangement, the local would lose its charter, and its members (former members now) would have a damn hard time finding work thereafter. It was strong-arm union management at its finest.

After Beck's toast, Merritt drank another Oly, had a quick snort of Scotch—rich guys always had the best liquor—and decided to call it a night. He considered finding Beck to thank him for the evening, but the bossman was in deep conversation with far more important men than Merritt, and besides, discretion was the better part of . . . *Fuck it*, he thought, unable to remember how the damn saying went.

He made his way to the front of the house and when the valet brought his car around, Merritt tried to tip the heckler a greenback, but the man scoffed and said, "Keep it," before turning away. Have it your way, pal, thought Merritt and got behind the wheel. As he drove off, he pushed the visor down against the orange glare of the late afternoon sky. He had no interest in returning to the apartment and thought he might swing by Sid and Amy's house in Laurelhurst. It was located at the tip of Webster Point overlooking Union Bay—a fine, lovely home, much like the one he longed to see him and Clara in someday. He missed the turn-off to Laurelhurst, though, and ended up driving past the university's Athletic Pavilion and Football Stadium, then across the Montlake Bridge and into the Arboretum. He rolled his window down and let the rushing air clear his head. The foliage throughout the Arboretum had turned yellow and russet, and the next big rain would bring the leaves down.

As he made his way out of the Arboretum and onto the narrow lane that was Interlaken Boulevard, heading up into the dark, ferny verdure of Interlaken Park, he turned on his headlights. With a glance in his rearview mirror, he saw a flatbed truck coming up fast behind him. The truck was combat green like the old Chevy flatbeds driven around the Naval Air Station at Sand Point. The driver flashed his headlights as if to signal Merritt to pull to the side so he could pass, yet the road was too narrow and steep. So Merritt sped up. Yet as he slowed down to take the sharp curve that lay ahead, the truck accelerated and without warning smacked his rear bumper at an angle that sent his car into a small skid. Merritt jerked the steering wheel, pulled out of the skid, and negotiated his way through the curve. He pressed on his horn and leaned out his window.

"What the hell," he shouted over his shoulder and threw his hand into the air at the truck driver. But the truck kept coming. The park dropped into a ravine to his right, and to his left a stand of large cedars interspersed with rhododendrons crowded the road's shoulder. If the truck rear-ended him again, he would have to veer into the trees and rhododendrons rather than risk plummeting over the edge of the ravine. He gunned it on the short straightaway in front of him, but on the next curve the truck roared up behind him again, ramming his back fender with its grill. The car went into another spin and before Merritt could regain control, it careened off the road and plowed straight into a massive rhododendron. The gnarled branches and thick leaves thrashed across the hood and windshield before the car jolted to a stop, his head thunking against the steering wheel.

He remained slumped forward, half-dazed, for several moments. When he decided he was not hurt, he sat up and looked about. The car was stalled out and buried deep in the massive bush. He tried the ignition and the engine started, yet when he threw it into reverse, the back wheels spun in the soft loam and the car remained stuck. He tried twice more and gave up. Then as he tried to get out of the car, he found the driver's side door jammed against a branch and couldn't budge it more than an inch or two. It was the same with the passenger side door. He finally climbed into the backseat and kicked at the back door until it opened enough to let him crawl out.

He peered up the road, the flatbed truck long gone, and then looked at his white Plymouth DeLuxe wedged squarely into the middle of the cottage-size rhododendron. It was going to take a wrecker's winch to get the car unstuck, he thought as he touched his forehead and felt a welt rising just below his hairline. He couldn't say whether the truck driver meant to kill him or just give him a good scare, but he obviously wanted to do one or the other. And as he walked up the dark road that led out of the park, all he knew for certain was that anyone who drove a flatbed truck in Seattle was damn sure a card-carrying Teamster.

THIRTY-FOUR
Clara, Fall 1948

Clara tried as she could to keep her spirits up. She insisted she would not spend their first-year anniversary in the "san." She told Merritt he would have to sweep in and steal her away, slipping past the vigilant Firland attendants, to take her someplace magical where they could fully and freely celebrate their *annus matrimonium*. To this end she did her best to convince him she was up to such a daring tryst. She cleaned her plate each meal to put on weight, dressed every day (rather than putter about in her robe and slippers), and did up her hair and makeup prior to each of his visits. This effort alone buoyed her spirits, giving her a purpose and helping her take pride once more in her appearance. She petitioned the nurses to allow the lady patients more opportunities to take care of their persons, so that no matter how sickly they were they might feel better about themselves. Such physical vanity, she'd long ago learned from the fashion mavens at Frederick & Nelson, was almost always worth the trouble and, indeed, carried virtues all its own.

Sadly, though, three days before their first-year anniversary, she experienced another setback—more coughing, more fever, and more night sweats. At times she could barely walk, and instead of absconding away with her, Merritt sat beside her in the common room, stroking her forearm and reassuring her that he loved her more than ever. He presented her with a heart-shaped gold pendant with a red ruby set in the center. He placed the chain about her neck, fumbling with the latch until it caught, and she vowed to wear it everyday until she was released from the sanatorium. She also expressed how sorry she was that she had no gift for him, but then gave him a charcoal portrait of the two of them on their wedding day, standing before Reverend Shelton. Merritt admired the portrait for the longest time and then lifted his face mask, took both her hands in his, and kissed her palms.

The kisses surprised Clara, and they were almost more than she could stand. They reminded her how much—at least until her most recent setback—she had been thinking about sex. "I want us to be together," she said as he lifted his face from her hands.

After their engagement, they'd had sex all the time—new, eager, excited sex—and after their marriage they seemed to have even more sex—tender, leisurely, knowing sex. Then she became pregnant and shortly afterwards there was the miscarriage. And some weeks later, just as they were reaching out to one another again, she received her TB diagnosis. All the same, even when she was homebound, they made love several times, guardedly, tentatively, their mouths never meeting. But even that tepid, nervous sex had been months ago, and now, more than anything, more than health itself, she longed for an uninhibited hour or two of warm and delirious lovemaking with her husband.

It was no wonder to her then that her daytime fantasies over the next few weeks became so much more vivid and insistent. She would lie in bed reminiscing on her three lovers—four, if she counted the one-night fling with Blake Hamby, the manager of Men's Wear at Frederick's. She reviewed each man's body in scrupulous detail. Each set of eyes, ears, and lips; each neck and pair of shoulders; each chest; their biceps, forearms, and hands (even Blake, who gnawed his fingernails); thighs, calves, and feet; buttocks, of course; and finally each male organ, pendulant or retracted, wrinkled or smooth, straight or curved. She also compared and assessed their lovemaking. Eliot was too agitated, and Guy too subdued, while Blake just plain forgettable. Merritt, however, was always just right. Savory and sweet. Energetic, attentive, tender, and virile. And always the perfect temperature.

Twice she woke in the middle of the night aroused by lurid sex dreams. The first dream involved a man she didn't know who had intercourse with her and was gone. The second dream was one of those long, lingering dreams that are remembered long after waking up. It involved her and Beverly, the 27-year-old former Army nurse two beds down from hers. Of the ten women on the ward, she and Bev were the youngest. They became fast friends, sharing girlie talk and gossiping about the older patients. They had their heartfelt moments as well. When Clara revealed how much she missed Merritt and Beverly admitted how lonely her unmarried life had always been, they held and comforted each another for the longest time, despite the sanatorium's strict prohibition on patient touching. Two nights later, Clara dreamed she and Beverly shared the same bed on an empty ward. They were both naked, spooning, cupping one another breasts. When Beverly rolled over and kissed Clara on the mouth, Clara draped a leg over Beverly's hip and reached behind and between her thighs. She awoke in the dark rubbing herself, mortified that someone might have heard her moans and rustling, yet already replaying the dream in her mind as she turned over and nuzzled her pillow.

Four weeks after their wedding anniversary had passed and she'd recovered from her last setback, Clara resolved to make a dash for it. She wrapped herself in her wool overcoat, donned an accordion-pleated rain bonnet she borrowed from Beverly, and snuck outside to the front verandah to await Merritt's arrival. When she saw his white car pull into the parking lot, she walked down the cement steps and across the wet lawn to greet him.

"I'm ready," she said as he walked toward her. Without another word, she took his arm and turned him about. He tried to ask her how she was feeling, whether she was up to this, and whether she let anyone know, but she ignored his tiresome questions and pushed him back toward the car.

"It's all right," she assured him. "I've been cooped up in that sickhouse for almost three months now, and I'm breaking out. And my one true love, the man I've promised myself to for all eternity, is going to be quiet and drive."

He paused to look at her as they stood beside the car, obviously weighing the situation against everything reason told him was wrong with it, then she placed her hand over his crotch and pressed.

"Whatever your heart desires," he said, relenting, and opened the passenger side door for her.

They drove in happy silence through the drizzle and when it finally occurred to her where he was taking her, she laughed.

As they pulled into the parking lot of the Pine Lodge Motel on Aurora Avenue, she was glad he hadn't taken her back to their apartment. It would have been too sad, she knew, and waited in the car as he ducked into the front office and a moment later came out flashing a room key. They drove around the horseshoe parking lot to one of the replica log cabins, pulled up to Cabin #8, and jumped out of the car. He fumbled with the key as rain dripped from the shaggy boughs of the enormous cedar towering over their cabin. When he finally opened the stubborn door, they hurried inside.

The musty interior was dark with knotted pine paneling and a single floor lamp, the lamp shade displaying a western mountain scene. They tossed off their clothes, pulled back the quilted covers on the bed, climbed between the chill sheets, and quickly wrapped their limbs around one another to share their mutual ardor.

The day after adventuring off with Merritt to the Pine Lodge Motel, Clara received a succinct reprimand from Firland's assistant administrator and promptly resigned herself once more to the routine of sanatorium life. This meant, of course, only one thing: rest, rest, and more rest. Everyone at the san insisted it remained the best cure for TB, not only restoring patients' strength but, more importantly, preventing them from disrupting the lungs' delicate fibrosis process, which kept the tuberculosis bacterium from spreading. This was why the rest regimen was enforced with the precision and authority of a German prison camp. One's diagnosis determined whether a patient remained in bed all day, most of the day, or just part of the day. It determined whether one was permitted to sit in the common room, venture out to the verandah, or had to remain strictly indoors. In Clara's case, she was allotted three hours a day in the common room, and when the sky was clear and the temperature above fifty-five degrees, which was rarely, she was allowed to sit on the verandah for thirty minutes. Otherwise she remained in bed, chatting with the other gals, listening to the radio broadcasts of Jack Benny, *Box 13* mysteries, and the Metropolitan Opera, and leafing through the fashion magazines that Merritt faithfully brought her. But mostly she slept, even when she wasn't tired, which likely accounted for her fantastically vivid dreams.

At one point early in her confinement at the sanatorium, she and Merritt had discussed transferring her to a private facility east of the mountain, near Ephrata, where it was so much drier and sunnier. Yet the cost was prohibitive. It was also far away, which would mean Merritt could only visit her on weekends, which for Clara was out of the question. So she stayed on at Firland and made the best of it. It heartened her to know the sanatorium had improved in recent years. Some of the long-term patients considered it a veritable vacation resort compared to times gone-by. Her friend Angela—whom the nurses called Angel—had been in and out of Firland since the late 1930s. She told tales of incompetent doctors, cold-hearted nurses, under-heated wards, shared baths, and restrictions on everything from reading to talking to peeing, all of which set Clara's hair on end just to hear of it.

"Of course," Angel added, "there were none of the fancy medicines they have now," saying this as if it accounted for the horrendous conditions she'd had to endure.

Clara still received her weekly injections of streptomycin, and then, just one week ago, the doctor started her on two new bactericides—horse tablets she had to break in half to swallow. She could never be sure if it was the TB or the drugs that gave her the nausea she experienced more frequently now, and the doctor couldn't tell either. She found it increasingly difficult to keep her food down and again started losing weight. Her worst fear—as it was every patient's—was that she would develop the dreaded miliary tuberculosis, which attacked every part of the body, from bladder to bones, without discrimination. Miliary patients had to be quarantined from the rest of the population and were not allowed any visitors whatsoever. Clara figured if that ever happened to her, she would just as soon die. After all, hadn't she always been taught that death, like sickness and sorrow and every other source of misery in this world, was mere shadow, a passing cloud, a wisp of nothing to be dispelled by the divine light of Christ Jesus the Way-Shower and Savior? Perhaps dying—even more than living and health and love efficacious—would have to be the lesson that brought this point home for her once and for all.

THIRTY-FIVE
Merritt, Fall 1948

By mid-October, Merritt could see that all bets were off in regard to Boeing and the Teamsters. The machinists voted down the Teamsters' newly-chartered Local 451 by an overwhelming margin and chose to stay with the International Aero Mechanics union. This not only meant Hoyt Bennett was gone, but it effectively ended Beck's raid on the IAM. He now stalked the Teamsters Hall liked a wounded bear. To make matters worse, Harry Bridges was returning to town. The longshoremen's union had hit the bricks two weeks earlier, and now Bridges aimed to rally the rank-and-file in Seattle, one of the ILWU's most stalwart ports. Yet when President Truman threatened to call up the Naval reserves to work military cargo ships for the duration of the strike, Merritt feared he might be forced to cross the picket lines. Upon hearing the news, Ken immediately phoned demanding to know what he would do if it came to that, and Merritt told him the honest-to-god truth—he didn't know—which only infuriated Ken.

The effects of the longshoremen's strike were felt throughout the city. The unaffiliated ferry workers walked off in support of it, as did the Shipwrights, Inlandboatsmen, and Masters Mates and Pilots unions, all of which belonged to the CIO. With the docks idled and no cargo coming in or going out, a good many truck drivers had nothing to haul. Transport and deliveries throughout the city and region slowed to half their rate. This incited Dave Beck to order all his drivers to make their deliveries even if it meant crossing picket lines—just as he had in '34—which inevitably led to skirmishes between longshoremen and Teamsters. If a driver parked his truck within five blocks of a picket line, a longshoreman would liberate the air from the tires with an ice pick. If a longshoreman wandered five blocks from the picket line, a driver would run a red light before the longshoreman could cross the street. Even the newspapers took sides, the *P.I.* calling on the maritime companies to settle the dispute and the *Times* demanding Harry Bridges' resign and the CIO expel the ILWU.

And once again, just as he had with the strike against Boeing, Merritt wanted to see what the action looked like from the front lines. So one night, after visiting Clara at the sanatorium, he removed his Teamsters union card from his wallet (being that much wiser since the IAM strike) and drove down to the waterfront to get a first-hand look at what the *Times* referred to as Seattle's "ghost port." The ILWU had picketers posted around the clock at every major pier, closing the port down tight, and an eerie atmosphere prevailed along the docks. Through the steady, dreary rain, Merritt could see fires burning in large metal drums, sparks flying up over the heads of the dark figures milling about them. The men who worked the picket lines looked wet and testy. The sole operating pier was Pier 2, which belonged to the Alaska Steamship Company. As in '34, the union had consented to load ships bound for the territory to keep Alaskan children from going hungry.

The largest throng of picketers, several dozen in all, congregated at the Port of Seattle's Central Terminal. Here the mood seemed almost jovial. As Merritt drove past, a handful of men standing about one of the drum fires, their caps tugged down and their collars pulled up, raucously sang out verses from "The Song for Bridges," which Ken used to sing in front of Merritt to needle him:

> *Oh, the FBI is worried, the bosses they are scared.*
> *They can't deport six million men, they know.*
> *And we're not going to let them send Harry over the sea,*
> *We'll fight for Harry Bridges and build the C.I.O.*

Merritt scanned the faces, looking for either of his longshoring in-laws. He'd heard that Ken had signed up to help man the flotilla of small boats sent out to block freighters from docking at any of the three exception ports—particularly Tacoma—that refused to back the strike. So he figured if he saw either in-law it would be Carl, down here doing his part. Instead he spotted Pete Bolotoff, the old-timer Carl had introduced him to last year. Pete's ratty old watch cap sloped down one side of his head as he stood about with his hands in his pants pockets as if, not having a freighter to discharge, he didn't know what to do with himself. Merritt pulled his car to the curb, leaned across the front seat, and called out to him. Pete ambled over to the car, dropped his forearms across the open window, and stuck his head in the car.

"Hey, young fella. Come down to walk the line, have yeh?"

"Not tonight, Pete," said Merritt. "I was hoping to spot Carl. Have you seen him?"

"He was hereabouts a while ago. Must've gone home. Us bachelors, we just stay on all night."

"It's going to be a cold one," Merritt informed him with some concern, especially since it was already darn cold. His breath was visible in the car as he spoke.

"'That's all right," Pete said, scratching his grizzled chin and not sounding too worried. Undoubtedly it wouldn't be the first time Pete Bolotoff had spent a night out in the cold rain.

Merritt reached over and popped open the glove compartment. Beneath a road map of Washington State, he kept a pint bottle of cheap Four Roses whiskey that he sometimes took a nip from after leaving the sanatorium. He handed the bottle to Pete.

Pete raised it to the light to inspect its contents. "More'an half full," he declared, his face brightening. "That'll keep the chill off." He gave Merritt a partial salute and stepped away from the car. "I'll let Carl know you were looking for him."

"Thanks, Pete," Merritt called out and rolled up the window. If for no other reason, he wanted the longshoremen's strike to succeed so Pete might earn a few extra cents an hour and have half a decent pension to draw on when his days on the waterfront came to an end. Who, after all, could be more deserving?

It was only as he was driving away from the waterfront, wending his way toward Beacon Hill, that the prospect of his being followed again occurred to Merritt. Yet after everything else that had happened—being run off the road last month, Carl's hit-and-run incident, being tailed to the ILWU meeting, and of course all the business with the Smitsons—he couldn't take such a possibility for granted.

As he checked his rearview mirror, he felt as though he were in an Edward G. Robinson movie. He made a u-turn on Dearborn and headed back toward the waterfront, zigzagging through Chinatown and keeping a close watch behind him., and just as he turned onto Jackson Street, a big sedan made the same turn—just as in the movies—and seemed to hold back as he drove past Union Station. With its elongated front hood, Merritt thought it looked like an old Studebaker. He took the next right onto Occidental, drove half-way down the block, and waited for the car to make the same turn. As it did, he sped up, turned again, crossed the railroad tracks, and made his way back onto Alaska Way along the waterfront. As he drove past the first several piers, a jolt of recklessness shot through him, just as it had when he jumped behind the anti-aircraft gun aboard the USS *Washington* and began firing at the Jap fighter planes. Then as now, he felt he had nothing to lose.

He slowed down as he cruised past the picket lines and drum fires, and then rolled down his window, leaned on his horn, and yelled out, "Stick it to 'em, men!" When the picketers cheered, he looked in his rearview and saw the sedan about sixty yards back. He crept forward, still watching behind him, and when the car tailing him came right to the spot where the picketers stood, he made a sharp u-turn and gunned the Plymouth straight toward it. The picketers looked up, startled, and pushed one another back from the street. Just as the other driver turned to avoid the head-on collision, Merritt veered directly at him and rammed into the car's front fender and left wheel well. The fender ripped free and locked with Merritt's and the two cars, now stuck, came to a stop. Thirty or more longshoremen instantly surrounded the two vehicles.

"You out of your friggin mind, buddy?" someone shouted at Merritt, who sat behind the steering wheel wondering the same thing and wishing he had the half-pint of whiskey back from Pete.

As he opened his door, someone grabbed him by the shoulder of his jacket and pulled him from the car. The other driver already stood beside his car, inspecting the damage. As several men pushed Merritt forward, he looked over the faces of the longshoremen.

"Pete," he shouted. Pete was standing on the curb, just beyond all the commotion.

At that moment, Merritt glanced again at the other driver and goddamn if it wasn't the heckler, the guy from the union pharmacy, the parking valet at Beck's house. One and the same. And from the way he was dressed—baggy dungarees and leather jacket, a ball cap on his head—he was a truck driver all right. Probably drove a flatbed truck, too. He also looked about Merritt's same age.

"This guy's a Teamster," Merritt said excitedly, pointing at him. "He drove me off the road in his truck a few weeks ago." He didn't know if this was true or not, but it made sense that it was. "I saw him cross the tracks back there. I thought maybe he was going to drive his car into the picket line or something. Maybe take a few men out."

The fellow started to speak, but seeing everyone's eyes on him, he stammered and couldn't get the words out. He looked scared and the best he could do was mutter a few curses and point to his damaged car.

"What about it?" a longshoreman asked him. "You looking for trouble down here? 'Cause if you are, you found it."

"Get out of my face," he shouted as more men crowded around him. "That pansy bastard *works* for the Teamsters. He's down here snooping around for Beck. Go ahead, ask him."

The longshoremen shifted their attention back to Merritt, who knew he had to play his hand just right. Then, as if on cue, Pete Bolotoff pushed forward and said, "This one's married to Cap Hamilton's girl, the one that's sick."

Merritt had never heard Carl called by this nickname before. *Cap Hamilton.* It thrilled him now to hear it. Another longshoreman looked hard at Merritt and said he recognized him from a meeting some time back, that he'd come with Cap and his boy Ken Hamilton, who worked Harbor Island. "That's right," Pete said and came up to Merritt and slapped him on the back. "That was quite a game of chicken you played there." He grinned at Merritt as though he'd probably already finished off the half pint of whiskey.

"We don't need Teamsters snooping around our picket lines," someone

268

called out, and someone else proposed they settle the question by checking both men's wallets for their union cards. Then the longshoreman who held Merritt by his jacket told him to turn it over, and Merritt readily obliged, handing the man his wallet.

Yet the other guy backed away and, apparently out of sheer panic, began telling them all to go to hell. "I'm not handing over anything to any lowdown dirty pier scum," he said, and just that fast four longshoremen had him pinned face-down against the hood of his car and were tearing his wallet from the back pocket of his dungarees.

Merritt watched as a longshoreman riffled through his own wallet, finding only his driver's license, Navy discharge card, and a photo-booth snapshot of Clara (*Cap Hamilton's girl, the one that's sick*), and handed him back his wallet. He watched then as another longshoreman went through the other guy's wallet. A moment later a card was thrust into the air. "Got it," the longshoreman shouted and read the card aloud for all to hear. "Allen Arda Smitson. Local 38 of the International Brotherhood of Teamsters, Chauffeurs, Warehousemen and Helpers. Tacoma, Washington." There were boos and catcalls. "Whatdaya know," said the longshoreman. "All the way up from Tacoma to pay his Seattle brethren a friendly call."

The name made Merritt do a doubletake, as did the fact that the guy belonged to the Tacoma local. *Did he hear right?* he asked himself. This was Smitson's son. The one in the Navy, just as Smitson Sr. had said in the bar in San Francisco. Though Merritt couldn't place him, they must have crossed paths somewhere during their service in the Navy, probably through the Recruitment Station, and it was Junior here who knew all about his incident with Ensign Rivard and had told his pops, the same guy who had it out for Carl for the past dozen years. He almost started laughing at having finally figured it out—and also at how ridiculous it all was.

Meanwhile, Allen Arda Smitson began cussing in earnest and kicking at the longshoremen who kept him pinned to his car. His face turned fierce with rage, veins bulging from his neck. He was practically foaming at the mouth as he glared at Merritt and called him a faggot and traitor and stoolie. Yet before he could say anything more, a longshoreman stepped forward and shut him up with a fist to the jaw.

Merritt now feared they might kill him, which he knew would end his ordeal with the Smitsons once and for all, yet might also set off an all-out war between the longshoremen and Teamsters. So as they dragged the half-conscious Smitson away from his car, Merritt stepped forward and told them to hold on a second. "I think he might be Navy," he said in a half-hearted effort to defend Smitson. As part of the alliance of greater maritime workers, longshoremen generally maintained a special respect for Navy men—his brother-in-law Ken being the sole exception to this rule.

"That's right," Smitson said, spitting out blood from the cut on his lower lip. "Your ensign boyfriend told me all about you," and he waggled his tongue lecherously at Merritt. "His best cabinboy ever."

"Fuck you," Merritt sneered back at him, and just like that changed his mind about Allen Smitson. Let them kill him and throw his body in the drink for all he cared. As Carl Hamilton had said, *Good riddance*.

He pushed past several longshoremen to get to his car, then jumped into the Plymouth, ground the gears into reverse, and stomped on the gas, ripping his front fender free of Smitson's car before gunning it down Alaska Way.

The next day Carl Hamilton telephoned Merritt to let him know the longshoremen had roughed up Smitson Junior pretty good, but nothing too serious. "He'll heal," was the way his father-in-law put it. His car, on the other hand, was another matter. By the time the longshoremen were through with it, a wrecker had to come in and haul it off to the junkyard.

Carl then warned Merritt again, much more sternly this time, to steer clear of Smitson—father and son alike. Yet as Merritt knew by this point, that wasn't so easy, and sure enough, three days later he received another letter, unsigned, saying, *Kill Bridges when he shows in Seattle or we will, and then we'll come for you. Count on it*," and that was all.

THIRTY-SIX
Clara, Fall 1948

Shortly after their second tryst at the Pine Lodge Motel, Clara had her worst setback yet. Merritt didn't say anything, but it was clear to her that he felt responsible. She assured him their time together had been the best possible medicine for her and she would get over this latest spell just as she had all the others. According to the sanatorium doctor, her sputum sample had a high mycobacterium count and her x-rays indicated cavitation deep into the lower lobe of her right lung. He was now recommending thoracoplasty—removal of several ribs to achieve a full pulmonary collapse of the right lung—since the lung appeared damaged beyond recovery and might severely hinder the healing of her left lung. The operation would also help keep the disease from seeding elsewhere in her body.

"I'll have only one lung?" she asked the doctor as she and Merritt consulted with him.

"Your left lung is still relatively strong," the doctor replied. "You'll be restricted in the kind of physical exertions you can undertake. But yes, the lungs are one of those organ pairs, like kidneys. When it comes right down to it, there's one to spare." He told them the operation had its risks, but that it had been performed on tuberculosis patients so often over the past thirty years that it was fairly routine by this point.

She and Merritt told the doctor they would consider his advice and a week later came to the decision to schedule the operation for November 15, which would give Clara time to recuperate before the Christmas holiday. In the three weeks preceding the scheduled operation, Clara's parents visited her much more regularly. Ken also returned and brought his wife, Cynthia, a lovely woman whose long, black hair and thick eyebrows made her appear almost Spanish. Clara's friend Jenny visited, too, as did her friend Callie.

Even though Callie's efforts to stage an exhibition of Northwest women's art had been repeatedly dismissed about town, she'd successfully begun to represent individual artists from the proposed show, including Clara, taking several of her portraits around to various gallery owners and curators. Now she brought Clara the good news that she'd found an interested buyer, a very prominent one in fact. They sat in the common room to discuss the matter while Merritt, who

271

already knew about it, ran out to the package store for a bottle of champagne to celebrate.

Callie was almost giddy as she explained to Clara that Mr. Walser Greathouse, who oversaw the Frye collection in town along with his wife Kay, was keen on developing the collection's Northwest holdings. "I showed them three of your portraits as well as works by several other artists"—Here she struck the note of a businessman, something Clara had never heard before in Callie, who had always seemed rather wild and untamable—"and now they want to view the *entire* series!" She turned excited again and leaned over and squeezed Clara's knee.

"*Really?*" was all Clara could think to say and pulled her bathrobe more tightly about her body. "*All* of them?"

"Yes! All fifty-seven"

"For a show?" Clara was incredulous. What could anyone want with her silly portraits. With the exception of her portraits of Mark Tobey and Guy Anderson, she had never painted anyone famous.

"No," Callie cried out and looked flustered. "I mean *Yes*, I suppose they do, eventually." She composed herself and looked at Clara. Along with her friend's new business demeanor, Callie had begun to dress more conservatively, wearing a charcoal pants suit with a matching jacket. Her hair, though, was still splayed about her head like so much tree moss. "Clara, sweetheart, Mr. and Mrs. Greathouse may wish to purchase the entire series for the Frye collection."

Clara could still not fully comprehend what Callie was telling her. Were there really fifty-seven paintings in all? She couldn't remember. And why in the world would the Greathouses want them all? Where would they store them? Would they keep them in their basement as she did at her parents' house in West Seattle? Furthermore, she'd never imagined actually selling the portraits. Not one, not two, and certainly not all fifty-seven. The project had been something that just came over her, a four-month trance, something she couldn't avoid even if she'd wanted to. That's how it seemed to her now at any rate, when she looked back on it.

"What you and Merritt will need to discuss," Callie explained in her businessman's voice, "is whether you wish me to negotiate a deal with the Greathouses. And if so, we'll have to write up a contract."

Still dumbfounded by the whole idea, Clara said she thought that would be best and that she trusted Callie entirely. Callie told her how the Greathouses planned to build a new museum to house the Frye collection and that her paintings would be much better off stored there than in her parents' basement.

"Would I still be able to see them?" she asked.

Callie answered that matters such as those would all be worked out in the contract. She added that the Greathouses might wish to buy only a portion of

272

the series initially, while retaining the right of first refusal on the remaining portraits, and then explained what that meant.

When Merritt returned, Clara and Callie were still discussing the details of the prospective purchase. Clara wanted to know more about the Greathouses and the Frye collection, so Callie reminded her of Frye's Prize Lunchmeat, which Clara's mother used to make sandwiches with for her school lunch. When Charles Frye died, his last will and testament dictated that his fortune be used to build a free art museum for the people of Seattle, and so Walser Greathouse, the executor of the estate, appointed himself and his wife to oversee the project.

"It's hard to imagine," Clara said as Merritt carefully uncorked the champagne without the attendants noticing and poured it into three papers cups so they could toast the good news.

By week's end, Merritt had enlisted his friend Sid to write up a contract giving Callie the standard art dealer's cut—ten percent—on any deal she negotiated with the Greathouses to which he and Clara agreed. Then Clara transferred her power-of-attorney to Merritt, and he and Callie signed the contract before a notary public.

The prospect of not owning her own paintings still left Clara rather mystified, though she very much liked the idea of her and Merritt having a little extra money. She agreed with Merritt that however much the paintings sold for—and they had no idea since Callie did not present them with a dollar figure yet—they would buy several government bonds and put the rest of the money away in a savings account for their future. Other than that, Clara's only stipulation was that she also be allowed to pick out several new suits for Merritt.

THIRTY-SEVEN
Merritt, Fall 1948

As much as he might try to laugh it off, Merritt couldn't ignore this last threatening letter from the Smitsons. It was too serious. He considered handing it over to the police, but he couldn't say for sure where the union allegiances of the Fraternal Order of Policemen lay. Maybe the FBI, he thought, except that J. Edgar Hoover had it in for Harry Bridges as much as anyone and as far as Merritt knew, Smitson father and son might be on Hoover's payroll as well as Dave Beck's. Bridges was due to arrive in Seattle in ten days, and if the Smitsons believed Merritt wouldn't assassinate the union leader for them, they might actually try to do it themselves—and then knock him off in the bargain. And based on the run-ins he'd had with them so far, they were probably crazy enough to try.

The fact was that Merritt no longer feared his own exposure, at least not in respect to his job, which he could readily quit, or his personal reputation, which was what it was. Yet in regard to Clara and her family, the matter of the blackmail was another story altogether. Given Clara's condition, he could never forgive himself if she found out, and as for Mr. and Mrs. Hamilton, they didn't need to know such things about their son-in-law. Warranted or not, whatever shame he had was his alone—and should remain that way. No one other than he should have to bear the consequences of it. Yet the more he pondered the situation, the more he realized the Smitsons were not just targeting him. They were going after Carl and Ken Hamilton. And what's more, whether they thought so or not, they were also going after Clara. It was this realization that turned his shame and apprehension into deep loathing for the Smitsons and settled his mind once and for all to put an end to the whole grubby business.

When he telephoned his brother-in-law several nights after receiving the last blackmail letter to arrange a meeting with him, Ken complained that he'd been working all day and it was cold and wet outside, and couldn't they meet another time? Merritt said no, he badly needed to see him that night. He also insisted on meeting at Duwamish Head, where Harbor Avenue curved away from Elliott Bay toward Alki Point, the most isolated spot in the city he could think of.

"I'll bring you an umbrella," Merritt said sarcastically.

Ken responded by telling Merritt if he was going to be a fathead about it, he could forget it, and Merritt apologized, adding, "I really appreciate your doing this, Ken. It's important."

"Sure it is," Ken replied and agreed to meet him.

When Merritt arrived at Duwamish Head, the wind was blustery. He arrived early and waited at first in his car. When nine o'clock rolled around and Ken didn't show up, he got out of the car and walked to the end of the point. The city lights across the bay reflected off the dark water and illuminated a slow-moving marine cloud layer skimming the top of the downtown buildings. He could make out several of the drum fires along Alaska Way where the longshoremen kept their vigil. Half a dozen freighters sat anchored in the bay unable to dock, while a skiff from one of the freighters transported crew members to shore. Otherwise, the whole waterfront from Smith Cove to Harbor Island was as quiet and calm as on Christmas Eve.

Merritt considered whether Ken had stood him up and even thought that if he had, it might be for the best. His brother-in-law could be such a self-righteous SOB when he climbed onto his Christian Science soapbox, so maybe he wasn't the right person to go to with this thing. Maybe no one was. He decided to give Ken another ten minutes, and if he didn't arrive by then, he would find a payphone and call it off.

A few minutes later, Ken's car pulled in next to Merritt's and his brother-in-law got out and walked toward him. They shook hands and Ken told Merritt he had to get back to the union hall for a 10:00 p.m. meeting to vote on the latest contract offer from the maritime companies. "It's a real crock," he said out of the side of his mouth. "They want us to go back to the company hiring hall, and there's no way we're going to—" He caught himself up short as if just then realizing he wasn't speaking to another longshoreman, but a Teamster, his sworn adversary. "What's this all about?" he asked.

Merritt looked across the Sound, away from the Seattle skyline, where the sea was indistinguishable from the land, the land indistinguishable from the sky—all just solid darkness. He then turned to Ken and faced his brother-in-law straight on. "Your father tell you about my run-in with a couple of fellas named Smitson?"

"He mentioned it," Ken said, watching him closely.

"Well there's more to it."

"Go figure," Ken said and cracked the vertebrae in his neck with a twist of his head the way a fighter might.

"They've been putting the screws to me for a while now." Merritt pulled out a cigarette, cupped a hand over it, and fumbled with his lighter to get it lit. "Plain and simple, they're trying to blackmail me." Ken remained silent, still watching him, waiting for what came next. Merritt knew he couldn't stall any longer.

"It's like this," he managed finally, tossing his cigarette into a puddle at their feet. "They know something about me from the service, something I'm not proud of." He looked up at Ken, who scrutinized him like the judgmental bastard Merritt knew him to be. He continued nevertheless. "There was this ensign, see . . . and we were out drinking. It was just after I'd met Clara actually, and just before I shipped out. I don't know why, or how, maybe something just came over me, but I went to this ensign's room for a drink, right, and—"

"*Hey*," Ken said sharply, stopping him mid-sentence.

"I need to tell you that . . ." Merritt looked him squarely in the eye. He was family after all. Clara's brother.

"Listen," Ken said, interrupting him again. "I don't need to know and I don't want to know. We were in a fucking war and things happened. Some good, some bad. Some really bad. Probably a lot worse than anything you went through. I know for a fact that a whole lot of things from that time won't ever make sense to me, and they don't make a shitload of difference anyhow now that it's over, know what I mean?"

Merritt didn't know how to respond, but it didn't matter, because Ken didn't give him a chance to.

"Anyone who wants to drag out what went on during the war to try to get at someone today, well, that's a helluva rotten thing to do. You served your country just like the rest of us. As far as I'm concerned, that's all that matters. And screw everything else."

Merritt hung his head and kicked at a stone with the toe of his shoe. He'd never seen this side of Ken before. He didn't sound like the brother-in-law or longshoreman or churchman he thought he knew. For one thing, he'd never once heard Ken swear. For another, Ken almost never spoke about the war.

"I mean it," Ken said as if to put a final exclamation point on the words he'd just spoken. He shivered and muttered, "It's damn cold out here."

Merritt nodded. "Yeah," he said but knew the matter wasn't finished. "There's this, too." He took the letter from his coat pocket and handed it to Ken.

Ken squinted at it and said, "I can't read this. It's too dark."

Without having to look at it, Merritt told him what the letter said.

"That's it?" Ken asked.

"That's it."

"These idiots can't be serious, can they? They want you to murder Harry Bridges?"

"I wouldn't put it past them," Merritt answered and recounted how he'd been driven off the road by the flatbed truck and followed down to the waterfront. He also mentioned Carl's hit-and-run incident, figuring this was as likely the Smitsons' doing as not. "The older one already had a grudge against your dad, and now they've got a grudge against me—for whatever reason."

Ken crumpled the letter in both hands and hurled it like a baseball pitcher into the bay. Merritt watched it float on the inky-black water before being swamped by the chop and disappearing. "It's not the first time someone's threatened Harry's life," he said. "And won't be the last."

His dismissal of the matter startled Merritt. "Bridges might be used to it," he said, "but I'm not."

"First time for everything," was Ken's quick retort and began walking back to his car. "Don't worry about it," he called to Merritt over his shoulder. "It's a union matter now."

THIRTY-EIGHT
Clara, Fall 1948

In the sanatorium's depthless nights when haggard coughing or tortured throat-hocking were the only sounds, Clara imagined herself escaping. She and Merritt would run away to New York City. They would lease a cozy walkup in Greenwich Village. Merritt would study for his Ph.D. at Columbia University while she would work as an illustrator at Bloomingdale's on Lexington Avenue. They would attend the Met to hear the live radio broadcasts in person, and on weekends they would visit the famous art galleries along Fifth Avenue and afterward stroll along the leafy pathways of Central Park.

Or maybe they would flee the country and escape across the ocean, all the way to Paris, where they could join her friend Adel and her Romanian composer in their life as bohemian expatriates. Merritt would write novels, as he told her he once fancied doing, and she would have a small atelier with a gas heater where she would paint every morning before going off to the Louvre in the afternoon to make studies of 18th-century masterpieces in her sketchbook. In the evenings they would meet in the cafés and drink pastis and on weekends take a picnic basket of bread and cheese and a bottle of red wine to the banks of the Seine to watch the fishermen dangling their lines in the river while the *bateaux mouches* glided by.

Ah yes, she mused, lying in the darkness of the ward. *Escape.*

Maybe, though, what she and Merritt really needed was to get away from city life altogether, as Guy Anderson had. Away from the galleries and museums, schools and universities, unions and strikes, churches and church people. Away from the hospitals and sanatoriums, the doctors and nurses, and all the ailing and dying people in the world. Perhaps they could find a remote mountain glen in Vermont somewhere. Yet other than the autumn foliage Merritt always talked about, she didn't have the faintest idea what life was like in Vermont. So perhaps they ought to find someplace closer to home, maybe near Willapa Bay, which they drove around on their pre-honeymoon road trip. They could build a cabin deep in the woods. Pull salmon from the rivers that coursed into the bay, rake clams from the mudflats, gather berries and mushrooms and root plants in the woods and pastures. Learn to make salmonberry wine (the kind of sour sauce they got tipsy on last year with J.P.). Merritt could learn to hunt and they could roast wild duck in their fire pit at night. They might acquire a goat or two to milk and shear. Build a chicken coop and keep a few hens. Have a big dog to chase away the black bears. And a cat. Clara had always wanted a cat. A big fluffball that would rub its whiskers against her face and curl up in her lap. She would give up painting and draw only landscapes. No people. And she would knit. Socks, sweaters, caps, gloves, and mufflers, all of which Merritt would wear happily as he gathered firewood for their stone fireplace. If family came to visit, they would have to trek into the woods to find them, even her dear, sweet mother.

But most of the time, as the seasons changed and months went by, she and Merritt would revel in the solitude of their sylvan hideaway. They would make love as freely as they had on their honeymoon. And kiss ceaselessly. Day and night. Little, tender kisses and wet, rapturous kisses. Because she would no longer be infectious—no more coughing, no more sputum. In fact, they would experience no sickness whatsoever other than the most commonplace aches and pains, nothing more than what a couple of aspirin, a hot water bottle, and a good night's sleep could cure. Maybe they'd have children, or maybe not. Yet as the years passed, they would gradually slow down, growing older and wiser. And when the time came, they would each die, first one, then the other, in close proximity to one another's passing, with very little bother and almost no notice.

And why not? she thought with eyes closed. *Why shouldn't that be?*

THIRTY-NINE
Merritt, Fall 1948

Following her most recent setback and the decision to proceed with the thoracoplasty, Merritt let himself believe Clara would get well and return home. There was always that chance. She believed as much herself, and he didn't want to dampen her hopes. Privately he worried about the disfigurement that would follow the procedure. The doctor had shown them photographs of people who'd had thoracoplasty, a portion of their chest concave, their torso off-center, but Clara and he agreed that if it meant she would recover and be able to leave the sanatorium, the disfigurement was a small price to pay. The doctor even remarked that since Clara was such a tall woman, the loss of an inch or two after a couple of her ribs were removed wouldn't make much difference. Mostly, though, Merritt hated to think of her continuing to suffer.

He knew his days with the Teamsters were numbered, a fact that declared itself even more loudly when he learned the university's Board of Trustees had voted against the ten professors hauled before the Canwell Committee—that is, had voted to fire or censure them in brazen defiance of the Faculty Union's recommendations and the general will of the student body.

The day after the news appeared in the papers, Merritt encountered Beck in the courtyard of the Teamsters Hall, and after they exchanged good mornings, he confronted him on the matter. He asked Beck straightout whether as an active university trustee he had voted against the ten professors.

Beck's face wavered from its typically stolid expression. He blinked several times and seemed to puzzle over the question. Merritt had caught one of the most powerful men in the nation off guard. But only momentarily. Beck recovered his demeanor as he scowled at his questioner, took a wide stance with his stocky frame, and thrust his hands deep into his overcoat pockets. *Proceed with Caution*, his posture seemed to proclaim. He sized Merritt up and asked him to repeat the question. "My hearing's not what it once was," he said.

Merritt steeled himself to go on. "The ten university professors," he said. "Did you vote to fire them?"

Beck stared at him hard. No one had probably ever asked him such a blunt question, and for just an instant Merritt thought the 51-year-old labor boss might actually slug him, and then once he was down give him a few swift kicks for good measure. Yet Beck didn't flinch. He didn't take his eyes off Merritt either. Only after a long pause did he withdrew his hands from the pockets of his overcoat and cross his arms over his chest. "The vote of the Board is confidential," he said as if making a prepared statement. "I can't discuss it."

"I understand," Merritt said, trying to sound conciliatory but knowing he had to press the point further. "I read about it in the papers yesterday, and that's why I'm asking you just the same."

Beck squinted at him, his nostrils flaring, and took a deep breath and let it out slowly. "Do you believe it's right for avowed Communists to be on the state payroll?" he asked Merritt, who again noticed how thick and mottled Beck's hands were.

Though he hadn't honestly expected Beck to give him a straight answer, the question threw Merritt. Yet he knew if he let Beck browbeat him now, if he backed down, he would regret the day for the rest of his life.

"I believe in the First Amendment," he replied, his heart thudding in his chest. "A person has the right to his beliefs and affiliations, without recrimination." He sounded like a schoolboy in a civics class and waited for Beck to dismiss him with a pat on the head. But that wasn't going to happen. He'd already shown his willingness to stand up to the labor boss and there was no retreating now.

"You're going to lecture *me* on the constitution?" Beck said in an imposing voice. "What do you know about a person's rights? I've spent my whole life fighting for men's rights. Those professors of yours were members of the Communist Party, Mr. Driscoll. So go ask Joe Stalin about your precious constitutional rights and then we'll talk about the First Amendment."

I fought for those same damn rights, he wanted to yell back at Beck. "Do you mean the rights men fought and died for?" he heard himself saying instead.

Beck turned into a slab of granite right before Merritt's eyes, frozen like a piece of statuary, glowering at him. Finally Beck uncrossed his arms, pursed his lips tight, and replied, "You're a real whizz-bang, aren't you? So you fought for your country, is that it? Saved the world from fascist dictators like Hitler and me. Well tell me this, war hero, what else were you doing during the war?"

A sardonic glint came into Beck's eyes. Merritt understood his meaning perfectly. *So that's it*, he thought.

"I'm proud of my service," Merritt said and left it at that. A cold silence fell over them both as they waited one another out.

Beck stuffed his hands back into his overcoat pockets and nodded. "You deserve to be," he said frankly as he brushed past Merritt and walked into the union hall—and just like that the stand-off was over.

* * *

281

For the remainder of the week, Merritt arrived late to the office and avoided passing anywhere close to Beck's office. On Sunday he visited Clara. She suffered once more from severe backaches and nausea and remained extremely weak in the days leading up to the thoracoplasty surgery. Because she could no longer be wheeled into the common room for fear the exertion might set off another coughing fit and weaken her further, Merritt was allowed onto the ward during visiting hours to sit beside her bed. She slept through most of his visits now, except for when she bolted upright to cough, grabbed at a tissue to cover her mouth, and collapsed back onto her pillows. Beneath the blue chenille bedcovers, she seemed to physically disappear before him. Her voice, once so clear and confident, was barely audible, and her eyes lost their focus and seemed almost opaque. It became difficult for Merritt to tell whether she knew he was even there with her. Still, he remained optimistic about the surgery, as he believed she did.

On Monday morning he was back at his desk at the Teamsters Hall. He put in a couple of hours before stepping down the hallway to see Leo. When he paused to glance at the Joint Council bulletin board, the first item he saw was a small clipping from the *Everett Herald*. According to the five-paragraph notice, Mr. Arda Smitson had drowned over the weekend in a boating accident in Possession Sound, near Everett. He'd been out in a small lapstrake skiff that, according to his son, Allen Smitson, of Local 38 of Tacoma, the two had built themselves before the war. Smitson had hauled the boat up from his home in Ballard on his truck—a flatbed, Merritt assumed—to go fishing with a friend from the Weyerhaeuser mill. When the friend didn't show up, Smitson went out alone and the boat capsized. According to a Coast Guard officer quoted in the notice, the winds weren't especially strong that day, and yet, as the officer added, strong crosscurrents passed through Possession Sound that often caught boaters by surprise.

Upon reading the newspaper clipping, Merritt double-backed to his office and straightaway called Ken Hamilton at the Todd Seattle Docks on Harbor Island where he worked.

"I don't know anything about it," Ken said after he came to the phone and Merritt recounted what he'd just learned. "People go out on the Sound all the time and drown."

There was nothing Merritt could say to Ken except that he hoped that was the case. At the very least, he suspected his dealings with the Smitsons were finally over. The father was dead and the son should realize the game was up.

Shortly after lunch, however, as he typed a letter to the president of the IBT local in Spokane, a ruckus broke out in the hallway and when he stepped out of his office to see what was going on, he spotted Allen Smitson wielding a baseball bat and coming at him.

"Come on, Driscoll," Smitson shouted and charged him. He swung the bat at Merritt's head and missed, but then came back around with it and caught him squarely across the right shoulder. Merritt staggered against the wall just as two men jumped Smitson from behind and wrestled him to the floor.

"That faggot killed my father," he kept screaming with the same rabid look he'd had the night the longshoremen roughed him up on the waterfront.

Merritt gripped his shoulder and could tell it wasn't right. It also hurt like hell. The two men wrenched the bat from Smitson and lifted him to his feet as Dave Beck approached from down the hallway.

"Is that Smitson's boy?" Beck demanded. His sharp gray suit didn't have a wrinkle in it.

"I think so," said one of the men, who Merritt now saw was Leo Reinke.

"Get him out of here," Beck ordered. "And make sure he's suspended. We don't need hotheads like that driving the streets." He looked at Merritt slumped against the wall, holding his shoulder, and without saying a word turned to face the people gathered in the hallway, told them to go back to work, and returned to his office.

Merritt stumbled into his own office and dropped into his desk chair. He tested his shoulder and winced when he tried to raise his arm more than a few inches.

He put an icepack on his shoulder that night, and it took several days for the swelling to subside to where he could lift his arm over his head again. On Tuesday and Thursday when he visited Clara in the sanatorium, his shoulder had mended enough to keep her from noticing the injury.

On Sunday she slept through most of the visiting hours. Yet just as the attendant was ordering Merritt to leave, she woke up and with half-lidded eyes asked him to give her a hug. He leaned over the bed, afraid of pressing her too hard, and looked into her face.

"Hold," she said, and reached up and pulled him toward her, prompting him to tuck his arms beneath her body and embrace her more firmly. After several long moments during which she kept her arms around him, she let go and sank back into the sheets. He then kissed her forehead, whispered he'd be back on Tuesday, and stepped away from the bed.

Early the next morning, just as it was turning light outside the bedroom window, the telephone rang, waking him from an already uneasy sleep. He made his way into the living room, sat on the couch, and held the receiver to his ear. As he listened to the nurse on the other end of the line, he remained silent, and finally the nurse asked if he was still there.

"I'm here," he muttered, then thanked her for calling, and let the phone fall to floor as he slumped forward with his head in his hands.

The doctor said Clara's body simply gave out, that it didn't have the reserves to sustain her any longer. This sounded to Merritt too much like an auto mechanic's description of a car engine, though maybe the doctor was right—and maybe having one's body simply give out was the best anyone could hope for when their time came.

"She appeared to be sleeping normally," the night nurse reported later that morning when Merritt arrived at the sanatorium. The nurse had made her hourly rounds of the women's ward at 4:00 a.m., flashing a small light across the face of each patient to determine whether they were breathing regularly or not, and Clara seemed to be. So in all likelihood she did not die of what the doctor called "pulmonary failure"—meaning she didn't suffocate, as many TB patients did—and that was something to be thankful for. Together the doctor and nurse estimated she had stopped breathing at about 4:30 a.m., while she slept.

Accompanied by Clara's parents, Merritt viewed her body that afternoon at the mortuary not far from the sanatorium, and two days later, according to Clara's wishes, he had her body cremated and her ashes delivered to him in a pewter urn. On Saturday the family and a small gathering of friends, including Callie and Jenny, held a brief memorial service at the Hamilton home in West Seattle, during which Ken and his wife each read from the Bible and *Science and Health* and her mother saw to it that everyone was well fed. Carl Hamilton shook Merritt's hand several times but said little throughout the course of the gathering. The next day Merritt had Sunday dinner with Clara's parents, and before he left that evening he accepted their offer to come to Sunday dinner every week for as long as he wished.

On Monday morning, he received a card of condolences signed by several Teamster officials, including Leo Reinke and Dave Beck. He took several more days off from work, during which time he spoke long-distance twice to his parents in Vermont, visited with the Hamiltons, and sat in the apartment looking at Clara's painting of sunflowers on the kitchen wall and her sketch of him from his Navy days.

When Friday rolled around, he forced himself out of bed to shower, dress, and go into work. As he drove down to the Teamsters Hall, he decided this would be his last day with the union. He figured there was no need to give the standard two weeks' notice, since almost anyone could do his job, and decided that at the end of the day he would simply tell Leo he wasn't coming back. In the meanwhile, to get through the day, he would try to tie up as many loose ends as he could from the paperwork piled on his desk.

Yet when he arrived at union hall, made his way to his office, and sat down at his desk, he couldn't concentrate. He typed half a letter, leafed through some file folders, and smoked several cigarettes. By noon he knew his efforts were pointless and that's when he picked up the framed photograph of Clara he kept on the corner of his desk and looked at it for the first time since returning to his office that morning.

In the color photo, Clara stood on the narrow shoreline of Lake Quinault, just past where the lawn sloped down from the lodge. The blue lake waters were spread out behind her, with a dark green ridge rising up from the opposite shore. She wore tan linen pants and a light blue blouse and her hair was tied back off her shoulders, her bangs loose in the breeze. What struck Merritt most was the playful manner in which she posed for the camera, her fingertips set coquettishly upon her thighs, her hips turned at a come-hither angle while she smiled at him, laughing even, divinely alive.

Acknowledgements

I am indebted to the following institutions for access to their special collections: The Seattle Public Library, the University of Washington Libraries, the Museum of History and Industry, and the Washington State Historical Society. As for primary and secondary texts, three works that were especially valuable were *The War Years: A Chronicle of Washington State During World War 11* by James R. Warren, *Seattle Transformed: World War II to Cold War* by Richard C. Berner, and *A History of Seattle Waterfront Workers, 1884-1934* by Ronald E. Magden. My understanding of Dave Beck derives from original research as well as various studies of the Teamsters on the West Coast. In respect to Christian Science, *Blue Windows: A Christian Science Childhood* by Barbara Wilson (Sjoholm) offered important insights. Online I was aided by usswashington.com, sponsored by the USS *Washington* BB56 Associate Unit, Inc. I am grateful to David E. Johnson, Duane Pasco, and Murray Guterson for sharing with me their adventures in Seattle during the 1940s, and to Dr. Peter Podlusky for his help with the clinical aspects of tuberculosis. For time to write, the artist residency program at the Willard R. Espy Foundation in Oysterville, Washington, and the Escape to Create program at the Seaside Institute in Seaside, Florida, were invaluable. For support through summer research grants, travel funds, and sabbatical release time, Birmingham-Southern College proved as generous as ever. Finally, I want to thank David Memmott of Wordcraft of Oregon for believing in this work.

About the Author

Jay W Shoots, 2008

Peter Donahue is the author of the novel *Madison House,* winner of the Langum Prize for American Historical Fiction, and the short story collection *The Cornelius Arms.* He is co-editor, with John Trombold, of the anthologies *Reading Seattle: The City in Prose* and *Reading Portland: The City in Prose.* He writes the Retrospective Reviews column on Northwest literature for *Columbia: The Magazine of Northwest History,* and teaches creative writing and journalism at Birmingham-Southern College in Alabama.

For more information on this and other titles
please visit our website at:
www.wordcraftoforegon.com

Breinigsville, PA USA
26 April 2010
236835BV00001B/6/P